THE AIR BEGAN SHIMMERING

The shimmering tightened down to pinpoints of glowing light, then erupted into more than a half-dozen gaping entries. There was no doubt the entries led to another world; mottled beasts I'd never seen before jumped through, muzzles snarling and hackles raised.

Then each of the two dozen beasts turned and charged at the nearest life it intended to take.

Even as I watched, my reflexes were already changing my body form and composition. My throat was now lower and thicker and covered with fur, but it was still there to be jumped at.

A huge brown and white beast raced toward me. I bared my own fangs in a snarl of contempt, then launched myself in counterattack . . .

D0835177

Other Avon Books by
Sharon Green

DAWN SONG

Coming Soon

THE HIDDEN REALMS

SILVER PRINCESS, GOLDEN KNIGHT

SHARON GREEN

AVONOVA

AVON BOOKS • NEW YORK

SILVER PRINCESS, GOLDEN KNIGHT is an original publication of Avon Books. This work has never before appeared in book form. This work is a novel. Any similarity to actual persons or events is purely coincidental.

AVON BOOKS
A division of
The Hearst Corporation
1350 Avenue of the Americas
New York, New York 10019

For Chris Miller
A great editor, a great friend

CHAPTER ONE

"Whatsa matter, girl?" a raspy and belligerent female voice demanded. "Ain't this place decorated t'suit ya?"

I leaned farther back against the stone wall behind me, and looked up at the woman who had spoken. Her long skirt and tight, low-cut blouse were grimy, her body had spread into an unattractive middle age, and her face . . . Topped by raggedy blond hair, her face was blurry, showing just how drunk she was.

"As a matter of fact, it doesn't suit me," I answered, keeping my voice smooth and even. "All those iron bars are way out of style, but they probably don't have enough taste to know that. I think we'll have to tell them."

"Bars out of style," the woman repeated with a snort. "We'll hafta tell 'em. Thatsa good one. We'll hafta tell 'em."

She started cackling at the big joke, then stumbled away to pass it on to someone else. There were about fifteen women in that large, dim dungeon of a cell, so she had her choice. Two or three of the women were crying, but the rest seemed to be as disgusted as I felt.

"Nice going, Alex," I muttered to myself. "This is what you get for not paying attention. If you're very, very lucky, they'll hang you before Father finds out."

I looked around again at the dingy stone cell, knowing

1

I wasn't about to have *any* kind of good luck. The city
guardsmen had arrested me for horse stealing, but the
High Magistrate would not have a chance to sentence me
to hanging. My father would want to discuss the matter
with me first, and only then would come the question of
whether or not I hanged. And by what.

I'd kicked all the straw away from the place on the
floor I'd picked to sit on, but it hadn't done all that
much good. The dungeon cell was under the city jail
and courthouse, with tiny slits of windows high up in
the walls. The slits let in just enough air to keep us
from suffocating; to clear the stench of fear and unbathed
bodies, they would have needed to knock out a wall. The
bugs and vermin were another story, and a roaring fire
might have done some good. Even if I got out of there,
my clothes would probably have to be burned . . .

All of which did nothing to change the fact that I
had a problem. I sighed deeply, wondering again how
I could have been so careless. Had I gotten so bored
that I no longer cared whether or not I got caught? If
that was true, then it was well past time to pack and
leave. I'd been thinking more and more about traveling
during the past year, but I'd been reluctant to leave the
family. Now . . .

"I don't like people who think they're better than me,"
a voice stated, but not the same voice as earlier. Even
before I looked up I knew this was a younger woman,
and she certainly was. Closer to my age, she stood with
fists on hips as she glared down at me. She wore the
same kind of sandals, long skirt, and low-cut blouse that
the first woman had, but she was larger, dark-haired, and
definitely not drunk.

"Did you hear me?" she demanded. "I said I don't like
people who think they're better than me. You better hurry
up and tell me how wrong I am, that you're *not* better
than me. And you better hope I believe it."

Most of the other women were paying very close attention, ready to be entertained by the antics of the cell bully.

The girl's faint prettiness had a hardened edge to it, often one of the signs of a professional prostitute. She was obviously used to pushing around the girls of her house, an arrogance that possibly had led her to steal from a customer. Or into beating up on a co-worker.

"I do hope you'll believe me," I said as I rose smoothly to my feet to look down at her. "In this place *nobody* is better than anybody else, and if you don't understand that, then you're stupid. And if you still think you want a fight with me, then you're beyond all hope."

"Big doesn't have to mean good," she blustered, but there was doubt in the yellow eyes looking up at me. "I've taken bigger than you, and *they* weren't virgins. You'd never stand a chance against me."

"If you think I'm a virgin at Shifting, then what are you waiting for?" I asked very mildly, seeing her flinch just a little at what must have been in my own eyes. All the disgust and annoyance I felt at myself was being redirected toward her, the anger inside refusing to let me do anything to stop it. "I prefer cat shape for serious fights," I told her. "How about you?"

Although her expression didn't change, she swallowed hard, and I could almost see her mind moving behind her eyes. Professional prostitutes aren't accepted in working houses unless they're better than average at changing shape; after all, they serve a large number of men with different tastes. If a girl can't change herself to accommodate most of the range, she's better off finding a different line of work. Or getting married, which isn't at all hard to do.

"Where would *you* get into a serious fight?" she asked at last, giving me a deliberate up-and-down. "If you were a professional, you wouldn't be wearing pants and boots—not to mention a shirt instead of a blouse. If you had to hide in a fruit orchard, you'd probably turn yourself into an apple."

Our audience chuckled at the insult, happy to see that the girl was regaining her self-confidence. I'd called her stupid, and now she was saying the same to me. Only an idiot would try to hide in an orchard by changing into a piece of fruit. Anyone in pursuit would just have to look for the apple or pear with a hole in the ground under it. You can change your size and shape, but not your mass; only very young children don't understand that the smaller you make yourself, the more concentrated your mass becomes. An apple massing a hundred and thirty pounds or so will put a respectable dent in the ground it lies on. Assuming, of course, that you're able to Shift down that small, which most people can't.

"And you'd be a bowlegged bird on a bending branch," I returned with the next thing to a yawn. "Does that take care of the kiddie dialogue, or do we also have to get into a spitting contest? Make up your mind, you're starting to bore me."

"You mean you're too bored to answer my question?" she countered, cheeks flushing with anger. "I asked where someone like you could have gotten into a serious fight, but I didn't hear an answer. Does that mean you can't remember—or there *aren't* any fights?"

"You think that because I'm not poor I've never gotten into a fight?" I asked with all the ridicule I was feeling. "Have you any idea how unfriendly an upper-class crowd can be? Some of them aren't capable of full-range changing, but most are. I know professional girls have to be adaptable, but how close to full-range do *you* get?"

She hesitated over that, her frown telling me she'd forgotten that full-range abilities show up more often in the nobility. It's the reason they're considered nobility in the first place, but a lot of people miss the point. Those who complain about being low-class prefer to think they've been cheated out of something otherwise due them.

"If you're trying to say *you* come close to full-range, you're lying," she said after the pause, her mind finally made up, her yellow eyes hard. "I wouldn't believe one of you rich brats if you told me the sun is high at noon.

Since you're so sure you're better than me, I'm going to give you a chance to prove it."

She started to step back, her faintly eager expression saying she'd seen through me: I'd been trying to talk her out of a fight because I couldn't fight, and that meant she was about to have some fun. Telling her she was wrong would have been a waste of breath, so I didn't bother. I gave a little shrug, folded my right hand into a fist, then socked her right in the mouth.

Vast surprise covered her face as she sat down hard, and then it was gone and she stretched out the rest of the way, completely unconscious. It was very quiet in the cell as I rubbed my knuckles, pairs of widened eyes staring at me from all sides. It isn't often that you see people using their hands or feet alone in a fight, not unless they're no more than chameleons. Most have at least one fighting shape to Shift into, and doing it is second nature.

But there are times when you can't let nature rule. The dark-haired girl would have had no chance against me, and her disbelief was no excuse for my hurting her. I knew enough people who would have used the excuse to have some fun, but that didn't mean *I* had to. I tend to do as I please, and let others worry about approval or disapproval.

Which, in a major way, was why I was behind bars just then. I'd been distracted from the problem for a short while, but that hadn't made it go away. I turned to go back to my piece of wall and a bit more brooding, but even that didn't work out. I heard a few sets of booted feet out in the corridor, and then a duty squad stopped in front of the cell. A small, well-dressed man was with them, and when I saw him I groaned.

"There she is, Sergeant," he said at once, his very dark eyes calm. "The tall young woman with the red hair. With your permission, I'll take her now."

"It's the Magistrate's permission you need, my lord, and you have that," the duty sergeant answered, already unlocking the cell. "All I have to do is sign her out in your custody."

"Come, Alexia," Merwin said in his soft, undemanding voice. "No sense leaving you in here for the night, when I shouldn't expect you would spend the night. Are you all right?"

"That's for you to tell *me*, I think," I responded, seeing that the men around him hadn't caught what he'd said. The cell they'd put me in had *bars*, for pity's sake. If they'd left me there overnight, I would have been gone as soon as everyone was asleep.

"Yes, you're quite right," he said as I moved through the cell door, his sharp, dark gaze looking up at me. "I would say the state of your health is in very delicate balance at the moment, and the prognosis isn't good. Your father wants to see you as soon as I get you home."

"I knew I wouldn't be lucky enough to hang," I muttered, at which Merwin chuckled. "And I wish you would stop enjoying yourself so much. When he kills me, you'll have the bother of attending a funeral."

"Let's see to the rest of your release, and then we can discuss the matter," he soothed with a gentle smile. "I have a coach waiting outside."

Where we'll have privacy, was the unspoken addition. At that point, it didn't matter to me one way or the other, but I knew my father's views on discussing private matters publicly. Rather than add fuel to an already raging fire, I shrugged and went along quietly.

With the number of times Merwin had to sign his name, I'm sure he could no longer spell it by the time he was through. They even turned over my personal possessions to him, but he made no effort to pass them to me. He carried the small pouch as he led the way to the waiting coach, stood aside to let me climb in first, then followed. When he slammed the door, the coach began to move, but not very quickly.

"Quite a lot of people in the streets today," Merwin observed, glancing out the window to his right. "Since it will be raining tomorrow, they're undoubtedly seeing to extra chores before then."

"I enjoy traveling in the rain," I observed back, watching him in the same casual way he looked at the populace. "Those who can stay inside do, so the streets and roads aren't crowded."

"No, you will not," he pronounced, now giving me the full weight of those eyes. "You will *not* take off for parts unknown, not when *I've* been made responsible for you. Whatever possessed you to take a prize racing stallion from your father's stable? Did you believe no one would notice, or simply that no one would care?"

"I borrowed the horse to win a bet," I said, leaning back on the very uncomfortable coach seat. "The people involved were thieves, stealing the money of everyone they raced their horse against. The animal was also a stallion, and it terrorized every horse running in opposition. Gray Thunder is pure ego, and he's faster than their nag. They said they would win against any and all comers, so I introduced them to a comer."

"There's something you aren't saying," Merwin decided, now studying me through narrowed eyes. "And it occurs to me to wonder where your winnings are. Your possessions include only five gold pieces, two silver, and a few coppers. I was under the impression the race had long been won by the time the city guard caught up to you."

"It had," I said, taking my own turn to study the people we were passing. In that neighborhood the buildings were mostly of stone, and a lot of the people matched. Stiff, formal, very full of self-importance—Why was being important so important to them?

"You gave your winnings to those you considered 'cheated,' " Merwin said, and there was no questioning in his tone. "You had no interest in keeping the gold for yourself, only in righting a wrong. Child, child, what in all the worlds is there to be done with you?"

"What's wrong with hanging?" I asked, my gaze still

on the scenery. "Since my nefarious schemes bother so many people, put an end to me and have done with it."

"You have no idea how truly tempted I am," he answered, the words very dry. "You persist in taking up all sorts of personal crusades, and never once stop to consider the consequences. Will you never understand you have a position to maintain, and righting wrongs is no part of it?"

"That's your opinion," I told him bluntly, bringing my stare back to his face. "*You* may enjoy having other people define your position and activities, but I don't. I find it intolerable and boring, just like living in this kingdom. As soon as my father is through handing me my head, I'm going traveling."

"So that's why you made no effort to cover your tracks," he said, his round face abruptly startled. "You made the decision to leave, and then sought a way to show your father how little he would be losing. Do you truly believe he'll allow you to go off all alone?"

"I'm beyond the age where I need his permission," I said, only faintly surprised to find that Merwin was right. I *had* been laying the groundwork for leaving, or at least my sneaky inner mind had. The rest of me still felt reluctant to take that major a step, no matter how necessary it was.

"With certain fathers, no daughter grows beyond the need for his permission." Merwin was now amused, but only distantly. "My dear Alexia, what you really need is a home and family of your own. We've had peace so long that the male population has risen out of all proportion to the female, so you can't say there isn't a wide selection. Find a man who suits you, and settle down with him."

"Settling down has never been the standard cure for boredom," I told him. "There are a lot of worlds out there to see, and all I need is a magic user to open the gates. When I get back I'll probably write a book."

"And if I believe *that*, you have a wonderful tract of swampland to sell me," he returned with a snort. "Your father won't believe it either, nor will he care whether or not it's true. He'll simply forbid you to go, and that includes sightseeing as well as adventuring."

"He *can't* forbid me to go," I returned wearily, feeling as though I'd been repeating myself for an hour. "He can't direct the life of a fully grown adult, and he knows it even if you don't. And I'm sure he also knows it wouldn't be very smart to try, not when I'm the adult."

"That has all the earmarks of a threat," Merwin noted, then narrowed his eyes at me again. "Let me see now, what could be in . . . Yes, of course. Your escapades until now have been for the most part innocent. If you aren't permitted to leave quietly, they'll change to—what? The deliberately destructive, the indelicately embarrassing? What did you have in mind?"

"I haven't found it necessary to make a decision about that," I said, beginning to feel annoyed. "I'm sure my father will be a lot more sensible than you're being. Even he doesn't push my temper too hard unless he's already lost his own."

"More threats?" he asked with raised brows. "At least this one is vague enough to be no more than a warning. Is this the point I'm supposed to become frightened?"

"That choice is entirely yours," I answered very softly, locking eyes with him. "I would never think to impose my beliefs on others."

"Stop that!" Merwin tried to snap, but the words came out a squeak. "I've seen you speak softly to others like that—Child, I *know* you won't harm me no matter how vexed you become, but a part of me deep inside knows nothing of the same. You will therefore do an old man the courtesy of sending that threatening gaze elsewhere—*before* it becomes necessary to call a healer."

The sweat on his forehead told me he wasn't joking. That meant he would probably leave me alone for a while, which was what I'd been trying to accomplish. I nodded obligingly, then looked out the window again.

My eyes saw the better neighborhood we were beginning to move through, but my mind registered nothing of
the large private houses and neat grounds. Instead I heard
again the words Merwin had used, about the position I
was supposed to maintain. Social position, he'd meant,
as well as public stance, remaining above the mundane
at all times.

I felt tempted to make a very rude noise, one to show
my opinion of the entire concept. Why was it supposed to
mean anything to *me* that my father was a king? I hadn't
made him a king, and I wasn't his eldest child or even
his eldest daughter. Was he likely to lose his place as
king because I didn't happen to agree with the accepted
standard for a princess? If I let myself be bored to death,
would that make his position more secure?

Since the answer to that was "no," I honestly couldn't
understand why everyone was making such a fuss. Who
got hurt when I lived my own life? No one, not even
those who thought I shouldn't. Who would be hurt when I
picked up and left? No one, not even my mother. She was
a good person and I knew she loved me, but I wasn't her
only child. She might miss me for a little while, but that
would hardly keep her from going on with her own life.

I sighed as I saw that we were drawing closer to the
palace, closer to the place where my father waited to
"discuss" my latest "escapade." He was a strong king
and a strong man, and really hated it when I got into
trouble. My being a girl had something to do with his
attitude, but not entirely. He came down just as hard on
my brothers if they got into trouble, but that didn't often
happen. *I* was the black sheep of the family, and that
was a thought that made me smile. What would he do,
I wondered, if I Shifted into the form of an actual black
sheep before going in to see him? Laugh his head off, or
turn me into lamb chops . . . ?

Considering the mood he'd been in lately, it wasn't
reasonable to expect him to laugh. I shifted around on
the coach seat, wishing the argument was already behind

me. And it *would* be an argument, that I knew for certain. We were so much alike, he and I, but he already had what he wanted. Now I wanted it to be my turn, and that's what I would be fighting for.

The rest of the ride passed with an inner silence to match the outer one, not precisely brooding, but not far from it. Other coaches passed us on the wide street, but when it came to the right-of-way, it was always ours. My father's sigil on the coach doors saw to that, and also brought servants running when we pulled up in front of the palace. Let's not waste time getting the condemned to the execution . . .

Merwin got out of the coach first, turned to give me a hand I didn't need, then led the way inside. Half the servants were staring at me while the other half avoided eye contact, a sure sign that they'd heard the latest. I would have been surprised if they hadn't, and it made little difference to my plans. If after I was gone everyone believed my father had thrown me out, it might do more good than harm.

"Lord Merwin," I called after the nervously hurrying little man. He paused and turned back to me. "I'm going to my apartment to bathe and change my clothes. You'll let me know when my father is ready to see me?"

"Your Highness, His Majesty is ready to see you *now*," Merwin replied immediately. "You're to accompany me to his study, then wait while I speak to him first in private. That will take only a moment, and then the audience will be yours."

"Audience?" I repeated, tickled by so diplomatic a word. "And he doesn't care to wait until I've washed off the dungeon stink. It looks like you might have to reconsider your opinions about whether or not he'll let me leave."

Merwin began to answer the semi-challenge, then realized we were no longer alone. He closed his lips again, gave me the most neutral bow I'd ever seen, and went back to leading the way.

My father's favorite study was in the middle of the palace on the ground floor, beside an inner court filled with grass and flowers. Merwin let one of the two door guards knock and announce him before disappearing inside with the door closed behind him. I usually visited my father's private garden when I was that close to it, but at the moment I wasn't in the mood. I took a seat on the nearest stone bench instead, and studied the declining day through the terrace windows opposite. The clouds were already gathering for the rain due tomorrow, and that felt extremely appropriate.

Merwin hadn't been lying about how short a time he would be. No more than five minutes passed before the door opened again, and he gestured to show it was my turn. I took my time getting up and walking over, and when I stepped through the doorway my father's stare was on me immediately.

"We thank you for your assistance, Lord Merwin," he said, making no effort to look at the man he addressed. "You may retire now."

"Yes, Your Majesty," Merwin acknowledged, and then a sound came of the door closing. It felt exactly as it had when they'd closed the door to the dungeon cell on me, something that made that whole situation even better.

"Come over here and sit down," my father said very flatly, gesturing to the chair about three feet away from him. "We have a long discussion ahead of us."

To say his tone was unfriendly would be like saying I'd made a minor mistake. His stare should have melted me as I walked across the floor and sat in the chair, or at least shriveled me a little. My father, King Reynar III, was a big man with full knowledge of who and what he was; when he lowered himself into his own chair, you would have sworn he was settling onto his throne.

"I want you to know how much I enjoyed being told my daughter was in the city lockup," he said after a short pause. "Most people didn't know she was my daughter, they just thought she was an ordinary horse thief. And, strangely enough, I didn't even have to ask which of my daughters it was."

His deep voice was perfectly calm, but I could see the anger smoldering in his golden eyes. I was the only one of his daughters to have inherited his red hair, but like both of my sisters and two of my brothers, I had our mother's silver eyes.

"You seem to have nothing to say to that," he observed, not particularly pleased. "Would you have been insulted if I *hadn't* known it was you? Just what is it you're trying to do?"

"Why does simply living my life mean I'm trying to 'do' something?" I asked, working to match his calm. "I realize I should have told someone I was taking Gray Thunder, but no one was around and I was in a hurry. If you're interested in apologies, I have one all ready. This time I owe at least one."

"This time, but not any of the others," he said, his words fractionally less even. "You disrupt the lives of everyone around you on an almost daily basis, but none of that calls for apology. You're simply 'living your life.' "

"That's right," I agreed, shifting just a little in the chair. "Maybe I don't do it the way people think I should, but I don't tell anyone else how to live. What gives them the right to try telling me?"

"The fact that you live among other people means you have to consider them," he pronounced, leaning forward a bit. "How many times have I told you that? As long as what you do affects others, you can't blithely dismiss upsetting them by claiming you don't tell them how to live. Your inconsiderate behavior forces them to deal with you, and that's worse than telling them things."

"Inconsiderate behavior," I echoed, seeing that we were finally getting down to it. "What you mean is that I refuse to act the way they expect me to. If I held lunch parties for all the fine ladies of the city, then went out to comfort one or two poor unfortunates in the needy section, that would be fine. People *like* to see a princess wasting her time that way. But let her try to take the training her brothers are given, or dare to walk around without an escort, or actually get to know some people who don't have even a single title to their name—"

"It isn't *safe* for you to do those things," my father interrupted with something of a growl. "Why can't you understand that? By the time I found out you were taking battle training, you were already past the worst part and I was advised to let it continue. The children of a king are always at risk, so against my better judgment I let you learn how to defend yourself. But that *doesn't* mean I gave my approval to your running around all over the kingdom by yourself. Are you under the impression I have no enemies who would strike at me through you?"

"If all they want to do is give themselves away, let them try," I answered with a shrug. "I heard a couple of your courtiers talking once, and they seemed to think I was a decoy set out by you. I only seemed to be running around on my own, and was actually being watched very carefully. If anyone tried for me, your guardsmen would pounce. I thought that was rather funny."

"You would," he said sourly. "We've been trying to figure out where your so-called sense of humor comes from ever since you started talking. But that absurd rumor, if true, doesn't mean you're safe. You're a very pretty girl, Alexia, and there are a lot of men in this world who think they're entitled to take whatever they like. If you believe they'd have to come at you one at a time, you're being naive."

"Father, I *don't* believe that," I said with a sigh. "But I also don't believe I'd be at much of a disadvantage. Just because I can defend myself doesn't mean I'm too stupid to know when I'm outnumbered. It isn't beneath my dignity to run, and I can probably Shift through a wider range than people like that. I'm not in anything like the kind of danger you've been picturing."

"Then it's only my imagination that just this morning

you were in danger of hanging?" he countered with raised brows. "What would you have done if I hadn't been told it was you in that cell?"

"Oh, I would have managed," I said with a vague gesture, not about to admit I'd been going to break out. Those cells had never been designed to hold someone capable of full-range Shifting, and once everyone had fallen asleep . . .

"I refuse to ask *how* you would have managed," he said. "I promised your mother not to lose my temper— Alexia, we're just wasting time here, and right now I can't afford it. I spent half the day thinking about you when I should have been concentrating on a problem that affects the kingdom, but I did come to certain conclusions. The difficulty you represent has to stop right now, and there's only one way to make that happen."

"It looks like we finally agree," I said as I watched him get up and head for the wine decanters. "But before we get into that, I'm curious. What sort of problem affecting the kingdom are you working on?"

"If you stayed home a little more, you'd already know," he told me, pouring two cups of wine. "You hadn't heard that we've been contacted by one of the gate realms, one of the places lying beyond our world's gates?"

"I heard a rumor to that effect, yes," I conceded, trying to dredge up details. Gate realms are those places just beyond a given world's gates, some really close by and therefore almost the same as our world, some so far away they're nothing familiar at all. Each gate offers a choice of worlds for your destination, but ordinary people can't make the choice for themselves. Only the Sighted can perceive the gates and use them, and they're supposed to be able to tell what lies beyond once they step into a gate. Everyday people like me needed a Sighted to go through with, and I'd sometimes wondered about that. What if the Sighted of a world didn't tell their people about the gates, or for some reason were afraid to admit to their people that they were Sighted . . . ?

"Their realm lies in a place where, entrywise, it's right next to ours," I went on, coming back to the point. "If our magic users created entries that are, for all intents and purposes, shortcut gates, we'd be right on top of each other and could trade with no trouble at all."

"Essentially correct," he agreed, handing me a cup of wine before returning to his chair. "Trading would be made so simple and inexpensive it would be like trading with ourselves at a profit. But that's only part of the story, the easy part."

He paused to sip at his wine, then shook his head.

"The primary reason they approached us has to do with weather," he said. "They did some research, and discovered that when they have a drought, we have floods. When we have a drought, *they* have floods. If we both set up the proper entries across the countryside, our floodwaters can irrigate their farmlands during a drought, and vice versa. It would save acres of crops on both sides, and put an end to famine caused by the vagaries of the weather."

"But?" I prompted, knowing there was a but. "If the arrangement is so beneficial, what's bothering you?"

"The fact that the arrangement can also be harmful," he answered with a sigh, golden eyes showing weariness. "Once the entries are created, they have to be left in place. If only water comes and goes through them, there's nothing to worry about. But what if an army suddenly comes through? I'd have people watching, of course, but that would still provide very little warning. I'd need a standing army of my own, already on the alert."

"And keeping a standing army of any size is very costly, but not only in gold," I said with a nod of understanding. "Filling the ranks takes men out of the work force, disrupting the economy. The army has to eat, but can't contribute any effort toward its feeding. And if they have to sit around for any length of time—Well, there's that saying about idle hands. If I'd ever been silly enough to think I'd enjoy taking your place, this would have done a good job of changing my mind."

"Two of your brothers are coming close to agreeing with you," he said with a humorless smile. "I can't simply refuse to consider the offer, not when so many people would benefit from the arrangement. I also can't forget my doubts and agree, not when it could put my people in such danger. I have to find out what these strangers are really like, without visiting their realm to see a possibly prepared picture. Our people have no interest in war unless we're attacked; how do *their* people feel about it?"

"More to the point, how do their leaders feel?" I countered. "And if they do happen to be into conquest at the moment, how good is their word? Would they die rather than break their oath, or is lying their favorite pastime? I think you really do need someone to take a close look at them, Father."

"I've already taken care of that," he said, ruining my plan to volunteer for the job. "I've sent an official embassy to match the one from them on its way to us, and also a few *un*official ones. Between them we ought to get some answers, but I want something more. The people they've sent will have been handpicked; if I can somehow get true, honest reactions out of them . . ."

His voice trailed off as his brows rose, and I didn't need to be told he'd gotten an idea. That was one of the things that made him such a good king: the ability to improvise. If he couldn't get things done with what he had at hand, he reached out as far as necessary to find other things.

"If I can help with that idea you just got, please let me know," I said, trying to sound suitably supportive. Playing politics bores me, but right then I owed my father more than a token apology. If he needed my brand of sneaking around, he'd have it.

"As a matter of fact, you're fully involved in the idea," he said, those eyes now looking at me rather than into the distance. "Using my major problems to solve each other is an idea I really enjoy. I'm going to ask the arriving embassy to be judges for the competition."

"What competition?" I asked, suddenly feeling as though I'd been caught not paying attention. "The spring games were three months ago."

"Alexia, I had a long talk with your mother," he said, ignoring the question I'd put. "My solution to the problem you present upset her, but she had to admit there was no other choice. If you keep going on like this, you'll eventually be hurt. Neither she nor I want to see that."

"Then we should be able to come to an agreement," I said, relieved that he had raised the subject. "I've been doing some considering of my own, and everything comes down to the fact that I'm bored. I hope you know I love you and Mother, but I just can't stay here any longer. I've decided to go traveling, and see what I can of the worlds."

"Before today you could have done that," he answered, suddenly looking pleased. "I would have been furious with you for even thinking about it, but legally I couldn't have stopped you. Now that you're a horse thief, though, you're subject to the courts just like everyone else. The High Magistrate has taken official notice that you had Gray Thunder when you were arrested, and even admitted taking him. If you go to trial, you'll certainly be found guilty."

"Are you saying you've decided to let me hang?" I asked, trying not to look as wide-eyed as I felt. My own father and mother, *agreeing* to let me be executed?

"You have no idea how seriously I considered it, even if for only a moment," he growled, briefly an annoyed king rather than an exasperated father. "I've started believing you *want* something to happen to you, just to make some sort of vague point. But no, you won't be hanging. The High Magistrate agreed to impose a lesser sentence. If you're tried and found guilty, you'll spend the next ten years as a city worker. The city hires out prisoners for menial jobs cheaply, and the coppers or silver they earn goes into the city coffers. You'll sweep, sew, scrub, and wash, and you won't be given the opportunity to escape."

"I think I'd rather hang," I muttered, but a nasty idea was threading its way through the shock I felt. "You said *if* I'm tried and found guilty. Let me make a wild guess and say you have an alternative choice."

"I knew you'd understand more quickly than someone else in your place," he commented with a grin. "The only other choice you have is a decision that's already been made for you. Come the day after tomorrow, notices of a full-range competition will go up, the sort that hasn't been held in more than four hundred years. The object of the competition will be to find the most adaptable single man in this kingdom—and his prize will be your hand in marriage."

My jaw headed for the floor along with the cup of wine I'd been holding, and I could feel the blood drain out of my face.

"You can't be serious," I choked out, suddenly wondering if Merwin had been trying to prepare me for this. "You'd force me into marriage, and with some stranger? I don't want to get married, and I'm sure you know it."

"Alexia, you need a man to bring some normal interest into your life," he said, and now his words were gentle. "Your mother and I have introduced you to every eligible male in a five-world, thousand-mile radius. Most of them you ignored, and the rest you insulted. Don't you ever want to know a strong man's love?"

"I've already tried it and wasn't impressed," I told him bluntly, hoping to shake him off-balance. "If you were picturing your baby girl as innocent, you're a few years too late. Now that you know you can't offer a virgin, let's forget about this competition thing and get down to serious negotiation. We—"

"I never said I was offering a virgin," he interrupted, his skin faintly mottled from suppressed anger. "And I wasn't referring to physical love, although that's another point to consider. To paraphrase an old saying, if you weren't impressed, you weren't doing it right."

"Let's find something else to disagree over," I suggested, too embarrassed to care about being clever. I'd been trying to shock him; instead of being shocked, he sounded as if he were ready to send me somewhere for lessons. It's a hell of a world when a father discusses his daughter's affairs calmly.

"There isn't anything *for* us to disagree over," he immediately disagreed. "At the end of the competition I'll declare a celebration feast, and we'll combine that with the wedding ceremony. That's when you get to decide whether you'd rather be married or sentenced."

"And if I decide on the sentencing, you'll let it happen for my own good," I summed up, "just the way you let Kinel use up a month's allowance to buy a horse when he was fifteen. You knew the horse wasn't as good as Kinel thought, but when he insisted, you let him buy it. And afterward made him go the entire month without a single copper to spend. He had to stay home while his friends were out enjoying themselves."

"And even after ten years, he remembers the lesson clearly," my father agreed with a nod. "It taught him to act responsibly, which is the same lesson I expect you to learn. My children will always be free to do as they like—as long as they're willing to accept the consequences of their freedom."

"If I simply picked up and left, I'd no longer be a problem to you," I pointed out, swallowing down a sick feeling. "I *want* to travel, Father—it's all I've been thinking about for the past year. You have my solemn word that I'll never cause you trouble or embarrassment again. I won't even come back without your permission—"

"Alexia," he said, interrupting again. There was a lot of compassion in his eyes—right behind the determination. "I'm not doing this to hurt you, child. I'm doing it to *keep* you from being hurt, and it doesn't have to be the end of your dreams. After you're married you can travel with your husband, as often as he's able to leave his responsibilities. Don't you see . . ."

By that time I was out of my chair and heading for the door, in point of fact not able to see much at all. It had been quite a while since the last time I'd cried, and privacy would be much more suitable to the occasion. I took a back way up to my apartment, happily finding it completely empty.

My apartment had a small sewing room that I'd done very little sewing in, but the room hadn't been neglected. Its wide casement had a padded window seat, and I'd spent a lot of hours watching the world through that window. It was a perfect place for thinking—or dreaming, or brooding—and no one else used it. It was *my* place, and just then I very much needed a place that was mine.

I closed the door behind me and walked slowly to the window seat, no longer crying, but not far from it. I'd been *so* clever in my planning to get away from home without argument, so really brilliant and creative. Things were working out so well it was a miracle I was still alive.

But not a good miracle. I slumped down onto the seat, no longer caring *how* my clothes smelled. Outside it was getting to be late afternoon, darker than it should have been because of the gathering clouds. Sometime tonight the rain would start, and tomorrow there would be a sea of mud . . .

"I refuse to let him force me into this," I whispered to the diamond-shaped panes of the casement. "I would rather hang than accept either of his alternatives, and if I really have to, I'll make it happen."

The only trouble with that was that I didn't want to die. There was so much I hadn't done or seen— and now probably never would. One way or the other, my life would never again be mine to direct. I'd done something wrong and had been condemned for it, the reason behind the wrongdoing making no difference at all. My father hadn't even asked *why* I'd taken Gray Thunder, and I understood the reason. He didn't care what had put my life into his hands; he was too busy being delighted *something* had.

A knock suddenly came at the door, but company was the last thing I was in the mood for. I ignored the noise in the hope that the knocker would give up and go away, but no such luck. Rather than give up, the knocker opened the door and walked in.

"I knew you were in here," my mother said, advancing across the carpeting. "This has always been your favorite haven, but today it's much too gloomy. Why don't we light a lamp, and lighten the scene at the same time?"

She was trying very hard to be cheerful and pleasant, but I wasn't in any mood to join in the effort. I continued to sit there and stare out the window, and she quickly got the message.

"It always upsets your father when he has to be strict with you, but today was the worst," she said in a very gentle voice, her hand coming to my shoulder. "He was so disturbed, he didn't even notice his favorite carpet had been ruined by spilled wine. Alex—"

"If you think he's bothered now, wait until he finds that I won't go along with his little plot," I couldn't help saying. "When that happens, you'd better have healers standing by."

"To tend whose bloody carcass?" she asked, her hand gone with the gentleness. "His or yours? Why must you two be so alike, and why must you always fight? I always have to make peace between you, but if I get in the middle *this* time, I'll be the one needing a healer."

"He's the one trying to force people into things," I muttered, trying to forget all the times my mother *had* intervened. "I offered to solve his problem by leaving, but he refused to even consider the idea. He likes his own too well to want to abandon it."

"I should hope so," she said, moving to her left to sit opposite me in the window seat. My mother was a very beautiful woman with reddish-brown hair and silver eyes, and her riding outfit said she'd been out on horseback.

Her gloves were still tucked into her belt, and she held the pouch with my belongings that Merwin had had.

"I should hope so," she said again, tossing me the pouch after she was seated. "You don't solve a problem by running away from it, and that's what you'd be trying to do if you left. You know you're not happy here, but you don't know *why*. Find that out, and you won't have to leave."

"I'm not happy here because I want to travel," I told her, ignoring the pouch. "There, now that I know the reason, I can stay here and travel to my heart's content."

"I think if you'd been my first child, I'd probably have refused to have any more," she commented with a sour look. "Even as a baby—Well, that doesn't really matter. What does matter is the fact that your father has broken one of his own personal rules in an effort to help you. Being free and on your own hasn't helped you in the least, so now he's trying it the other way. Don't you think *you* might try it, just to see how it works?"

"You make it sound as simple as trying on a pair of boots," I scoffed. "If they feel good, go ahead and keep them. If they don't, toss them out into the trash. Don't you think the winner of a full-range competition might protest just a little over being thrown into the trash?"

"Is that what's bothering you the most?" she asked, one dark brow arched. "The virtual certainty that you won't be able to treat your husband the way you've treated your boyfriends?"

"What's that supposed to mean?" I asked, honestly puzzled. "And what boyfriends are you talking about?"

"Maybe I should have called them passing male aquaintances," she responded. "Considering that they were all rather good-looking I can't fault your taste, but as far as personality goes—I'm sure they were all adequate in bed, but were you ever able to talk to any of them?"

"As far as I know, they were all capable of speech," I answered, beginning to get annoyed. "I just didn't happen to want them for discussions. Don't you and Father have anything better to do with your time than catalog the men I've had sex with?"

"If you ever have a troubled child, we'll see how well *you* do at minding your own business," she countered, not in the least embarrassed. "But you're still avoiding my question. You made no commitment at all to any of the men you've been with, not even to the extent of treating them as equals. Is—"

"But they weren't my equals," I interrupted with a laugh. "They knew that as well as I did, so what would have been the point in pretending? You think they never tested their range against mine, or tried to see how far my battle skills extended? They hated admitting it when they couldn't measure up, but they still had to do it."

"Could *that* be it?" She looked abruptly startled. "You were born with a great deal of ability, and your nature forced you to improve yourself in every way you could. Then one day you looked around and discovered no one could match you. It had to make you feel terribly lonely, and that's why you want to travel. To search for someone who can be a full companion. But Alex, your father must have seen that, and that's why he decided on the competition. To find you the best man available."

"The best of a bunch of second-raters is still a second-rater," I pointed out. "Even if what you say is true—and it strikes me as being too simple—that competition won't solve a thing. I'd be stuck with someone who resented me for being better than him, and I refuse to allow that. I really would rather hang."

"I don't think I blame you," she muttered, brows raised over troubled eyes. "I would myself. But what if you're wrong? What if the competition does find someone your equal? Why not wait and see?"

"And then what?" I asked with a snort. "Find myself needing to decide between bitter resentment and ten years at drudge labor? Especially when I'll know I could have beaten the winner without half trying?"

"Alex, dear, I'm sorry," she said as she put a hand out

to me, obviously serious. "If you're thinking about running away, I'm afraid that won't be possible. Your father is having a team of Sighted watch you, just to prevent something like that. I'll have a talk with him—"

"To accomplish what?" I interrupted again. "If there's one thing I've learned, it's that strong men will laugh at the idea of any woman being stronger. Trying to tell him differently would be a waste of time."

"You're probably right, but I still have to try," she responded with a sigh, then got to her feet. "Maybe I can point out how silly we'll all look if the winner of his competition is made a fool of by his wild, undisciplined daughter. He might decide to forget the idea rather than let that happen."

She smiled and gave my hand a reassuring pat, then left the room with a definite sense of purpose. I knew she would try speaking to my father, but when he thought he was right he had a habit of not hearing opposing opinions. If anyone was going to get me out of that mess it would have to be me, but right then I couldn't see how. If only I could get my father to believe me without using force . . .

At that point I sat up slowly on the seat, the glimmering of an idea beginning to show itself. I'd have to spend part of the next day doing research, but if I found what I needed, the time would be well spent. My father would be furious, of course, but that couldn't be helped. Better him furious than me stuck between two impossible situations.

I stared out my favorite window while the plan began to solidify, and actually found a smile. It would rain tomorrow, and what better way to brighten the gloom than to ruin someone's plot to take advantage of the helpless . . . ?

CHAPTER TWO

Tiran leaned his chair back against the inn wall, full satisfaction covering him like a blanket. He and Encar had gotten to that city the day before, soaking wet from the rain, exhausted from days and miles of travel, starving for a decent meal. After a very good dinner, a night's undisturbed sleep, and an excellent breakfast, Tiran was beginning to feel human again.

"I wish you would stop looking as though you're ready to settle in for the winter," Encar said around a mouthful of eggs. "It's only the middle of the summer here, Tiran, and summer is when you go and do."

"We've been going and doing together for more than five years, En," Tiran pointed out, his deep voice held low. "Or at least *I've* been doing. Your only contribution to the partnership has been opening gates for us to go through."

"What else was I *supposed* to do?" Encar whined in protest, his narrow face wounded. "You knew when we formed the partnership that opening gates was just about the limit of my magical ability. And why would I need more? *You're* the one everybody wants to hire, to train their army or lead it into battle. I do my part by getting you to them. Like the next employer, who happens to be waiting for us at this very—"

"Encar, not now," Tiran all but growled. "You do nothing but count profits while I work my butt off, so going from one job to the next doesn't bother you. Right now I want a short vacation, so I'm going to take it. Unless you'd rather dissolve the partnership."

"And give up my share of all that beautiful gold?" Encar asked with a snort. "Really, Tiran, I'm not stupid. But why would you want to take a vacation in *this* dull place? I hear there's a beautiful world just beyond our next employment, all white-sand beaches, blue-green ocean, lots of beautiful—"

"I think I'll take a walk," Tiran interrupted again as he stood. "If I'm not back in time for lunch, don't force yourself to wait."

"Well, of course I won't," Encar agreed. "But where are you going? What if there's an emergency and I have to get in touch with you? Tiran—"

By then the big mercenary had left the inn, and the relief he felt was incredible. Encar was worse than a wife, constantly nagging and complaining and helplessly lost without him. And he couldn't even be used to provide the pleasure a wife would. The one thing he was good for was opening gates, and Tiran was beginning to be very tired of even that.

Outside was a pretty day with a lot of people hurrying in all directions. It made Tiran feel good that *he* didn't have somewhere to hurry off to, at least not immediately. He hadn't yet accepted that next job, even though Encar had been working on him to agree to the very generous terms being offered. He had the feeling the terms were a little *too* generous for the simple assignment it was supposed to be, and he'd take a good look around before sending for his company.

"You fool!" the man in front of him suddenly snarled when the crowds forced Tiran to bump into him. "Why don't you watch where you're—oh."

The man had turned around looking for a fight, but the sight of Tiran quickly changed his mind. The man was tall and husky; Tiran was a lot larger. The man wore a dagger at his belt; Tiran wore a dagger *and* a sword. The man had blond hair, yellow eyes, and stubble on his face; Tiran was clean-shaven, black-haired, and green-eyed. Only in places like that did his green eyes bother people, but it had been a long time since anyone had remarked about them.

"Sorry about the push, but everybody out today seems overeager," Tiran drawled. "They must have all stayed inside yesterday because of the rain."

"Uh, yeah, right," the man agreed, trying not to stare up at the big mercenary. "No offense meant, no offense taken. Wasn't anybody's fault . . ."

Wiping one hand across his face showed he was giving up on the small talk, and then he pushed away through the crowds as fast as he could go. Tiran was just as pleased to go on with his walk unbothered. After all, he *was* trying to vacation.

And that city seemed to be just the place for it. The heavy stone buildings and cobbled streets reminded him of his own hometown, in a world little different from that one. The people he walked among were also familiar, an echo of home that affected him strangely. It was a lot of years since he'd last been back, and that time he hadn't even tried to find anyone he knew. Chances were they wouldn't have been very happy to see him . . .

Tiran abandoned that thought with a sigh and went back to sightseeing. It was useless to regret what once had been, and the city provided an opportunity he didn't want to waste. There would be stores to buy familiar things in, a racetrack to lose some money at, a pleasure house to spend an enjoyable evening in. And without Encar, definitely without Encar.

It was a very pleasant summer day, still too early for the heat to be unbearable or all the puddles to be dry. Tiran strolled along, looking for a shop window that would tempt him into stopping, and then he noticed something else. He'd been letting the crowd carry him along, and it suddenly came to him that he was being carried in a definite direction. Most of the people around him were heading for some place in particular, and he wondered where that was.

"Say, can you tell me where everyone is hurrying to?" he asked a man on his left. "I'd hate to find myself volunteering for something just by being there."

"Like the army?" the man came back with a chuckle. "Don't blame you a bit, but you have nothing to worry about. We're all heading for the town square, to hear the details of the proclamation posted this morning. There's a copy of it on that board over there."

The man pointed to a notice board ahead and to Tiran's right, then increased his pace toward the square he'd mentioned. Tiran could just see it over the heads of the crowd, and that helped the mercenary make up his mind. First he'd read the proclamation, and then he'd decide whether he wanted more detail on the subject.

It took only a little effort to make his way to the board, and he stopped there among the others who had gathered to read. The proclamation glittered faintly in the morning sun, showing it had been created magically rather than printed. That probably meant it was posted all over the kingdom, and once he began reading, Tiran understood why.

"His Majesty King Reynar III of Golran is pleased to announce a Competition," the proclamation read. "In the Tradition of Olden Times, a Full-Range Contest is decreed among any and all Unmarried Individuals in the Kingdom. The Prize to be awarded the Ultimate Winner is the Hand and Dowry of Her Highness Princess Alexia, daughter to King Reynar. Registration will be held for three days, and then the Competition will begin."

At the bottom was the signature of some lord or other, high this-and-that to the king. Tiran read the thing through, then shook his head.

"Why would a king make his daughter the prize in a contest?" he muttered to himself. "If he wants to marry her off, why doesn't he just do it?"

"Because she's ugly as a boil and twice as mean," came the unexpected answer in a silken-smooth voice. "Since he can't marry her off to any man who's seen her, he's now trying to give her away."

The woman who had been speaking turned, and Tiran could feel his brows rise. "Girl" would be a better word than "woman," but however you said it, she was beautiful. Long, heavy red hair, glittering silver eyes, a fully curved body that suited her unusual height—The other men there were just as interested, but her ability to look them straight in the eye seemed to quiet some of their enthusiasm.

"If you know what that princess looks like, you must be from around here," one of them offered before Tiran could comment. "So your advice would be to stay away from the competition?"

"If you like the idea of lots of land and gold, go ahead and give it a try," the girl answered with a shrug. "If you're fussy about what you take to bed, though, you'd be smart to think twice. If the lady tells her daddy her new husband isn't performing . . . Well, there'd always be the runner-up."

The man who had asked the question grimaced, then moved closer to the silver-eyed girl.

"If it was you I had to perform with, there'd be *nothing* in the way of complaints," he murmured, lifting his arm to slide it around her waist. "Let's get out of here and find someplace quiet, and I'll show you what I mean."

"I'm not interested, friend," the girl returned calmly, refusing to let herself be drawn closer to the man. "Be smart and let it pass."

"Now, you don't mean that," the man coaxed with a grin, starting to tighten his grip. "It won't take any time at all and you'll be thanking me—"

Tiran was a breath away from stepping in when suddenly all interference became unnecessary. With lightning speed the girl brought her knee up into the man's crotch, catching him square with a move that her eyes hadn't warned was coming. It was such an old move that many of those watching groaned to see the man taken by it. The man himself *didn't* groan; first he choked as his eyes bulged, and then he folded to the ground, clutching his wounded parts.

"Thanks, friend," the girl murmured, faint amusement now in her eyes. "You were right about it not taking very long. My advice would definitely be to forget about the competition. And that goes for any of you who aren't better than this gem. If you risk your health, it should be for something worthwhile."

She looked around at her listeners with a faint smile, then walked off to disappear into the crowd. One of the men standing near the board bent to the fallen, but another let out a deep breath.

"Well, that's the end of *my* wanting to join the competition," he announced. "If that's how the *girls* around here handle themselves, I don't think I'd care to face the men. And I'm going to spread the word to everyone else I know. Ugly as a boil and twice as mean. The gold wouldn't be worth it."

Murmurs of agreement came from all around, and then the small crowd began to disperse. Tiran glanced up to see they weren't standing far from a transients' hostel, and then he noticed something much more interesting. Two young street urchins were taking turns reenacting the way the girl had downed her erstwhile admirer, at the same time quietly laughing their heads off.

Tiran was curious, and experience had taught him he was usually smart to indulge his curiosity. He strolled over to a place about ten feet from the two boys, crouched down, then began to flip a coin. The golden color of it caught the rays of the sun, and also quickly caught the attention of the boys.

"Hey, lord, you shouldn't oughta do that," one of the boys said after sidling closer. "Somebody could take it away from you, and you wouldn't like that. What you need is a city guide, to tell you what not to do and where not to go."

"Two guides," the second, younger boy corrected, glaring at his friend. "Two's always better than one."

"The only kind of guide I'd be interested in is one who knows more than most people," Tiran said, still flipping the coin. "If he can't answer a few easy questions . . ."

"I can answer anything," the first boy announced, his friend chiming in with "Me, too!" a moment later. "You just ask something and *see* if I don't know."

"That man the girl floored," Tiran drawled. "You think he's staying at the transients' hostel?"

"I *know* he is," the second boy put in triumphantly when the first hesitated. "I seen him come out the door this morning."

"But you've never seen the girl before," Tiran prodded gently. "*She* isn't staying at the hostel."

"Hell, no," the first boy said with a grin. "That was Alex. We don't know *where* she sleeps, but it ain't at the hostel."

"We seen her a few times and asked who she was," the second boy added. "We know *everything* going on in the city."

"I'll bet you do," Tiran said with a grin. "And I also bet you'd know the best places to spend a gold coin. Why don't you go ahead and do it?"

With that he flipped the coin to them, and their grimy faces lit up as the first boy closed a tight hand around the gold.

"Hey, thanks, brother!" the boy said with a laugh, then he realized he might have gone too far. "I mean, thanks, lord."

"*Brother*'s good enough," Tiran allowed as he straightened. "Make sure no one knows you have that before you get it spent."

"They won't have *time* to know," the second boy said with his own laugh, and then the two were gone in a figurative cloud of dust. Tiran stood thinking for a moment, then he turned back to consider the notice board.

So a girl named Alex just "happened" to be near the board closest to the transients' hostel. Luckily for the transients of the city, she was able to warn them away from entering the competition. None of them had known how ugly and bad-tempered the princess Alexia was until she'd told them, thereby saving them from a fate worse than death. The word would now spread to *all* transients in the city, and they'd stay away from the competition in droves.

"Why do I have the feeling she wasn't just trying to keep the competition local?" Tiran muttered to himself. The idea that a princess would be running around the city alone, discouraging men from competing, seemed scatterbrained. But so did the idea of that kind of competition, which was supposed to be used to find a fitting mate for a *crown* princess. If the girl had been a crown princess, the proclamation would have said so.

Curiosity stirred in Tiran again, stronger than it had been in quite a while. He was supposed to be on vacation, but didn't people look for interesting things to do while vacationing? And didn't they sometimes follow pretty girls to see if they stood a chance with them? Of course they did, so why shouldn't he?

Whistling tunelessly and almost soundlessly, Tiran headed for the square to get more details on the competition.

"Yes, we slept extremely well, Your Majesty," Lord Arthon assured his host. "After we dried out, of course."

The laughter from those around them was polite, not too enthusiastic and not too stiff. King Reynar thought the embassy from Vilim put forward a very good face, but there was a faint tension just under the surface that he didn't know the reason for. Not yet, anyway.

"We're pleased to welcome you to Golran, my lords and lady," Reynar said with a pleasant smile. "Do help yourselves to refreshments, and then We will explain the task We would have you perform. As soon as the task is done, we may all concentrate on the agreements you've come to negotiate."

None of the four members of the embassy went so far as to stop and stare, but Reynar could see he'd surprised them. The three men, Lords Arthon, Fregin and Moult, covered their reactions by turning toward the refreshment table. Arthon was tall and muscular, Fregin average in height and weight, Moult short and stout. Fregin and Moult both had brown hair and eyes to go with undistinguished features; Arthon was blond with *blue* eyes but, aside from that, was rather handsome.

Their fourth member, however, could not be dismissed with a few words of general description. Lady Wella was exquisite, and the way she carried herself underscored the attraction of her rich, dark brown hair and glowing, dark brown eyes. She was dressed in a day gown of blue trimmed with white, and she seemed to have the habit of accepting what she heard without criticism. Not that she seemed pliable or unintelligent. Just uncritical.

And without a doubt she's the most dangerous of the four, Reynar thought. Her purpose has to be to dazzle or even seduce me, at the very least to distract me from being too critical of their agreement. Or maybe she represents a test I'm supposed to pass, to show how competent a king I am. We'll just have to see.

"I hope you'll join us, Your Majesty," Lord Moult said after showing the servant which of the cakes he wanted. "We brought this coffee as a gift for you, as well as a supply for us. It's a drink one comes quickly to appreciate, especially in the morning."

"We'll be pleased to join you," Reynar said, glad that he'd already had his sorcerers test it for poison or general ill effect. In its natural state the brew looked evil, but its aroma was positively enticing. His guests drank it with sugar and cream, and so would he.

"After that breakfast we had, Your Majesty, the coffee alone will do me," Lady Wella told him with a warm, incredibly attractive smile. "And it looks as though Lord Arthon and Lord Fregin agree with me."

It was true that only Lord Moult had taken a sampling of the snack cakes, but the portly man was unconcerned. He seemed to be beyond self-consciousness, at least as far as his appetite went. The four took chairs not far from Reynar, and as soon as he was handed his cup of coffee he dismissed the servants.

"Now we can be a little less formal," he told his guests. "Using the royal 'We' is required of me, but only in public. I know you're wondering what task I'm going to ask you to perform, so let me set your minds at rest. I need a panel of judges for a competition about to be held, and that's what I want you for."

"Judges?" Arthon asked with raised brows, whatever relief he felt completely masked. "What sort of a competition is it, Your Majesty?"

"It's a full-range competition open to all unmarried men in the kingdom," Reynar replied. "The entrants don't have to be citizens of the kingdom, but they do have to be single."

"There must be a reason for that requirement," Lady Wella observed prettily.

"Certainly," Reynar agreed with a smile. "The winner of the competition has to be unmarried, because what he'll win is my daughter Alexia."

Wella's dark brows rose, but she wasn't alone in that reaction. The three men stirred and glanced at one another, and Arthon cleared his throat.

"I presume you have reasons for offering so precious a treasure as the prize," he said, showing his diplomatic ability. "I, however, would like to know what 'full-range' means. Does it refer to the events the contestants will have to win at?"

"Only in a manner of speaking," Reynar told him, suddenly getting a very odd feeling. "Full-range refers to the shape-shifting abilities of my people, as opposed to limited-range. The events of the competition will be weighted heavily in favor of the most versatile of the entrants—Why do I have the feeling I'm telling you something you've never heard before?"

The three men seemed to be struggling to control their disturbance, and even Wella looked bothered. All amusement was gone from her eyes as she held out a hand toward him.

"Please forgive us, Your Majesty, but this *does* make us rather confused," she admitted. "We knew your people were shape-shifters, but we assumed you were like the shape-shifters of *our* world. You know, with only a single link-shape to shift into, most often accompanied by the ability of Persuasion?"

"Yes, it so happens I do know," Reynar said, cautiously relieved. "We seem to be cousins to those people, and some consider us poor cousins because we lack the ability of Persuasion. We, however, prefer being able to Shift into almost any shape we care to, as opposed to influencing those around us. There's less temptation involved in the Shifting."

"There certainly is," Fregin agreed comfortably, the first words he'd spoken since the embassy had arrived. Reynar's people had told him the man was a magic user, and that was probably why he was there: to make sure the others weren't unduly influenced by Persuasion.

"You say your people are able to Shift into almost any shape they care to?" Moult asked, his round face now showing curiosity. "That, of course, must mean within reason."

"That means within range of each individual's ability," Reynar corrected. "Just about anyone can draw a stick figure, but not everyone is an artist. Most of my people can Shift into half a dozen different forms, but some do a better job of it than the rest. And then there are those whose only limitations are knowledge, experience, and imagination. Not including copying people, of course. With that we're all stuck with the mirror-image effect. Happily."

"What's the mirror-image effect?" Arthon asked, his polite question just a shade too casual. Disturbance had flickered in his odd blue eyes, and Reynar thought he understood why.

"It's the reason my people can't Shift to look like someone else and then commit a crime," Reynar told him. "In copying other people, we always end up with a mirror-image reflection rather than a true copy. Once you've seen it a time or two, it isn't possible to mistake the reflection for the real thing. There's an imbalance of sorts that's a dead giveaway."

"We'd certainly be interested to learn how to recognize that imbalance," Arthon said, confirming Reynar's guess. The embassy from Vilim didn't want to say something indiscreet to anyone but each other.

"I'll have one of my people see to it," the king promised, considering it best to set their minds at ease. "Do you understand now what I'm asking of you? We'll supply a copy of the rules of the competition, and you'll need to make sure those rules are followed. If there's a dispute in the sector one of you is responsible for, you have the final word on settling it. Clear?"

"Our parts in it, yes," Moult fretted, obviously still confused. "What I fail to understand, Your Majesty, is how far this changing business goes. Our people don't have that talent, you see. Are we likely to be called upon to judge the merits of two—bushes, say? Or the beauty of the plumage of two birds in flight?"

"I can see I'm going to have to arrange a basics-session for you," Reynar answered with a sigh. "Lord Moult, if I were to change myself into a bush to hide among other bushes, you would have your choice of ways to find me. You could push at all the greenery in sight, and I'd be the one who fell over because I wasn't rooted into the ground. Or I'd be the one leaning on the other bushes because I can't stay upright without roots *or* feet. If I were a bird, I'd be the bowlegged one that *couldn't* fly."

"But why couldn't you fly?" Wella asked in surprise. "If you're able to change into an exact copy of a bird, you should be able to fly. And why would you be bowlegged?"

"Both of your questions have the same answer," Reynar said, noticing that he was smiling again. "Even if I copy the *shape* of a bird, I can't copy its weight. I'll still have the weight of a man, which will keep me firmly anchored to the ground."

"And the thin legs of a bird could never support the weight of a man!" Arthon exclaimed with satisfaction. "That's why you would be bowlegged."

"Exactly," Reynar agreed, then noticed that he hadn't tasted his coffee. He braced himself inwardly before taking a cautious sip, but the bracing was unnecessary. The warm liquid was excellent, as pleasing to the palate as its aroma had been to the nose. He took a larger swallow, then nodded his satisfaction.

"I'll have to find a suitable gift to thank you for this one," he said, gesturing with his cup. "In the meantime, I've arranged a tour of the palace and grounds you should enjoy. We'll speak again later."

Knowing they'd been dismissed, the four rose and bowed before heading toward the refreshment table to leave their own coffee cups. Wella sent him a glance and a smile before following after her male companions, and that made up Reynar's mind. From now on Josti, his wife and queen, would have to sit in on these meetings. There was no sense in trying to resist temptation alone, not when he knew he wasn't likely to win against it. He was a healthy man, after all, and the best way to resist a beautiful woman was to stand behind another beautiful woman.

Reynar laughed softly to himself as he enjoyed another sip of his coffee. If their new friends had understood about his people's kind of shape-shifting, they wouldn't have bothered trying to tempt him with Wella. After all, if he decided he really had to have her, he could. Josti was the most understanding of wives, not to mention versatile and accommodating. He'd just ignore the mirror-image effect . . .

I got back to the palace too late for formal lunch, so I went to the kitchens and just scrounged. I'd done the same often enough in the past that no one paid any real attention, which left me free to consider the morning's work.

I'd visited the three or four most usual places the transients frequented, those who were only passing through the kingdom or were here for a limited time. After telling them the "truth" about Princess Alexia, not many of them were likely to sign up for the competition. That still left a lot of local men—with the proclamation going up magically in every town and village in the country, *no* one would miss hearing—but I thought I had that covered.

I sliced off another sliver of cheese and ate it, reviewing my plans and trying to find flaws in them. They'd begin registering entrants that very afternoon, and would continue signing up those straggling in over the next two days. The vast majority of those intending to enter would be at the tables set up on the parade grounds, the party due to start in less than an hour. I was sure no one involved expected it, but I would be attending that party.

"If you'd asked, Your Highness, I would have sent a tray to your apartment." Tringo's voice came suddenly from behind my left shoulder. "A princess has no business bruising her dignity with a hastily swallowed meal at a scullery table."

"I know kitchen masters are supposed to be snobs, Tringo, but you abuse the privilege," I said without turning. "If the day ever comes that my dignity depends on where I'm eating, we'll both know I'm in trouble. And stop fretting. I'll be out of your way in just a few minutes."

"I'm sure you're welcome to remain as long as you care to, Your Highness," he returned stiffly, his thin body undoubtedly held rigidly straight. "It's certainly not my place to tell you where you may or may not remain. You do, however, need a small bowl of stew to go with that bread and cheese. I'll have it brought to you immediately."

With that he stalked off across the room, looking around for a victim to delegate stew detail to. I sighed as I turned back to what I was eating, wondering if I would ever live long enough to find an acceptable point of compromise with the man. When I was polite to him, he tried to run me over; when I refused to be run over, he went rigid and insulted. It was almost as if he didn't *want* to get along with me . . .

I stopped that thought cold, knowing it was only a reaction to what I was in the middle of. Tringo didn't get along with anyone, and he had nothing to do with the case of nerves I was developing. What if my plans didn't work? What if I ended up having to decide between an impossible marriage and an impossible captivity? What if death became my only way out? It could happen, I knew it could . . .

I put the knife down and closed my eyes, needing every ounce of concentration to struggle my way back to control. My own half-thought-out planning had gotten me into that mess, but if I lost confidence in myself I'd never get out again. Maybe my new plans *would* fail, but if I didn't try them, they couldn't possibly succeed. It was a matter of not lifting a finger and accepting failure, or fighting for the chance to win.

Taking a deep breath let me open my eyes again, and by then the struggle was over. If the worst happened, I'd worry about it then. Until it happened, I'd fight with everything I had.

"Here's your stew, Alex," a whispered voice said, and I looked up to see Fini holding a large bowl. She'd whispered to keep Tringo from hearing what she called me.

"You can put it down, Fini, but I won't be eating any of it," I said, wiping my knife before resheathing it. "All

I wanted was a snack to cut my hunger. If things work out, I can eat as much as I like later."

"If what things work out?" she asked as I stood. "Are you all right? While I was walking over here, I thought—"

"I'm fine," I interrupted with a smile and a hand on her arm. "I'm so good, in fact, that I'd advise you not to be anywhere near my father for the next few hours. When he finds out just how fine I am, I guarantee he'll be looking for blood."

"Since it's your blood he'll be after, why should *I* worry?" she countered, more exasperated than amused. "I swear, Alex, somebody would think you were in enough trouble without needing to look for more. Don't you have *any* sense?"

"That's something we'll be finding out, Fini," I said with a grin, then waved good-bye over my shoulder as I left. I still had to find Gromal and talk him into going along with my plan, which could be the hardest part of all. I'd still be able to use one of the others, of course, but I wanted Gromal's standing. In an hour or so it would start, and then we'd all see . . .

Tiran had thought he would reach the parade grounds early enough to look around while doing some serious thinking; it was a simple idea, but it turned out to be simple in another way. When he arrived, it looked like more than half the city had gotten there ahead of him.

To get a look at who the entrants will be, he realized, stopping on the fringes of the crowd. This is probably the most excitement they've had in years.

Which was a point he ought to keep in mind. Life in a place like that was usually quiet, no problems, no excitement. Was he so sick of the life he'd been leading that that sounded good to him, or was he just tired? Would he feel differently once he'd had some sitting-around time, or was he seriously looking for something different and better?

A short way around to the right of the crowd was a bunch of hastily erected booths. People were selling food and drinks and sweets as though it was a fair, and the odor of hot meat pies was magnetic. Tiran hadn't stopped for lunch in the city, a fact his growling stomach kept reminding him about. First he'd get something to eat, and then he'd do some serious thinking.

After buying two meat pies and a small flask of ale, Tiran made his way to the stand of trees surrounding the parade grounds. The noon sun was hot enough to make the shade feel good, but very few people were taking advantage of it. They'd started putting out registration tables, and most of the crowd was more interested in that than in getting out of the sun.

Which meant he could get in some undisturbed thinking while eating. Keeping his scabbarded sword out of the way without using his hands as he sat carefully in front of a tree was tricky, but the pies and ale left him no choice. He slid and sidled more than sat, but as ridiculous as it probably looked, it did work.

The first pie went down fast to satisfy his hunger, and it was good enough to make him want to savor the second. A swallow of ale from the flask smoothed the last crumbs along, but it didn't do much to lubricate his reasoning. Why was he there, and what did he hope to accomplish? Had he really decided to enter a contest that would end in his marriage? Wasn't he more used to avoiding marriage? And how long did he intend to ask himself questions without coming through with some answers?

"This is all happening because of that girl," he mumbled around a mouthful of the second meat pie. "If I hadn't seen her and realized she was the one being given away . . ."

But he *had* seen her, and the sight had brought him more interest than he could ever remember feeling. He usually took small and dainty women to his bed, shy and trembling females who would faint at the mere thought of challenging him. He'd been certain that was the sort of woman he preferred, but now he'd been kicked in the teeth with the truth. That was the sort of woman he felt safe with, the sort that would never tempt him.

And now he'd been caught by the real thing. That silver-eyed redhead was magnificent, and Tiran had the sinking feeling he was almost to the point of being willing to do anything to win her. She might have been made to his personal specifications—except for that temper. Even a blind man would have known she had one; that she'd learned to control it only meant she probably blew up twice as hard when she did let it go.

So why had thoughts of her been haunting him since that morning? She wasn't happy about the competition, and unless someone cast a spell on her, she would *not* greet the winner as her personal hero. Entering the competition and besting all opponents would win her, but it would not win her over.

"And I feel sorry for any man who tries forcing himself on her," Tiran murmured with a private grin, remembering that morning. "Even I would have to work at besting her. The average yokel from around here would be unconscious before he realized his mistake."

Unconscious—or dead. There had been that unmistakable air about the girl, the attitude that said her training had gone beyond simple fighting. If pushed hard enough she would respond with deadly force, and the man who couldn't match her would lose more than a fall.

Match her. Tiran paused in the middle of chewing, suddenly wondering if *that* was the reason for the competition. Was her father looking for a man who could match her, one who could protect himself long enough to collect the first kiss? That seemed like an excellent possibility, and would even explain why *he* was there. Tiran had always been most attracted to those things that had to be fought for. The harder the fight, the sweeter the eventual win.

And he couldn't imagine a woman who would make him fight harder, after the competition as well as during it. He'd have to really work to get her to accept him, and he'd never be able to take her for granted. If he ever did she'd be gone, without warning and without tears. Whether he retired from hiring out his skill or decided to go back to it, he'd never be bored again.

"It looks like I've made that decision," he told himself with a chuckle. "I'm going to spend my vacation winning a permanent cure for boredom. Assuming I can talk her into letting me live."

That made him laugh, but didn't interfere with the hasty finishing of his meal. He wanted to be one of the first to step up and register, but he had to return the ale flask and get his deposit back. For what he'd been made to leave, he could have bought three flasks.

Having had to wait on line at the ale booth meant he found a line when he reached the registration tables. No one had made any announcements about being ready to take names, but the number of men ahead of Tiran said an announcement was unnecessary. Those who had decided to try their hands were eager to be started, almost as eager as the big mercenary.

"Rust leather," a voice said from behind Tiran. He turned to see that two more men were on line behind him, and the closer of the two had spoken.

"What about rust leather?" he asked, noticing that both men, as well as the ones ahead of him, had on cloth shirts and trousers. "Don't tell me there's a law against wearing it?"

"Rust leather says you're a mercenary and not from around here," the man answered, a lot of bluster in his tone. "This competition is only for local men. They won't let you register."

"The proclamation specified unmarried men," Tiran returned, swallowing his annoyance. "It didn't say anything about a required place of residence. I think you'll find you're mistaken."

"It didn't *have* to say anything about that," the man insisted as Tiran began to turn away. "If you're not from around here, how will they know you're not married? You could have a dozen wives in half as many worlds."

"That's what the magic users are for," Tiran pointed out with rapidly fading patience. "See those men behind the ones taking names? Silver to copper they're checking each man as he steps up, using a minor truth spell to see if he's lying. Why would they guess and hope when they can know?"

The heckler finally ran out of what to say, leaving Tiran free to face forward again. He knew that the man was probably trying to cut the competition before the contest started, but the big mercenary wasn't feeling charitable. He was more personally involved than the yokel behind him, and resented the attempt to best him with words. Anyone wanting to win would need skill to do it, the kind of skill Tiran would use.

And thinking about skill caused him to look around again, estimating how many of the hopefuls wore belts like his. For those who shape-shifted, there were two options when it came to clothes. Either you took them off and folded them neatly before changing shape, or you went ahead and changed and either tore the clothes or got trapped in them.

Those who used their Shifting skills regularly—and sometimes abruptly—needed a third choice. Centuries earlier, someone had gotten the bright idea of using magical talismans made in the shape of a silver belt. The talisman took your clothes and weapons when you Shifted, and held them in some nonspace until you Shifted back. The talisman wasn't cheap to buy, but for those like Tiran it was worth twice its weight in gold.

And there were more belts around than he'd been expecting. It was years since he'd last been in a community of shape-shifters, and even then the number of talismans hadn't been disproportionately high. People didn't spend gold on something they would rarely use, not in a place of only average wealth. If that many men had talisman belts, it could only be because they used them . . .

Tiran was shocked at what he was suddenly feeling, the teeth-baring urge to begin attacking everyone around him. That reaction usually came only in the midst of battle, and only if he found himself outnumbered. Why would he be feeling it now, with nothing more threatening around than lines of men . . . ?

"Damn it, get a hold," he growled at himself very low, frustration and foolishness now fighting for his attention. "You have no intention of letting them take what's meant to be yours, so stop being a fool. Their presence is *not* a personal insult, and taking them on here and now won't do anything but get you arrested."

It was good advice, but he was only just able to take it. It was ridiculous to think of the other entrants as active rivals, but his mind was seeing them in just that way. It didn't matter that they were after a princess and her dowry rather than a woman; if one of them won the princess, Tiran would lose the woman.

The line was moving slowly but steadily, so he fixed his attention on the forward progress. He didn't enjoy acting or feeling like a fool, but that seemed to be what he'd be doing until the competition was over. If he accepted the fact, he'd hopefully be able to control it where other people were concerned.

It was only a few minutes before Tiran was able to step up to the table. The man sitting there finished writing something, then looked up at him.

"Name and occupation, please," he said with a smile that abruptly froze before fading away.

"I'm Tiran d'Iste, military adviser," Tiran answered, knowing what was coming and dreading it. Ordinarily he could handle the comments, but right then the hold he had on his temper was less than firm.

"You're aware that this is a full-range competition?" the man asked, exquisitely polite. "If you need the phrase explained to you—"

"I don't need it explained," Tiran cut in. "I know what full-range Shifting means, and I'm capable of it. Is there something that makes you believe I'm not?"

"My dear young man, you *know* what's causing the doubt," came the reply from a second source. The Sighted standing behind the registrar had stepped forward, and he smiled at Tiran through his neatly trimmed white beard.

"You have green eyes, young man," the Sighted went on, looking directly at Tiran. "Do you have any idea how rare that eye color is among our people? One in ten thousand at the very least, possibly even one in fifty thousand. We must be certain that no one enters this competition unless he's qualified. If he isn't, it could well mean his life."

"I think I've already proven my eye color has nothing to do with my ability," Tiran replied, fighting to keep his tone from going stiff. "I'm not unknown among the worlds, so please feel free to check on me as much as you like. Right after you accept me as an entrant."

"He believes he's speaking the truth," the Sighted told the registrar with a sigh. "He's also absolutely determined, so you might as well register him."

The man seated at the table looked as though he were signing a death warrant, but after taking a deep breath he plowed on. Age, marital status, world of origin, competitions entered, competitions won, life standing thus far achieved—Tiran answered everything as briefly as possible, but the registrar still filled almost the entire sheet of paper. It was taking longer for him than for most of the others—which thought made Tiran smile.

"All right, that should do it for now," the registrar said at last. "Collect your possessions and come back here. All entrants will be guests of the king until the competition begins."

Tiran nodded and began to turn away, but never completed the step. Sounds of astonishment were coming from all around, undoubtedly caused by the abrupt appearance of the woman he knew as Alex. She had an obvious fighting man with her, and she strode into the middle of everything before holding up both hands to claim everyone's attention.

"For those of you who don't know me, I'm Princess Alexia," she announced in a voice that carried. "Those of you who do know me won't be surprised at the reason I'm here. Since my father has seen fit to hold a competition with my future as prize, I've been given no choice. I'm entering the competition with the rest of you, and I intend to win."

At that point pure bedlam broke out, but Tiran was too stunned to move. His greatest rival in the competition for the woman he wanted would be the woman herself!

CHAPTER THREE

My announcement brought the uproar I'd been expecting, so I just stood there while they got it out of their systems. Gromal didn't say a word, but his amusement was almost thick enough to feel. He'd grinned when I'd told him what I intended to do, and had nodded his agreement to go along with it. He knew my father might have his hide for a rug when that insanity was over, but he'd worry about that when the time came.

Right then his attention had been taken by an entrant at one of the tables, someone he seemed to recognize. The man in question was big, even taller and broader than Gromal, and he wore the rust leather of a professional fighter. His hair was as black as Gromal's, but instead of yellow eyes—or any other normal color—his were green. I seemed to have a vague memory of having seen a man with green eyes, but couldn't remember where.

"All right, who is he?" I asked Gromal, the hullabaloo almost drowning my words. "You're not amused any more, and I'd guess he was why."

"That's Tiran d'Iste," came the deep-voiced answer, a flicker of yellow eyes accompanying it. "I saw him in action once. You'd better hope he's doing this just for the fun of it. You're good, Alex, but he's probably better."

"*Probably* better," I said, filing the information for later consideration. If anyone knew enough to judge, Gromal was it. "So my best bet would be to get him to withdraw. Later I'll want everything you know about him, and then I can—"

"Your Highness, please!" someone interrupted. "I'm sure we all sympathize with your position, but what you intend is impossible."

"What makes you think so?" I countered immediately, certain I didn't know the man. Tall, thin and nervous he was, as well as instantly aware of the way the remaining noise died down. Everyone wanted to hear what was being said, and that made things worse for my challenger.

"It's—ah—impossible because you're not—not a man," he stammered, obviously hating that he was the one on the spot. "The competition is for men, so—"

"Oh, but it's not for men," I interrupted with a pleasant smile. "I checked the archives, and the rules call for 'unmarried individuals' as entrants. *I'm* an 'unmarried individual,' so I qualify. They didn't use the specific word 'men,' so you can't either."

"But that's ridiculous," the man said as he blinked. "When the prize of a competition is the hand of a princess, who else but men would *be* entrants? Everyone understands—"

"Understandings are all very well, but rules are written down," I cut in again, still smiling. "The only reason my father can get away with this is that the competition is part of very old tradition. If you won't accept the rules as they stand, you're also rejecting the tradition. Well, that's fine with me. Which one of you gets to tell my father the competition is off?"

Most of the men in my line of vision paled, including some of the Sighted. My father was one of the best kings our country had ever had, but he was still an absolute ruler. When he decided on something, he didn't care to hear dissenting opinions.

Gromal gave me a glance that said I was playing dirty, and he was perfectly right. The way they all began clearing their throats showed how eager they were to change the subject, so I helped it happen.

"I don't know why the word 'men' isn't used in the ancient rules," I said, looking around at them. "It's possible someone decided to be literary, and paid the usual price in confusion. Whatever, you now have a decision to make. Either I'm allowed to enter the competition, or everyone will know it's fixed and therefore invalid. What do you say?"

People in the watching crowd began muttering; although nothing specific could be heard, the men I addressed jumped to the conclusion I'd hoped they would. The last thing they wanted was for word to spread that the competition was fixed, so they chose their only way out. The previous spokesman conferred briefly with his fellows, then stepped forward again.

"Very well, Your Highness," he gave in with a sigh. "We seem to have no option but to register you as an entrant—subject, of course, to a study of the rules. After that, the duly appointed judges will render a final decision. Is this course acceptable?"

"For the moment," I allowed with a regal nod. "I'll expect that final decision as soon as possible, and the announcement is to be made public. If these good people don't hear about the decision, I'm sure they'll know what happened."

"The announcement will certainly be made," the spokesman hastened to assure everyone in hearing, sweat now beading his forehead. "Now, why don't we get back to—"

"There's one more thing," I interrupted again, hating the way the poor man cringed. "Has anyone been told yet about what happens if more than one entrant makes it all the way through the competition? No? Then it's something all you eager—unmarried individuals—ought to hear. To me, it sounds like a lot of fun."

The other entrants seemed to be all ears, so I switched my cat-about-to-eat-the-canary smile to them.

"If more than one entrant makes it through, there's a final—tiebreaker contest, so to speak. The first one back gets to choose his—or her—favorite mode of combat, and must be defeated at it by one of the others. If he is, then the winner chooses *his* favorite, and the fight is on again. If he isn't, then he's the ultimate winner. Or she is. I thought I'd give you all some idea of what I'll choose if there are others who finish with me."

Gromal came along as I walked out beyond the tables and lines to give us some room. I was also making it easier for everyone to watch, and the crowd wasn't shy. The prospective entrants were closest to us in the circle that formed, but the people in the crowd were right behind.

"This circle isn't wide enough, so everybody had better step back," I called to them. "The man with me is Gromal Sihr, Master Combat Instructor to the Royal Princes— my brothers. He's also been my instructor since I was ten. The weapons we're wearing right now are practice weapons, created for the purpose by magic users."

Gromal and I drew our swords, and the glint of the blades in the sunlight helped widen the surrounding circle by a couple of feet.

"These swords look and feel like the real thing, but the blades are actually only illusion," I explained. "When they come in contact with each other they behave normally, but they won't cut flesh and blood. Like this."

I used my sword to chop at my left arm, and could feel the tingle as the illusion blade passed through without a trace. The crowd gasped and oohed, but they still hadn't heard all of it.

"For this demonstration we're using practice weapons," I went on when the exclamations had quieted. "If the time comes that I have to fight another finalist, the weapons will be real."

There was a lot of muttering as that comment sank in, but Gromal and I weren't waiting for reactions. I turned to him as we both brought our weapons up, and the demonstration was on.

Now, most people have seen sword fights, either real ones or practice bouts. The mind takes on a certain set as it expects certain movements, but Gromal believed a mind-set like that could get someone killed. Our people had special abilities, after all; to refrain from using them in self-defense was stupidity and suicide.

Gromal came at me in serious attack, and when I blocked the blow with my own weapon, I could feel the shock of contact all the way up my arm. The instant his sword shifted, though, I attacked over it to the right. With his longer reach I wasn't really in range to connect, so I extended my reach—by Shifting my arm longer.

There was a united gasp from the audience as Gromal blocked high and backed, but that was only the beginning. When he came too close on my left, I compressed a third of my body width to the right. When he swung at my neck in an effort to decapitate, I was suddenly and briefly three feet shorter. The practice clothes we wore were tight knits that contracted and expanded instantly and easily as the need arose; they'd been designed and made for the purpose we were now putting them to.

After ten minutes of showing our audience what to expect, Gromal began using the same fighting style. At one point he overextended—on purpose, of course—and I was able to figuratively slice through his arm. By that time our audience wasn't making a sound, due to shock, I think, rather than boredom. In between Shifting, Gromal and I were putting on a very pretty fencing exercise.

It wasn't many minutes later when I called a halt and finally looked around. I wanted to see how everyone was taking it, and I wasn't disappointed. The shock was clear on most of the faces watching, and a few had even slid over into fear. It takes a lot of practice to be able to Shift-fight effectively; if even two of the people watching had that practice, I'd eat my boots. But as I looked around a second time, I knew my ordinary diet was safe.

"Wasn't that fun?" I asked into the teetering silence. "It's probably what I'll choose for the finals, but I haven't completely decided yet. I may be in the mood to go for something that takes a bit more skill. Well, we'll all find out together, won't we? Thanks for giving me your time and attention."

Everyone came out of it then, and there was muttering and exclaiming and even a smattering of applause. I resheathed my sword as I turned back to Gromal, then asked low, "What do you think? Is it going to work all the way?"

"Sorry, Alex, but I don't think so," he rumbled in answer, his gaze still moving over our erstwhile audience. "More than half of those who were on line are walking away as fast as they can go, but that still leaves too many. And Tiran d'Iste isn't one of those quitting. I'll swear he watched every move you made with a grin, and now those eyes of his are gleaming. I think he likes what he sees."

"Wonderful," I said with a weary sigh, not about to turn and look for myself. "All I needed was an admirer. Are you telling me he knows how to Shift-fight?"

"Only as well as I do," he said, and then those yellow eyes were looking down at me with a grin. "When you make that face, you look ten years old again. Doesn't it help to know who the most likely winner of the competition will be?"

"Only if that most likely winner is me," I answered, not terribly pleased with the way his grin broadened. "Why do I have the feeling you've suddenly switched your support to *him*?"

"You know I'm a Traditionalist," he said with a shrug of his broad shoulders. "I agreed to go along with your schemes because I don't approve of seeing you paired with someone who's your inferior. Most of this dross couldn't stand against you for a minute, but that doesn't apply to d'Iste. He's better than good, so if he's serious he ought to win."

"That's the second time you've suggested he might not be as determined as the others," I said, ignoring the outrage I felt. Gromal *was* a Traditionalist, which meant he'd always back a man against a woman. I was the only female he'd ever taught, and I'd first had to outgrow the other instructors. "Why would the man be entering if he wasn't seriously interested?"

"If for one reason or another he's stuck here for a while, he could be entering to stave off boredom," came the answer with another shrug. "He could also be curious about what a traditional competition is like, and has decided to find out firsthand. If he wants to, he can come within one step of winning, then do something to have himself disqualified."

"And in that way turn it into a game," I said, feeling more than a little angry. "Doesn't he care that the rest of us don't consider it a game?"

"It isn't guaranteed that *he* does," Gromal warned. "All I said was maybe. If it turns out that he *is* seriously interested, he'll be going for the win with everything he has. Which way would you prefer it?"

I opened my mouth to answer, then decided not to be an idiot. I might not like the idea of someone entering for fun, but if the man was that good, I certainly didn't want him to be serious.

"I'm impressed," Gromal said, his broad face showing a faint smile. "It looks like you're finally learning to think before sounding off. What do we do next?"

"You go back to what you were doing before I dragged you away from it," I said, glancing around to see that the depleted lines had formed at the tables again. "I get to go back to my apartment and wait for my father to drop a ceiling on my head. If we both survive his mild displeasure at this demo, the next one is scheduled for whatever guest quarters are put up for the entrants."

"And that's when we go hand-to-hand," he said with a nod before grinning. "Right now they're seeing you with a weapon in your fist, but wait until they see what the emptied fist can do. We might not even have to use the positional Shifts."

"We might not have to, but I'll probably want to," I said with a grin of my own. "A few of them might decide they can pin me down anyway, so I want them to see what they'll be pinning. It might start out as me, but what happens if I Shift to wolf or tiger form? Instead of a kiss, they'll get a face full of fangs. Or maybe I'll go python, and give them a little hug and squeeze."

"Your Shifting speed will bother them more than number of shapes," he said, as usual taking the professional point of view. "Anyone in a full-range competition can Shift to any form necessary, but how fast they can do it is what separates winner from loser. Since your speed is even better than mine, they could sprain something trying to keep up."

"I don't think I have to tell you what I hope they'll sprain," I said, making him chuckle. "Now don't forget: I *ordered* you to come with me and put on this little show. Since it's the absolute truth, it won't kill you to say it if you're asked."

"I'll keep it in mind," he commented, promising nothing. "Next time try to give me some advance warning. I'd rather get one of the others to stand in for me with a group than have to cancel the session entirely. Those trainees need all the practice and teaching they can get."

"Advance warning it is," I agreed. "I'll see you then."

He nodded and walked off, leaving me free to do the same in another direction. I glanced around before starting, curious to see if that Tiran d'Iste was still staring, but there was no sign of him. That in itself was encouraging, which meant I hadn't done badly for one afternoon's work.

"She did *what*?" Reynar roared, only distantly noticing the way the man in front of him flinched. "She *can't* enter the competition!"

"Your Majesty, Argol pointed that out," Merwin ventured. "Her Highness countered that the traditional rules call for entrants to be 'unmarried individuals,' and say nothing about men. I'm afraid she's correct."

"She would be," Reynar muttered, rubbing at his face with one hand. "She never lies about something that can be checked. So Argol let her enter?"

"Only on a provisional basis, Sire. Providing the rules support her and the designated judges agree, she's then a registered entrant. She—ah—made certain to elicit a promise from Argol that the final decision would be made public. By now the entire city is waiting to hear."

"Because of the crowd that heard the first of it," Reynar growled, this time seeing Merwin flinch. "It's too bad tradition doesn't call for drowning excess daughters at birth. Right now I'd like to do a little retroactive drowning. Maybe our judges will find something in the rules that will let them exclude her—Damn the girl! What more can she do to ruin this?"

"Ah, Your Majesty?" Merwin said hesitantly. "There's—ah—one other thing she did."

"I hate it when you try to break things to me gently, Merwin," Reynar growled. "Spit it out and do it fast."

"Yes, Sire," Merwin quavered. "Her Highness mentioned the rule covering multiple finalists, then showed the other entrants a demonstration of Shift-fighting. She'd brought a combat instructor with her, and together they—"

"Together they scared the hell out of half the men there!" Reynar roared as he stood up from his chair, feeling an overwhelming need to do serious damage with his bare hands. "I'll kill her! It's not bad enough she forces her way into the competition! To ice it she lets the men know what they'll have to face if they win! Are there *any* entrants left? If she ends up winning by default, I'll—"

"No, no, Your Majesty, there are quite a few entrants left," Merwin assured him. "We even seem to have attracted a professional fighter, one with a respected reputation in a large number of worlds. He invited us to check his credentials, so we did. His name is Tiran d'Iste."

"I know that name," Reynar said with a frown, more diverted than soothed. "He can just about name his own price, and once two worlds bid themselves into debt in an effort to get him. If anyone can match strategy and skill against that daughter of mine—You're positive he didn't withdraw? If he decides she isn't worth the effort—"

"No, Sire, I'm certain he didn't withdraw," Merwin quickly assured him. "As a matter of fact, he's already returned with his belongings and has been given an apartment in the guest palace. When last I checked, seventeen others had also returned."

"I want all of them here for dinner tonight," Reynar said, beginning to pace around the room. "Make certain our judges have been given copies of the competition rules, and then tell them about the first decision required of them. After dinner they'll make a formal announcement about Alexia's eligibility. And make triply certain that girl is also at dinner. By then I hope to have control over the urge to kill."

"Yes, Your Majesty," Merwin acknowledged with a bow, then left as fast as he could move. Getting out while the getting is good, Reynar thought with a snort. Wise man, Merwin.

But that Alexia! Reynar wished he had his hands on her, even though it would do no good at all. She made him want to commit violence, but he loved his children too much to ever harm them. Or want to see them harm themselves.

"What's the *matter* with that.girl?" he whispered, wishing he could find at least one person who understood her. She'd even managed to talk her mother around, and it had hurt him to have to refuse seeing it Josti's way. He could believe Alexia was worried about having to marry a man with less skill than she had, but that was the reason for the competition in the first place. Her objections were no more than an excuse.

"There's something else bothering her," he muttered, dropping into a chair. If she would talk about it, they'd certainly be able to work something out. But rather than talk she preferred to attack, striking hard with the element of surprise. If his kingdom ever went to war, his first act would be to draft Alexia as strategist. The war would be over in less than a month.

But right now, he faced something a lot more complex than war. He had a peace to negotiate with Vilim, and watching their embassy act as judges for the competition would help enormously. That he also had his daughter's future to settle made it unbelievably worse, but there was no help for it. Both problems needed the proper solution, and it was his job to find them.

"I wonder if there's any precedent for a king running away from home," he muttered and closed his eyes.

Tiran glanced around the cozy reception room he and the other entrants had been ushered into. They would have drinks before dinner there, be introduced to the king and queen—royal treatment for the entrants in a royal competition.

"This room is big enough to hold a hundred people," one of the others whispered to the man beside him. "And look at all that gold!"

That the second man shared the same awe of the first made Tiran realize he was spoiled. He'd spent so much time in palaces over the years, he was more likely to notice the artwork than the gilding and jewels. And this room had all three in abundance. The paintings were excellently done, the small sculptures exquisite even without the encrusting gems, and the inlaid gold in furniture and fixtures—just enough to suggest opulence without overdoing it.

Realizing he sounded like an interior decorator, Tiran silently laughed at himself. What he was really doing was trying not to anticipate the arrival of a silver-eyed redhead. He'd dressed in black suede trousers and boots, with a wide-sleeved tunic of turquoise silk, hoping hard that he wasn't overdoing it. None of his fellow entrants was able to match the peacock splendor, but the question was how well the girl Alexia would match. Tiran had set his hand to trying to anticipate her, and he'd soon see how well he'd done.

"Wine, sir?" a passing servant asked. Tiran turned to see a tray with hand-etched crystal and silver goblets, each one filled with a different wine. "Stronger drink is also available if you prefer it," the servant added.

"Let's hope I won't need anything stronger," Tiran answered with a smile, knowing the man had no idea what he was talking about. "Is that blue from Ixval Mountain?"

"Why, yes, sir, it is," the servant responded, immediately swallowing his surprise. "It happens to be one of His Majesty's favorites."

"Mine as well," Tiran said, taking the cup of red wine that was so dark it was almost blue. "Thank you."

"My pleasure, sir," was the response along with a bow, and then the man was moving on to the others. Tiran tasted the wine and found it was undeniably a first pressing, but he was still too distracted to give it the appreciation it deserved. He'd spent half the day with his mind in a turmoil, and the whirling hadn't stopped yet.

He strolled over to a painting and stared up at it, but saw nothing of the gray landscape hidden in swirls of gray fog. What he saw again was the girl Alex announcing her intention to enter the competition, and his own shock at the idea of having to compete against her. She was certain to be *the* entrant to beat, but Tiran didn't want to beat her. He wanted to win her and then win her over, but how was he supposed to do that if she lost to him?

She'd hate me then as a matter of principle, he told himself, knowing there was very little chance for any other attitude. But if I lose to her, I lose *her*.

It was a clear damned-if-you-do, damned-if-you-don't kind of situation. Before the competition had been declared, he might have gone courting; if he had, he would have stood the usual even chance. Now . . . if the idea of being given away as a prize hadn't soured her on marriage entirely, she wasn't the woman he thought she was.

Maybe I *am* crazy for getting involved in this, just like Encar said, he admitted silently with a sigh. Only Encar had yelled rather than said, and had still been whining and shrilling at him as he walked away. His Sighted partner had gone into hysterics when Tiran went back to collect his belongings, and hadn't enjoyed being ignored.

"Tiran, you're being impossible!" Encar had shrilled. "Stop that packing this instant and listen to me! If you enter this competition you'll almost certainly win. Have you thought at all about what will happen after that?"

"Yes," Tiran had answered without pausing or turning. "I'll then have a wedding to attend. Don't you like weddings, Encar?"

"As a matter of fact, I love weddings," Encar had huffed. "Other people's weddings. Not yours. After all this time I know you better than you know yourself, and you'll hate being married. She won't want you to keep taking on commissions—it won't be important enough for the husband of a princess. She'll make you sit around looking stupid in her father's palace, and that will be the end of our partnership."

"How do you know she won't be glad to see me go?" Tiran had asked, then regretted being so hard on the man. "Look, Encar, there's no guarantee I'll win. This is a full-range competition, and when you have to go full-range anything can happen. If I lose, this discussion becomes a waste of breath."

"But if you don't, then it becomes the last words we'll ever speak to each other!" Encar had screamed, so far out of control that his hands trembled. "I don't know what full-range means, nor do I care! I only know that you're being more selfish than I would have believed possible! What will happen to me if you're killed? I know you haven't considered that, because you're not taking even a single moment to think of *me*. I forbid you to do this!"

"That's not how partnerships are supposed to work," Tiran had answered with a sigh. "Partners support each other, they don't tell each other what to do. Can't you understand that this is something I *must* try? If I don't, I'll regret it for the rest of my life."

"You don't know the meaning of the word 'regret,' " Encar had returned bitterly, his narrow face twisted. "We could have accepted that next commission by now, and all that gold would be in our hands. *Not* having it: *that's* what regret means, and I won't allow you to do this to me. You are *not* entering that competition."

"We'll speak again after it's all over," Tiran had said with another sigh. "Just think of it as an extended vacation and try to be patient. If that commission is as good as you think, it'll wait for us to get there. I've paid for your room and meals for the next week, so don't worry about having to spend your own gold. I'll see you."

He had taken his belongings and left, but Encar hadn't stopped whining until there were two doors between them. That was the first time Tiran hadn't let himself be talked out of something unusual he wanted to do, but it wouldn't be the last. He'd given Encar too much control over his life—doing it had been easier than being whined at and wheedled—but that was the end of it.

Encar, however, wasn't his major problem. The Princess Alexia was, and he still didn't know what he could possibly—

"Excuse me, sir," a servant said. "The king and queen are about to arrive, and you and the others will be presented right after that. If you would be so kind as to rejoin the group?"

The seventeen other entrants were standing clumped together looking uncomfortable, so Tiran nodded and went back to them. If the evening's festivities were about to start, he couldn't be happier.

The man who had been introduced to them as Lord Merwin came in, and he was the one who announced the arrival of King Reynar and Queen Josti. Behind those two came the four people who were to be judges of the competition, and Tiran had the strangest feeling they were almost as uncomfortable as his fellow entrants. The new arrivals accepted glasses of wine, and then the entrants were called over to be presented.

Tiran considered it a coincidence that he was the last of the group to be called, but that impression didn't continue for long. When he straightened out of his bow he expected to go on to meet the judges, but instead the king gestured him closer.

"Tiran d'Iste, We welcome you to Our kingdom and Our competition," Reynar said, his voice too low to carry to the others. "We've heard of your many exploits, and find Ourselves pleased at your interest. Have you met Our daughter Alexia yet?"

"Not formally, Your Majesty," Tiran answered, faintly surprised at the true warmth in the king's voice. "You could say I've run across her, though."

"This afternoon at the registration," the king said with a nod, strong annoyance flashing briefly in his eyes. "We were told of her escapade, and regretted that she's grown too big to spank. The experience would likely impress her in no more ways than one, but would certainly do *Us* a world of good."

Tiran grinned, but considered it more politic not to comment. Queen Josti was clearly annoyed with her husband for saying such a thing, and looking at her, Tiran could see where Alex got her beauty and her silver eyes. The girl's size and red hair clearly came from her father, who was almost as large as Tiran himself.

"Tell me, sir," Queen Josti said smoothly, pretending she didn't realize she was interrupting her husband. "Did Alexia's—'escapade'—bother *you* all that much? If what she did frightened away prospective entrants to the competition, isn't it good riddance to them? If they're that easily discouraged, they would have made a terrible showing anyway."

"That's very true, Your Majesty," Tiran granted with a polite bow. "It so happens I enjoyed watching the exercise, but I'm afraid I didn't enjoy what came before it. That *did* bother me."

"Her announcement that she would be an entrant," the king said with a nod while the queen raised her brows. "Yes, if *We* were trying to win her, that would disturb Us as well. A man has no wish to embarrass the woman he means to marry, my dear. It's a pity some women don't hold to the reverse."

"In what way will Alexia's presence in the competition embarrass the men?" Queen Josti asked, now looking very innocent. "The fact that she'll certainly win through while they might not? The fact that none of them will enjoy facing her if they're also finalists? There's a simple solution to that problem, my dear. Change the winner's prize to land or gold, and I'm sure Alexia will agree to withdraw."

"Why don't we see how that solution appeals to one of the entrants?" the king responded smoothly, then turned again to Tiran. "Tell Us, sir, would *you* prefer land or gold as your prize? Alexia would then withdraw from the competition, so your previous disturbance would be no more. Would you have Us do as Our Queen suggests?"

Tiran's first urge was to refuse the offer, even though he knew the king wasn't seriously considering it. That was because it was much too late to undo the damage, the bias Alex would now have against marriage. If he didn't win her, his only other option would be to forget her. And he didn't want to forget her, not before they'd even met.

He was rapidly shuffling through possible answers, trying to find one that would offend neither of the two people watching him so closely. It seemed to be a lost cause, and then he was saved by what must certainly have been the intervention of the EverNameless. Two servants opened the wide double doors to the room, and in swept the object of all that contention.

No, not swept, Tiran thought, having turned with everyone else. She's strolling in, letting all of us get a good look at her. I was right about what she'd do, but I wish I'd been wrong. This is going to be one of the hardest meals I've ever attended.

"Oh, my," Queen Josti murmured, wide-eyed. It was an opinion others were sharing, not just Tiran's fellow entrants but three of the four judges as well. That afternoon Alex had been wearing ordinary exercise clothes and boots; now she was dressed in a silver-and-smoke gown of clinging mist, her incredible body and neck hugged by the filmy material—in the places it happened to cover. Her shoulders and arms were bare of everything but flowing red hair, her long legs flashed enticingly from the side slits of the gown's skirt, her cleavage thrust down almost to her belt—

And that regal little smile on her face says she hasn't dressed that way for any of *us*, Tiran told himself, grudgingly admiring the move. We're supposed to understand she's too much woman for us in more ways than one.

"I'll kill her," King Reynar muttered, too angry to remember the royal We. "Look at those poor fools— they're tripping over their own feet with panic. There's not a backbone in the lot of them."

Tiran considered the condemnation harsh, but it wasn't far from true. The seventeen other contestants were dragging their tongues along the floor, but if Alex had stopped in front of one of them, the man might well have turned and run. She was trying to make them feel appalled at the enormity of what they were attempting, and she was coming close to succeeding.

"Silver princess," Tiran murmured, suddenly remembering a chess set he owned. It had been a gift from a grateful employer, and the pieces were cast in silver and gold. The silver queen had always struck him as being more aloof than the gold queen, more desirable but more unattainable. Alex was a silver princess, but a golden knight could still capture her.

And somehow he would.

*   *   *

The smile I wore wanted to falter as I approached my father, but I refused to let it happen. I'd been told—very diplomatically—that my continued good health depended on my showing up for dinner that night, so I had. I wouldn't have made that much of a show of it, but I don't like being threatened. If my father felt I was rubbing his nose in my defiance, he had only himself to blame.

"I'm surprised you forgot the trumpets," he said as I reached him, anger clear in his golden eyes. "And a line of servants with heavy sticks. If you're going to beat people over the head, why not do the job thoroughly?"

"All I did was walk into the room," I responded, trying for an air of injured innocence. "I didn't realize there was a law against it, or I would have stayed away. Would you like me to leave?"

"Now that the performance is over and the damage is done, you want to leave," he said, refusing to discuss my contention of innocence. "Well, you're *not* leaving, because everything *isn't* over. After dinner the judges will rule on your eligibility as a contestant, and you have to be here for it. If they say you can't compete, then you don't."

"If their decision is arbitrary rather than backed by a rule, I'll fight it," I told him flatly, beginning to share his anger. "This is my *life* you're playing with, and I'll be damned if I just stand around and—"

"Why don't we save the debate until the decision is rendered?" my mother interrupted, stepping smoothly between us with a smile. "Until then we have guests to give our attention to, and one of them is standing right here. Reynar, my dear, he really should be introduced to Alexia."

"Right as usual, my love," Father said after taking a deep breath and putting his arm around her. "Alexia, We now present to you Tiran d'Iste, a man of reputation and an entrant in the competition. We expect you to welcome him to our land warmly and graciously."

I took my time turning to look at the "man of reputation,"

already having seen him as I approached. At his size it would have been impossible *not* to see him, and I wasn't quite sure what to do. Tiran d'Iste was the one I needed *out* of the competition, but so far my efforts had accomplished nothing.

"You look—inspirational tonight, Your Highness," he said with a bow that didn't take his strange eyes off me. "I'm delighted that we've finally been introduced."

"You look delighted," I commented, throwing it back at him. "What is it that I inspire in you?"

"The same thing you inspired the *first* time I saw you," he answered with an easy grin. "A wish for a successful and speedy end to the competition. You and I will make a team no one can beat."

And there I had it, the answer I'd been hoping I *wouldn't* get. The man of reputation wanted me for something, and was therefore serious about the competition. I felt a lump of ice beginning to grow inside me, but couldn't afford to let it show.

"If you like, we can start forming our team right now," I told him with offhand friendliness. "Why don't you sleep with me tonight, and we can discuss what you have in mind."

I'd been so casual about it, the invitation almost passed them all by. Then my mother gasped, "Alexia!" while my father choked on his wine. The man I'd been talking to started, then closed his eyes and rubbed at them with one hand.

"I'll kill her!" my father growled, fury and embarrassment darkening his skin. "Did you hear that, Josti? Your daughter just invited a man to—a stranger to—I'm going to kill her!"

"Why are you getting wild?" I asked in the same casual way. "You told me to welcome him warmly, and you can't get much warmer than that. Besides, I've never tried a man with green eyes. Maybe he does it different than a normal man."

Words failed my father at that point, and all I could do was hope he didn't hurt himself. Since my mother took her turn at eye-closing just then, Tiran d'Iste was free to get on with other things. Those green eyes filled with annoyance, anger hovering sharp in the background.

"Good try, but it won't work," he said, briefly reminding me of Gromal during a teaching session. "I can't quite decide if you're trying to kill my interest or satisfy what you think is passing curiosity. But it doesn't matter. You won't get what you're hoping for, even if I do accept your invitation. And I do."

At that point it was my turn to stare, finding it hard to believe he'd have the nerve to say that. My mother was definitely upset, and my father was studying him with a calculation I didn't understand. My father should have been livid, and the fact that he wasn't made me begin to worry. Had there been agreements of some sort between my father and this man before I'd gotten there? What was he *really* up to?

"I do hope you'll forgive our intrusion, Your Majesty," a smooth baritone interrupted, and we all looked around to see the four judges. A good-looking man with blue eyes seemed to be their temporary spokesman, and he smiled winningly. "If this is a bad time to ask to be introduced to the last of the contestants, we'll certainly—"

"No, no, not at all," my father returned with attempted friendliness, reminding me that they were that embassy from Vilim he'd mentioned. "This could be the best possible time. Lady Wella, my lords Arthon, Fregin and Moult, We present to you the last of the entrants registered today, Tiran d'Iste and the girl Alexia."

So I was now "the girl" Alexia, demotion obviously stemming from having entered the competition. Gestures toward each of the men had separated them as they were named, and the woman didn't need separating. Lady Wella's smile was more amused than haughty, which led me to wonder if she was really that sure of herself. She was a beautiful woman, and most beautiful women don't like competition of any sort. If her thoughts were on something other than appearance, though . . .

"I've been eager to meet Princess Alexia," the spokesman, who had been introduced as Arthon, said. The immediate re-promotion amused me, as did the way the man looked at me. The high-heeled sandals I wore added very little height, but it was still enough to put me eye to eye with him.

"*We've* been eager to meet the princess," the small, round Moult corrected, but with a smile. "I must say that the wait was worth it."

"I understand more clearly now why your people don't have Persuasion," the man Fregin said, taking his turn. "The princess is clear proof that you don't need it."

"And I, of course, admire the princess's spirit more than her other attributes," the Lady Wella put in with a sexy, tinkling laugh. "I appreciate meeting other women who don't let the politics of the worlds simply roll over them. One doesn't always succeed, but one must always try."

"Yes, of course," Lord Arthon said with his continuing smile. "One *must* always try, or one will never forgive oneself. I do hope you'll allow me to escort you in to dinner, Your Highness. And perhaps grant the time to exchange a few words afterward? In an effort to establish friendly relations between our kingdoms, you understand."

"I certainly do understand," I said with my own smile, one crammed as full of delighted interest as I could make it. It had come to me that Lord Arthon was giving me a chance to walk away from Tiran d'Iste, so I added, "Wherever did you get those beautiful blue eyes? I'm dying to hear all about it."

By then I'd taken his arm, and if his chest had swelled any more, his blue dress jacket would have exploded. My father was quietly furious, but he couldn't very well yell at me. He knew I was using Lord Arthon to rid myself of his "man of reputation," but he didn't care to ruin his chances for dealing with Vilim by saying so out loud. My mother wasn't very happy with me and neither was the "guest" she'd insisted I be introduced to, but that was too bad. I wasn't the one who had started that nonsense, but I'd do my damnedest to finish it.

Just then dinner was announced, so we all headed for the double doors leading to the informal dining room. You entered the room on the ten-yard-wide carpeting lying between the high table to the right and the low table to the left. All members of our family sat at the high table along with special guests, and everyone else sat low. That didn't mean you weren't served the same food and wine by the same servants, just that you weren't quite important enough to sit high. It was simple protocol that I'd known almost from infancy, but this time there was a change I hadn't anticipated.

"Just a moment, Lord Arthon," my father called, stopping us as we were heading for the high table. Arthon had been chatting charmingly about nothing, but he stopped immediately and turned us back to those who were following.

"Yes, Your Majesty?" he said, his free hand on the arm I had wrapped around *his* arm. "May I do you a service?"

"We're afraid We must do *you* a *dis*service," my father answered with a sad smile of regret. "We and Our Queen and your embassy will be sitting high, but the balance of Our guests—those who are entrants—will be sitting low. That, unfortunately, includes the young lady you're escorting in, so you must continue your conversation at another time. This gentleman here will escort her the rest of the way."

The "gentleman" standing next to him was too controlled to show smug satisfaction, but that didn't mean it wasn't lurking in his ice-green eyes. I was being tossed back to the man I'd tried to leave well behind me, and I didn't like it one little bit.

"Oh, what a pity," Lord Arthon said, the experienced diplomat bowing to inevitability. "Your Highness, I'm devastated, and the only thing sustaining me is your promise about after dinner. We *will* be able to speak then, I hope?"

"Certainly, Lord Arthon," I agreed with a smile. "I'm looking forward to it. Just as I'm looking forward to the decision you and the others will be announcing. We'll get together after *that*."

"Until the moment," he murmured, bending over my hand to kiss it. The other two men from his world grabbed the opportunity to do the same, and then all of them were following my father and mother toward the high table.

"And what did you expect to accomplish with *that* little routine?" a voice asked from behind me, mildly curious. "Whatever it was, I don't think it worked."

"Guess again," I said, not bothering even to glance at my father's "man of reputation." "I wanted to know what their decision was, and now I do. My registration in the competition will be allowed."

"What makes you think that?" he asked, a big hand coming to my arm when I began to walk away. "And in case you've forgotten, I'm the one who'll be escorting you the rest of the way."

"Since my father was the one who agreed to that, go and escort *him*," I suggested, stiffening my arm in his grip. "And don't be afraid to ask. As much as he likes you, you *have* to be his type."

"And since I'm *his* type, I can't possibly be yours," he concluded, looking down at me with those strange green eyes. "Don't you think you're blaming me for something that isn't my fault? I met your father only minutes before you arrived, and still don't understand why I have his approval. Maybe he did it so you'd *dis*approve."

"I make up my own mind about things, thanks," I said. His was a good try, suggesting my father really didn't like him so *I* should. That sort of thing had never worked on me, not even when I was very young.

"Then why don't you make up your mind to give me a chance?" he said, his hand finally leaving my arm. "It's just possible you'll find out we have a lot in common. And

I meant it when I said we'd make a great team. We'll make a fantastic one."

"Really?" I returned, raising one brow. "Doing what? Just what exactly do you picture us teaming up against?"

"Anything and everything there is," he answered after the briefest hesitation. "Whatever comes against us won't have a chance, not when you and I are full partners."

"In other words, you have no idea," I said, ignoring the hand that had come to lightly touch my arm. "The line sounded good, so you used it. There's nothing for us to team up against, and if there was, I don't have to wonder who would see most of the action. Why don't you go and waste someone else's time?"

Frustration flashed briefly in his eyes as I turned away, but there was nothing he could say. Any words he used would show what he was really after—gold, lands, a title, or maybe just an attractive female for his bed. Whatever his reasons for entering the competition, it wasn't because he needed a "partner."

The other entrants were already heading for the low table, and were only about fifteen feet ahead of me. I lengthened my stride to catch up—and hopefully leave the one behind me behind—but nothing worked out the way it should have. I heard his bootsteps on the carpeting, the pace sounding determined, and then—

And then the air began to shimmer all around, a definite clue that magic was being used. The shimmering tightened down to pinpoints of glowing light, and then erupted into more than half a dozen gaping entries. There was no doubt the entries led to another world rather than to other parts of ours; mottled beasts I'd never seen before jumped through, muzzles snarling and hackles raised.

Then each of the two dozen beasts turned and charged at the nearest life it intended to take.

CHAPTER FOUR

At times like that, you don't make conscious decisions. The brown-and-white beast racing toward me would jump for my throat, and that was all I needed to know. Even as I watched it my reflexes were already changing my body form and composition, Shifting me almost instantly into the most effective fighting form I have. A stray thought gave thanks that the talisman belt I always wore would save my favorite gown, and then there was nothing to think about but the beast.

The thing broke stride when it saw me Shifting, but it didn't abort its attack. My throat was now lower and thicker and covered with fur, but it was still there to be jumped at. I bared my own fangs in a snarl of contempt, then launched myself in counterattack.

The shock of contact told me the mottled beast was fractionally heavier, but I had the greater speed. Its teeth closed just short of my throat, but mine sank into its shoulder as my claws went for its underbelly. It howled as it tore away and stumbled back, then took a moment to glare at me.

What it saw was a cat usually called a puma, sand yellow, short-haired, and mean-tempered. The taste of blood teased my tongue and coated my claws, blood I'd drawn from the thing that had dared to attack me. A growl of pleasure rolled out of my throat as I realized victory would be mine, and

I started forward. The beast watching me hesitated, then began to back away.

By then I could smell its fear as well as its blood, and that did it. It had no choice but to meet my immediate attack and fight, but it wasn't expecting to win. It knew it was going to die, and when a rake of my claws opened its throat, it did. I watched it thrash around on the carpeting for a moment, life leaking out of its wounds, and then I looked around for my next opponent.

But the action was already over. Two dozen beasts had come through the entries, and some of those lay unmoving without a mark on them. The rest were torn up the way my opponent was, and all trace of the entries was gone. I saw a big black cat with green eyes flexing claws into the motionless carcass at its feet, but its attention seemed to be on me. *His* attention. The big cat was male, and his stare made me suddenly want to roll on the carpeting and stretch lazily.

Which was the last thing I would ever do. Instead I flexed the desire to change back into my natural form, which took almost no effort at all. It's changing *from* your natural form that takes practice and strength; going back is like rolling downhill.

"Alexia, are you all right?" The question came abruptly from behind me, and then I thought I was under attack again. My mother was there and throwing her arms around me; my father was right with her, and in a towering rage.

"I want to know who did this!" he roared, glaring around at the guardsmen and courtiers who hadn't even gotten into action. "If Lord Fregin hadn't banished the entries and stopped some of the beasts— Do you hear me? I want answers *now*!"

The poor men flinched at his roar, bowed hastily, then began running in all directions. There had been none of *our* Sighted there, which was simple courtesy when dining with those who were supposed to be friends. All but saying you need a magic user to protect you is an extreme insult, and my father would never be that heavy-handed except on purpose. Had someone known it would be that way and taken gleeful advantage?

But advantage to accomplish what? Even as I soothed my mother I wondered, trying to make sense of the thing. Was someone opposed to the competition and therefore trying to stop it? But why would anyone be opposed? It was possible the entrants had become accidental targets, and the real victims were supposed to be my father and the embassy. But why would anybody be against an alliance, especially an alliance that wasn't guaranteed to be made? Everything I thought of was blind guesswork, but what more can you get without any facts?

"The guardsmen will get a change of clothes for *that* fellow, but there's nothing anyone can do for the other," my father said in a lower voice, gesturing with his chin. "Neither of them wore their belts, but at least the first had the good sense not to worry about his clothes. The second—I watched him reach frantically for the bottom of his tunic, then change his mind and start to Shift. By then it was too late, and the beast had its teeth in his face. In natural form, he didn't have a chance against it."

"I just thank the EverNameless Alex isn't that foolish," my mother said, now inspecting me narrowly for damage. "But her safety is no thanks to *you*, Reynar. If you hadn't insisted she sit low, she wouldn't have been in the middle of that. If anything terrible had happened to her—"

"Josti, weren't you watching?" my father broke in, more surprised than impatient. "The poor beast didn't have a chance against her, and even *it* knew that. My daughter is a good deal better than average, and it would take more than an animal like that to harm her."

"So now she's *your* daughter," my mother said, flames kindling in her eyes as she turned to him. "Ten minutes ago she was *my* daughter, and someone you wanted to kill. Now you're proud of her again, and all because she successfully risked her life! Well, let me tell *you* . . ."

By that time I had backed away out of range, just the way everyone else was keeping clear. I'll face a wild beast any day of the week, but I'm not stupid enough to get between my parents at a time like that. The point my mother was arguing made no sense, but my father would still try to defend himself against it. If that was what having children did to normally sane people, I was glad I didn't have any.

"Your fighting form is as attractive as your natural one," I heard, and then Tiran d'Iste was standing beside me. "Would it be prying to ask what the king and queen are arguing about?"

"I think they're arguing about me," I said, not at all certain. "The only problem is they've shifted sides from the last version, which means it could be something else entirely. They don't argue often, but when they do it seems impossible to follow."

"I'd be willing to bet your mother is just shaken up," he said, studying her in a casual way. "She's probably never seen you fight seriously before, and it frightened her. Lucky for you she didn't notice how sloppy you were, or she would be screaming at you rather than at your father."

"What do you mean, sloppy?" I demanded, turning to glare up at him. "Who the hell do you think you are to say something like that? I wasn't sloppy, I *won*!"

"There are wins and there are wins," he said, bringing those eyes back to me. "I happened to be keeping track of your fight, and I noticed a few things. Like the fact that your arm was scored during your first exchange. Shifting back to your natural form healed the scoring enough so that only faint lines are left, but that doesn't mean it didn't happen."

His finger flicked down my left arm over the lines he'd mentioned, probably to show he wasn't guessing or making it up. Since I already knew he wasn't, I didn't follow the gesture; that, however, wasn't the end of it.

"You also let the taste of blood turn you faintly feral," he continued. "If you make a habit of doing that to win form fights, one day you'll lose control and it will go too far. You've probably never had any trouble pulling back from the edge, but just because you haven't had trouble *yet*, that doesn't mean you never will."

"Is that all of it?" I asked, folding my arms as I looked up at him. "If there's anything else, please don't hesitate. I'm finding this *so* instructive."

"You also waited too long with your first attack," he obliged, ignoring the daggers in my stare. "You should have known there was a good chance your opponent would outweigh you, so you needed to be moving faster to take full advantage of your own body weight. That thing only just missed taking you in the throat, and if it had you wouldn't be feeling so cocky now. As a matter of fact, you'd be feeling nothing at all."

"Oh, is *that* what this lecture series is all about?" I said, finally seeing the light. "The grand prize of the competition looked like it was about to be chomped, and that scared you. Well, get yourself a drink and calm down. This grand prize isn't *about* to be chomped, not that it'll do *you* any good."

I started to turn away from him in disgust, but that hand came to my arm again. The gentle pressure of his fingers didn't add much to the soreness in my arm, but I still had to keep myself from flinching.

"I don't want a grand prize, I want a woman," he said, his eyes hard. "If the only way I can get her is to win her then I'll do it, but you won't be able to blame *me*. Get to know me before this thing starts, and let me get to know you; if nothing sparks between us, I'll turn around and walk away."

"And if something does spark?" I countered, knowing better than to feel hope. "Or, specifically, if it sparks for you but not for me? Will you give your word to walk away anyway? Come on, let me hear it."

"You know I can't give my word for something like that," he just about growled. "You're all ready to hate everything about me, just to get one more competitor out of your way. Can't you forget about the competition and simply concentrate on us?"

"Us?" I echoed with a sour smile, pulling my arm free. "There ain't no such animal. And even if there was, it would have no purpose. Or maybe I should say it would just have *your* purpose, whatever that is. Have you figured out yet what we'd team up against?"

The muscles in his jaw tightened, giving his handsome face a hardened look, but he didn't answer.

"That's what I thought," I told him, then couldn't help twisting the knife. "Not very creative for someone who's supposed to be full-range, are you? I hope you have better luck in your next competition."

I managed to walk away from him then, even though it looked for a moment as though he would try to stop me again. When I got away clear, I was close to sweating; I was also prepared to throw a fit in case he came after me, most of which would *not* be acting. I was scared clean through, and didn't mind admitting it.

Servants were circulating with wine again while the bodies were being cleared away, so I helped myself to a glass and used its contents to steady me. Gromal had been right about how good Tiran d'Iste was; I had to get him out of the competition or, barring a miracle, I would lose to him.

And I couldn't bear the thought of losing to him. I looked down into my glass of wine, demanding silently why I found him so attractive. He didn't really want *me*; from what he'd seen of me, he should have been running in the opposite direction. His still being here meant he wanted something connected to me, something he couldn't get without accepting me as well. That would be just as bad as being married to someone inferior, and maybe even worse. I wasn't likely to begin caring about someone inferior . . .

I finished the wine in a swallow, then put the glass aside. There would be no change in my general plans, only in some of the specifics. Getting rid of Tiran d'Iste was my primary concern, but I also had to find out about that attack. If it really was aimed at the competition, I might not have to worry about anyone else being a finalist. If it was aimed at my father and the embassy instead . . . Well, I'd have to do what I could to help, even if it interfered with my other plans. Delays can usually be worked around . . .

I looked up to see Lord Arthon watching me. My father and mother had moved to the side of the room for a bit of privacy, so I suppose he had to look *somewhere* other than at them. And then it came to me: the man really liked what his eyes showed him, and he was one of the judges of the competition. If he was looking forward to our date after dinner—and he was—then he expected it to be pleasant. If they refused me entrance to the competition it would be anything but, so they had agreed to let me stay registered.

Which meant I might be able to coerce a little help against Tiran d'Iste. If some basis could be found for *his* disqualification, after the competition was over I'd still be single and available. Lord Arthon was certain to be interested in an outcome like that, and maybe even the other two men as well. Lady Wella considered herself independent, and would probably help me on general principles. I'd have to talk to her and find out.

A glance showed me that Tiran d'Iste looked ready to pester me again, so I quickly crossed the room toward Lord Arthon and the others. The fact that my father seemed to approve of d'Iste would make it harder to avoid him, but it still had to be done. He'd seen more of what I was doing during a fight of his own than Gromal would have seen while doing nothing but watching. The last thing I wanted was for him to see the wrong reaction or expression . . .

Tiran stopped short and cursed under his breath when it was clear Alex had escaped him. She'd had too much of a head start, and would reach the judges before he reached her. Unless he ran, which he'd almost considered doing. The woman was driving him crazy, something that should have been obvious to anyone watching.

Instead of running he accepted a glass of wine, then sipped at it while looking around. The sixteen who were left of his fellow entrants were shaken, but for the most part it didn't seem to be anything they couldn't handle. The attack had been a complete surprise, yet the only one to go down under it was a fool who couldn't think. Everyone else would be fine, even the man who needed his clothes replaced.

And thinking about the attack was almost enough to distract him from Alex. What possible reason could anyone have for doing such a thing? Considering the people who had been attacked the move was stupid, so maybe the contestants weren't the hoped-for targets. The judges, they'd been told, were from a world interested in developing relations with this one. Maybe some dissenting faction from one side or the other . . . ?

Dissenting faction. There was one dissenter Tiran was getting the urge to strangle, and that thought led right back to Alex. He'd finally met her, and things had promptly gotten worse instead of better.

"No one here would ever believe there are a lot of people in the worlds who consider me a smooth talker," he muttered to the wine in his cup. "Every time I open my mouth, she makes me feel like a tongue-tied liar."

Which was a new experience for Tiran, especially with a woman. He'd told his share of embroidered stories, but no one had ever doubted him when he'd spoken the unvarnished truth. With Alex it seemed to be a matter of finding the *right* truth, which he hadn't yet been able to do. What would they be partners in? Everything, damn it, but that answer didn't suit her. How in hell was he going to find one that did?

He sipped at his wine as he let his gaze move around the room, then nearly choked on an unexpected flash of rage. Alex had taken possession of that Lord Arthon's arm again, and the way the man looked at her made Tiran want to challenge him on the spot. That Alex was encouraging Arthon seemed to make no difference to Tiran's fury. It was Arthon he wanted to tear into, fighting form or natural, with weapons or without.

That's because he's taking dishonorable advantage, Tiran thought, fist closed tight around the cup. He knows damned well she's meant for the winner of the competition, but until then, he intends having his fun. If I let him live that long . . .

Exerting superhuman effort, Tiran forced himself to look away. The girl didn't belong to him yet, and if he wasn't careful, she never would. He knew she would be allowed to enter the competition; if they were going to refuse her, Arthon would hardly be so sure of himself. But that meant Tiran would definitely have to compete against her, specifically in the finals.

"Why does she have to be so damned good?" he growled, a question that brought him memory of her fighting form. He'd almost lost control of his own form at the sight, and had thanked the EverNameless that she'd Shifted back so fast. He'd called her performance sloppy, and in the ways he'd mentioned it had been, but that wasn't the whole story. She'd been sloppy because she'd faced nothing in the way of a real challenge; if she'd been seriously threatened, he had no doubt that she'd have come out without a scratch.

And in the finals she'll put everything she has into winning. I can probably best any of the others without seriously hurting them, but only because they're not in her class. What do I do when I'm face to face with *her*? Let her rip me to shreds? Rip *her* to shreds? That's a loss whichever way it goes, and I can't afford to lose. There's not another woman like her anywhere.

Tiran sighed and finished his wine, pointing out to himself that at least part of his aim had been successful. He'd wanted something to cure his boredom, and he'd found it. Now all he had to do was accomplish the impossible by discovering a way to *keep* it. And, strangely enough, he was beginning to get an idea for a plan of attack . . .

"They're on opposite sides of the room," Josti said, breaking into Reynar's thoughts. "They were together for a while, but now Alex is back with Lord Arthon, and Tiran is chewing up his wineglass. You don't think she's really interested in Arthon, do you?"

"She's interested in disrupting the competition," Reynar answered in a low rumble. "If batting her eyes at Arthon will cause a disruption, it isn't beyond her to do it. Ah, good. Sisal and Limis just got here, and in a moment they'll have the room warded. By the time we finish dinner, they'll have spread the warding outward to cover the entire palace."

"It's fortunate we have sorcerers strong enough to do that," Josti said, her hands moving here and there. "I hope Lord Fregin isn't insulted by their presence—when he gets around to noticing them. Right now he's too involved with trying to get Alex's attention away from Lord Arthon."

"Josti, please try to calm yourself," Reynar said, putting one of his hands over both of hers to still them. "I know you're upset by what happened, but if you keep going on like this we'll have another fight. One a night should be enough entertainment, even for special guests like ours."

"You're right, Reynar, and once again I apologize," she said with a ghost of her old smile. "Besides, if we do give them a second fight we'll have to charge them, and that isn't polite. You think Lord Fregin might have had something to do with that attack, don't you."

"At this point what else can I think?" he responded with a shrug. "It took a fairly strong magic user to open those entries into this room, but the attacking beasts were inadequate. Either whoever did it wasn't able to find anything better—hardly likely, considering all the beasts in the worlds—or they didn't *know* the things were inadequate. Fregin and his embassy still have very little idea what we're capable of."

"But they're learning," Josti said with a sigh. "What I can't understand is why they would do such a thing. It was their idea to begin political relations with us. Why start in the first place if you're only going to do something to wreck it?"

"It's their government that wants to deal with us," Reynar reminded her. "One or more of these people may have their own ax to grind, or maybe they're trying to see how far they can push us, how long it takes before we stop defending and start attacking. When you don't know what to expect from people, you sometimes put them through a test."

"The way you're using the competition to test *them*," Josti said, her beautiful silver eyes sad. "I know it's too good an opportunity to miss, but that makes it very unfair for Alex. She won't stop fighting you on this, and she *could* be seriously hurt."

"*Our* daughter is much too capable to be casually hurt," he said as he put his arms around her, all the assurance he could muster in his voice. "She'll be able to more than hold her own, and *that's* what worries me. When she reaches the finals, she'll be holding her own against a very capable man who really wants her."

"Tiran d'Iste," Josti said with a nod and a smile. "I like him, Reynar, and I noticed that you do, too. The way he looks at Alex says he's attracted to everything about her. I'm afraid I wondered briefly if that was because of some head wound he'd gotten."

"Shame on you, Josti," her husband said with a deep rumble of a laugh while she grinned. "Tiran d'Iste is the kind of man who's attracted to danger and challenge. Ordinary women must bore him to yawning after he's—made their acquaintance. One look at Alexia told him she'll *never* be boring or easy to manage, so now he's hooked. If you want the truth, *he's* the one I feel sorry for. Our daughter has managed to put him between a rock and a hard place."

"Because he'll have to face her in the finals," Josti said, no longer amused. "He said something about not wanting to embarrass her, but what he means is that he's afraid he'll hurt her. Oh, Reynar, you don't think he will?"

"He's probably more frustrated with the idea of her hurting *him*," the king said, reassuring again. "He can control his own actions, but not Alexia's. The competition has an added dimension where he's concerned, but it might be for the best. If he can figure out a way to win despite the handicap of Alexia's presence, he'll more than deserve everything he gets."

"Which includes something neither of them knows about," Josti said with a return of her sad smile. "The Oath won't let us mention it, but if we could it might make a tremendous difference. Can't you say *something* to Alexia? Just to ease her mind? I'm sure she feels she's being thrown to the wolves."

"Why would I do that to poor, innocent wolves?" Reynar asked with brows raised, then joined the smile he got from his wife. "I can't say a word, my love, and neither can you. If Alexia hadn't gone to extremes she wouldn't be caught now, and she needs to be taught a lesson. We won't always be there to save her from herself, so she has to learn how to do it on her own. You can see that, can't you?"

The queen gave him a weary nod, but her answer wasn't the complete truth. She could also see Alex's side, which colored the problem a nice gray. Her husband and daughter saw black and white, and she was caught in the middle with gray. Maybe *she* ought to think about running away from home or entering the competition. It would probably be easier and more pleasant than dealing with what lay ahead . . .

"Ah, we're finally ready to go to table," Reynar said, taking her arm. "The food had better not be ruined, or our unknown attacker will pay double when I get my hands on him. And I think I'll have the contestants moved into the palace, just in case the attack *did* have something to do with them."

"Good," Josti murmured. "That will put Tiran closer to Alex, which just might do some good. Doesn't she have the sense to see how attractive he is?"

Under other circumstances, Reynar the man might have felt a flash of jealousy. Even Reynar the king might have been bothered, but not Reynar the father. His wife wasn't looking at another man, she was approving a prospective son-in-law. Now if only Alexia could be made to do the same . . .

By the time I got back to my apartment, I felt I might have accomplished something. And while accomplishing, I had also enjoyed myself. Arthon was a delightful man, full of charm and fun and a very diplomatic lack of sincerity. After dinner Moult had announced their unanimous decision in my favor, and then Arthon and I had gone off for a short while to have our conversation.

But not the conversation he'd been hoping for. I laughed softly as I stopped at the sideboard in my reception room to pour a glass of wine. Arthon had been almost as delighted with my fighting form as with my natural one, and had wanted to demonstrate his appreciation in an intimate way. Unfortunately for him, I'd been much too upset over what that brute Tiran d'Iste had said to go along with his intentions.

"Poor, dear Arthon," I murmured with another laugh. He'd been devastated that my mood had been ruined, but more importantly he'd also been annoyed. By the time I led him back to the others, he was more than ready to search the rules to see if there were grounds to disqualify d'Iste. I'd assured all three of the men that my mood would be marvelous once that big boor was permanently gone, and they'd quickly gotten the message.

And then I'd had a private talk with Lady Wella. I meandered toward my bedroom as I remembered how amused she'd been, and how willing to cooperate. There was something about that woman which went beyond the obvious, some secret she shared with herself and no one else. Her mystery was almost enough to distract me from my own problem, especially since it had to relate to my father and our kingdom. . . . It would probably be a good idea to call my servants and have a bath drawn, then think about it while I soaked—

"You're back later than I thought you would be," he said from the lounge to the right, inside my bedroom. "Nice apartment you have here."

I stopped just beyond the threshold to stare, trying to decide whether Tiran d'Iste was carved out of nerve or out of stupidity. He was comfortably sprawled on the lounge with a glass of wine on a small table near his hand, looking as though he had moved in for good.

"What in hell do you think you're doing here?" I demanded. As an original comment that one left a lot to be desired, but I couldn't help it. I was starting to get mad, and mad often turns me banal.

"I was invited here," he answered with casual surprise, green eyes filled with innocence. "Don't you remember issuing the invitation—and the fact that I accepted? We're supposed to discuss what a great team you and I are going to make."

His broad, handsome face showed a faint grin, and those eyes never left me. He was pretending to be completely at ease, but he wasn't *that* stupid. Behind the facade he was alert and ready—or so *he* thought.

"Does that mean you've finally thought of something for us to team up *against*?" I asked, staying right where I'd stopped. "If so, then go ahead and get it said. I'm dying to hear."

"My answer to that is still the same," he responded with a small shrug and headshake. "We'll be teaming up against anything that happens to come at us, no matter what it might be. Haven't you ever wanted someone you could rely on completely, someone to stand with you against whatever life happens to throw in your path? Like tandem fighting. Have you ever done any tandem fighting?"

"Yes, I have," I answered, sipping at my wine. "Gromal and I won a Guard competition once, but it really wasn't fair. We were so good, none of the teams we faced had a chance against us. And I already have someone I can rely on no matter what. Me. Do you intend retiring?"

"Retiring?" he echoed, now looking confused. "I haven't decided. Of course, as my partner *you'd* have a say in—"

"So it's possible," I plowed on. "If you retired, we could team up against the weeds in our garden or the rabbits trying to eat our lettuce. If you didn't retire, though, we could team up against—what? All those people fighting to shower you with hire money? The troops you would be training and leading? Oh, wait, I know. Against the people you were hired to defeat. That's got to be it. I could join you in—training and leading? Running the battles? My goodness, I don't know if I could handle all that."

The amusement he'd been showing was gone, replaced by more than simple frustration. He ran both hands through his thick black hair, then got slowly to his feet.

"How can I convince you that a real, true partnership doesn't have lists of things the two are each responsible for?" he asked, the words halting but intense. "It's a blending, a togetherness that goes beyond the needs and demands of others. You're each there for the other, and because of that nothing is too hard to accomplish. I know I can hold up my half of the team; what I need is a woman capable of doing the same. You're the only female I've ever seen who has any chance to become that woman. Don't tell me you're not even going to try."

The last of it was said with an odd kind of coaxing worry, the coaxing half hopeful, the worried half frightened. I'd never heard anyone say something like that before, and when he stopped no more than a foot and a half away, I barely noticed. Was he telling the truth about what he was after? Did I *care* if he was telling the truth? What in hell was he trying to do to me?

"You look confused," he commented, bringing my gaze up to his face. "I'm not trying to fool you or corner you, so if you need to talk about it some more, let's do it. I *know* we could be great together. Just give me the chance to prove it."

His hand came to stroke down my bare arm, the touch gentle and no more intimate than a pat on the cheek. But it *was* intimate, somehow, so much so that it was all I could do not to shiver. He was so very masculine, tall and broad and—

"But what if I don't *want* to give you a chance?" I asked, fighting to keep the words even. "What if I don't want to be great with someone? Where is the law that says I have to get involved just because *you* want it? Show it to me, and then we can talk again."

I moved to my left then, toward my wardrobe and dressing area, trying to get some distance between us. It was impossible not to be aware of the man even across a large and crowded room; standing right next to him . . .

"Are you saying you're not attracted to me in any way at all?" he asked in turn, his voice—and, unfortunately, the rest of him—following after me. "There's not the smallest spark of interest, the least amount of curiosity?"

I stopped to kick off my shoes, but didn't turn to look at him. He was a man who, at the very least, matched my skills and abilities; how could I *not* be interested? But that wasn't the point, not as far as I was concerned.

"Why are you still here?" I demanded, ignoring what he'd said as I rounded on him. "Aren't you bright enough to know when a subject is closed? Besides, I'm expecting someone, and I want you gone before he gets here."

Not a single emotion showed on his face or in those strange eyes, but I would have put gold on the fact that he wasn't as calm as he looked. Two or three heartbeats passed without any reaction, and then he raised one brow.

"I think you need to hire someone to keep track of your appointments," he said. "I dislike repeating myself, but I was invited to spend the night and I accepted. Did you expect me to go out for a walk while you entertained, or stay here and offer criticism and advice?"

"Neither," I returned, trying to match his casual air while ignoring the heat I could feel in my cheeks. "I thought you would be bright enough to know my invitation was a—a—

joke. If you took it seriously I'm sorry, but the mistake can be fixed. I now formally withdraw the invitation."

"You can't, not after it's been accepted," he said, turning to look at my bed. "There's enough room in there for three, I suppose, but not much beyond that. Is your second date also staying the night, or just stopping by for a visit?"

I closed my eyes and put a hand over them, trying to understand what I'd done to deserve this situation. I know the entire universe works on the concept of balance, but I'd really thought you had to destroy a world or two—or wear an outfit that was three seasons out of style—before you earned someone like Tiran d'Iste.

"Well?" he prodded. "Are you just not saying, or don't you remember? It's a good thing we'll be married soon. A memory as undependable as yours can cause a lot of embarrassment."

"Married!" I echoed with all the outrage I felt, dropping my hand to glare at him. "Are you stark, raving mad, or do you think I am? I wouldn't marry you even if—"

"Even if I was the winner of the competition?" he cut in, raising that single brow again. "You know that's what I'll be, so why act as if you don't? I tried to make the inevitability easier on you, but you prefer doing it the hard way. Do you *like* doing it the hard way, or is it just something that happens to you?"

"Things like you are what happen to me," I grated, rapidly approaching the point of true hatred. "I want you out of here, and I want you out now."

"You seem to be saying your word is worthless," he mused, moving nearer again to look down at me. "When you invited me here I took you at your word, and now you're telling me I was a fool to do that. Let me hear it straight out, and I'll go. Tell me your word isn't any good, and I may even drop out of the competition."

That was all I needed to hear. I parted my lips to say the words that would get rid of him for good—and found that I couldn't speak them. I'm not above lying when a situation calls for it, but somehow I . . . couldn't . . . quite . . . lie about that. Keeping my word is important to me, but I hadn't realized how important.

"I didn't 'give you my word' about anything," I tried, now hating *myself* for not being able to take the easy way out. "If you don't know a joke when you hear one, that's not my fault. You—"

"I wasn't the only one who didn't see it as a joke," he interrupted again. "Even your parents believed you were serious, so I repeat: I took you at your word. Are you going to break that word?"

"What if I broke *you* instead?" I asked with a growl, putting my fists to my hips. "Let's fight right now, and see which one of us gets their way."

"I don't think so," he returned immediately, grinning as he folded his arms across his chest. "If you win, I'm out of here. If I win, I might as well be out of here. I accepted an invitation to your bed, not to a fight. Are you or are you not going to break your word?"

"Damn it, stop saying that!" I raged, feeling as cornered as I had when my father had first mentioned the competition. "How can I break a word I never gave?"

"Aren't you paying attention?" he asked, doing that eyebrow thing again. "We've already established that you did give your word. The only question left to answer is—"

"I have a headache!" I blurted, which at that point wasn't entirely untrue. "That's it, I have a headache, so you can't possibly stay tonight. We'll continue this discussion tomorrow, and then I can—"

"Alex," he said, so gently and warmly that my words stopped by themselves. "You don't mind if I call you Alex? After all, we *are* going to be married. Alex, my lovely, I have a headache remedy that never fails, and since I'm now yours, so is the remedy. Why don't you slip into something more comfortable, and then we'll get started."

He gave me a smile filled with warm encouragement before turning away with his hands on his belt. A moment later the belt was off, and then he began on his tunic. I looked down at the wineglass in my hand, wondered where it had come from, then said to hell with it. I didn't *care* where it had come from, just as long as it was there for me to empty.

Good wine sometimes does an equally good job of bracing you up, but not if you swallow it whole. I could feel the last of it burning its way down as I put the glass aside, but at least it was helping to unscatter my attention. I hadn't been put that much on the defensive in a very long time, not since I'd first been introduced to strategy and—

Strategy and tactics. I sat down on my padded dressing bench, letting my toes and feet enjoy the deep-piled rug the bench stood on. So that was the way Tiran d'Iste won his battles, by continually attacking to the weak side. It was sound and classic strategy, combined with the creativity of half inventing a weak side when a real one wasn't easily available. No wonder he'd earned a reputation.

But I had a reputation of sorts too, even though it wasn't as well known as his. He might have been given hints about it, but now it was time for specifics. Without moving I Shifted just a little, then got ready to play Monster.

My worthy opponent stood with his back to me until his tunic was off and put to one side, and then he turned. He still wore that encouraging smile, but no other woman would have noticed it before the rest. Without a shirt it was possible to see how massive and beautifully muscled he was, broad-shouldered, deep-chested and lean-waisted. Black hair covered his tanned chest, emphasizing the deep cuts of muscle that also meant strength. The sight was enough to make me want to hum, but all I did was smile.

Which immediately killed *his* smile. His eyes widened as he stared, and then he shook his head in bewilderment.

"What in hell did you do?" he demanded. "Is there something wrong? Are you sick?"

"Aside from that headache I mentioned, I'm perfectly fine," I replied with a shrug. "Why do you ask?"

He parted his lips to answer, but this time he was the one who couldn't find the words. My smile wanted to change to a laugh, but overconfidence is too often the kiss of death. I intended to win that battle against Tiran d'Iste, and then see if it was possible to also win the war.

"Your appearance," he managed after a moment. "There's still a vague resemblance to your natural form, but you've—really changed yourself. Is this your next try at getting rid of me?"

"Whether or not you leave has become your decision," I pointed out with another shrug. "I wouldn't dream of trying to influence you."

He snorted in disbelief over that outright lie, and it suddenly came to me that he'd never played Monster. When shape-shifter children first begin to have control over their natural abilities, the most popular game is usually Monster. The object is to produce the most horrible being you can think of, without changing yourself so much that you're unrecognizable. The game sharpens a child's ability while it stimulates his or her imagination, and a contest between older kids can be downright grotesque.

But it isn't usually as subtle as the efforts of a full-range adult. What I'd done was Shift myself far enough out of true to be repellent, to make an observer want to look away. My body was now short and dumpy, uneven and very unattractive. My face was puffy and also uneven, the result of a bad sculptor's attempt to copy life. None of my features were quite the way they should be, either in placement or in form. The effect should have been enough to turn the stomach of the average person, and that's what it was doing to Tiran d'Iste.

"How long do you intend to stay in that—that—disguise?" he demanded, trying not to look away. "It has to be the most dishonorable thing I've ever seen, a blatant attempt to go back on your word after—"

"But you said it was the invitation I'd given my word about," I interrupted, prepared for that argument by having expected it. "You can't claim I did more than invite you to spend the night, not when there *are* witnesses to the exchange. You may not like what I did to myself, but I never said I wouldn't. And my Shifting doesn't change a thing. You're still free to go or stay, as you please."

"And what if I decide to stay after all?" he challenged, now looking straight at me. "What if I take you to bed just as you are? Will there suddenly be spikes sticking out of you to keep me away?"

"Say, I never thought of that," I exclaimed with a grin that made him flinch. "I'll have to remember the idea for next time, but using it now wouldn't be fair. I'll let you take me to bed just as I am."

I watched the muscles in his jaw flex as he clenched his teeth, a sure sign of the struggle going on inside him. His mind wanted to answer my challenge by ignoring what I'd done to my appearance, but men are too vision-oriented for that. He might be able to force himself to take me to bed, but his body would refuse to let him do anything once we got there. It didn't mean he was too good to bed a woman who wasn't beautiful; he was simply too male to overcome his basic drives and preferences. Women have their own built-in prejudices, but most men are stuck with that one.

"Marriage vows usually require a woman to obey her husband," he said at last, his voice a growl. "I wasn't going to insist on that part being included in *our* ceremony, but now I've changed my mind. Think about *that* when you start to congratulate yourself on what a good idea *this* was."

His movements were jerky with anger when he reclaimed his tunic and belt, and then he was striding out of my bedchamber without looking back. I followed him to the door to make sure he was leaving the apartment entirely, and once he had I Shifted back and went to ring for my servants. I still wanted a bath, but not for the original reason.

"Damn that man!" I snarled as I picked up one shoe and threw it as hard as I could. So he was going to make me obey him, was he? And all because of what I'd done to get rid of him? He had no special right to anything, not when he wasn't my husband yet! Who did he think he—

The words in my mind ran into a wall of shock, which stopped them dead. Where had *that* thought come from, that he wasn't my husband *yet*? It meant I'd accepted his winning as a fact, not as a distant possibility. Why was I thinking that way, when I knew as well as anyone that attitude made all the difference? Expect to win and you probably will; expect to lose and you certainly will.

I sat down on the bench again and searched my mind, and it took only a moment or two for me to come up with the answer. That miserable man! While coming at me openly with his weak-side attack, he'd also sneaked around to the rear with a potentially more devastating maneuver. I'd been so busy defending myself against an accusation concerning my word, I'd done nothing to counter his assumption of victory. Not arguing the point had given it validity and reality to me, and that's why I'd—

"Damn him!" I hissed, getting more furious by the minute. "He was *cheating*, and I nearly fell for it!"

Only then did it come home to me just how dangerous Tiran d'Iste was. If I hadn't found a way to get rid of him, I would have had to let him take me to bed. I'd caught myself reacting to his presence when he was still a foot and a half away; did I have to wonder what it would have done to me to be held in his arms and made love to? It would have been like nothing I'd ever experienced, and afterward . . .

"Afterward he would have had me good," I muttered, finding it useless to deny even so embarrassing an idea. My body would have wanted more of what he offered, and that would have ended my effectiveness in the finals. Why fight when surrender will be so much more pleasant?

I stood up from the bench when I heard my maids entering the apartment, my mind now firmly made up. I had to get rid of d'Iste no matter what, or one way or another I'd end up married to him. *That* was the main reality to be faced, one that would totally destroy my plans and my life. Even if I believed his intentions were good, he had no idea what was really involved.

But I did. And I had to continue remembering it, since no one else would. I *had* to win my freedom, no matter how much it hurt . . .

Tiran left Alex's apartment and strode up the hall seething. He still carried his tunic and belt, and once he reached the outer guards to that wing, he would be stared at. Not that he really cared. He was mad clear through, and most of the anger was aimed at himself.

"And you call yourself a decent human being," he muttered in disgust. "Shallow is what you are, and wasn't it fun having her rub your nose in it. You deserve the tossing you'll do tonight, wishing you were in *her* bed instead of alone in yours. And wasn't it clever the way you blamed it all on *her*."

That part of it bothered him as much as the rest, and he knew he'd have to apologize. Blaming someone for showing you your shortcomings was downright vile, and he—

"Tiran d'Iste." The low-voiced call stopped him in his tracks, and he turned quickly just in case it was an ambush. He was prepared for anything—except the sight of the king beckoning to him from an open doorway. Feeling like a conspirator, Tiran walked quickly into the small sitting room, and the king closed the door behind him.

"So you let her throw you out," King Reynar said, disappointment more than censure in his voice. "I was hoping . . . Well, Alexia is Alexia. Where did it go wrong?"

"Your Majesty, I don't understand what you're asking," Tiran temporized, very aware of the clothing he carried rather than wore. "I'm not in the habit of discussing the ladies of my acquaintance even if a lady was involved, which it so happens there—"

"All right, all right, stop being the defensive gentleman," the king grumbled, leading the way to two chairs. "You won't be getting Alexia into trouble, not when I was the one who told the guards to let you through if you came. The Queen and I were hoping you would, but it doesn't look like you got very far. I'd like to know what happened, and I ask it as a favor."

Tiran waited for the king to sit before he took a chair of his own. So that was why the outer guards had let him through—not because he'd told them he was invited by an unnamed lady, but because the king had left orders.

"What happened, Your Majesty, was that I really messed up," Tiran admitted, tossing aside his tunic and belt. "She was willing to let me stay, but I couldn't do it. I picked up and walked out."

"Qualms about touching her?" the king asked with raised brows. "She didn't make you think she was innocent, did she? Her mother and I wouldn't have encouraged this if she were."

"No, Your Majesty, she didn't make me believe she was innocent," Tiran conceded, more embarrassed than he would have thought was possible. "I—isn't there one of your people I can discuss this with? She's your daughter, after all, and talking about my intentions . . ."

"Listen to me, young man," the king said gently, relaxing back into his chair. "I can appreciate how uncomfortable you are, but Alexia isn't your average father's-precious-pink-bundle. That girl can tie most grown men into knots, but beyond that she's abysmally unhappy. Her mother and I believe you can change that, that you really *want* to change it. Isn't it your intention to marry her?"

Tiran nodded as he blinked, more than surprised to realize that the king was serious. His concern for his daughter overrode *everything* else, prejudices and parental outrage alike. He wanted Alex to be happy, and wouldn't quibble over the means producing it.

"Well, if you intend to marry her, why are you Shifting from pillar to post? Am I supposed to believe you'll be shaking hands with her when you go to bed as man and wife? If I were that far out of touch with reality, I'd hardly make a very good king."

The man was still being calm and reasonable, and Tiran decided he might as well go along. Right then he did need someone to talk to; if he said the wrong thing and Reynar had him executed . . .

"All right," he agreed. "I'll give you the whole story, and then you can tell me that you've changed your mind. About me being acceptable husband material for your daughter, that is. I would have sworn I was deeper than that, but I'm starting to believe—"

"From the beginning, Tiran," Reynar interrupted gently. "Alexia invited you to spend the night with her in an effort to shock all of us, but you shocked *her* by accepting. I'm sure she didn't believe you would actually show up, but you must have gone there with a purpose beyond the obvious one. What *was* the purpose?"

"I'd decided to mount an offensive against her," Tiran answered with a shrug. "I had to play most of it by ear, but my main objective was to get her to accept the idea that I *would* be her husband. She's harder to maneuver against than anyone I ever fought, and not simply because of her physical skills. If she had an army to direct, I don't think I'd care to be her opponent."

"It's a wise man who realizes he may be out of his depth," Reynar said with a grin. "Most women are appallingly good at strategy and tactics, but they don't usually call it that, so men tend to misunderstand. And they forget that women take no prisoners."

"Unless that's their primary aim," Tiran agreed with a grin of his own. "But everyone beyond their target is expendable. Well, I thought I could breach her defenses by distracting her with a feint, but she caught *me* instead by shifting her center of balance. I backed her into a corner and got her to agree that I could stay the night—but then she showed me what I would be staying with."

"You're not amused any longer," Reynar observed as he studied Tiran. "What do you mean, she showed you *what* you would be staying with? What would it be if not her?"

"Oh, it was her," Tiran said with a sigh, using one hand to rub at his eyes. "The problem was she'd Shifted into this— grotesque—*thing*, the most repellent object I'd ever seen.

I'd planned to take her to bed and make gentle love to her, letting her know I wanted to do the same for the rest of our lives. I intended to gain her trust—and then discovered I couldn't go through with it. She was the same woman I'd decided to make my wife, but just because she was no longer as beautiful as she had been . . . How can she possibly learn to love a man who's interested in nothing but her looks?"

Tiran hadn't been able to watch the king while he admitted his deep shame, and for a moment there was silence. He wouldn't have been surprised if Alex's father got up and walked out without another word, but it didn't happen.

"Tell me about this grotesque thing she Shifted into," Reynar said after the pause. He sounded thoughtful rather than condemning, and Tiran was confused.

"Don't you understand?" he demanded, needing to look at the older man again. "I couldn't bring myself to touch her because she was ugly! *Boys* concern themselves with physical beauty! Grown men are supposed to be wiser."

"Grown men aren't expected to be the same as the EverNameless," Reynar countered, his tone sharper. "The EverNameless have been around long enough to understand themselves almost completely, and have learned how to work with that understanding. That's why their version of humanity is almost perfect. We haven't been around nearly as long, so we're entitled to mess up now and then. You said Alexia made herself ugly. Just how ugly?"

"On a scale of one to ten?" Tiran responded wearily, running a hand through his hair. "About three hundred. Every part of her was—*wrong*, somehow, a horrible mockery of her true appearance. I think it even scared me a little, the way a nightmare will."

"I should have known," the king said, and *now* he looked angry. "She stopped playing Monster because she won all the time and none of the other children would compete with her. And all those lectures she went to, on the true natures of men and women. When one of her brothers teased her about her interest in philosophy, she laughed. It wasn't philosophy, she said, it was extended battle strategy. Damned if she wasn't telling the truth."

"Telling the truth about what?" Tiran ventured with a frown. "And what were you saying about monsters and children?"

"Obviously you never played the game," Reynar said with a sigh. "But even if you had, I don't see how it would have helped." He explained the rules of Monster, then went on. "So the one who becomes most repellent while still remaining himself wins. The effect goes beyond ugly; it touches something deep inside that makes you need to look away. Those lectures said men are vision-oriented, and I think it's obvious that we are. You had no choice but to react so strongly; it's the way your nature forces you to go. Think about that, and then remember that Alexia knows this even better than I do."

That got him. With rational thought finally replacing emotional reflex, Tiran's mind was in high gear; because of that, implication immediately became explanation.

"She did that to me on purpose!" he growled. "She *knew* I'd never get past the prejudice. She pretended the decision was mine, but she literally forced me away from her!"

"Now do you see why I don't worry about her ability to protect herself?" Reynar asked. "The brat's more of a menace than most could easily believe. Have you changed your mind about wanting to marry her?"

"Right now I'd be happier murdering her," Tiran muttered, leaning back in his chair. "She even had me believing I owed her an apology. Now I *will* insist that an oath of obedience be included in her part of the marriage vows. It might help me survive to father a family."

"I admire a man who stands his ground even in the face of reversal." Reynar grinned. "What do you intend to do now? Go back and confront her?"

"To what purpose?" Tiran countered with a snort. "I march in and tell her I know what she's doing, and she smiles and does it again. I still won't be able to touch her, so what have I gained? No, this is going to take some thinking."

And better planning than he'd managed until then. If he'd ever performed so badly with a paying client, the showers of gold would have quickly dried up. Showers of gold. Alex had said that, and more besides. Why did he have the feeling he'd almost heard what she *hadn't* said . . . ?

"I'd like to ask one more favor before you go," the king said, drawing Tiran's attention back. "That attack on you and the other entrants—I have people looking into it, but another pair of eyes and ears can't hurt. If you come across anything suspicious at all, have one of the guards bring you to me. And if I can be of some help on that other matter . . ."

"Thank you, Your Majesty," Tiran said, standing up to bow. "I'm not too proud to ask for help, but if I don't do this on my own, it won't mean anything. But I'll certainly keep alert while I'm working on my main problem, and if I find anything interesting I'll pass it on."

"Thank you, my boy," the king said with a smile. "I suggest you dress before you leave here, though. That way you can pass the guards with some *small* amount of dignity."

Reynar watched the younger man wince before he nodded wearily and began to dress. He and Alexia hadn't been together long enough for anyone to believe something had happened, and the guards would certainly gossip. As a father, Reynar was pleased that his daughter hadn't—welcomed—a man she didn't yet know; as that same father, however, he would have enjoyed being able to insist on her immediate marriage to a man he approved of.

He watched Tiran offer a final bow and then leave, and all the king's hopes went with the man. He was exactly the sort the competition was to have supplied in the way of a winner, and he'd even passed the test of an unmentioned Truth spell. After dinner it had been, when Alexia had been paying all that attention to Lord Arthon. Sisal had keyed the spell with a gesture, then had begun discussing Tiran's intentions during the competition. Sisal, a very promising young sorcerer who worked well with Limis, another of the same, had told him afterward there was no doubt. It was Alexia herself Tiran wanted, and the more she fought him, the more determined he became.

"The EverNameless must surely have taken pity on me and sent you, Tiran d'Iste," the king murmured as he rose. "But if it's their fault you're here, they'd better follow through and give you a hand. I have a very strong feeling you'll need it."

Reynar sighed, then headed for the door out of the sitting room. The first thing he wanted was something to drink, and then he would review the appointments he had for the following day. Lady Wella had asked for some of his time, and he was curious about what she would do with it . . .

CHAPTER FIVE

I had breakfast in my apartment, sent word to Gromal, then began getting dressed. As one of the entrants, I'd been told that the exercise fields used by the palace guard would be available to us twice that day. Two hours in the morning and two this afternoon would help the entrants to stay loose while waiting for the competition to begin. I intended to use the afternoon hours for more than exercise; by then today's arrivals from the outlying districts would be registered and settled in, just in time to see the show.

"Alex, why are you wearing exercise clothes?" My mother's voice came abruptly, startling me. "Have you decided to join the men during their two hours on the field? I was going to ask if you wanted to ride with me, but if you have other plans . . ."

"Sorry, Mother, but I do have other plans," I said, noticing that she wasn't dressed for riding. Slacks and a tunic and short boots are for loafing, not for climbing into a saddle. "And when am I going to be old enough that you'll knock before walking in? One day you'll find me with a naked man—or is that what you're hoping for?"

"When I want to see a naked man, I speak to your father," she answered with a grin. "He's never been too busy to provide me with one. And you'll be old enough to have my arrival announced when you're old enough to keep your servants here full time. If the apartment hadn't been empty, I wouldn't have simply walked in. What sort of other plans do you have?"

"I have some reading to do," I replied with a pleasant smile, refusing to respond to the servant question. Everyone in the known universe seemed to believe that if you had servants at all, they ought to be around all the time. I preferred to do things my own way, and discussing the point usually led to an argument.

"You need exercise clothes to do reading?" my mother said, her brows high. "It must be very heavy reading."

"The clothes are for when I do use the exercise fields," I responded with the same smile. "You know how I hate to change a million times a day. It's enough that I'll have to change again for dinner."

"Alexia, I hate your style of lying," she stated, fists on hips and anger in her eyes. "You make no effort to get your listener to really believe you, just as if their opinion is unimportant! It's as though you're announcing beforehand that you *are* lying."

"Most people seem to like it better than being told to mind their own business," I observed. "If you really hate it that much, Mother, I can always make you an exception."

"And simply tell me to mind my own business," she said, not noticeably happier. "Alex, what am I going to do with you? You've got some plot or other up your sleeve, and you don't believe you can confide in me. Can't you understand that I'm on *your* side?"

"I know you are," I assured her with a better smile. "Would you like a cup of that coffee the Vilim embassy brought as a gift? There was a pot of it on my breakfast tray, compliments of Lord Arthon. I find I really like it."

"Yes, thank you," she responded absently, following me to the table the tray still sat on. "Lord Arthon sent you the drink? I know you impressed him at dinner last night, but I didn't expect him to be sending you gifts. Under the circumstances, I don't think it's quite proper."

"These circumstances make it entirely proper," I countered, beginning to fill two cups. "Arthon knows I intend to win the competition, and when I do my life will be mine again. Besides, I find him very attractive."

"Alex, he's a very successful *diplomat*," she said with a sigh as I handed her a cup. "I agree that he's charming and attractive, but I can't believe he would commit himself to a serious relationship. He's the sort of man whose career means everything, leaving nothing but second or third place for a woman. Do you think you'd enjoy always being second in his life?"

"Really, Mother, I have no plans for sharing his life," I said with a laugh, adding cream and sugar to my cup. "Right now he and I are working on a mutual attraction, and chances are nothing will come of it. If something does, I can worry about it then. Why waste time agonizing over remote possibilities now?"

"Now I see," she said, continuing to study me as she sat. "You don't intend to *let* it become serious. Is that because he isn't your equal in skill and ability? That was your main objection to marrying a winner of the competition, I recall."

"Arthon's skill and ability don't enter into this because he hasn't any," I half agreed, taking a chair of my own. "That's not the same as being my inferior, you understand. He's different from the rest of us, so he can't be judged by the same rules."

"Different," she echoed. "With those blue eyes, 'peculiar' would be a better word. I'd never be able to stand it, but that's probably what attracts you to him. And if *that's* true, why aren't you attracted to that man Tiran d'Iste? Green eyes aren't as bad as blue, but they're still strange enough to be noticed."

"If it's all the same to you, I'd rather not discuss Tiran d'Iste," I said, pausing to sip at my drink. "The man's too arrogant to live, but he refuses to have the good grace to quietly fade away. Let's find a more pleasant topic, like plague or torture."

"I'm having trouble understanding your attitude," she protested, reaching for the sugar spoon. "You were terrified of being married to a man who was your inferior, so you should be delighted that Tiran d'Iste is here. If he isn't your superior he's at least your equal, and chances are excellent that he'll win the competition. Why aren't you even a little bit delighted?"

"Because I don't like the man," I pronounced clearly, swallowing my annoyance with another sip of coffee. "I never said I'd automatically like someone who wasn't my inferior, so you can't claim I did. I don't like him, and I won't marry him."

"If he wins the competition, you will," she contradicted, no longer trying to look confused. "The only reason you don't like him is the fact that your father does. He's never insisted that you pay attention to his choice before, so you've gotten the idea you can do anything you please. Alex, none of us do exactly as we please, not even your father. If you put your effort into making the most of what you *can* do, you'll be surprised at how happy it's possible to be."

"But that's exactly what I *am* doing," I told her, flatly refusing to let myself be drawn into an argument. "I'm going to make the most of what I have by winning the competition, and then I'm going to leave. After that you and Father will no longer think you *have* to marry me off, and I can get on with my own choice of life."

"Which will be what?" she asked, clearly fighting to stay reasonable. "If you had any idea at all, you would already have started doing it. Do you expect to go searching for it? Where will you look first? And what happens when you discover that most of the worlds in the universe are just like this one? Even the ones with big cities and mechanical wonders still have the same kind of people you'll find here. What happens when you don't agree with their ideas any more than you agree with ours?"

I put my cup aside and got up to walk to the windows, looking out but not seeing. Problems are always so easily solved by those who don't have them; choices are clear and made without effort. What they don't seem to understand is that *your* choices are entirely different, otherwise you would have already solved the problem yourself.

"Alex, I'm not trying to upset you," my mother said, following me to the window to put a hand to my shoulder. "I know you don't fit into any of the usual life niches, but that just means you have to adapt a niche, not go off looking for a new one. I don't want to think of your spending a very long life searching for something that isn't there."

"But what if it *is* there?" I asked, turning to look down at her. "What if it's just around the next corner, but I never find it because I don't bother to look? How much better will that very long life be if I spend it trying to forget how desperately I hate what I settled for? If you try you may not win, but if you don't try, you'll *always* lose."

"But what do you expect to find?" she asked, her disturbance putting a begging note into her voice. "Please, just tell me that much!"

"I can't," I said with a sigh, reaching out to hug her to me. "There's a definite drawback to being superior. Other people can't see what you do, even if you point it out. What I want would make no sense to you, and you'd double your efforts to talk me out of it. As far as I'm concerned, you're persistent enough right now."

"Young lady, you make me mad enough to spit!" she stated, leaning back after returning my hug. "You're trying to awe me with your 'wisdom' so I'll leave you alone, but I still remember which of us is the mother. And which of us has been conning people with sober consideration ever since she was a little girl. All that talk still boils down to the fact that you insist on getting your own way."

"What's so wrong with wanting my own way?" I demanded, beginning to lose the firm grip I'd had on my patience. "You want me to do things *your* way, Father wants them done his—hell, even that Tiran d'Iste of yours is trying to join the game. What makes me so unimportant that I'm supposed to skip my turn?"

"Now *that* is your main problem," she pounced, pointing a finger at me. "When you get right down to it, you consider everything a game. Taking a horse isn't theft, it's simply borrowing someone else's piece. You could have avoided all this unpleasantness by telling someone what you were doing, but that would have ruined your game. An adult would have paid attention to consequences, but all you did was ignore them."

"So you think I'm still a child?" I asked, heading back to my coffee. "Now that's a point I can make use of. If I'm still a child, I have to be too young to get married."

"I wish your father had heard you say that," she growled, stalking after me. "Just last night he was saying what a shame it is that you're too grown up to spank. Would you like me to pass on your theory about still being a child?"

"Mother, what he probably said was 'too big,' " I corrected, trying not to laugh. "And considering what my reflexes are like, that's the last thing I'd encourage him to try. Do you want me executed for denting my sovereign?"

"You are absolutely impossible," she pronounced, not far short of fuming. "When I first got here I wanted to help, but now all I can do is wonder why I bothered. You *are* a brat, and I can't wait until Tiran d'Iste wins and claims you. I seriously doubt if you're too big for *him* to spank, with or without reflexes. I intend to stand there cheering him on."

She gave a very firm nod, turned around, and marched out of my apartment. I stood there for a moment just in case she decided to come back, but when she didn't I was able to sit down and drink my coffee. It was cool enough to really enjoy, and when I finished it I poured another cup.

"To celebrate avoiding a close call," I muttered as I added sugar and cream. "If she had ever guessed . . ."

I loved my mother very much, and believed she wanted to help; the only problem was, whatever she found out would certainly be passed along to my father. If I'd told her I meant to use the morning for loosening up before that afternoon, the afternoon would never have come off. My father would have had no trouble finding a way to stop me—*if* he'd found out about my plans.

And my mother had refused to stop asking questions. The day will never come when I insult her by telling her to leave, but I had to do *something*. Leading her on a run through the woods had drawn her away from the original trail; getting her mad at me had made her forget about the trail entirely.

"But it almost worked *too* well," I muttered, staring down into the tawny-brown liquid. I didn't even want to *think* about my father deciding to spank me. It had been years since the last time, but it isn't an experience you forget. Not so hard that you're really hurt, but hard enough to make a lasting impression. And I couldn't defend myself against the father I loved, even if my life depended on it. What I know is too devastating, too damaging . . .

"But that doesn't hold true for Tiran d'Iste," I growled, leaning back in my chair. "If *he* ever tried it, I'd—"

Rip his ears off and feed them to him? Well, he wasn't so big that I couldn't reach his ears, but ripping off takes time. With someone as good as he supposedly was, it would probably be smarter not to try to get fancy. In order to attack he has to open up, and that's when you make your move.

And hope like hell it works. I sighed deeply, wishing I were better at lying to myself. It would be nice to believe that none of my competition stood a chance, but unfortunately I knew better. And once again I'd been accused of disliking the man simply because he had my father's approval. It was pure luck no one had realized that that made him *more* attractive to me. I admire my father and respect his opinion in most things; how could I *not* be interested in a man he really approved of?

But none of that changed the basic fact that I couldn't allow myself to be married off. My mother hadn't believed the absolute truth I'd told her, that I knew what I wanted but couldn't find it here. I wished I could, but wishing doesn't make it so for anyone but magic users. We lesser mortals have to do it the hard way . . . the hard way . . . Did I *like* doing things the hard way, or did it just happen . . . ?

I sat forward abruptly to finish the coffee, then got to my feet. I still had things to do, and more plans to make. The following day would be the last for registration, and the very next morning the competition would begin. If Gromal and I put on another show tomorrow for the last of the entrants, what should it be? Bare hands again? Demonstrations of a wide range of weapons? Shift-fighting with a different twist?

I'd have to discuss it with Gromal. And it might have to be something I could do alone. My father would be furious when he heard about today; if he didn't have Gromal put in chains to keep him away from me . . . Maybe I could use someone else, someone who would pretend to be a real attacker—but who else besides Gromal was good enough to protect himself?

My head was already spinning as I started out of the apartment. If I'd had any brains, I would have insisted on being hanged before any of that got started. After all, how much planning do you have to do to be hanged . . . ?

Tiran stopped near a bench to one side of the exercise fields, looking around as he dropped his drying cloth on it. Their ranks had been swelled by another six men, those who hadn't reached the city until that morning. Four out of the six looked likely enough, but the last two would never make it to the finals. They were brothers who would be happier cooperating than competing, but the chance had been too good to pass up . . .

"So you're the one all the rest of us are supposed to measure up to," a voice said, causing Tiran to turn. "Funny, but I don't see anything to be impressed about."

The man was one of the newcomers, a brawny, red-eyed country-gentleman-about-town who stood with four of the others behind him. He was bare-chested and almost Tiran's size, and might very well make it all the way.

"You're not the one I have to impress," Tiran said, in no mood to worry about keeping the peace. "Not unless you stumble through to the finals, that is. If you do, I'll take care of it then."

"Good," the newcomer said with a grin the girls must have found very attractive. "You don't believe in keeping modestly quiet, then. I hate taking that kind apart to show everybody what they're made of. There aren't any words I can make them eat. Where did you get those funny-looking eyes, big man? Don't tell me your mother got kinky when she fooled around."

"That's not very original," Tiran said, holding the flash of rage tightly in check as he moved closer to the newcomer. "Try again, little man, but this time make it really good. I'll need a solid reason as an excuse for what I do to you."

He stood no more than two feet away from the other, and by then his voice was very soft. The man's grin faded and died as he looked into the eyes he'd mentioned, seeing there what so many others had seen before him. Tiran d'Iste wasn't afraid to spill blood, and if he did it, he would make no excuses. A man like that had to be killed to be stopped, especially if he was answering a challenge. The newcomer realized *he'd* been challenging, and the four who had accompanied him had rapidly backed away.

"I—don't think this is the time or the place," he said at last, refusing to do his own backing away. "We'll need to be in top form to get through the competition, and even a sprain could make the difference between winning and losing. When we reach the finals, it'll be a different story."

"No, only a different place," Tiran said, but he moved back to let the other man do the same. What the man had said happened to be true, and Tiran also didn't care to take any chances. If it wasn't him facing the field in the finals, it would certainly be Alex. Could she take a hulk like this big-mouth? Damn it, now he had something else to worry about.

The man moved away to let the others rejoin him, but none of them seemed ready to start exercising. They appeared more interested in sizing up the competition—a waste of time if Tiran had ever seen one. Studying someone you might never have to face can only cause confusion if you remember the wrong thing about the wrong man. Better to wait until he's in front of you; if you can't size him up then, you shouldn't be facing him.

"Okay, calm down," he ordered himself in a mutter. "She didn't show up this morning, so she's guaranteed to make it now. She's got to go on with her campaign of discouragement, doesn't she? Of course she does, so she'll be here."

Waiting for Alex to show up was getting on his nerves, not to mention making him proddish. The plan he'd come up with was the next thing to ridiculous, but he couldn't even start it until she showed up. It was all he could do not to go looking for her, although that would probably be the worst thing possible.

Or it could be the best thing. At that point he no longer knew, not after realizing how many times he'd lost to the girl. She was more talented in turning the tables on him than anyone he had faced professionally. All she needed was the merest hint of what he was trying to do, and then zap! He was countered. The only time he had come close to besting her was when he had simply been playing it by ear.

So his plan was to work without a plan. She couldn't figure out what he was up to if even he didn't know, and at the very least not knowing should rattle her. Just the way he was rattled, not to mention frustrated. His mind insisted on constantly calling up a picture of her, the prize that stood just beyond his reach with her tongue stuck out. She hated the idea of being considered a prize, but to him that was what she was growing more and more to be.

Tiran looked around again with an impatient breath, then stepped onto the grass to do a little stretching. The area was littered with arms racks and target posts and chinning bars and all sorts of tables and things, but none of their group were using any of it. Three of the men were stretching gently, seven were jogging slowly around the outer track, and the rest were strolling along examining everyone else. It was clear no one intended to overdo it and lose his place because of a pulled muscle.

It had been that way during the morning hours as well, before the newcomers had joined them. Seventeen of them, including Tiran, and no one had spoken a friendly word to anyone else. They were *afraid* to become friendly with their rivals, he knew, a typical amateur outlook. They'd never be able to face a friend in serious combat, which would be the case if both they and the friend made it to the finals. It was a point of view Tiran had never been able to understand— until he had entered that competition.

And I still don't know how I'll handle facing Alex, he thought, twisting his body to loosen his back muscles. How do you stomp all over the woman you want to marry, and what good would it do even if you did? Could he get away with facing her bare-handed? If she wasn't very good at unarmed fighting, maybe it would be possible to—

The babble of voices brought him out of deep reflection, and he looked up to see that his guess had been correct. Alex had arrived, and the other entrants were already flocking around her—or at least the newcomers were. Those who had been there at dinner the night before kept a respectful distance, dogged determination clear in their eyes. Since this was what he'd been waiting for, Tiran walked over to join them.

" . . . to meet those of you newly arrived," Alex was saying as he got there. "Has anyone told you yet that I've been accepted as an entrant?"

"Most beautiful Princess, it was mentioned in passing," the hulk who had approached Tiran said. He stepped forward, bent to kiss her hand, then grinned one of those practiced grins. "I'm Sellin, Baron West, and as soon as I heard, I hurried here to enter. I think it's marvelous that you want to experience what your future husband has to do in order to win you, but isn't it too dangerous? No man here would want to see *you* hurt."

"Hurting me isn't all that easy, Baron Sellin," Alex answered with a matching grin. "And you seem to be missing the point. I haven't entered to experience things, I've entered to win. I don't happen to want a husband, and once I've bested all of you, I won't *have* to have one."

The newcomers exchanged startled glances filled with confusion, all but the man Sellin. He grinned that grin again, and chuckled indulgently.

"So you're going to best us," he said, an adult hearing a small child boast of its prowess. "What you really mean is that you're testing us, and any man who backs down proves he doesn't deserve to have you. Well, you needn't worry about that, my sweet. The best man here won't *be* backing down."

"Neither will the best woman," Alex countered, her smile hiding the fangs of annoyance growing behind. "And just to prove it, I've arranged a small demonstration. I haven't yet decided what fighting method I'll use in the finals, but I have lots of choices. Yesterday I showed everyone Shift-fighting with weapons. Today I think I'll try the unarmed variety."

She started through the group toward the open ground on the far side, leaving Sellin still amused and Tiran cursing silently. Once again she'd gotten him, and this time she didn't even know it. If she was about to give a demonstration of unarmed combat, she had to be better than just fairly good. So much for his vague idea of facing her empty-handed.

But at least she was here. Tiran followed her along with everyone else, his senses drinking in the way she moved, spoke, gestured, smiled. If you looked at it right, it was a damned good thing her smiles weren't aimed at *him*. His reactions to her were already making him trip over his own feet; if she ever went so far as to *encourage* him . . .

"For those of you who haven't already met him, this is Gromal, Master Combat Instructor," Alex said once she had reached the man who was clearly waiting for her. The two of them were in light tan exercise clothes, and sweat stains said they'd probably already warmed up. "Gromal and I will need some room, so why don't you all spread out in a wide circle."

"By the EverNameless, I don't believe this," one of the men near Tiran muttered. "As soon as I decide I'd only have to keep weapons away from her, she shows up to prove she doesn't *need* weapons. If this goes the way I think it will, I'll probably withdraw. Why go through hell just to be killed on your wedding night by your bride?"

Wordless sounds came from two or three others as they began to spread out, wordless but suspiciously like agreement. Their original number had seen Alex in action twice, and understood all too well that she wasn't simply making a gesture. She had taught them she was really good, and now she was putting it on a personal level. If they won the competition, they would also win *her*; did they really think they were up to it?

"This should be entertaining," Baron Sellin said in a murmur to those around him. He stood a few feet to Tiran's right, and the smile hadn't left his face. "The man is the one with the skill, of course, and he'll use it to make her look good. Any fool who takes this seriously deserves to lose her for his bed."

Two of the men with him were part of the original group, and one of them snorted.

"I may not be a baron, but I've seen enough combat to know when someone isn't carrying their weight," he murmured back. "She's deadly with weapons *and* in fighting form. If she has to marry one of us, it will be against her will; she could decide to keep only to her own bed, and which of us would be able to argue the point?"

"I could," Sellin breathed, his eyes unmoving from where Alex stood. "To have a woman like that, I could do anything. And don't forget what comes along with her. A man would be a double fool if he gave up, which is why I won't be quitting. Once she's taught to respect her husband, there won't be any more nonsense."

The man he spoke to didn't answer, probably because he was wondering why Sellin had told him that. Everyone else wanted to *discourage* other entrants, but Sellin was providing reasons to stay with it. The man didn't understand but Tiran did, and the knowledge made him clench his fist in an effort to keep silent.

The bastard didn't simply want to win, he wanted to do it over the bodies of as many rivals as he could. If everyone else dropped out he would win by default, and where's the fun in *that*? And when he won he intended to make Alex *respect* him? Fear him would be more like it, and the thought put a growl deep in Tiran's throat.

"All right, we're ready to start," Alex called after she and Gromal had removed their boots. "Please make sure you all stay out of the way. It would be a pity if one of you was hurt before he actually had to be."

She grinned around at the watching men, twisting the knife deeper, then gave all her attention to her opponent. There was no bowing or other gestures of respect, not with a demonstration like this. She'd suggested it was just a friendly exercise, but it was really meant to be a nose-rubbing in unpleasant reality.

Without warning Gromal attacked her, his left leg lashing out in a kick that was aimed for her middle. If it had connected it would have broken her up, but she blocked it and countered with a kick of her own. The strike was lightning-fast and almost reached the man, but he threw a block and danced out of reach.

Take it easy, they're only sparring, Tiran told himself desperately, appalled at the way he was fast losing control. When Gromal had attacked Alex, it was all Tiran had been able to do to just stand there and watch. He wanted to kill the man who had come so close to hurting her, end him to make sure he never tried again. The fight was Alex's idea, Tiran knew that, but his idiot reactions didn't. All *they* wanted to do was protect the woman meant to be his.

The woman who didn't *want* to be his. As he watched the two sparring, he tried to put that out of his mind. In a way he was just as bad as Sellin, the self-important baron. That Tiran wanted to make it good for Alex as well didn't count, not unless he thought of a way to actually do it. And just then he couldn't . . .

Those who were watching made a joint sound of interest, and Tiran brought his attention back to see that the sparring was over. The two had warmed up enough to get down to it seriously, and in an unexpected way. They were no longer facing each other like trained fighters, but were circling like a couple of street brawlers. Fighting like that would be more dangerous for Alex, and Tiran's insides tightened at the thought.

Gromal reached out with a big hand and tried to pull the girl closer to him, but she broke the hold with a single move, then threw an elbow into his middle before retreating. She had been careful not to put too much strength into the blow, but it was clear the man had still felt it. He reached out again, this time for the front of her tunic, and got his hand grabbed and his arm twisted for his trouble.

They went through a few more hold-breakers, then began getting fancy. When Gromal grabbed a fistful of the front of Alex's hair, she didn't simply use a crossed double knifehand to lean down on his wrist and almost break it. Once his grip was loosened, she grabbed his hand, twisted it, and kicked sideways into his middle.

Right after that was when Tiran ran into trouble. Alex was defending while Gromal attacked, and she'd been doing a thorough job. But there can always be a time in a fight when you get knocked down, and she obviously wanted to show she could handle that as well. Gromal came at her fast, but this time he bent and reached for her knees. Alex went down hard on the back of her head, but still managed to draw her legs back and kick Gromal in the chest and face.

Even as Gromal staggered back and Alex rolled to her feet, Tiran was moving. He was in front of the combat instructor before the man had regained his balance, planted between him and Alex.

"This time you hurt her," Tiran said very softly to Gromal. "The exhibition is over."

It never occurred to Tiran that the other man might argue, and he didn't. He simply looked at the big man who had spoken his decision like an incontestable order, swallowed, and said, "Yes, sir."

But that didn't mean there was no argument to be had. Alex was suddenly there on Tiran's right, annoyance covering her like a cloth.

"What in hell do you think you're doing?" she demanded. "Get out of the way so we can finish this."

"And a good afternoon to you, too," Tiran answered mildly. "Nice day, isn't it."

"I said, get out of the way," she repeated, and Tiran could see a shadow of confusion over the annoyance in her silver eyes. "I'd like to be finished before dinnertime."

"You *are* finished," Tiran told her pleasantly. "Gromal here pulled a muscle, and now he can't go on. How about a walk in the gardens? You can show me the artificial lake everyone says is more than worth seeing."

"Gromal," she said, her stare now on the other man. "Since when do you pull muscles? We still have the form fighting to do, not to mention the rest of *this* exercise."

"Forgive me, Your Highness, but I really can't continue," Gromal responded, looking her straight in the eye. "It would definitely be bad for my health."

A silver dagger-stare immediately fastened itself on Tiran, forcing him to admire how quick she was. Gromal hadn't said anything about the order Tiran had given, but she still understood exactly what had happened.

"Take back whatever you said to him," she counter-ordered in a very flat voice. "Take it back and make him know you mean it."

"But I can't do that," Tiran objected, still pleasantly reasonable and mild. "Even if I said the words I'd be lying, and he'd know it. You'd never ask me to lie, would you?"

"Why not?" she challenged, not in the least amused. "There's nothing wrong with lying to save your own life. Which you'd better do fast before I—"

"Your Highness," a voice called, interrupting whatever threat Alex was in the middle of. "You and the others won't mind if we watch, will you?"

Tiran turned along with Alex to see three of the four judges approaching, the male three. Lord Arthon seemed to be leading them right to her, but Tiran wasn't about to be moved in on again.

"I'm afraid there's no longer anything to watch," he said at once, his tone friendly and comfortable. "Princess Alexia's exhibition is over, so she and I are going to walk in the palace gardens. I'm really looking forward to it."

"Your Highness?" Lord Arthon said with brows raised high, just as though he'd been told she planned to shave her head. She, on the other hand, had just started to growl, "Now you listen to me, you dirty son of a diseased street walker!" and Tiran knew she wasn't talking to Lord Arthon. In the midst of it all Baron Sellin came over to announce that he meant to join any garden-walking excursions, bringing the noise level way up beyond intelligible.

It was anyone's guess where matters would have gone to from there, but just as Tiran wondered how long it would be wise for him to simply stand there and smile, everyone's attention was diverted by the unmistakable sound of entries popping into existence. The group looked up to see large balls with knives sticking out of them come sailing through the midair entries, balls that began to spin as soon as they were through.

"Take cover!" Tiran bellowed in his best parade-ground voice, and then he grabbed Alex and began running with her toward the nearest table. Whoever their secret attacker was, his game had now grown deadlier.

CHAPTER SIX

King Reynar looked around the room, satisfied with the arrangements. It was a very small meeting room filled only with chairs, nothing of couches. Each chair had a small hand table next to it for refreshments, although none had been provided for *this* meeting. Reynar meant to keep it friendly, but strictly business.

He resisted the urge to rise and pace as he thought about how pleasant a glass of wine would be. Ordinarily there would be a decanter and cups, but that might make things *too* friendly. He had no idea what Lady Wella wanted to talk to him about; his sole determination was to keep political relations *in* the political and *out* of relations.

Without realizing it he got to his feet, wishing Josti could have been there. He'd promised himself his wife to stand behind if Wella got too close, but Wella had specifically asked for a meeting between just the two of them. He'd considered refusing, but that would have been an insult with no supporting reason. She hadn't actually said or done anything, not that he could point to. Was it *her* fault he found her incredibly attractive?

Yes, it was, he realized with surprise, stopping in the middle of the small room. She *works* at it, just as though she's laying siege to a man. I'm worried about what she might ask for because of the political situation, but that's stupid. If they consider it proper to ask for the wrong thing, they're not the sort of people we can afford to deal with.

That revelation lifted a large burden from Reynar, so much so that he rang for a servant and ordered a pot of chai. That should set the tone of their meeting perfectly, and anything that happened afterward would come under the heading of necessary knowledge.

Lady Wella and the chai arrived together; by then Reynar was seated again, studying some business papers he'd brought with him. He looked up to see Lady Wella's curtsy and the servant's bow, acknowledged both with a nod, then allowed the chai to be served. When he and his guest both had a cup and Wella was seated opposite him, he waited for the servant to leave and then smiled.

"We hope you and your countrymen are finding your time here pleasant as well as necessary," he said, deliberately using the royal "We." "You have something you wish to speak to Us about?"

"There are a number of things, Your Majesty," she answered with a dazzling smile. "I appreciate this time you've given me, and yes, I certainly am enjoying myself."

Reynar watched her sip at the chai, trying to understand what it was about her that attracted him. Her dark hair and eyes were nothing extraordinary, nor was the beauty of her face and figure. There was something else involved, something he couldn't quite pin down . . .

"Your Majesty, I feel I should tell you that Lord Arthon is quite taken with Princess Alexia," she said, still smiling warmly. "You have my word that nothing will come of the matter if you don't want it to, but I felt we would do best by bringing the subject into the light."

"We are already aware of Lord Arthon's interest," Reynar answered carefully, trying not to show his surprise. "We are also aware of the encouragement given him by Our daughter. It might perhaps benefit our two kingdoms if the encouragement indicated a returned interest, but We fear this is not so. In Our opinion Alexia simply encourages the interest of a judge in the competition, not of a man she finds attractive."

"You seem to have a rather . . . *poor* opinion of your daughter," Wella said, the smile gone, but not so the waves of femininity emanating from her. "Is that the reason you named her as prize in an open competition? Forgive me, Your Majesty, but I'm having difficulty understanding this whole thing. Our own kingdom has nothing like it."

"Lady Wella, We appreciate your concern," Reynar said, hastily juggling possible answers. Could he admit that coping with Alexia was beyond him, and not end up looking like a fool? "It may seem that We have a poor opinion of Our daughter, but this is not so. We love her dearly, and the competition was declared for *her* sake. We were hesitant, true, and yet . . ."

"And yet you still declared it," Lady Wella finished when he didn't. "May I ask in what way it's to *her* benefit? Especially since she seems to be totally opposed to the idea?"

The woman's whole attitude told Reynar she was all but begging for enlightenment, not trying to put him on a spot. He *knew* she was humbly asking for his help, so there was nothing to become insulted over. Still and all, some part of him wondered how a woman that self-effacing had ended up with a highly placed political career.

"Our daughter Alexia has no choice but to be opposed to the competition," Reynar said slowly, carefully watching his words as well as the way his guest took them. "We are all of us chained to the natures we were born with, but some natures are more easily adjusted to than others. Alexia, unfortunately, has the most difficult sort, a nature that insists on doing for itself. Were she older, she would likely have learned to accept the help of those who love her."

"Those who love her and know what's best for her," Lady Wella said, her tone suggesting complete agreement. "We can often see things that our children are too immature to see."

"Yes," Reynar murmured, caught in the faint smile she

showed, then abruptly pulled himself out of it. "No," he corrected firmly. "It has nothing to do with knowing what's best for her. If I had the sure ability of *knowing* what was best, I'd be emperor of the universe rather than king of one small country."

"I—see," Lady Wella responded, clearly taken aback. "But I don't see. If you're not trying to force her into your idea of what's right—"

"Dear lady, We have no hidden ambitions to be a tyrant," Reynar interrupted, the sense of being back in control making him stronger. "We allowed Alexia most of her life to find what was best for herself, but she's been unable to do so. Are We to stand by and watch her continue to flounder, simply through the desire not to interfere? Certainly she opposes the competition; her nature insists on it. It remains to be seen whether it continues to insist once the competition is won."

"But what if *she* wins?" Wella asked, for the first time looking sincerely concerned. "We'll be the judges, after all, and none of the others will hesitate a moment before declaring her the winner. She's a very beautiful girl, and I'm forced to admit that Lord Arthon isn't the only one taken with her."

"Ah, your disturbance begins to be clear," Reynar said, allowing himself a satisfied sip of chai. "Alexia's attempt to win all of you over hasn't failed, and you fear the political implications of a decision such as that. Are We correct?"

"I would say 'seriously disturbed' is a better term than fear, Your Majesty," Wella answered, her renewed smile rolling over him like a boulder. "We are, after all, supposed to be establishing friendly relations between our two kingdoms. A wrong decision on our part could destroy that even before it's properly begun. It would be of *so* much help if we had some idea about the outcome you would most prefer."

She was asking humbly for his help again, but this time there was an almost overwhelming sex appeal wrapped around the humility. Reynar all but felt her soft hand gently caressing his face, ready to slide down to other parts of him . . .

Pouring the hot chai deliberately down his throat helped, as did dredging up a picture of Josti at her most provocative. Giving in to this woman in any way at all would be a slap in the face to the woman he loved, and Reynar refused to do something like that. The strength he'd previously felt was still there, and he grabbed it firmly with both mental hands.

"It would be contrary to the spirit of the competition if We were to voice an opinion on the desired outcome," he said at last, his voice actually not far from normal. "We expect you and your fellow judges to render decisions according to the rules, and afterward We will all speak again."

"About those decisions," she said, understanding him perfectly. "But, Your Majesty, what if we—"

"And now you must excuse Us," Reynar continued as if the startled woman hadn't spoken. "Pressing matters of state demand Our attention, and We must return to seeing to them."

Her mouth opened as she struggled to pull herself together, but she couldn't argue with the dismissal. It seemed to Reynar that she felt shocked at the outcome of the meeting, and at a total loss as to how to turn it around. She looked rattled as she stood and curtsied, and then she was gone from the room.

"Probably only until she remembers she said there were 'things,' plural, she wanted to discuss," Reynar muttered as he poured himself another cup of chai. "Then she'll ask for another appointment, one where she won't let herself be surprised. I wonder how long I'm supposed to miss the fact that she's working on me with some kind of Talent. And how long, politically speaking, I should keep from mentioning it."

But that was only a matter of curiosity, and not nearly as compelling as the thought that the embassy from Vilim might be feeling threatened. At least one of them was worrying what their decision as judges might mean to the negotiations they were involved in. Would that make them refuse to judge, thereby taking them out of harm's way?

Not after I asked it of them as a favor, Reynar decided. Wella came to try to wheedle some answers out of me, and the others are doing—what? Hoping she succeeds? Thinking about being taken gravely ill? Or trying to do something to end the competition before it starts? They'd be off the spot if there *was* no competition, and Alexia would also be free to be courted. Was it possible? Would they really—

"Your Majesty, please forgive this intrusion!" a breathless guard gasped as he burst in. There had been the briefest of knocks, but no time to acknowledge it. "There's been another attack!"

Reynar cursed as he surged to his feet, instantly chilled. Was Alexia there and involved? What had happened? Was anyone dead? All those questions fought to be asked, but they could be answered on the way.

"Show me where," he ordered, then ran after the guard, who obeyed immediately.

By the time I was thrust under a table with a big body diving in on top of me, I was beyond furious. It felt like the EverNameless had designated me "it" for some incomprehensible game of theirs, the rules of which I had to discover for myself as the game progressed. My father's declaring the competition and naming me as prize was part of it, right along with this mysterious attacker. Those two things I could understand and even accept, but that didn't go for the part that I was beginning to think of as The Last Straw. *Him* I refused to accept, and damned well didn't *want* to understand.

"Will you stop squirming around?" the fool muttered, tightening those arms around me. "For all we know, those ball-knives are attracted to motion."

"Well, if they're attracted to brains, you have nothing to worry about," I snarled low. "It so happens you're crushing me, and if I have my choice I'd rather take my chances with the knives. Let go of me, or I'll—"

"Look out!" he shouted, and then he was completely on top of me. I heard a faint whirring sound, just before the table above us was attacked by at least two of those things. Splinters began flying as they tried to chop the table to pieces, but happily it was too thick. After a long, teeth-aching moment they backed off, whether temporarily or permanently it was impossible to tell.

"Are you all right?" Tiran d'Iste whispered as he shifted over a little. "Did any of those splinters reach you?"

"No," I answered shortly, not trusting myself to say any more. He'd actually protected me with his own body . . .

"If nobody's going to stop those things, we've got to get out of here," he whispered next. "Even if some of us were armed, we couldn't very well defend against *those*. Can you see what your magic-user admirer is doing?"

"He's trying to speak a spell while under attack," I reported after peering around the table end. "He and Arthon and Moult made it to the next table."

"I notice you're not denying that he's your admirer," the man whispered, a sigh behind the words. "Sometimes I have the feeling you're trying to discourage me."

"Nonsense," I whispered back, leaning forward to peek out the other way. "It's all your imagination. Everyone seems to have found something to hide under, but how much longer will those things keep attacking from above? We'd better be out of here by the time they discover they can fit underneath."

"Then pick a direction and let's go," he said. "By rights they should already be under here with us—unless whoever's doing it is also here. If the rest of us are chopped and he isn't . . ."

"Maybe only *some* of us are supposed to be chopped," I suggested, peering out again to see who was under attack and who wasn't. Those knife-balls were something, what looked like metal spheres with serrated knives almost a foot long sticking out in all directions. It had been bad enough when they'd just been hanging in the air; once they started turning, it wasn't hard to picture yourself minced as well as diced.

Four of the entrants had overturned two weapons stands and tented them, leaving a narrow gap the balls were trying to attack through. A couple of tables over another group was getting the treatment, and to the right—"Fregin must have made a mistake," I added. "Most of those things seem to be after him and the others."

"But not all of them," Tiran said hurriedly, hauling me back and covering me again. More splinters came flying through the air, but for a shorter time than the last. When the attack was over and he drew back to his own piece of ground, I made up my mind. Leaning out slightly to the left, I cupped my hands around my mouth.

"It's time to aerate plant roots!" I shouted. "All of you, do it *now*!"

There might have been one or two quizzical glances sent back, but most of them understood what I'd said. I could almost see them preparing shallow tunnels in the ground with their fingers, and then they began Shifting out of easy sight.

"Worms," Tiran d'Iste said, almost like a revelation. "You told them to become worms. Once they get down far enough, they should be all right."

"They can't go *too* far down, or they'll never come up again," I disagreed. "Haven't you ever tried moving through the ground like a worm?"

"No," he answered, his tone strange. "When the kids my age were trying it, I was—otherwise engaged. Well, I guess it's our turn now."

"You go ahead," I said, peering out to the right again. "I've got to think of something to help Arthon and the others. Shifting down and leaving them to fend for themselves wouldn't be right. They aren't *able* to Shift."

"But they have Lord Fregin, who's Sighted," he argued, now sounding annoyed. "If *he* can't keep them safe, what do you think *you* can do?"

"Whatever it is, it's got to be better than what *he's* managing," I countered, refusing to turn to look at the man. "They're just huddling together while those things attack, and that table isn't going to last much longer. They came out here because of *me*; I can't just crawl into a hole and leave them to die."

"I knew having a woman with a sense of honor would be trouble," he responded with a sigh. "Women are always practical—except when they should be. Move back and let me take a look."

"Don't put yourself out," I said, feeling vast annoyance as I stayed right where I was. "Just consider it your good luck that you *don't* have a woman with a sense of honor. This is *my* problem, so I'll work it out all by my—hey!"

Those big hands had pulled me back from the table edge, and on top of that had turned me to face him. Impatient green eyes stared down at me, the broad face below them showing a trace of annoyance.

"You listen to me, my lady princess," he growled, making me feel very strange. "Whether you like it or not, you're not alone any longer. You may not belong to me yet but you will, so your problems are also mine. If your sense of honor says something has to be done, then you and I will do it. I'd no more soil your honor than I would my own, something you would do well to remember. Now, stay here while I take a look."

He crawled a couple of steps beyond me to peer out, leaving me to struggle with what he'd said. I felt the definite urge to shudder, but that would have been stupid. What I really needed to do was figure out what he was up to *this* time, then find a way to counter it. I was absolutely certain he intended conning me as well as winning me, so *I* had to—

"You're right, they're *not* doing anything in the way of self-defense," he said, returning to his piece of ground beside me. "You said Lord Fregin was trying a spell before. Whatever it was, it obviously didn't work."

"I don't understand that," I said, letting the very real

problem distract me. "Last night he had no trouble stopping
the beasts that weren't already engaged with one of us, so
why would he have a problem now? Because these things
aren't living, the way the beasts were?"

"Magic doesn't work like that," he said with a
headshake. "Or at least it isn't supposed to. But maybe
that's the problem. Last night he went on the offensive,
so he must have done the same today. If these things were
warded by whoever sent them, they can't be stopped by
offensive magic. What's needed here, I think, is a little
defense."

I turned over to watch him crawl forward again, feeling
the ache in my teeth from the noise those balls were
making. They seemed to be taking turns attacking the next
table, just as though no one else mattered.

"Fregin!" Tiran d'Iste shouted, trying to make himself
heard through the noise. "Expand your personal warding
outward to cover the others! Hurry, before the table col-
lapses!"

Rather than wait to see if he'd been heard, he pulled
back fast and grabbed me again. An instant later there were
more splinters flying, and this time the attack lasted a little
longer. There was still some table over us when it ended,
but not much.

"I think they were telling me to shut up," d'Iste commented with a grin, having moved back only a short way.
"What do *you* think?"

"I think you can let go of me now," I supplied, too aware
of how close he was. It was mindlessly stupid to notice how
wide his arms and chest were when we were no more than
half an inch from being killed . . .

"But why would I want to let go of you?" he asked, his
expression now carved out of innocence. "Five minutes
from now I could be dead, and then I'd have missed the
opportunity."

"Five minutes from now you could be dead because you
didn't miss the opportunity," I countered, trying to squirm
loose from his arms.

And then all words were stopped, buried under the weight of lips pressing against mine. I couldn't believe he had the nerve—the *insanity!*—to kiss me in the middle of an attack, but there was no doubt about it. My hands were flat against the hardness of his chest, his arms had pulled my body against his, and his lips were taking the kiss I never would have given.

I tried to use outrage to force myself to fight harder, but outrage dribbled away beneath the strength of that kiss, the pull of something my body had wanted practically from the moment I'd first seen the man. My mind was outvoted and shoved aside, and then there was nothing but how good it felt. Strong arms, hard chest, soft lips . . . being kissed and returning that kiss . . .

Where it could have gone from there I don't even want to think about, but a distraction came just in the nick of time. The buzzing whine of the knife-balls began shifting up to a screech, getting really painful before it chopped off entirely. By then d'Iste and I were apart and cringing, hands to our ears in an effort to stop the pain. When it stopped by itself, I blinked and looked out, only to find Limis bent over and looking down at me.

"Are you all right, Your Highness?" the sorcerer asked anxiously, offering me a hand to get up if I wanted it. "Sisal and I came as soon as we heard those entries appear, but we were still almost too late. We temporarily extended a corner of the palace warding and forced them and the balls away from this area, and now Sisal is banishing the entries. Once the last one is gone the balls will disappear, you know, because—"

"Please don't bother to explain," I interrupted as I crawled out on my own and stood up. "You'd be wasting your breath, and I'm too grateful to want to see you waste breath. I hate Shifting to worm form, but I would have had to do it if you and Sisal hadn't shown up."

"Why do you hate worm form?" d'Iste asked as he straightened up behind me. "I thought it was a pretty good idea."

"Eating dirt makes me sick," I answered without turning, determined to act as if nothing at all had happened. "What about the others, Limis? Was anyone seriously hurt?"

"The entrants are still in the midst of Shifting back to natural form," he answered, then turned to the right. "The Vilimese are unharmed, of course, as their magic user spread his personal warding to cover all three of them. You would think they'd have had the decency to also include a royal princess."

My father's sorcerer was seriously put out that I'd had to survive on my own, but his anger wasn't noticed by the three men it was aimed toward. As soon as they were on their feet they hurried over, their relief and gratitude just about mixed half and half.

"Thank the EverNameless you two are all right," Arthon exclaimed, looking between me and d'Iste. "You risked yourselves for us, and if anything had happened to you because of it—"

"I can't believe I needed to be *told* that," Fregin said, looking only at d'Iste. "I threw everything I had at them, and all it accomplished was to attract their attention. I was so frightened, I completely forgot about my personal warding."

"And I've never been so grateful to a table that had no food on it," pudgy Moult added, his amusement real even though he was shaken. "If the one above us hadn't been so strongly made, we wouldn't have survived long enough to be saved. Can you tell me what they're used for besides hiding under?"

"When the guard units are out in the field for siege or storming exercises, their food is brought out here," I explained, seeing he really wanted to know. "Those pots are *big*, so they need heavy tables to support them—as well as metal plates and cups and things. Not to mention kegs for their daily ration of brew."

"Now *there's* a good idea," Moult said, suddenly swaying on his feet. "Strong drink and lots of it. Not to mention a place to sit down."

"You'd better get him back to the palace," d'Iste said as Arthon and Fregin grabbed for Moult. If they **hadn't** caught him, he would have sprawled on the ground. "He's feeling the reaction now, but if you walk him back he ought to be all right when he gets there. Don't let him sit down until he can stand by himself."

The other two men nodded and began helping their countryman away, a chore they were probably very relieved to have. Their color would have to come back before they could even be described as pale, and if they hadn't had Moult to distract them they might have fainted. A glance showed their refuge table completely destroyed, and if Fregin hadn't been told to spread his warding . . .

"Your Highness, here comes the king," Limis warned, and I could almost see him flinching. "He's going to be very upset with Sisal and me, and he has every right. We should have foreseen something like this . . ."

"Nonsense," I disagreed, turning to look at the wave of agitation that was my father and about a dozen of his guard. "You two alone can't ward the entire kingdom, and you know it. Were you *asked* to stand guard during exercise time?"

"Well, no," Limis admitted, still obviously thinking about becoming invisible. "But—"

"But nothing," I interrupted again. "Let me handle this, and he'll end up giving you medals."

My father told three of his guard to escort the Vilim embassy back to the palace, then he came on looking like a storm about to happen. I wasn't quite sure who he was furious with, but the guard unit meant to protect him was having a hard time keeping up.

"Alexia, are you as unhurt as you look?" he demanded as soon as he was close enough. "What about the others?"

"Everyone still seems to be in one piece," I answered, having looked around a moment earlier to be sure. "It's a good thing we have sorcerers with more sense than whoever arranged the exercise times. Limis and Sisal were listening for trouble even though no one told them the entrants would be leaving the palace warding."

"They weren't told?" he all but bellowed, causing everyone in sight to flinch. "What do those idiots of mine use in
place of brains? What's the good of having magic users of
the second highest level if we keep secrets from them? It's
a miracle they got here at all!"

Limis glanced at me at that, but it was nothing he
shouldn't have been expecting. When my father has all
the facts, he can't help being fair. It's the way he's made.

"I'll get that part of it straightened out later," he continued, happily no longer shouting. "Right now I want to
ask again: are you certain you're all right?"

"I'm dirty and I have wood chips in my hair, but aside
from that it's the same old me," I assured him. "But come
to think of it, dirt and wood chips are *part* of me. Without
them you'd probably have trouble recognizing me."

"Why don't you go back to your apartment and get
cleaned up," he said, putting a gentle hand to my face.
"I'll take my chances on recognizing you, and I want to
say a few words to the men over there. Go on now, scat."

He smiled before heading toward the group of entrants,
all of whom stood clumped together looking confused.
They weren't the only ones who didn't understand what
was happening, or why someone was making it happen.
I would have enjoyed getting my hands on the miserable
coward, especially if Limis and Sisal could find a way for
me to get around his or her personal warding . . .

"Alex." The sound of my name and a hand on my arm
stopped me just as I was starting back to the palace. I
didn't have to wonder who it was; I'd been trying to
forget that particular person, but it hadn't worked. I still
remembered him all too well, so I'd have to settle for
selective forgetting.

"Yes?" I responded politely, turning to look at him.
Those green eyes were staring down at me, all but
swallowing me whole.

"Why don't we get together later and take up where we
left off?" he suggested, his smile trying to let me know

exactly what he meant. "It should be a lot more fun when we aren't under attack. I'll come to your apartment."

"For what?" I asked, raising puzzled brows. "The demonstration? What good will continuing with it do without the others there to see it?"

"Of course not the demonstration," he said, now looking faintly less assured. "I was talking about the kiss we shared. You responded to me, and I'd like to do it again."

"Kiss?" I echoed, brows still high as I smiled. "You expect to make me believe we kissed and I responded to you? That's the funniest thing I've heard in a long time. Me, ever kiss *you*? I really don't think so."

"What are you trying to pull?" he demanded, thunder gathering in the green pools glaring at me. "I didn't imagine that kiss, and you'll never make me believe I did. What's the matter, are you afraid of what was starting to happen between us?"

"Ah, I see," I said with a nod. "Something was starting to happen between us, just the way you're guaranteed to win the competition. Aren't you getting bored trying to make me believe your opinions? I'm getting damn bored hearing about them, I can tell you."

His head came up at that but there were no more words, so I turned away and resumed my unhurried retreat toward the palace and my apartment. Gromal, apparently undamaged, had hung around long enough to be sure I was the same, and then he had disappeared. Trying to avoid my father, probably, and maybe even Tiran d'Iste . . .

Tiran d'Iste. I brushed casually at my clothes as I walked, but it was all I could do not to turn around and stare at him. Was I afraid of what might develop between us? No, actually I was terrified. My mother had been right to suggest I'd been avoiding suitable men on purpose; I *had* been, and I fully intended to continue. The last thing I needed was a man who could make me forget what I'd decided I wanted out of life.

Which meant I had to stay well away from Tiran d'Iste. I should have been long gone before someone like him ever showed up, but I'd foolishly hesitated over leaving. Now I was stuck until the competition was over, but once it was . . .

I could walk away, and spend my free time working to forget him.

Tiran watched Alex until he could no longer see her, and then he turned away to think. The brat had actually had him close to believing he'd imagined that kiss, but if he'd been into imagining things, it wouldn't have been a kiss. Or at least not only that. No, he was sure about what had happened, but Alex's behavior had confused him.

Until he realized what her denial really meant. He'd gotten to her, made her respond, and now she was even afraid to acknowledge the incident. She found him as irresistible as he found her, and the only way to handle it was to insist it had never happened!

"But don't start patting yourself on the back too hard," he advised himself in a mutter, fighting to hold down premature delight. "*Your* admitting it means nothing. The problem is to get *her* to admit it."

Which, at that point, wasn't likely to happen. He had no idea why, but she wasn't about to let her interest show. He finally had her on the run—and she'd picked a direction he hadn't even known was there.

Now all I have to do is head her off before she reaches any sort of foothills, he thought with a sigh. There's *some* mountain she means to climb, but I'll be damned if I let her do it without me. Solitary mountain climbing isn't what it's cracked up to be, and I know that better than most. But how do I make *her* believe it?

CHAPTER SEVEN

By the time we all gathered for the start of the competition, my mood was foul enough to corrode rock. It was a pretty morning and the spectators had turned out in excited droves, but they were keeping their distance from us. Every entrant wore gray exercise outfits and stood armed, but not with practice weapons.

The previous day and a half hadn't been at all pleasant, starting with dinner the night after the attack. I showed up wearing sandals and my oldest tunic and trousers, a perfect match to the way my hair was tied back. My father wasn't pleased, not even after I reminded him how he'd disliked my previous outfit. If my best gown hadn't met with his approval, I'd thought surely . . .

Rather than being thrown out, I'd been banished again to the low table. Waiting to come after me there had been Tiran d'Iste, and I'd had to use that obnoxious Baron Sellin to keep d'Iste away. It hadn't helped when the embassy from Vilim had given formal thanks to d'Iste for saving the lives of three of their members. They'd wanted to thank me as well, and I'd had to refuse in order to avoid being put right next to my co-hero.

During dinner that night I'd gotten a hunch, so I'd reluctantly sent my apartment staff instructions to move back in. The hunch paid off when not only Tiran d'Iste, but also

Baron Sellin and Lord Arthon tried to follow me afterward. The staff had no trouble keeping the three men out, but the situation had also kept me in. In the company of people who considered chattering as natural as breathing . . .

"Nice day for a competition," Tiran d'Iste commented from behind me to my right. We'd all been assigned places in a line, and his was next to mine. It seemed to bother him that I was standing silently and staring at the crowd . . .

It had also apparently bothered him that I hadn't shown up in public the day before. I'd meant to put on another demonstration the last afternoon when the final entrants were settled in, but hadn't been able to find Gromal. The combat master had disappeared after arranging for his duties to be seen to by others, leaving not a single word for *me*. That was something else I had Tiran d'Iste to thank for.

"Have you noticed there are only twenty of us?" came the next comment. "Four more men were registered yesterday, but the rest from the first two groups dropped out. We all noticed that at dinner last night. When you didn't show up, we wondered if you'd also decided to drop out."

"Fat chance," I muttered before moving away from him. I'd had dinner in my apartment the night before to be certain I didn't spill blood at the wrong time. Happily, though, the right time was fast approaching.

"Ladies and gentlemen, may I have your attention, please," a magically overloud voice called. Everyone turned to look up at the high platform built above and behind the line of twenty entries which had been called into being. The parade grounds had been used as the starting point of the competition, to allow enough room for everyone who wanted to watch. It would also be the ending point—for anyone who managed to reach the end.

"Please quiet down now, we're just about ready to start," the man with the very loud voice said. Behind him on the platform were the four judges of the competition, with Lord Merwin for company. I'd wondered if my father would be there, but he wasn't *that* insensitive. He must have known I was ready to tell him exactly what I thought about that situation—with everyone listening—and had taken the easy way out.

"For those of you who don't know how this competition works, I'll briefly summarize," the man on the platform said. "Each person competing has been assigned an entry which will lead to the start of their individual trail. Following the trail will take all of their ability and skill, but they must find the end of it in order to qualify for the finals. Traps have been set along the way to catch the unwary, and any entrant so caught will be released after the finalists are established."

The crowd cheered and applauded that idea, caring not at all that the rest of us weren't quite so enthusiastic. They weren't the ones who would have to face those traps, but they also hadn't been silly enough to enter the competition. I spotted Limis and Sisal to one side, their battery of less talented assistants scattered across the area. There hadn't been another attack after the second, and they meant to keep it like that.

"I'm sure most of you have heard that the competition has a very special entrant," the man continued once the crowd had quieted. "Her Highness Princess Alexia has elected to compete, pitting her own skill and ability against those who seek to win her hand. I'm sure we all wish the princess luck in her attempt, and I, for one, admire the effort."

He then led the crowd in polite applause, and it was all I could do not to sneer at the lot of them. They all considered me a silly female for challenging men, not believing for an instant that I had any sort of chance. I wondered if they were noticing that my fellow entrants *weren't* applauding, then I shrugged off the question. They'd find out how silly I was when I got to the finals.

"Now for a last point before we wish all the entrants well and start them on their way," the man said. "You've been told that we'll see them off this morning and watch them emerge this afternoon, and that's correct. What you may not know is that a lot more than half a day will have passed for them when they emerge. The trails have been set through worlds with different time frames, so don't be surprised at their appearance. They will have lived more days than the one."

This time the crowd muttered in surprise, many of them noticing that none of us carried extra clothes, food, or drink. We were expected to live off the land we passed through, and what clothes we wore would have to do.

"I'll introduce our judges once the entrants are on their way, and explain how they'll be spot-checking the progress made," our announcer finished up. "Right now—will the entrants please stand directly in front of their respective entries."

Our line had been somewhat haphazard while the preliminaries were going on, but it straightened out fast. The entries were set like a series of doorways, one against the next all down the line. Tiran d'Iste was to my left and some man I'd never seen before to my right, and they both seemed to be as eager to start as I was. We lined up almost shoulder to shoulder, and then—

And then the world started to go crazy. The ground under my feet began to ripple and rise, rocking me around as if I were in the middle of an earthquake. Screams and shouts proved the same thing was happening all across the parade grounds. I stumbled as I tried frantically to keep my balance, at the same time catching a glimpse of the swaying, wiggling platform above the entries. Only the entries themselves weren't moving, which didn't help in the least.

I stumbled again and almost went down, and then everything happened so fast it was nearly impossible to follow. With screams ringing in my ears, an arm clamped itself around my waist—just as the ground rose really high. I felt myself being thrown forward, which quickly changed to flying through the air. Flying, flying—and then a landing that turned the lights out.

*   *   *

This time when Reynar came storming out of the palace, he knew that nothing short of the blood of the attacker would calm him again. Dozens of people had been hurt, the competition proceedings were a shambles—and most of the entrants had disappeared. Of *course* Alexia had to be one of those gone; it would have made things much too easy for Reynar if she weren't.

"Your Majesty, please, it could be dangerous for you to be out here," said a voice, and Reynar noticed it was a bothered-looking Merwin. "Everything possible is being done. Why don't you return—"

"Limis!" Reynar roared, taking advantage of the prerogative to hear nothing he didn't care to. "I want a report, Limis, and I want it *now!*"

The sorcerer hurried over, wary at Reynar's having dropped the royal "We." The king did that only when he was relaxing—or furious.

"The plan seems to be working, Your Majesty," Limis reported, not as happy as his words should have made him. "The attacker had to come inside our protective warding to strike again, and now he's trapped. We don't know which one he is yet, but we'll find out."

"Wasn't there any way for you to stop what he did?" Reynar demanded, hardly mollified. "According to the plan *I* remember, you and the others were supposed to trap him *before* any damage was done."

"Sire, we promised to do what we could," Limis answered, making no effort to avoid Reynar's eyes. "The miscreant obviously prepared his earthquake spell earlier, keying it to a single sound. Once he spoke the sound, it was all we could do to quiet the heavings *and* seal the area."

"All right, I'll grant the point," Reynar grudged. Ever since the sorcerer had spoken to Alexia after the last attack, Limis seemed like a different man. "What about my daughter and the others? Have you found out where they disappeared to?"

"All but one of the entrants passed through the entries," Limis said, pleased that he had *some* good news. "It was the most logical—and safest—thing for them to do, not to mention the easiest. The last man would have done the same if he hadn't fallen and broken his neck. Apparently he tried to fight the wave instead of going along with it."

"The earthquake wave moved the contestants *toward* the entries?" Reynar asked, immediately suspicious. "Why would it be set to do that, when in another moment they would have gone through by themselves? Could the attacker have done something to the trails—or to the worlds the trails pass through?"

"I don't know," Limis admitted, now looking worried. "It hadn't occurred to me. If you'll excuse me, Your Majesty, I need to speak to Sisal."

He hurried away without waiting for permission, but Reynar noticed it no more than he did. If something had been done to the prepared trails, the entrants might have noticed it and refused to step through . . . but now they *were* through . . . including Alexia.

What a wonderful idea I had, Reynar thought as he looked around at the frightened, bruised—and trapped—people on the grounds. I'd better apologize as soon as Alexia gets back . . . and she *will* get back . . . please, *please*!

Tiran hit the ground, but the actual fall was no more than a couple of feet. He'd taken worse and he was sure Alex had too, but she'd collided with a tree branch just inside the entry. He scrambled over to her immediately, worried about the way she just lay there. She was unconscious, but nothing seemed to be broken. He'd have to wait until she woke up, but what if—

Hold it, he ordered himself sternly, sitting down next to her. Acting like a hysterical fool would help no one, least of all Alex. He would have to wait until she was conscious before deciding how badly hurt she was.

It was hard advice to follow, but Tiran was used to having to do things the hard way. He preferred it when life slid along smooth and easy, but that didn't often happen. He'd had to fight for everything he had, and that meant he had experience in making events go his way.

Like the way he'd managed to get himself and Alex through the same entry. Just as they'd been about to be flung apart he'd gotten an arm around her, and after that things had grown blurred. He'd been certain they had to stay together, even though originally they were meant to separate. He'd acted on a spur-of-the-moment hunch, one that he couldn't explain.

But in just a little while he'd *have* to explain it, he realized as Alex began to stir. She'd worked hard to avoid him the last day and a half, and she wasn't likely to enjoy seeing him now. Especially when one of them was supposed to be elsewhere. Tiran sighed, wondering why being near Alex made life so complex for him. He might be trying to avoid boredom, but that didn't mean he was interested in courting chaos.

And that's *not* the same as courting Alex, he thought as her stirring turned into actual movement. She's just a victim of chaos, and together we'll—"Okay, take it slow, Alex. You hit your head and you were knocked out."

Silver eyes blinked and then opened all the way, more confusion than vagueness in them. Tiran was very glad to see that, but a moment later there was less to be glad about.

"This isn't the parade grounds," she stated, looking at the foliage all around. "I must have fallen through an entry, but if I did, what are *you* doing here? Entries are supposed to be one to each of us."

"You and I got tossed through together," he answered with perfect, if less than complete, honesty. "With the way the ground was rolling, I'm surprised it was *only* us. And I thought the mysterious attacker had given up."

"What's wrong with this place?" she asked, one hand to her head as she sat up slowly. "Or is it my eyesight that isn't working right?"

"No, it's this place," Tiran answered, frowning at the scenery. Brooding bushes, looming trees, a gray and sinister sky . . . "I'd gotten the idea that the worlds we passed through would be trapped but normal, but this strikes me as—wrong, somehow. It also seems vaguely familiar, but I don't remember from where. If I'd gotten a look at it before moving completely through the entry, I might well have gone back."

"Then let's do it now," she said, obviously getting ready to stand. "They must be waiting for us to get back before starting the competition for real."

"Alex," he interrupted, one hand on her shoulder to keep her seated. "We can't be more than five feet from the entry. Do you see it anywhere?"

This time she looked around deliberately, but the outline he himself had looked for earlier still wasn't there. There should have been *some* indication of it, but there wasn't even a shadow.

"A one-way entry?" she said, looking confused again. "Why would they do *that*? There's nothing in the rules that says you can't change your mind even after the competition starts. You're immediately disqualified, but you can still change your mind."

"Well, for whatever reason, *we* can't," he said. "Our only option seems to be to follow the trail to its end and get out that way. Why don't you rest for another minute or two, and then we'll get started."

"What's this 'we' business?" she asked with a sound of annoyance, raising her knees to rest her forearms on them. "This competition isn't supposed to be a group effort. When I decide I'm ready to get started, I'll be doing it alone."

"How?" he asked in turn, working hard to sound reasonable. "There's only one trail to follow, so we can't split up. One or the other of us could go first, but then the second will be open to charges of following after the first rather than following the trail. I don't know about you, but I'd dislike having someone charge me with that."

Those silver eyes watched him without shifting around, but Tiran could see he'd scored a point. He'd as much as said he refused to go second, and she felt the way he did. That was a problem, with no easy solution at hand.

"If we can't split up and we can't play follow the leader, there's only one thing left that we *can* do," she said after a moment. "One of us stays here while the other goes on to complete the course, and then we both demand that the one left be allowed a course of his own. Considering the unusual circumstances, they'll have no choice but to agree."

"Does that mean you're volunteering to stay?" Tiran asked, annoyed with how fast she'd found a loophole. He preferred to deal with intelligent women, but not at *all* times . . . "Because if it doesn't, we still have a problem. I joined this competition to win, not to hand over my chance and *hope* there's a provision for unusual circumstances. If you do decide to stay, you have my word that I'll explain what happened as soon as I find my way out."

"What good will *that* do?" she countered at once, just the way he'd hoped she would. "All *you* can do is explain. I can insist, and as a princess and the supposed prize in this farce, I'll be listened to. You can't think you have more influence than I do."

"Maybe, maybe not," he replied with a neutral shrug. "The point is that I'm not staying. Are you?"

"No," she answered in a mutter, now giving him a baleful look. "I suppose that means we have to hold our own final, to see which one of us gets to go. There isn't much in the way of clear space, but—"

"I have a better idea," Tiran said quickly, before she offered him his choice of weapons. "Why don't we *share* following the trail, taking turns as we go from one world to the next? Each of us will be responsible for finding his or her own segment, and if at any time we can't, then that one is disqualified. If we both make it through, we can both be there to demand individual chances."

"That's your concept of a better idea?" she said, not terribly pleased. "If we do it that way we'll have to stay together, and frankly I've already had enough of your company."

"Frankly, you haven't had *any* of my company," he countered, suddenly needing to be blunt. "You've spent all your time avoiding me, so how can you possibly make any value judgments? Do you think if you ignore me long enough, I'll simply go away?"

She made no answer to that, other than running a hand through her hair. Obviously she *had* been hoping for something along those lines, and might be wondering why it hadn't worked.

"I can imagine how many men you've managed to get rid of like that," he said, certain the number wasn't small. "Most men do need to be encouraged to keep them hanging around, but Alex—I'm not most men, and you're very special to me. I won't let you go without more of a fight than you're currently able to give me, not unless we really can't get along. We can find out about that while we're taking turns."

"Do you mean that?" she said, refusing to let him see any of what she was feeling. "If we go along taking turns but don't get along with each other, you'll drop out of the competition? Whether or not you get disqualified along the trail?"

"If it becomes clear that we really don't blend, there's no sense in my continuing," he said, trying to make her believe him. "You're the only thing of interest to me in this competition, the only thing that matters. Don't you remember what I told you? Did you think I was lying?"

"I don't know," she admitted, apparently being open about it. "Are you saying you never lie?"

"Hardly," he conceded with a snort. "I may have a strong sense of honor, but I'm still as human as the next man. So what do you say? Do we have a deal?"

"On one condition," she countered, a little too quickly for Tiran's liking. "I want your word that you won't try to take advantage of our being together to take advantage of *me*. You'll stay on your side of the trail, and I'll stay on mine."

"I can't agree to that," he refused just as quickly. "What if something happens that *requires* me to be closer to you? If I give my word, I'll be stuck with doing the wrong thing or soiling my honor. And what do you mean by 'taking advantage' of you? What specifically are you worried about?"

"I'm not 'worried' about anything," she gritted in answer, her silver eyes beginning to flare. "Or maybe I'm worried about the possibility of decking you at the wrong time. If you refuse to give your word that means you're up to something, and I'll be damned if I just let it happen. You—"

"What do you mean, 'up to something'?" he demanded, deciding it was time to feel insulted. "You make it sound as if I'm sneaking around behind your back, trying to hide my intentions. Since I expect to marry you, what do you *think* my intentions are? What would *any* normal man's intentions be?"

"*You*, normal?" she shot back, a flush starting on her face. "Don't make me laugh. Normal men don't enter a competition like this, so that lets you and the others out. The whole bunch of you are disgusting and depraved. You—"

"Depraved?" Tiran repeated, real feelings of insult starting. "And disgusting? That's the most childish thing I've ever heard, but perfectly fitting considering the source. It's—"

"Childish?" she stormed, obviously intent on overriding his words. Rather than allow it, Tiran just kept shouting, the argument getting louder and louder. It might have gone on for hours, but suddenly they were both silenced by something felt rather than heard.

"What is *that*?" Alex asked, putting a hand to her ear while gritting her teeth. "I've never felt a sound like that."

"Damn it, *now* I know why this place looks so familiar," Tiran said, also feeling the ache in his teeth, bones and ears.

"We've got to get out of here, and as fast as possible. Do you know the cheetah form?"

"Not a cheetah," Alex disagreed at once, rising to her feet just as he did. "An ostrich. Cheetahs hear too well."

Tiran had no time to admire how quick she was to understand things. Instead he nodded curtly and said, "The trail is right there. If it fades out before we find the next entry, we stop to confer. Otherwise we keep going."

This time it was her turn to nod, and then her form began to blur and shift. His own mind had already pictured the ostrich form, so he willed his body to match. That was what Shifting felt like, *willing* yourself into another form. There was a lot more to it than that, of course, but most of it was automatic to the nervous system of a shape-shifter. He'd been given an explanation once by someone who seemed to know what he was talking about . . .

But there was no time for dwelling on nonessentials. The feathered bird shape beside him with her long, sexy, bald-looking neck and head began to move off at a trot, so he followed. His taloned feet dug into the ground of the faint trail, he held his short, flightless wings out for balance, and very quickly he was moving as fast as his thick, awkward-looking legs would go.

Which was incredibly fast, and luckily so. The two of them raced along just ahead of the deadly sound that was definitely in pursuit refusing to let the pain throw them off gait. The brooding forest watched the race dispassionately, offering no hindrance but also no help. In that place you helped yourself—or you died.

They ran on for what seemed like a very long time, and then, finally, Tiran was able to make out what looked to be an entry. It was still a good distance away, but Alex had also seen it and was heading straight for it. Tiran's ostrich body was trembling with fatigue and fear, making him want to stop, dig a hole and bury his head. He overrode the feeling even as he wondered how those creatures had managed to survive with such a deadly-to-them fear reflex. If he and Alex stopped for any reason at all, they were done for.

And that, of course, was when the animals attacked. They were fairly large for anyone who didn't have the size of an ostrich, and were covered with a heavy blue-gray pelt that looked inches thick. They came charging out of the surrounding brush with fangs bared and dark eyes eager, ready to take down this fleeing prey or simply delay it long enough to let what was in pursuit catch up.

But an ostrich didn't use its legs only to run. Even as Tiran watched, Alex broke stride to kick at one of the beasts, catching it so hard that it flew into a small group of its friends. They went down in a tangled knot, silently flailing all around, and Alex was already running again. Tiran hurriedly did some of his own kicking then followed her, knowing the beasts that had been directly kicked were probably dead.

Another few minutes of running brought them to the entry, and Alex lowered her head before plunging through. Tiran, since he was larger, had to do the same, but once through he didn't continue running. When a glance around showed nothing in the way of immediate danger he stopped, Shifted back to his natural form, then drew his sword. If one or more of those beasts tried to jump through after them . . .

It didn't take long to notice that I was suddenly the only ostrich around, so I Shifted back to natural and returned to the entry to do my part. This time the outline was fully visible, and Tiran d'Iste was standing braced as he waited for one or more of those animals to jump through after us. Since he didn't need any help staring at the entry, I turned my attention to the world we'd crossed into.

It was early afternoon of a nice day, and meadow stretched away from us in all directions. The wild grass was fairly high, but it didn't feel as though anything was stalking us through it. The sky was an off-blue and the sunshine somewhat on the pale side, but other than that it looked like a perfectly normal world.

Unlike the one we had just left. I hadn't had much time to think about it sooner, but that first world made no sense at all. The competition wasn't supposed to be easy, but it also wasn't supposed to kill an entrant before he'd even had a chance to look around. And if d'Iste hadn't known what was happening, we probably *would* have been killed.

And that made my original problem much more difficult. My hand tightened around the hilt of my sword at the thought of having to stay with him, at not being able to take off alone. There was no doubt he intended to take advantage of the situation, and I wasn't finding it possible to think of too many ways to stop him. If only more of me *wanted* to stop him . . .

But most of me didn't, and the rest refused to desert someone in the face of extreme danger. My companion probably could have gotten away safely if he'd been alone in the previous world, but what about the worlds to follow? If any of them turned out to be worse—at that point a distinct possibility—could he make it without someone to help? I was certain *I* could, but arrogant self-assurance is part of my nature. If I left him to his own devices and he didn't survive, his death would haunt me for the rest of my life.

So I was stuck with feeling responsible for a man who was supposed to be better than me. Put like that it sounded ridiculous, and just might give me a way out. If something happened to *prove* he was better, my sense of responsibility might decide to take a hike. It was a slim thread to hang a hope on, but what choice did I have? Along with spending the intervening time keeping him away from me . . .

"If they were coming through after us, they would have done it by now," his voice came suddenly from behind me. "Let's move a few yards away just to be sure, then figure out which direction to take next."

"You haven't told me yet what we were running from," I pointed out as he moved in front of me. "I could certainly feel it, but I wasn't able to see anything."

"I'm not sure *anyone* knows what the things look like," he answered, glancing around as he beckoned me farther from the entry. "They're a life form that uses sound vibration, either as a general weapon or in order to hunt. The closer they come to you the stronger the vibration gets, until the sound is enough to tear you apart. I happened across that world years ago, but at that time I was using a gate. We got back through the gate just in time, and that's as close as I ever want to come."

"Those animals that attacked us," I said, suddenly understanding more than I had. "They didn't make a sound even when they were hurt, not to mention when they jumped us. I'll bet they're not only mute but deaf as well. And those really thick coats—insulation against the vibrations, maybe?"

"It could very well be," he agreed, looking thoughtful. "How else could they work with whatever causes the vibrations? They could very well be the equivalent of trained hunting dogs."

"Or they could be a hunting party using the whatever-it-is to flush quarry into their waiting teeth," I countered. "It isn't smart to make assumptions when you don't have any facts."

"You're absolutely right, and I bow to your wisdom," he said with a grin, actually performing a short bow.

"My wisdom tells me we ought to get moving," I said, refusing to be diverted into a "friendly" conversation. "Since you were in charge of the last world, this one has to be mine."

"Yelling 'Run!' is hardly my idea of being in charge," he disagreed immediately, holding one hand up. "I suggested cheetahs, you countered with ostriches and we went with the ostriches. You were also the one who followed the trail while I followed *you*. With all that in view, this world gets to be mine."

"But you were the one who recognized the last world, and knew enough to yell 'Run!' in the first place," I returned just as fast. "You also pointed out the trail, and told me to stop if I lost it. That's not my idea of doing it by myself. If it happens to be yours, we have another problem."

"Okay, then there's only one way to settle this," he said, digging inside his swordbelt to come up with a golden coin. "I'll toss and you call it."

"Go ahead and toss," I agreed. "I'll call it once it's in the air."

"What a terribly suspicious nature you have," he observed with a faint grin, but didn't argue the point. It looked like we both knew people who could manipulate the toss—if they knew which side was theirs before the coin went up.

"Tails," I said as soon as he flipped it, once again not taking any chances. Most people automatically choose heads. The coin came down into his palm, got clapped to the back of his left hand—and when he uncovered it, I could see the face of some sovereign I didn't know.

"Just to avoid any further argument, here's what the reverse looks like," he said, turning the coin with two fingers to show a large building of some sort. "Does that satisfy you, Your Highness?"

"Not as much as it will satisfy me if you can't find the trail," I answered as sweetly as possible. "Shall I wish you luck?"

"Not unless you specify *good* luck," he came back with a snort. "I can find the other sort on my own. Let's see what we have to work with."

He put the coin back where it came from and looked around, leaving me to resheathe my sword and ignore his choice of words. If he expected to get any helpful suggestions by talking about what "we" had to work with, he was due for disappointment. I'd already made a guess or two, but since he was in charge I'd be keeping them to myself.

"There's nothing in the way of a visible trail," he murmured, almost to himself. "In the first world it could be seen easily, so we're faced with two possibilities. Let's check them out."

He Shifted into his cat shape, looked around again, Shifted into a wolf, did the same, then went to a bird. After that he went through toad, lizard, worm and dragonfly, pausing after each Shift to check. The snake was the last, and then he Shifted back to natural.

"Okay, we have to head toward that distant stand of trees," he said, gesturing to the left of where we stood. "I'll check again as we go, but that's where the scent seems to be coming from."

He gave me a pleasant smile and started off, possibly expecting me to ask what he was talking about. I followed without saying anything, mostly because I didn't have to. The two possibilities he'd spoken about checking had to be that in this world the trail was *in*visible to the human eye, or it wasn't a trail to be followed by sight. Shifting through all those shapes had given him the answer: this time the trail was composed of scent.

Which had been one of my original guesses. I had also expected it to be relatively easy to find, and it had been. Each world we crossed into would be progressively harder, and I found myself getting impatient. Any child could do what we'd done so far; would it get so hard that it became a real challenge? If so, I wanted it to hurry up and do so.

"You'd better take it a little slower," I heard, and looked up to realize I'd passed our temporary leader. "When you have a long way to go, you're smartest pacing yourself."

"If you're tired from our run through the first world, you should have said so," I commented as I slowed down, suddenly impatient with being lectured. "When you start getting on in years, pride should begin to make room for common sense."

"What do you mean, 'getting on in years'?" he demanded, abruptly outraged. "You make it sound like I'm looking at my three-hundredth birthday! It so happens I'm not that much older than *you*."

"Of course you're not," I soothed, making sure my tone stayed sober. "You're a mere child as these things go, and the fact that our people don't start showing their age until they're past three hundred has nothing to do with it. That reputation you have was only built over the last year or two, so even that doesn't count. But when you're feeling tired, you really should let me know."

"That reputation I have was built over the last ten years," he growled, for some reason annoyed enough to be looking ice daggers at me. "That I started when I was a lot younger than you are now has to count for something. Is that why you've been giving me such a hard time? Because you think I'm too old for you?"

"Look, I was only trying to be considerate," I answered with a very visible sigh. "I was taught to be considerate toward my—toward other people, but if it bothers you I'll stop. Bickering over unimportant things isn't smart in a place like this, so we'll simply take it slow and no more need be said."

I quickly returned to scanning the landscape, pretending I didn't hear the sounds of pure vexation coming from him. That I hadn't changed my "opinion" should have been clear, as clear as the fact that I refused to discuss it. Whatever he said I would certainly agree with—just to keep the peace.

I had to make sure my expression didn't show how delighted I was with that turn of events. It wasn't possible to really consider Tiran d'Iste old; but if it bothered him to believe I thought he was, then I would go on fostering that impression. And add to it with other "casual comments," as many as I could think of. If I kept him in a constant rage, he ought to be too busy to think about taking advantage of that situation.

And of me. I bent to pluck a blade of tall grass, and played with it as I walked. With nothing attacking us, it was a really pretty world, all meadow beneath sunshiny sky— and very private. Truthfully, I was a little tired from that run myself, and wouldn't have minded a short rest—if I'd been alone. Since I wasn't I'd just keep going, and continue to protect myself with everything I had. If he'd been willing to give his word . . . but he hadn't, so whatever happened was his own fault.

We continued on for quite a while in silence, with my companion Shifting twice to wolf form to check the trail. We couldn't yet see the next entry, but it wasn't likely to be very far. I was also beginning to get hungry, and hopefully the next world would offer more variety. Shifting form to a grass-eater isn't one of my favorite options.

"When we go through to the next world, we'll stop for a short rest," d'Iste said abruptly, all but reading my thoughts. "If we run ourselves into the ground now, we'll regret it later."

"I thought I already agreed to stop whenever you wanted to," I answered, then held up a hand. "Sorry, that was uncalled-for. What I meant was, of course we can stop to give you a rest."

"We'll be giving *us* a rest," he corrected almost absently. "Little girls need it as much as old men do, a truth you'll be able to admit once you grow up."

"Oh, I'm already grown up enough to admit *that*," I said with a warm smile. "Little girls do need their rest—only not as often. Let me know when you're ready."

Nothing in the way of expression crossed his face, but that doesn't mean he wasn't feeling anything. Trying to turn the tables on me hadn't worked, and now he was in the position of having called himself an old man. If he got really wild and decided to settle the matter with a forced march, he'd end up regretting that, too. Women are built to take forced marches better than men, and the most usual reason they don't is that they're not in shape for it. I was, and was ready to prove it.

Another period of silence strolled past, and then we were just about up to the stand of trees. I automatically loosened my sword in its scabbard as I looked around, absently noticing that d'Iste was doing the same. When he held up a hand I stopped, paying almost no attention to the entry we could now see. If there was a trap in that world, it had to be very close.

Once again my companion Shifted to wolf form, then spent a number of minutes testing the air. A wolf has a fairly good sense of smell, but if it had been me, I would have used a bloodhound. And maybe even a coin to toss. The entry was directly ahead of us on the other side of the trees. Would the best approach be straight ahead, or circling the trees? If circling felt easiest, would left be better, or right?

"The scent trail definitely circles to the left," d'Iste informed me after Shifting back. "Since we're supposed to follow that trail we'll do the same, but walk directly behind me. Something around here feels like it's waiting."

He didn't go into more detail after that comment, but he didn't have to: I was also feeling that something. The closest I can come to defining it is what a cage smells like when you're in animal form. Even if you can't see the cage, you know it's there.

We moved around the stand of trees to the left, all senses alert, examining every inch of ground before trusting our weight to it. It took a while to go that short distance, but finally we were right in front of the entry. D'Iste gestured that he would go first, and I nodded. When it became my turn at leader, then firsts would also be mine.

He hesitated a moment, and then stepped quickly through the entry. It seemed as though there was a small resistance that he first had to overcome, but then he was gone and it was my turn. Waiting a second or two gave him the chance to clear out of the way, and then I went . . . pushing through the slight, unusual resistance . . .

Directly into water so deep I could almost feel it crushing me. I threw my left hand back in an effort to grab the entry to return, but one touch showed it was blocked. *In* was all it could be used for, and we'd already done that.

And then I saw Tiran d'Iste hanging in the water not far away, proving we were still together. Wonderful, I thought as I struggled to sheathe my sword. All I needed was company to drown with . . .

*   *   *

Reynar truly wanted to pace, but the rage he was in the grip of refused to allow it. Somewhere in that crowd on the parade grounds was the person responsible for what had been going on, the person he would not let escape. If he paced the fool would believe he was indecisive, and could conceivably make even more trouble. No, the situation called for him to sit where he was, staring broodingly at those who weren't being allowed to leave . . . considering what he would do to the guilty one when they found him . . .

"Your Majesty, Limis sends his apologies," Merwin reported from Reynar's right. "He hasn't yet unraveled all there is of the situation, but he'll report to you as soon as he does so."

"What has he got so far?" Reynar asked, and this time the growl in his voice didn't bother Merwin at all. The short, round man *knew* the growl wasn't aimed at him and, even more, seemed to share the mood.

"At least one of the trails has been tampered with," Merwin answered, anger clear in his words. "Exactly how he doesn't yet know, nor has he finished checking them all. He's working with the judges to check the trails each is responsible for, which means he has to do it one at a time. Sisal and two of the others have begun to go through the crowd."

"Which also means one person at a time," Reynar said, struggling to control the flare of furious impatience. "All right, there's nothing else that can be done. Just make sure Sisal knows no one is to leave even if he or she has been cleared. And have the cleared group guarded, to be certain no one joins it unofficially."

"Yes, Your Majesty," Merwin acknowledged with a bow, then hurried away to see that the orders were obeyed.

Reynar let his eyes move to the four ambassadors working with Limis. He would wait until Sisal had sifted through the crowd, and if nothing was found, it would then be their turn. Once he found out who, he would demand to know why. Not that it really mattered. Limis hadn't reported to him because Limis hadn't yet found Alexia; that Reynar knew beyond all doubt. And if anything serious had happened to Alexia, the one responsible would be days dying. The law didn't really allow for an execution of that sort, but no one would try to stop him . . . or at least wouldn't try for long . . .

CHAPTER EIGHT

As soon as I got my sword sheathed I Shifted to killer-whale form, and it was none too soon. Tiran d'Iste also Shifted immediately, and he must have needed to breathe even more than I did. He'd waited until I was through the entry, probably to be certain I knew which fish he was. As if I would have wondered when one fish stuck close to me . . .

Breathing water felt as strange as it usually did, especially in a body so much larger than my natural one. Going a lot larger means stretching your working material—yourself—extremely thin, and usually isn't wise. If you stretch beyond your limit there will be gaps, and gaps can kill you as surely as any weapon. The bodies of living things are whole, each according to its species; put a gap in the wrong place, and the living thing dies.

But a killer whale isn't nearly as large as a blue whale, and whale form was what I needed. I'd been able to hear the call as soon as I Shifted, whale song with a difference. It *had* to be the trail, and I wasn't certain a smaller fish would be able to pick it up. I also had no intention of experimenting; spreading out to whale size once doesn't mean you'll be able to do it twice.

Tiran d'Iste floated not far from me, undoubtedly able to hear the song but waiting for me to lead off. I did so at once, but it bothered me that he was playing fair. That world was mine to lead through, and he was stepping back to let me do it. Even if he'd guessed—as I had—that this time the trail would most likely be sound, he hadn't tried to jump in with help. As I moved along in the proper direction, I had to suppress a shudder. If he was going to use fair play against me, how would I ever counter it?

Moving through the water as a fish isn't swimming, not as a human defines the word. It's a marvelous glide through the most fantastic colors, greens and blues and grays that can be seen even that far down. Brighter colors may be lost, but the richness of what's left lets you forget the loss easily. As I looked around, I had to constantly remind myself to keep going. Whales need to rise to the surface on a regular schedule, and we didn't have the time for long side trips.

Following the call led us through schools of tiny, darting fish that looked delicious, and I was a little too hungry to resist. I discovered that they also tasted delicious, and I didn't even have to stop for the meal. Sailing through with my mouth open made the snack effortless, and I almost laughed. *That* was my concept of perfect food service, and I'd have to remember to tell Tringo about it.

Time is a lot less meaningless underwater than many people believe, especially if you're a whale. By the time we got close enough to see the next entry, I was very aware of my shortness of oxygen. I had only a few minutes left at most, and then I would have to rise to the surface or drown. Tiran d'Iste couldn't have been doing much better, and might even be doing worse. I stopped and gestured toward him, telling him I wanted him to go through first, but he didn't seem to understand. Or didn't *want* to understand. If he was refusing to take my orders, things were looking up . . .

And then, suddenly, they were looking down. A dark shape glided past me, one of a number of shadow-shapes that were suddenly all around. That they were a bit smaller than me didn't matter; sharks have enough teeth to make up the difference, not to mention how much more they weighed. I might have looked and swum like a whale; my weight was that of a human.

But so was my mind, and that tilted the balance in my favor. The sharks weren't attacking yet; they seemed to be checking the lay of the land—or water—before starting anything, which meant we had a chance. A glance at d'Iste showed that his path to the entry was as clear as mine, so I didn't hesitate. I went straight for it, and just before it would be necessary to veer, I Shifted back to human. My momentum carried me right to where I needed to be, but putting an arm out stopped me. I had given an order earlier, and I meant to be certain it was obeyed.

Just as I'd hoped, d'Iste was directly behind me. He'd known immediately what I was up to, and thought he'd be guarding our rear the way he wanted to. Rather than go through the entry I ducked aside, then slid around to end up behind him. Putting my feet in his now-human back shoved him through the entry, and then I was following right behind.

Into what, despite the fall, I almost thought was another underwater location. It took me a moment to realize I was sprawled in the mud, under the sort of downpour that looks like it's good for the rest of the day. Ah, well, it wasn't as if I had come through dry.

"And what in hell was *that* little trick supposed to mean?" a growly voice demanded as I started to get to my feet. "You knew I wanted *you* to go through first."

"And I wanted the opposite," I answered, reaching up with both hands to push the sopping hair out of my face. "Since I was leader, I made sure we did it my way."

"Without once stopping to wonder if I had a reason," he said, staring down at me narrow-eyed through the rain. "Or if I'd had a plan you might not have had."

"A plan such as what?" I demanded, beginning to get annoyed. "Pretending you really were big enough to handle those sharks? Or were you going to *talk* them out of attacking?"

"I was going to Shift to barracuda form," he returned, using one hand to wipe his face. "Not only would breathing have been easier, but I could have taken a chunk out of one of those sharks before it had a chance to dodge. After that the other sharks would have attacked it, and I would have had the speed to reach the entry during the confusion. But it would have worked only if you went through first."

"And my plan *didn't* work?" I countered, folding my arms. "Are you making an issue of this because we were both killed?"

"No," he answered shortly, as though the question had been put seriously. "We'll have to talk about this, but not here where we're still in danger of drowning. Let's pick up the trail and see if we can find some shelter along the way."

He turned away from me then to look around, but it was a moment or two before I could do the same. He had something in mind that I wasn't going to like, and I couldn't decide how to feel about that. I should have been pleased to find a point of dissension, but I was also ready to feel irritated. As though I'd been happier when he was playing fair. Which I hadn't been. Or maybe I had. Maybe I was going senile from too much water on the brain.

Whatever, I pushed the muddle of thoughts aside and paid some attention to our surroundings. It was hard to see much beyond dripping trees and a road of mud, but there did seem to be buildings in the near distance. Could this world be inhabited by real people, ones who might be willing to share the warmth of a fire?

Tiran d'Iste moved under some nearby trees, but not to get out of the rain. It wasn't possible to find a dry spot, but it *was* possible to shield what he was doing from casual observation. It seemed to be very close to sundown in this world, but there was no sense in taking chances. He started going through the cat-wolf cycle again, stopped to think about it, then Shifted to owl form. The big bird blinked and shook damp feathers, sidled out to look down the road, and then there was a man again in its place.

"The trail seems to lead to the other side of that bunch of buildings," he reported as he walked back to me. "It's not quite dark enough for the best vision from owl eyes, but at least I was able to see a suggestive smudge. The cat and wolf saw nothing."

"So we're back to a visual trail," I said with a nod. "It was either that or one of the remaining unused senses. A visual trail that needs special vision to see it. If a pattern is being developed, the same will hold true for the next world with smell."

"We still have this world to cross," he pointed out. "And the trap here may be pneumonia. I don't know about you, but I started out soaked to the bone and now I'm going downhill."

"Ditto," I agreed, trying not to shiver. The world and the rain weren't precisely cold, but sometimes cool can be enough to reach you. "Do you think we can get going now?"

"Excellent idea," he said, starting to put an arm around me. "Let's see if we can find some body heat to share."

"Sorry, but I'm too selfish to share," I said at once, moving quickly away from his arm. "Whatever I have left I intend to keep for myself."

"Baby," he taunted softly as he followed me. "What are you afraid of, baby? The big, bad man just wanted to put an arm around you. What's so terrible about one small arm?"

"You're the sort to have all kinds of communicable diseases," I said without turning, giving most of my attention to slogging through the mud of the road. "Do me a favor and communicate them to someone else."

"Poor little baby," he said in a soft singsong. "She's afraid of the man who's going to be her husband. Don't be afraid, baby. I won't hurt you."

"Damned straight you won't," I muttered, ignoring the flush in my cheeks. He was *trying* to make me feel small and helpless, and somehow was almost managing it. But I refused to buy into the belief that he would win. As long as I was still up and moving, it continued to be anybody's game.

"All right, slow down," he said with an amused laugh. "I'm not really chasing you yet. When I do start, I won't keep it a secret."

"I've already told you I don't want to be chased," I said, fighting to hide how appalled I felt. "Are you having trouble with the language, or is the idea too complex for you to grasp?"

"What I'm having trouble understanding is *why*," he said, now walking beside me to my right. "You're not an innocent who's desperate to stay pure, so I don't understand why you won't even give me a chance. And don't try claiming again that you don't like me. Your mind was made up even before you met me."

"It's my right to make up my mind about things like that," I said, wiping at the rain in my eyes. "You decided you wanted me, I decided I didn't want *you*. You're going with your wants, so I'm entitled to go with mine."

"You're still avoiding the question," he insisted. "All rights and wants aside, you're fighting this competition thing with everything you have. I think I've gotten to know your father well enough to doubt that he put you up as the prize on a whim. Did you do something to earn having it done to you?"

I couldn't see that the question was relevant. My father might have had reason to be angry with me, but not to ruin my life. I examined the buildings we were approaching, a poor collection making up a tiny town huddling in the rain, and didn't say a word.

"I'll take your silence to mean you did do something," he continued after a moment. "It couldn't have been a small something or a first something, or your father wouldn't have reacted so strongly. You finally did a big, serious something that you now have to pay for, but you've been refusing to cooperate in any way at all. Considering the fact that you have a fairly strong sense of honor, that doesn't make any sense."

"Having a sense of honor doesn't mean you also have to let your life be ruined," I couldn't help pointing out. "My father would have been within his rights to have me hanged, but not to have me married."

"Nonsense," he answered with a snort. "Any man who would let his daughter be hanged is no man at all. If she did something so terrible that she needed to be put down like an animal, it would be his job to do it. If the offense just brought him to the end of his patience, he's more than wise to look for a man who can handle her."

"And you think *you* can handle me?" I asked with a snort of my own. "Talk about living in a dream world."

"I think we both know it's no dream," he returned quietly. "And I refuse to let myself be diverted into an argument. *Why* are you fighting so hard to keep from being married? Honor should have made you go along with it even if you hated the idea. What's so important to you that you're fighting rather than paying your due?"

"My freedom is that important," I replied, still keeping my attention on our surroundings. "And I *am* paying my due, by going along with this ridiculous competition. When I win it, all debts will be square."

"*If* you win it," he corrected. "If you don't, marrying the winner will be the only honorable option left to you. And what makes you think marriage will end your freedom? If it's done right, you just find yourself exercising that freedom next to someone else."

"Right," I said with a ridiculing laugh. "I'll still be able to go where I please, do what I please—sleep with any man who interests me. No really dedicated husband would let any of *that* bother him."

"You'd sleep with other men without giving your husband a chance to hold your interest?" he asked, and I could *hear* that one eyebrow going up. "That doesn't sound like someone who believes in fair play, so I have to say I doubt that you would."

"Then you'd be wrong," I assured him. "There's nothing fair about marrying a woman against her will, so I don't have to play fair either. If I ever do end up married, my husband will spend a long time regretting the bargain."

"And if he doesn't regret it?" he pursued. "What if he takes everything you throw at him, and handles it with ease? What if he handles *you* with ease? You'd be feeling totally defeated, and there's no need for that. Why court defeat when you can share in a victory?"

"Who gets to define the concept of victory?" I countered, hating the way he was making me feel. "If it isn't me, then the concept isn't valid—or acceptable. And I'd rather not continue with this conversation. Arguing in circles tends to make me dizzy."

"Skirting all around an issue does that to most people," he pressed, refusing to drop the bone. "You asked for a definition of victory, but I want one of freedom. What exactly is involved with your concept of freedom?"

"Freedom means not talking about anything I don't want to," I replied. "And since you're leader in this world, how about letting me know if we're going straight through that collection of shacks or if we're stopping."

"We're stopping," he said, swallowed annoyance in his tone. "We need to dry off and get something to eat. If we don't fuel that stubbornness of yours, it might start to fade."

"Fat chance," I muttered, then let it drop. Despite the fish snack I'd had in the last world, I was beginning to feel hollow. Shifting takes a toll on the body's reserves, and the more you do, the more you need to replace what was used. So far my companion had done most of the Shifting, but I didn't intend to let that continue.

The little houses weren't really shacks, just small and wooden and belonging to people who didn't have much. Pouring rain and approaching darkness made the place look worse than it probably was; all towns look raw and uninviting when they're new. The road we'd followed to get there had widened some to become the town's main street, and the buildings we came to first were houses rather than stores.

My companion marched up to the first house on the right and knocked, but nothing came in the way of an answer. A second knock brought the same, so he moved on to the next house and tried. Despite the fact that we could see a light through the cracks in the shutters, no one seemed to be home there either.

"Maybe they believe in working in the rain," I suggested. "Since it isn't quite dark yet, they could still be out in the fields. Assuming they have fields to be out in."

"Leaving a lamp or candle burning, and the doors barred from the inside?" he countered as he came back to where I stood. "And why are the shutters also closed? I'm sure I saw glass through one of the cracks."

"Okay, maybe they melt in the rain," I offered. "As a matter of fact, I'm not far from that myself. Can we investigate a mystery some other time?"

"I don't like unanswered questions," he muttered, but still headed for the houses on the left. The first one he tried turned out to be the same as the previous two, but at the second he got an unexpected response.

"Whoever you are, go away!" a male voice rasped through the tightly closed door. "Nobody in this town's goin' t' be crazy enough t' open up, so go away!"

"We're a couple of travelers who need a corner near a fire and something to eat," d'Iste called back. "We're also able to pay. Are you saying there's no one in this town who needs silver?"

"Silver's just what we do need, but even gold don't help if you're dead," the voice retorted. "Take my advice and don't stop nowhere around here."

"I have a woman with me," d'Iste protested, all but pounding on the door. "If you won't let *me* in, at least—"

"Go *away*!" the voice said again, for what proved to be the last time. My companion kept trying for another moment or two, but there was no further response.

"Looks like we just get to keep going," I said when he finally stomped back to me. "I wonder what they're so afraid of? No, strike that. It doesn't matter what they're afraid of. Even if it's nothing more than a serious case of warts, it's still enough to keep us away from a fire and food."

"I refuse to accept that," d'Iste said, his light eyes hard. "There's got to be *someone* in this town more greedy than afraid, and I'm going to find him. Let's go."

After giving me my orders he moved on ahead, knocking on every door and offering gold for shelter. It so happened I had also brought a few coins, but I didn't offer to sweeten the pot. If we had simply kept going, we might have been almost to the next entry. I often admire men who won't give up on an idea, but not usually when that dedication brings me closer and closer to drowning.

"All right, that place up ahead looks like a store," he said when he'd just about run out of houses. "I'm going to try these last people here, and if no one volunteers, the store becomes *it*. Either they'll sell me food, or I'll break in and take it."

"Look, d'Iste, we're just wasting time," I began. "If we simply keep going—"

"No," he stated, giving me no time to say that the forest beyond would have animals to hunt. A quick change to cat form . . . "It's unreasonable of them to refuse to sell me food, and I'm long out of patience with the unreasonable. We'll do this my way."

With that he went back to knocking on doors, not even noticing when I shrugged and continued along the street alone. I didn't know what his problem was, nor did I care. If he wanted to play stubborn, he could do it by himself; I had better things to do with my time.

After the last building the street narrowed down to a road again, and a short distance along the forest resumed. The mud wasn't letting me move too fast, but that didn't really matter. I was more interested in finding a sheltered place to Shift to owl form, and after that I could worry about hurrying. First you want to know which direction to hurry *in*.

I spotted a place to the right under some trees, went to it and Shifted, then studied the—smear—visible to my owl eyes. It was a streak of light not painful to my vision, and it continued along the road deeper into the forest. Just for the hell of it I also tried one of the big cats that preferred hunting at night, and got only the hint of a smudge. Owl eyes were the best for this world, and that was that.

Shifting back to natural wasn't as pleasant as it usually is, not with how wet I was. It was a toss-up as to whether I needed food more than someplace dry, and the balance was beginning to tilt toward dry. Whatever, it had now become time to hurry a little.

But the mud of the road continued to force me to watch where I was putting my feet. If I'd fallen I couldn't have gotten wetter, but it's always possible to sprain something—or simply get covered with mud. Wet was bad enough, especially since I was already somewhat muddy from falling into that world . . .

It was about then that I noticed the fire off to my left, a small, polite cooking fire that seemed to be sheltered from the rain by something over it. As I got closer I saw that a canvas had been rigged in the trees, and there was also a dark form near the fire. The form noticed me at the same time, and stepped out of the tiny shelter to move closer to the road.

"Well, hello there," a cheerful voice called, and then the man had stopped about five feet away. "Another face at last. I was beginning to think I'd have to leave this area entirely before having any company but my own."

"The people around here do seem to be less than welcoming," I agreed, trying to make him out in the gloom. "Happily, I'm only passing through."

"I also consider it a happy chance," he returned with a chuckle. "Especially since you're a woman. Can I lure you into sharing my fire? You won't find anyone else around here willing to make that offer."

"So I noticed," I said, considering his suggestion. The idea of being near even a small fire was really tempting . . . "Do you happen to know *why* those people are sitting behind locked doors? What are they afraid of?"

"Something they call a loup-garou," he answered with the hint of a smile. "I don't usually scoff at people's superstitions, but this one has made life very uncomfortable for me. And for you as well, obviously. Will you join me?"

"You have no idea how much I'd like that," I told him honestly and a bit wistfully. "The only trouble is, I do need to continue on. Into what will hopefully be friendlier climes."

"You're breaking my heart," he said mournfully, putting one hand on his chest. "I can't leave here yet, otherwise I'd offer to go with you. How about staying for just a *little* while? A cup of chai will at least warm the cold out of your bones."

The temptation was getting stronger, and if I'd been alone I'd probably have done it. But the idea of getting comfortably ahead of Tiran d'Iste was stronger yet, and even more pleasant than the thought of being near a *large* fire. If I just kept moving he might never catch up, and I'd be able to complete the course without distraction.

"I thank you for the offer of bone-warming, but I'm afraid I have to pass," I told him with regret. "Time presses, and this rain has already made me waste too much of it. I hope you finish your business around here quickly so you can move on, too. It was nice meeting you."

"So I can't talk you out of leaving," he said without any amusement as I began to move on. "That's a pity, since I often hunger for companionship as much as I do for other things. I regret the need and apologize in advance, but I really have no choice. It's forced on me, you know, and holding it off becomes impossible."

"What's forced on you?" I asked, stopping to face him directly. The first thing his tone had made me think of was that my sword hilt was wet and therefore slippery. If I had to draw on him, I'd better do it carefully.

"Why, the change," he answered, the words easy and reasonable, his dark form also facing me. "If I could control it I would, but since I can't, why fight it? That's what those people refuse to understand. It's one of life's inevitabilities, so what's the good of fighting? I'll get them all eventually; with the moon full every night, they don't stand a chance."

"So you're the one they're afraid of, and it's because you change," I said, fighting off stronger chills than even a freezing rain could produce. There was a child's horror story I was beginning to remember, one I would have been happier *not* remembering . . . "They find the idea of someone changing frightening, or is there something else bothering them?"

"Oh, it's definitely the something else, pretty girl," he said, and as he grinned his eyes began to glow red. " 'When the change is complete, the newborn must eat.' That's a little rhyme I made up myself. Loup-garou, they call me. Almost everyone else says werewolf."

And then, with a slowness that was absolutely horrible, he began to change form. It took me a moment to be sure, but it was definitely a wolf that he was becoming . . . a werewolf . . . creature of the darkness . . .

Tiran forced himself to knock on every single door of the houses, and only then did he head for the store. He was hungrier than he'd been in a very long time, and being wet on top of it just made things worse. There was no way he'd be taking "no" as a final answer, not that time.

"You'd better open up," he shouted after pounding on the store's door. "I prefer buying food, but if I have to, I'll come in and take some. Don't think I'm bluffing, because I'm not."

"What—what d'you want?" a frightened voice asked from inside, this time a female voice. "I'm just a poor woman alone. If there's any decency in you—"

"None of you cared about the woman *I* have with me," he interrupted angrily. "What makes it so terrible for *me* not to care? Are you going to open up, or do I break this door down?"

"Why d'you hafta come in if all you wanna do is buy?" the woman demanded, no longer sounding quite so helpless. "You have silver t' pay, I'll sell what you want."

"Through a locked door?" Tiran asked with a snort. "A coin can fit underneath, but bread and cheese and meat can't. You—"

"I can put it out a window," the woman cut in. "I won't say which window, but one of 'em. That all you want?"

"And a jug of wine, if you have it," Tiran said, trying to be reasonable. "Any chance you have it?"

"Yeah, I got wine," the woman allowed. "Bread, cheese, meat and wine. Two pieces of silver. In advance."

Tiran was about to point out that he could probably buy her whole store for that, but it suddenly became not worth arguing over. He had gold with him as well as silver, and it would be a while before he was down to coppers.

"All right, I'll pay in advance," he said as he dug into his swordbelt. "Just make sure everything is wrapped against the rain and all of it is fit to eat. If it isn't I'll be back, and next time I won't stop to knock."

The woman didn't say anything, but the coins he slipped under the door disappeared immediately. Tiran straightened again and prepared himself to wait, but not too long. He'd already wasted enough time . . .

Wasting time. That was what Alex had called it, but he hadn't agreed. Actually, he hadn't been able to agree, not with the mood he'd been in. She'd stubbornly refused to tell him what he desperately needed to know, and then those people had refused to let them in. They hadn't cared that he was responsible for Alex's well-being, and they were making him fail miserably . . .

And there it was, the reason for his lack of reason. He'd discovered he needed to be responsible for Alex's safety, but she herself wasn't letting him do it. She didn't seem to care that he'd rather be hurt himself than see her even slightly harmed. He'd failed trying to be the guard for her back underwater, and now he couldn't even provide her with shelter and food. How could she possibly learn to care about someone who was proving to be a total incompetent?

All right, stop the breast-beating, he told himself sternly. You're just reacting to the way she keeps slipping out of your reach. And to what she'll say when you tell her the deal's off. If you continue to take turns as leader, she'll push the point by doing things like she did underwater. You can't live with that, but you don't know how to explain that it has nothing to do with her competence.

And has everything to do with the way you feel about her, he thought wryly. When a man discovers he's crazy about a woman, "crazy" becomes a very appropriate word. Every emotion he has turns fierce, especially the protective ones. If danger threatens he'll stand in front of her, even if she can handle four times the threat without batting an eye. *He* has to do it, or consider himself less than a man.

But Tiran might have been able to control the reflex if only Alex hadn't rejected him so thoroughly. He wanted to help, she didn't *want* any help—Damn it all, was he supposed to just walk away without knowing *why* she was refusing him? If she'd had a good reason she would have mentioned it, so it stood to reason it wasn't him she was rejecting. He knew that well enough, but it was so difficult to keep in mind . . .

Well, he'd have to do it, or the game would be lost even before they got back to the others. It wasn't him she was rejecting, so he had to get closer to her, let her know what she was trying to throw away. He'd never intentionally seduced a woman before, mostly because he'd never had to. To his way of thinking it wasn't quite fair, but what other option had she left him?

Left him . . . speaking of that, where the hell had she disappeared to? He was supposed to be the one in charge in this world, but he wouldn't put it past her to take off alone. And the worst was still ahead of them, he knew that with every trained sense that he had. If she went through the next entry by herself—

"I put the sack through the window around to the other side," the woman's voice came suddenly from behind the door. "If you really don't mean us no harm, you better stay outta them woods. *It's* out there, an' if you meet it the blood'll flow like the rain pourin' down . . ."

It, Tiran thought as he took off running. The sack lay on the ground beneath a reshuttered window just around the corner, so he grabbed it up as he went past. Alex *must* have gone ahead, and like the biggest fool alive, he hadn't even noticed. She could take care of herself, he knew she could—but what if *it* was too much for her? What if . . . what if . . .

"Your Majesty, Limis asked me to tell you what he's found so far," Merwin said, drawing Reynar's thoughts back to where he sat. "It seems that only one of the trails was tampered with, the one meant to be used by Tiran d'Iste. All the rest were left as they were supposed to be, and the entrants in them are carrying on in normal fashion."

"Normal fashion," Reynar echoed, finding that bizarrely amusing. As if anything about that situation could be considered normal. "Is that all he's found so far?"

"No, Sire," Merwin said. "It's also been clearly established that Princess Alexia is *not* following the trail meant for her. Since she's not there and she's not here with us, Limis feels certain there's only one other possibility. She must have ended up going through Tiran d'Iste's entry with *him*."

"Limis feels certain," Reynar repeated, fury beginning to glow back to life. "Are you telling me he doesn't *know*?"

"Your Majesty, it isn't possible for him to know," Merwin answered, compassion clear in his eyes. "None of them can see through to d'Iste's trail, which means he and the princess also can't be removed. If they're going to get out, they'll have to do it themselves."

"How was the trail tampered with?" Reynar asked next, partially relieved by knowing Tiran d'Iste was with his daughter. If anyone could keep the two of them alive and get them out . . .

"Limis says it was very oddly done," Merwin replied. "All of the traps and dangers of the trail have been intensified and made more deadly, but in a way Limis doesn't quite understand. That's what he's looking into right now. If he can find a key to the changes, he might be able to change it all back."

"Let me know immediately if he finds that key," Reynar ordered. "And in the meantime, how is it going with Sisal?"

"Slowly, Your Majesty," Merwin answered with a sigh. "There are a lot of people here, and Sisal wants to be certain."

"So do I," the king said with a nod, then dismissed Merwin with a gesture. All Reynar had to do was be patient, and the miscreant would be delivered into his hands. Patience, only the hardest thing in the world to achieve . . . but he would do it . . . and once the waiting was over . . .

CHAPTER NINE

Remembering horror stories at the wrong time is definitely bad for your health. I stood gaping at the stranger's slow-motion Shift so long, when he was finally changed all the way and jumping at me, I almost didn't throw myself aside in time. I'd *never* seen anyone change that slowly, and couldn't help wondering if it was deliberate.

But that was a question for another time. Right then I Shifted with every ounce of speed I had, and turned to face him in wolf form myself. He was already launching himself at me again, which would have shocked the hell out of most people. Not only should my own Shift have made him pause, he was also attacking a female of his species. Only the human male finds that easy to do—unless there's something really wrong.

As there was here. The stranger's charge almost knocked me down, but I rolled with it as I tore at his shoulder. My fangs ripped fur and flesh and he howled, but with madness rather than with pain. I wasn't being a good little victim; I should have stood there screaming while he took me down, and instead had gotten a piece of *him*.

But he was so far gone into the feral that he barely noticed his wound. He came at me a third time, aiming for my throat as he used his greater body weight. If I weren't better than average at form fighting he would have had me, and even so he managed to score along my side. Madness provides a kind of ability of its own, and worse, incredible strength. His wound should have slowed him at least a little, but it hadn't.

And the mud wasn't helping. Being four-footed was an advantage, but it didn't eliminate slips. My opponent was briefly off-balance so I attacked, but couldn't do more than score along his back. My own balance went flying before I could reach his throat, and it became a matter of score and get out or stay and die.

There wasn't really a lull in the fight; I had backed off and he was gathering himself to attack again when suddenly everything changed. A big gray form came flying wildly through the rain out of the dark, and the stranger found himself in a different kind of fight. The newcomer was a male wolf even bigger than he, and the fury being projected was a damned good match to madness.

I backed off a little more, then stood watching Tiran d'Iste and the stranger go through the fiercest fight I'd ever seen. Neither one of them hesitated, or stopped to plan, or made fancy moves. They bit and clawed at each other, rolling madly through the mud, savage snarls an almost constant backdrop. Each one wanted the blood and heart of the other, and each was determined to get it.

There's an old saying in unarmed combat that a good big man will take a good small man every time. The word "good" presupposes equal ability on the part of the two, properly ignoring the fact that you sometimes get lucky. As I watched Tiran d'Iste fight the stranger, I knew that in his place I would *not* have gotten lucky. With both body weight and madness on the stranger's side, even my high level of skill would not have saved me.

As it was, high skill, size, and roaring rage were the only things that saved Tiran d'Iste. The stranger continued to ignore his growing number of wounds, and the ferocity of his attacks seemed to have doubled in intensity. My trail companion was bleeding heavily, fighting in spite of the wounds rather than being unaware of them. All he seemed to want was one good opening—and when it came he moved with incredible speed. Fangs flashed into a throat, a head pulled back savagely, and then blood was gushing rather than simply flowing.

For a horrible moment I thought the stranger would ignore that, too, and he certainly tried. His jaws opened in a soundless snarl as he gathered himself to attack again, but there's a point beyond which none of us can go. Rather than attack he coughed and stumbled, coughed again and choked, then collapsed in the mud. Death tremors shook him hard before he subsided into stillness, and then his body shape began to flow back to natural. It took a long, ghastly moment, and not until then was I certain that it was over.

"D'Iste, are you all right?" I called as soon as I'd Shifted back and had begun to move closer. "Why are you still in wolf form? Shift back and get that bleeding stopped."

He was just about lying down in the mud, and when the Shift came it left him on his hands and knees. I reached down fast to keep him from going face-first onto the road, then got his arm across my shoulders.

"I'll do most of the work, but you've got to give me *some* help," I said as I fought to get him to his feet. "Since you enjoy being as ridiculously overgrown as you are—and you *do*—you can now pay the price for it. If you were normal, I'd have no trouble carrying you."

"If I—were normal—there'd—be nothing—left—for you—to carry," he gasped, exhaustion turning the words to a whisper. "Give me—a minute—and I'll—try."

He leaned heavily on me as he fought to get some breath and strength back, and it took more than a minute. Finally his weight shifted a little, and he made an effort to stand.

"Stop trying to do it yourself!" I snapped, immediately giving him my support. "If you pass out, I'll have to leave you here in the rain."

"Won't pass out," he answered huskily, weaving on his feet. "Where else but the rain?"

He meant where else would I leave him, which meant he hadn't seen his erstwhile opponent's shelter. Rather than point it out, I began helping him toward it, and when we got there I let him stretch out in the relatively dry space.

"You can rest here while I go back to that town," I said after glancing around the shelter. "Our late friend obviously didn't believe in keeping emergency rations handy, not even the chai he offered me. I wonder what he would have done if I'd agreed to have some."

"You don't have to go all the way back," he said, actually sounding stronger. "There should be a sack on the road not far from here, right where I dropped it before Shifting. If I wasn't cheated, there's two silver pieces' worth of food inside."

"A feast like that I've got to see," I said. "You enjoy the fire and I'll be right back."

I added some wood so there would continue to be a fire to enjoy, then went back out in the rain. Finding the sack on the road wasn't hard even in the dark, but I didn't have much hope for the food inside. No feast in the universe will do well in a downpour, and especially not the sort that can be gotten from a small, unfinished town. But I retrieved the soggy, muddy sack and took it back with me. D'Iste was sitting cross-legged by the fire, leaving just enough room for me to do the same.

"Okay, now we get to look inside," I said when the sack was positioned between us. "Do you want to do the honors, or should I?"

"I don't have the nerve," he answered, his hunched-over body obviously trying to soak up the fire's warmth. "You do it, and if the food is ruined, lie to me. If I hear the truth, I'll probably cry."

"Well, I really do hate to see a grown man cry," I said, rooting around in the sack. "But it looks like you'll have to save the tears for some other time. Whoever wrapped this stuff did a damned good job."

I pulled out one of the packages, and let him see the oiled paper the contents were wrapped in. The thing would probably have floated on a river, which frankly surprised me no end.

"That probably means the contents are inedible," he said, showing he knew how the worlds usually wagged. "I'll open that one while you check the others."

I handed him the thing and went back to the sack, but moving a second package uncovered treasure. I grabbed the treasure and pulled it out, uncorked it, then took a swallow of one of the worst wines ever pressed. But it still spread down and out from my throat in a warming wave, doing a better job inside than the fire was doing outside. I gulped a quick second swallow and reluctantly held out the jug.

"Small-town firewater," I said by way of warning. "Drink it and reap."

"Not until I've got more of this in me," he replied around a mouthful, referring to the wedge of cheese he'd uncovered and started on. "If I drink anything before I fill the void, I'll end up finding the next entry only by staggering into it."

"To each his own," I answered with a shrug, and put the jug down closer to me. I'd really needed the warmth it had provided, and now was able to think about more solid nourishment.

The remaining packages held bread and two kinds of meat, all of it simple but surprisingly satisfying. Between d'Iste's efforts and my more modest ones, there was nothing but crumbs left by the time we leaned back. The feast really had been a feast, and my companion was looking a good deal stronger.

"How are your wounds doing?" I asked while he took a long pull from the jug. Shifting back to natural tends to heal most wounds, but the more serious ones will sometimes re-form. They say it's the memory of the trauma that does it, the subconscious memory of a hurt too deep to forget about quickly. Since our memory does have a lot to do with the forms we Shift to, I suppose it makes sense.

"I'll have some aches and twinges for a while, but beyond that I'm fine," he answered, putting the jug down to study me. "How about you? I know he hurt you, and I've been hoping it wasn't serious."

"Nothing like what it was about to be," I admitted, then decided to get all of it said. "Look, d'Iste . . . I haven't thanked you yet, but that doesn't mean I don't know you saved my life. I've never come up against anything like that—thing, and he would have had me if you hadn't stepped in. I definitely owe you."

"Well, if you think you owe me, stop calling me d'Iste," he said, those green eyes amused. "My name is Tiran, and I'd enjoy hearing you say it. Go ahead, try it."

"Tiran," I repeated after a pause I hoped he hadn't noticed, trying to make the name sound effortless. It wasn't, but I was trapped.

"See how easy that was?" he asked with a grin. "Pretty soon you won't even notice yourself doing it. But there's something I'm curious about. Did I hear you say he offered you chai? I'd been thinking he simply attacked."

"No, he seemed to want some conversation first," I said, reaching for the jug as the memory came back. "He tried to talk me into stopping for a while, and when I said I didn't have the time, he turned really strange. I felt as though I'd stepped into one of those horror stories small children are told to keep them in line."

The swallow of wine only just managed to stop the shudder, and I was surprised it did. Between the wet clothes I was sitting around in and discussing madness, shuddering was the least to be expected.

"I know the story you mean, but it's no fairy tale," he said, all amusement gone. "Every now and then one of us goes insane like that, and when it happens the results are horrible. The victim focuses on one single animal shape, and uses that to act out his madness. The last time I came across it the form was a bear, and it took half a dozen of us to finish it off."

"But how can something like that happen?" I demanded. "And *why* would it happen? He said something about its being a full moon here every night. Even if that's possible, what difference would it make? Why would moonlight be a factor?"

"Moonlight, full moonlight, is the triggering factor in these cases," he answered with a shake of his head. "Why it is, nobody seems to know, but it's the same in every instance. If a victim ends up in a world without a moon, he isn't triggered. If it's a place where the moon is full all the time—and there *are* such places—not only does he get triggered, but the illness intensifies. He knows the full moon is there even when he can't see it. It can get to the point where his manic strength makes him almost impossible to best, and the only thing that will finish him is silver."

"Which has to be one of the worst ways of going," I said with a shiver. Silver worn as a decoration can go through a Shift with you and nothing will happen, but if even a sliver of it is *inside* you—The Shift apparently turns it poisonous, and the poison spreads immediately through your bloodstream. Not even raw iron will do as much damage, although iron produces its own problems. Silver is the metal to be most careful of, and that in spite of its beauty.

"All sorts of legends tend to grow up around instances like these," my companion was saying. "Some believe the poor cripple can't be killed by ordinary means, and that isn't surprising. He may have gone completely feral in his chosen form, but there's still a man's mind directing the body. You may not be able to use a weapon on him, but that's because he avoids it rather than that it has no effect on him."

"And you have to be able to think of using the weapon in the first place," I said with a frown. "The change startled me so badly, I never even thought of my sword. I followed blind instinct, which was to defend myself with natural weapons."

"By matching the form *he'd* taken," he said, nodding. "It's a standard reaction, and stories have even grown up over that. The nontalented—or the uninvolved—see one of us react like that, and immediately assume something the sick one did—like biting us—caused the change. They think the sickness is passed on that way, but it isn't. It's a sickness of the mind, not of the body."

"If it weren't, we'd end up taking his place," I said, relief rather than scorn in the words. "He didn't get me as badly as he did you, but he still got a piece of me. I wonder if those people will get up the nerve to investigate and find out that he's dead."

"They should get a hint when they notice people have stopped being killed," he answered with a shrug, and then those eyes were on me again. "Right after the fight, when I started to get back to my feet, you were annoyed with me for trying to do it alone. As a matter of fact, you yelled at me. Do you remember that?"

"I remember being somewhat firm," I replied with my own shrug, for some reason abruptly uncomfortable. "I seriously doubt if I yelled, but if I had you would have deserved it. You were trying to ignore my help, and by doing that could have made things worse."

"So you're telling me you don't approve of someone ignoring available help in a bad situation and trying to go it alone," he summed up, his stare unmoving. "Is that a fair recap?" When I nodded cautiously, he nodded, too, but not in the same way. "Then would you like to tell me what in hell you thought you were doing when you took off all alone? If I hadn't found out there was something out here killing people, I might not have made it in time. You even said you refused a cup of chai because you didn't have the time to stop. Were you in that much of a hurry because you wanted to leave me *far* behind?"

"I—You were being unreasonable," I stumbled, suddenly remembering what I'd been in the middle of when all that insanity started. "It made more sense to get on to the next entry and out of the rain, but you felt the need to pound on doors that weren't going to be opening. We don't have all the time in the worlds to get to the end of the trail, so I decided not to wait for you to come out of it. If you've lost interest in winning, I haven't."

"So you were the voice of sanity in the face of my unreasoning stubbornness," he said, sounding not in the least like he agreed. "I suppose it never occurred to you that my lack of reason was your fault in the first place, but that's beside the point. What *is* the point is that taking off alone could have gotten you killed, and there won't be any more of it. If you try it again and happen to survive, you'll really wish you hadn't. Do you understand me?"

He wasn't shouting, but only because he wasn't letting himself shout. I felt like a five-year-old caught in a joke no one else had found funny, and it was all I could do not to squirm guiltily. Going off on my own *had* turned out to be a mistake, but still . . .

"I understand that you're upset, and with good reason," I allowed. "But one unfortunate incident doesn't make a general course of action wrong. I'll certainly be more careful from now on, especially when considering options—"

"I said, you will *not* be taking off alone again," he interrupted, a growl now accompanying the green stare. "As an option for you to consider, that one is out. Have I made myself clear?"

"Very," I muttered, needing to look away from those green pools of anger. He hadn't pointed out that if we'd been together, he might not have had to fight so hard. If we'd stayed natural and had used our swords, the stranger wouldn't have had much of a chance to do us harm. Do him harm. It was my fault he'd been hurt so badly, and the guilt wasn't letting me argue the way I normally would have.

"Then I think it's time we got moving again," he said, taking a last swallow of wine and passing the rest to me. "We still have the end of a trail to find, and if you've lost interest in winning, I haven't."

I really wanted to say something to him about stealing my lines, but instead paid attention to getting a final swallow of wine without the dregs. I'd have to find some way to make up to him for what I'd done, and then things would be back to normal. Of course, I'd still owe him my life, but that was a problem I'd have to work around. Somehow. And honorably. It had to be possible . . . it just had to be . . .

Tiran let Alex leave the shelter first, but once they were back out in the rain he took over the lead. They passed the corpse of the poor creature he'd killed without comment, everything having already been said. Once they were gone the forest dwellers would see to the remains, the spirit inside having gone on its way. Adding his body to the biosphere would hardly make up for all the destruction the man had caused, but it was still proper.

And thinking about the proper, Tiran gave silent thanks to his former opponent's spirit. He'd gotten Tiran so furious by attacking Alex that Tiran had been able to hold out long enough to win the fight. Too often madness was able to best skill, but not that time. Tiran had known that if he went down Alex would be next, so he hadn't allowed himself to be beaten. *Had* come awfully damned close, though . . .

Being back out in the rain made his body throb harder, but Tiran was too pleased to mind. He'd been too angry to notice at first, but when he'd read Alex the riot act, she hadn't tried to jump down his throat in retaliation. That had to mean she was bothered by what had happened, and might even be worried about him. After all, those wounds had hardly been scratches . . .

And if she's too worried about my health to argue with me, I'll be able to use the reprieve to my own advantage, he thought. It's not likely to last long, so I'll have to move fast. Get her hooked on the line before she remembers about keeping her distance . . .

Tiran felt a twinge of conscience over the way he planned to exploit Alex's vulnerability, but logic promptly pointed out his lack of choice. If he played fair he would lose her, and how fair would *that* be? He had to try his best to give them a chance to be happy together, which he was sure they *would* be. If it turned out he was wrong they would both find it out, but first they had to try.

And that would start as soon as they were out of the damned rain. When you were cold and soggy to the skin, it wasn't possible to be interested in anything but getting dry. If the next world wasn't better than this one, he would probably commit murder once they got back.

"Am I indulging in wishful thinking, or does that look like an entry?" Alex asked abruptly, pulling him out of his thoughts. "Hold on a second, and I'll check."

She Shifted into owl form and looked around, then Shifted back. He did his own looking around while that was happening, but they were still alone. On a wet, miserable night like this, he would have been surprised if they weren't.

"That's it, all right," she reported. "Under normal circumstances no more than a ten-minute walk beyond that town."

"You're not entitled to say, 'I told you so,' " he commented without expression. "The phrase 'under normal circumstances' cancels out everything else. If the next world tries to drown us, too, I'll probably lose my temper."

"Thanks for the warning, but it's unnecessary," she commented back. "If the next world turns out to be wet, I'll be too busy losing my own temper to notice yours."

With that she headed directly for the entry, and Tiran lost no time in following. Whatever the next world held, they would go through it together—but dry would be so much easier to take . . .

Or so he thought until they'd both stepped through. Alex gasped at the incredible difference, and Tiran just managed not to. It was somewhere around noon in this world, and so hot it felt as if there were no air to breathe. A blue-white sun raged in the faded sky, trying hard to set fire to the sand and rock beneath it. The white sand threw back a glare that was almost blinding, making the newcomers squint as their eyes teared.

"Got to Shift," Alex gasped out. "Follow me."

Tiran realized she thought it was her turn to lead, that he'd forgotten to tell her he'd decided differently. By rights he should have said something then, but that sun was just too strong. Once they found forms capable of surviving here, they would have a "later" for any discussions they liked.

Alex Shifted into snake form, a beautiful cobra Tiran had no trouble matching. That made the heat lovely and lazy, but apparently it didn't suit Alex. She tasted the air with her tongue, looked at him with glittering eyes, then Shifted to lizard form. Once again he matched her choice, and that *was* better. Not only was he faintly less lethargic, but when he tasted the air with his own tongue, he found a very compelling odor. It had to be the trail, and the direction it went in was unmistakable.

He Shifted back to natural just long enough to say, "You lead off and I'll follow," then returned to the much more suitable shape of a lizard. Alex didn't bother Shifting back to answer; she simply turned and scuttled off in the proper direction.

Lizards are able to move fast when they have to, but not for long periods of time. Tiran could feel the heat trying to talk him into napping, and the way Alex kept slowing down said she was feeling the same. Continuing on became a battle of wills, but not against each other. It was the heat and a need to sleep they fought, enemies who grew stronger the farther they went. When Tiran's tail got too heavy for him to keep it out of the sand, he deliberately unlidded his eyes and looked around.

And was startled by what he saw. Ahead to their left seemed to be an oasis, but nothing in the way of water-scent came to him. Was it a mirage? Did lizards see mirages the way humans did? There was only one way to find out, so he moved up close to Alex and bumped her with his snout to get her attention. When she unlidded her eyes and looked at him, he nodded in the direction of the oasis. If it was a mirage, she shared the illusion; as soon as she saw what he meant, she began heading for it.

The smell of water finally came to them when they were about thirty yards away. It was a tantalizing tickle of wet and cool combined, enervating them and giving them the strength to continue. Shortly after that, it was as if they'd crossed an invisible line; the farther they went, the more moisture there was to fill the air. Then they reached the first line of shade trees, and it felt as though someone had turned off the sun. Tiran immediately Shifted back to natural, and after a brief hesitation Alex did the same.

"Ugh," she said at once, looking down at herself. "I knew this would happen. Our clothes have been perfectly preserved inter-transition—right along with the wet and the mud. I'd rather be wearing lizard skin."

"Then let's get the clothes washed before we do the same for ourselves," Tiran said, already looking around. "I can see three separate pools over there, which means one's for drinking from, one's for washing clothes in, and one's for bodies. There are also spots where the direct sunlight comes through unfiltered. Ten minutes in one of those spots, and the clothes will also be dry as sand."

"Don't use the word 'sand' to me," she muttered, starting for the pools of water. "If I never see another grain of the stuff, I'll live a long and happy life. I never knew anything could taste worse than dirt."

Tiran wondered how she had managed to taste the sand, then decided not to ask. If she told him and he laughed in the wrong place . . . And besides, he really needed to get out of his own clothes. The heavy damp was making his body ache, a reminder of the fight so recently past. If he didn't want the reminder made permanent, he needed to be out of the clothes fast.

A quick inspection of the three pools showed one to be relatively narrow but very deep, one reasonably shallow where the water ran like a busy stream, and the last to be wide, about four feet deep, and only moderately swift-moving. Even as Tiran began to take his clothes off in front of the second pool, a faint frown touched his thoughts. He'd been joking about the three pools and the use for each, but he'd turned out to be right. Wasn't that strange . . .

"We'll be best off not taking any chances," he heard from behind and to his right. "You go ahead and do your washing while I stand guard, and then I'll do mine while you watch. I mean guard. I don't mind waiting, so—"

"No," Tiran pronounced, turning to look at a fully clothed Alex. "Wet clothes can give you arthritis, and I think you know it. You should also know that with the flattened dunes around here, we'll have plenty of warning if someone shows up. Taking turns standing guard is ridiculous, but that's not what you really want. Would it help if I promised not to look at you, baby?"

"It would help even more if you dried up and blew away," she returned, her face flushing from something other than the sun. "I've been looked at by enough men to know it's nothing special, and neither are you. It just so happens I—"

"No," Tiran said again, unconsciously using the tone he did when commanding armies. "We both need to be out of these clothes, so that's what we're going to do. Together. If you're afraid you can't trust yourself not to attack me, don't worry about it. I'm pretty good at protecting my virtue."

Those silver eyes burned him down where he stood and a growl came from her throat, but she still turned her back and began to take off her swordbelt. It helped quite a lot that she *wanted* to be out of the clothes, so she'd accepted his challenge. If he'd had to forcibly strip her, he would have; wet clothes were nothing to play games with, but he was glad the need wouldn't arise. Wrestling matches too often turned into something else, and his newly formed plans didn't allow for that yet.

Boots, belts, and weapons went directly into the sunlight, and then they washed the muddy messes they had stripped off. Tiran noticed out of the corner of his eye that

Alex was giving full attention to her chore, not once even glancing in his direction. He'd done more than glance, and because of that had to keep very tight control of himself. It helped that he had something to occupy his hands; otherwise he might have found them caressing skin he didn't yet mean to touch.

Once the wash was wrung out and hung from branches in the sunlight, they went to the bathing pool. Alex had been looking more thoughtful than distant, and Tiran was almost afraid to wonder why. The woman's habit of picking up on his plans as soon as he made them haunted his expectations, especially since this was one plan he refused to abandon. He wanted Alex to *want* him, and if seducing her was the only way to accomplish that . . .

"Hey, you *are* still raw in a couple of places," she said suddenly, upset in her voice. "And look at those bruises. For a minute I'd forgotten."

He looked up to see her eyes directly on him, at least from the waist up. All traces of embarrassment were gone, and she made no effort to hide herself. Her large, beautifully formed breasts led the eye down to the curves of waist and hips, but that was as far as Tiran let his eyes go. Playing his new game right was essential, and there was no use in torturing himself.

"For a minute you'd forgotten what?" he asked, honestly curious. "And don't worry about these decorations. They'll be gone before you know it."

"I'd forgotten you got those—decorations—saving my life," she answered, letting her gaze meet his. "You were right about my acting like a baby, but that's all over with. It won't kill me to be looked at, so if you feel the urge, go right ahead."

"Because I saved your life," Tiran said, stiffening. "Not because you'll enjoy being looked at by me, but because you think you owe me something."

"There's no 'think' about it," she replied with a shrug he couldn't help but notice fully. "I do owe you, and there's nothing either of us can do to change that. Are you trying to say you don't *want* to look at me?"

She moved closer to him with the question, gliding through the cool blue water in a way that turned his mouth dry. Tiran didn't often consider himself slow, but it took him until then to understand what she was doing. By the endless glitter of the Diamond Realm, *she* was trying to seduce *him*!

"Your chest is so thickly covered with hair," she said, adding a toying finger to the observation as she looked up at him. "Men are always so proud of chest hair that they show it off at every opportunity. I've always wondered why that was."

"There's a law," Tiran answered, fighting too hard for control to pay attention to what he was saying. "The law demands that those with chest hair flaunt it, so we do. It's illegal to disobey the law."

"I like that explanation," she said with a delighted laugh, moving even closer. "And I *do* like the way you look at me, not in the least self-consciously or furtively. You look the way a man *should* look at a woman, encouraging her to do the same. And giving her ideas about what to do next. Doesn't looking give *you* any ideas?"

If Tiran hadn't been stronger than average, he would have groaned out loud. Alex wasn't trying to seduce him, she was blatantly offering herself; as much as he wanted or as little, the choice was entirely his. That showed how well she knew men, leaving it to him to make the first direct move. That soft and beautifully toned female body was his for the taking, a taking every nerve in his own body ached for.

But that was the one thing he couldn't do. She was offering her body in payment for the debt she saw standing between them, but he didn't want her that way. There was no debt between them, but if he got *his* way there would be something considerably better.

"Looking *does* give me an idea," he agreed almost immediately, putting his arms around her. "Let's see how it works."

If Tiran hadn't been watching for it, he would have missed the way Alex hesitated before letting their bodies touch. Her face was turned up for the kiss he started, her lips accepting his and quickly responding, but her body wasn't as eager. She *was* afraid of something, and that fact hardened his decision. When he did finally make love to her, there would be nothing of fear present.

The kiss progressed wonderfully well, and Tiran enjoyed every minute of it. Alex had relaxed against him, her hands on his arms, her breasts deliberately poking into his chest. His own hands were enjoying the smooth, strong feel of her—but there's a point where enjoyment stops and masochism begins. When Tiran reached that point, he let the kiss end.

"I'd say that worked rather well," he observed, smiling to himself when he noticed that Alex's eyes were closed. "Now we'd better get to the baths we're supposed to be taking. By the time we get out of here, our clothes should be dry."

"You want to—bathe first," Alex got out, then her eyes fluttered open. "Are you sure? I mean, we'll only have to bathe again afterward, and since we've already rinsed off . . ."

"Alex, bathing is *all* we'll be doing," Tiran said, firmly ignoring the arousal in her beautiful silver eyes. That wasn't the only place it showed, and his own body hadn't been left unmoved.

"How can you say that?" she demanded. "I know you're not uninterested, so why are you stopping us? You can't believe that *I'm* uninterested?"

"Has it ever occurred to you that 'interested' is *not* the same as 'willing'?" he asked, letting her go and moving past her into deeper water. "You said you owed me something, so I took a kiss. Now that we're even, I'm not willing to go on."

"You think one kiss makes us even?" she countered scornfully. "That's not only ridiculous, it's positively juvenile. Who's being the baby now?"

"Babyish or not, it's the way I feel," he answered with a shrug, then got down on his knees to be deeper under the water. "A kiss was what I wanted, and now that I have it I'm satisfied."

"Satisfied," she echoed disgustedly, and then she was around in front of him again and also going to her knees. That put her neck-deep until her arms circled *his* neck. "Your mind may be satisfied, but your body isn't and neither is mine," she told him bluntly. "You've been trying for this practically since the moment we met, and now I'm giving you the chance. Why aren't you doing anything about it?"

"I'm not so desperate that I need to be done favors," he said, trying to sound equally blunt. "Before I saved your life, I was barely good enough to breathe the same air; now I've become so acceptable you're offering me your body? Sorry, little girl, but things don't work that way in the real world. If I wasn't good enough before, I'm sure as hell not good enough now."

"But—I never said you weren't good enough," she protested, her arms slipping away as hurt confusion filled her eyes. "All I said was that I didn't want *any* man, you included but not in particular. What has that got to do with not being good enough?"

"It has to do with the fact that your mind wasn't magically changed until your life was saved," he countered. "And maybe not even then. Are you now willing to marry me—or simply willing to let me into your bed?"

The flash of guilt in her eyes answered his question without words, and Tiran would have felt depressed if he hadn't been expecting it. It was too soon for her to be seriously attracted, but how he wished it weren't.

"Why are you men so—so—*ridiculous*?" she suddenly demanded, close to exasperation. "You spend most of your lives going from one woman's bed to the next, and you're perfectly happy. Then one day you get the idea of marriage into your head, and from then on nothing else will suit you. What's *wrong* with my now being willing to let you into my bed? Why do I also have to promise to marry you?"

"You don't," Tiran told her with another shrug. "I'm not looking for promises—or anything else. If you like you can owe me another kiss, but that's as far as I'm willing to go. I don't enjoy feeling as if I'm being bought off."

"I *wasn't* trying to buy you off," she insisted, but a faint flush in her cheeks contradicted that. Rather than wait for more or give an answer, Tiran turned and dived under the water. His hair needed washing, it was true, but even more that conversation needed ending. Alex was feeling guilty, and right then that was the way he wanted her.

They spent only a little while longer washing, and then they crossed the grass to the patch of sunlight where they'd left their clothes. Even in that small amount of time their bodies were dry, so after Tiran took a quick field shave they began to dress in clothes that were also dry. Alex paid no attention to Tiran, but he realized that was because she was wrestling with her thoughts. He left her to it without comment, but mentally had his fingers crossed. If she would only give him a chance to prove how good they could be together . . .

By the time they'd replaced their weapons, Alex's expression had undergone a change. She now looked determined about something, and it wasn't long before Tiran heard about it.

"This is ridiculous, and I refuse to accept it," she stated, looking straight at him as she used her favorite word in challenge. "You're entitled to warning, and this is it. I flatly refuse to accept it."

"What is it you're refusing to accept?" he asked, wondering if he should pretend to be nervous. Her fierce expression was enough to cause most men to back cautiously away, but he found it delightful.

"I won't accept being turned down," she said, folding her arms as she examined him from head to foot. "I know most women find a man like you totally without interest, but I'm more broad-minded than that. I want you, dolly, and what I want I get."

"Am I supposed to be impressed by a spoiled brat?" he asked her grin, folding his own arms in annoyance. "If I say no it stays no, and you can warn me till you're blue in the face. I told you how I feel, and I expect you to accept it."

"But I've already said I won't," she answered lightly, strolling closer to him. "And how you feel is wrong, because I never said you weren't good enough. I tried telling you that in words, but you refused to believe them. Now I'm through with words."

"Stop that!" he snapped, smacking at her hand. She'd walked her fingers up his arm to tickle his neck, and it was all he could do not to grab her. "If you don't behave yourself, I'll—"

"What?" she asked, not in the least worried. "Something interesting, I hope. And I don't know what you're making such a fuss about. If my luck turns sour and I don't win the competition, you certainly will. After that we'll be married, and then you won't be allowed to refuse me."

"If that happens, I won't have to," he returned dryly, really disliking the way she was trying to coerce him. "If— when I win the competition you'll belong to me, and I can do anything I like with what belongs to me. Until then, my decision stands."

"Has anyone ever told you you're as stuffy as you are big?" she asked, clearly refusing to let herself get annoyed. "Take my word for it, sweetie, you'll enjoy what I do to you. And didn't you say we needed to get to know each other better? That's still the best way of doing it."

And that was when Tiran knew, beyond all doubt and argument. Alex wasn't accidentally turning him off, she was doing it on purpose! She'd been sincerely willing to give him her body in payment for an imagined debt, but when he'd refused her it had given her an idea. If he was too fastidious to accept charity, he'd certainly hate having it forced on him. And she was showing him a side of her no full man would find attractive.

But rather than get angry, Tiran grew thoughtful. Another woman would be doing nothing more than taking advantage of the situation. Alex, though, probably believed she was doing it for his own good, freeing him from desire for a woman who would not add joy to his life. He still didn't know why she thought that, but he was sure it was the reason behind her act. An act she was playing too damned well. He had to stop it, or his own plans would go right down the nearest bottomless pit . . .

"I wonder what that is," he heard her say, and looked up to see her staring at the distant sky. "It wasn't there five minutes ago, and now it's big enough to see."

He sent his own gaze to search the sky, and spotted a small blackness against the faded blue. It was still too far away to see clearly, but it did remind him of something. Years ago now, and it had only been mentioned in passing . . .

"Well, well, will you look at that," Alex drawled, obviously no longer distracted from her act. "I hadn't noticed it sooner, but doesn't that nicely shaded patch of thick grass look like a bed? We could take some time out for a short rest, and not worry about losing daylight. I think that sun is nailed to its place in the sky."

Her grin was pushy and abrasive, but Tiran barely noticed. What he did notice was that she was right about the sun, something he should have seen himself. Damn it, the woman was distracting the life out of him, and if he didn't wake up it could mean both their lives.

"We've got to get out of here right now," he said, all the clues finally lined up properly. "I should have known this was a trap, but we needed it too badly to pass it by."

"What do you mean, a trap?" Alex asked with a frown. "I agree it appeared awfully conveniently, but—"

"Take it all together," he urged, beginning to lead the way back to the spot where they'd entered the oasis. "This place is *made* for tired and dirty human beings. A pool to drink from, a pool to wash clothes in, a pool to bathe in—and a bed of grass to encourage a nap in the shade. On top of that the sun isn't visibly moving, which gives the impression of no time passing. All of that was supposed to make us overlook the one sour note."

"Which is?" she prompted, nothing of the aggressively flighty female left showing.

"That dark spot you were sharp enough to notice is a sandstorm," he said, feeling his insides twist at the thought. Sandstorms could rip unprotected flesh from bones in a matter of minutes . . . "Under normal circumstances that would be bad enough, but we happen to be following the trail of a scent. Want to bet that scent will still be there even if we survive the storm? If it isn't, we won't find the entry either."

"Damn," she muttered, those silver eyes filled with self-annoyance. "And I was too interested in playing games to see any of that. If I'd been alone, I would have been trapped."

"If you'd been alone, you wouldn't have been playing games," he pointed out. "You also wouldn't have stopped for a rest, not with the amount of impatience *you're* filled with. But we can discuss that later. Right now there's an entry we need to find."

"And fast," she agreed. "Back to lizard form, and this time we don't stop for anything."

"Back to lizard form *first*," Tiran corrected before she could Shift. "We need it to find the trail, but we'll be better off following it as camels. They're able to move faster in sand, and we can Shift back every few minutes to check on the trail."

The glance she gave him was strange, but all she did was nod in continued agreement. They Shifted together to lizard form, scuttled far enough away from the oasis to pick up the trail, then went to camels. The storm was growing in the sky to their left, and it wouldn't take long before it reached them.

They made considerably better time as camels, but it was a good thing they constantly stopped to check their direction. The scent that had been in front of them suddenly started coming from the left, heading them directly into the approaching storm. If they didn't reach the entry before the sandstorm reached them—even camels needed a dune to hide behind, and that desert was unnaturally flat.

They had to close the nictitating membranes over their eyes before they caught the first glimpse of what *had* to be the entry. Sand was whirling around them with the sting of the storm's edge, and that meant they were out of time. Tiran used his nose to nudge Alex into an ungainly run, gambling everything on the entry's being there. And on the livability of the world on the other side. By that time he should have been checking before leaping, but time was the problem. No time to check, just to leap . . .

CHAPTER TEN

Shifting just as you reach an entry is easier when you can *see* the entry. All I could see was flying sand, so I had to work on memory and hope. I flew toward where the exit out of that storm should be, using what had damned well better be proper timing, then jumped and Shifted. A brief instant of sand tearing at my skin like nails, and then I was into calm and being caught before I could fall.

"Nice teamwork," Tiran d'Iste said as he let me go, first patting my shoulder. "We both made it, and in the proper order. If you were the one who had to catch *me*, I think we would have had a problem."

"Not unless you have something against being flat," I commented, looking around at our new location. "If this is a cave, where's the light coming from?"

"Maybe from the rock itself," he replied with a shrug, also looking around. "As long as it lets us see where we're going, what difference does it make?"

"As long as it keeps doing it, none at all," I allowed. "Have you spotted the trail yet?"

"I'm not *that* good," he said, faint amusement in his eyes. "Give me another second or two, and we can be on our way. But come to think of it, there isn't much confusion about that part. There's only one way *to* go."

Considering the fact that we stood at the end of a corridor of stone, that was rather obvious. To the left was the entry we'd just come through, behind us solid rock, and ahead a corridor stretching three-people wide. The rough, blue-gray rock defined where we could and couldn't go, at least until the corridor curved away out of sight.

"I think this worries me," I decided aloud. "It looks perfectly simple, so that means it can't be. There's something intricate involved, and if we miss it we're done."

"It could be that the intricate part is the *absence* of anything intricate," d'Iste suggested, and I couldn't decide if he was serious. "We go crazy searching for the catch, and all the time there isn't one."

"You have a very twisty mind," I said, at least part of the observation a compliment. "Let's see if we can find *another* trail, and then we can decide."

He agreed with a chuckle, and then began to Shift. I watched him take the standard path through forms for a moment, then started myself at the other end of the list. Aardvark and ant, bee and flower, everything but honey, nuts, and bran. We both worked our way all the way through, and finished up with nothing but wasted effort.

"Well, that does it," he said, leaning against the wall just the way I was doing. "I thought we had something in the bat, but there was nothing for it to sense. If we don't follow the corridor, our only other option is to stay here and stare at the walls."

"I don't like the way that breaks the pattern," I said, wishing there were something more definite to grab onto. "By rights the trail in this world should be sound, but instead it's switching back to sight. And *our* sight. I wonder . . ."

Looking around had brought my attention back to the entry, the only thing there not made of rock. It glowed softly in the directionless light of the cave, and I just had to try. Walking over to it took a second, and then I thrust my left hand through—but in and out as fast as I could make it. It still forced a gasp out of me, and my hand came back red and almost raw.

"Now that was smart," d'Iste growled, immediately there to examine my hand. "Do you also touch wet paint to be sure it really is wet?"

"I thought this might be a double entry," I said, pulling my tender hand away from his untender probing. "You know, leading someplace else from this side. There have been enough one-way entries to make the idea very possible."

"Then why didn't you stick your scabbard through?" he asked, looking at me the way some of my tutors used to when I was young. "Boiled leather takes a sand-scouring a little more easily than unprotected flesh."

"But it also can't tell you that it *is* taking a sand-scouring," I pointed out, thinking really fast. The truth of the matter was, it hadn't occurred to me to use something other than my hand. And it was all *his* fault . . .

"Maybe," he said, not in the least convinced. "But now that you've narrowed our options to only one, let's take it. Standing here won't get us to the end of the trail."

I shrugged and nodded, then followed as he led off up the corridor. It *was* the only choice we had left, and that cave offered nothing in the way of nourishment or comfort. Not like the oasis we had left, which had probably even had something for us to eat . . . if we'd bothered looking . . .

I was horribly aware of Tiran d'Iste walking beside me, a constant reminder that I ought to continue what I'd started in the oasis. I *did* owe him my life, and therefore also owed him the best I could give. It had been hell-hard offering him sex, but not for any reason *he* would have thought of. The truth was I did want him, very badly, but the idea of letting him make love to me was terrifying. I knew I would enjoy it, but what if I *really* enjoyed it . . . ?

The shudder I felt was only on the inside, but it certainly was there. Tiran d'Iste was the most attractive man I'd ever met, and the longer I stayed in his company, the more I wanted to feel his hands and lips on me. When we'd kissed in the bathing pool I'd really lost it, the desire for him overcoming everything in the way of good-sense reluctance. I was ready and eager for him . . .

But then *he* refused *me*. At first I'd tried talking him out of it, and then I woke up to what was happening. He'd misinterpreted how I really felt, and had therefore come down all insulted. It was what I needed to remind me how bad our getting together would be, not only for me but also for him. If I had to marry him I'd be miserable, and I'd surely make *him* miserable.

Which was why I began pushing him. He wasn't the sort of man who would like that, but—it meant I had to be close to him—and touch him—when more and more I really did want to touch him—by the EverNameless, it was driving me crazy—and what would happen if he ever agreed?

"Are you all right?" my companion asked, looking at me oddly. "You're awfully quiet all of a sudden. Is that hand giving you pain?"

"Not at all," I answered with a smile, at least telling the truth about *that*. "I was just wondering how far this corridor goes."

"We'll probably find out," he said. "Let's hope it's to the proper next entry."

"If it's that easy, I'll probably faint from the shock," I muttered. Things hadn't been working out at all lately, the way I felt right then being an excellent example. I knew what I wanted and I really wanted it, but I *didn't* want it. If you're lucky, clarity like that comes only once in a lifetime.

I spent the next few minutes silently debating whether or not to start the game again, and then, abruptly, the question had to be shelved. The corridor had twisted and turned through the rock in a gentle, harmless way, and then it did it again—for the last time. We rounded a curve and there it was, another dead end.

"And not an entry in sight," I observed as we slowed. "Looks like I won't be fainting."

"Maybe it's camouflaged into the rock," my companion suggested with a sigh. "If it isn't, we're going to be here for a while."

"I preferred the oasis," I said, then began helping him search the walls. I took one side, he took the other, and we met in the middle of the dead-end wall. Not only no entry; not even any cracks.

"I think it's time we searched for the trail again," he said, turning to look back the way we'd come. "If what we followed isn't it, it has to be *somewhere*."

He immediately began form Shifting again, so I took the other end of the list the way I had the first time. Once again we went through all of it, and when we were done I could really feel the length of the day we'd had—so far.

"Nothing," he said disgustedly while I leaned back against a wall. "The same exact nothing we found at the *other* end. If the trail is here, how can it have disappeared so completely? And why bring us this way if the trail *isn't* here? Could we have used the wrong entry in the last world?"

"Only if you were wrong about the oasis being a trap, and I don't think you were," I said with a headshake. "The sandstorm was there to wipe out the trail, so why add a false entry? That would be overkill, and totally wasted if we stayed at the oasis. No, this is the next leg of the trail. If we can't find it, we might have to go back to the oasis and wait to be retrieved."

"I don't think we'll be able to do that," he said while part of my mind drooled happily at the idea. "The oasis was directly in the path of the sandstorm, and it wasn't a natural oasis. Once the storm is over, there won't be much left of it."

"Then we *have* to go on," I acceded, the rest of me much preferring *that* idea. "And something you said struck a faint chord. You said we found the same sort of nothing here as we did at the other end. Since that happens to be so, what unchecked place does that leave?"

He parted his lips, probably to say it didn't leave anywhere, and then he understood. That dippy-minded part of me loved how quick he was, how fast to pick up on things other people never even noticed. And the way he didn't seem to mind when I was the one who had the good idea . . . as though he considered me a real, live person . . .

"Of course," he said with a sudden grin, those green eyes warmly approving. "If there's nothing at either end, that leaves the middle. I knew there was a reason to be glad you were along. Let's go check it out."

He put out an arm to me, and it was all I could do not to go and take it. I was getting too tired to remember just how far I wanted the game to go, which meant it was too dangerous to pursue at close quarters. Distance was what I needed, and what I meant to have. I leaned off the wall and walked up to him, but just behind rather than beside.

"After you, sweet stuff," I drawled, patting him on his southern region. "You have buns that are made to be watched."

The flare from those green eyes should have burned me and my dirty grin to a crisp, but he didn't come back at me in words. What he did do was withdraw the offer of his arm before stomping off, which was exactly what I'd wanted. Distance, blessed distance.

I trailed after him back to the approximate center of the corridor, and then it was time to be a team again. Considering the fact that that part of the trail should be some sort of sound, we started with the most logical form to pick it up: a bat. He took the side toward the end of the corridor, I took the side toward the beginning, and then we began to squeak. The sound came bouncing back the way it was supposed to—but mine, at least, showed an extra echo, different from the one bouncing off rock. I got it pinpointed at the outside of the last corridor curve, then Shifted back.

"Over there," I said when d'Iste followed my example, gesturing toward the curve. "On the outside, where this light is dimmest. We walked right past it."

"And couldn't reach it earlier because the corridor curves around too much," he said, this time following me. "With all that rock in the way—Well, hopefully we'll be out of here soon."

We still couldn't see anything, but feeling around showed us the entry, its glow hidden behind a facade of blue-gray rock. It probably would have been smart to check out the rest of the corridor, but there was just a little too much of it and I was close to the end of my strength. My companion couldn't have been doing much better, and we needed to save what we had for what lay on the other side of the entry. D'Iste managed to step through first, but I was right behind him . . .

Into a world that was a distinct relief. Just about late afternoon, pleasant in the quiet woods all around. Not far to the left was a road, and directly across the road stood a prosperous-looking inn. The sign in front of it said it was The Traveler's House, which made me lick my lips.

"Too bad that's also probably a trap," I said, forcing myself to be resigned to the loss. "I'll start looking for the trail, and once we find it—"

"No," d'Iste said at once, his own gaze on the inn. "I'm close to falling off my feet, and you can't be any better. If we don't stop for some decent rest, whatever's ahead won't have any trouble taking the both of us. Trap or not, we'll be making use of that inn."

"Am I supposed to bow and say, 'Yes, master'?" I asked, annoyed with the tone of authority he'd used. He'd done that to me once before, at the oasis, and I hadn't been able to argue. There was something about him at times like that, something that turned him worse than my father . . .

"You're supposed to say, 'Yes, *Tiran*,' and the bow isn't necessary," he came back, distantly amused. "There's no sense in wasting strength arguing, because we'll still end up doing things my way. You do remember what I said would happen if you ever try taking off alone again."

The green eyes looking down at me had lost even the distant amusement, letting me know I'd better be absolutely

sure of myself or firmly committed to suicide before trying
to disagree. I don't say he didn't have cause to feel like
that—as well as wounds that hadn't quite healed yet—not
to mention the size and ability to make the threat stick—

"Yes, I remember," I grudged, disgusted with myself for
backing down even that far. Why the man affected me like
that . . .

"Good," he said, putting an arm around my shoulders to
head me toward the inn. "Then let's get in there. Even if we
have to keep our eyes open—so to speak—we can still get
some food and rest."

The arm left me as soon as I was moving under my own
power, which was a qualified good thing. The fact that I
couldn't see it as a completely good thing annoyed me
more than Tiran d'Iste's high-handedness; it wasn't unreasonable to have no control over *him*, but more and more I
was having none over myself. If something didn't happen
soon to change that, the rest of the competition would be a
breeze compared to my personal problems.

I was just able to keep from muttering to myself as we
walked, and happily it didn't take long to cross the road
and reach the inn. We left the birdsong and sunshine for
the interior of The Traveler's House, and immediately had
the loss made up.

Inside there was light, polished wood all around with
bright curtains and homey knickknacks, everything fitting
well with the older woman who stood behind the registration counter. Short and stout with gray-streaked brown hair
in a neat bun, she smiled at us as though we were exactly
the people she'd been waiting for. Her red-and-white dress
was spotless and fresh, but she didn't even blink at our
well-worn clothes.

"Good day to you, sir and madam," she greeted us
warmly. "Will we be having the pleasure of serving you
a meal?"

"That and providing us with accommodations," d'Iste
told her with an answering smile. "This is a lovely inn you
have here."

"Thank you, sir." She beamed at him. "My sons and I take great pride in the efforts we've made over the years, and accommodations you shall have. Let me see now . . . Oh, dear."

She'd opened a registration ledger and had begun to read, then suddenly her smile had vanished. She glanced at us with disturbance, studied the page again, turned back to a previous page, then let out a sigh of relief.

"Thank goodness, there's still one left," she said, smiling again. "Spring is the time we close off half the rooms in turn for painting and repairs, so everything will be fresh for our summer trade. Half has always been enough to accommodate those who begin their traveling early, but this spring is so unseasonably warm—We've had more guests than we know what to do with, and my sons are working day and night to finish what they'd already begun. If we'd known, they wouldn't have started, of course . . . One room *will* be proper, I hope? This has always been a respectable house—"

"Oh, quite proper, ma'am," d'Iste hastened to assure her sudden worry, sincerity oozing out of every pore. "My wife and I have taken to the road just as you see us, our intention being to recapture the closeness we once shared—before material objects began to come between us. When we find again the passion we've lost, we'll return home renewed."

"Oh, how marvelously romantic," the woman sighed, her hands to her breast. "I *had* wondered why you carried not so much as a pair of saddlebags. Here, let me call my grandson, and he'll show you to your room. It's near some others that are still closed off, so you won't be disturbed. Would you care to have your meal served there?"

"Yes, ma'am, thank you, and as soon as possible," Tiran replied as the woman rang a pleasant little bell. "Our last meal is a good distance behind us—becoming reacquainted with the person you once loved is a distracting business."

"Oh, my, yes," she agreed with a dazzling smile as a boy about nine or ten ran through the doorway behind the counter. He was brown-haired and brown-eyed and as messy as boys that age usually are, but he wore a big grin.

"I won, Grandma, so I get to take care of these guests," he informed the woman proudly. "Dranka went out for more stove wood, so he couldn't outrun me this time."

"Well, I'm delighted to see that you've won, Rinni," the woman said with a laugh and a ruffling of his hair. "Get a pot of chai and two cups, and then you can show these nice people to their room."

"Okay, Grandma," he agreed, then dashed back through the door. My companion signed the register while we waited for the boy to return, then he insisted that the woman accept some silver as partial payment in advance. She was trying to refuse when the boy reappeared, so the argument ended with her taking the coin. The boy picked up the key she'd prepared and glanced at it, put it in his pocket, then headed for the stairs. If we hadn't followed right after, we probably would have been left behind.

Our room was on the third floor toward the back of the house, and was larger than I'd expected it to be. Straight ahead four windows let in the afternoon sunlight, which warmed the newly whitewashed walls. To the left was a large canopied bed, with the curtains drawn back to show fresh linens and quilts. The bed and the wardrobe and the washstand were all polished light wood, as were the table and chairs to the right. The tablecloth was snowy white with tiny red flowers, a perfect match to the window curtains, bed-curtains, and linen. It radiated the same kind of homey comfort the woman downstairs had, and there were even fresh flowers on the mantel above the hearth. The stone fireplace stood beyond the table and chairs, and wood had been laid in but no fire started.

"Here's your chai and your key," the boy Rinni said, putting everything down on the table before turning to look at us. "Anything else you want, you just let me know."

"We'll do that," d'Iste told him with a grin, then flipped a copper in his direction. The boy caught it with a whoop of delight, remembered to bow his thanks, then raced out leaving the door open. With his new fortune clutched in his hand he'd apparently forgotten everything else, and I could hear him clattering down the stairs until my companion closed the door himself.

"You and your *wife* have taken to the road to recapture lost *passion*?" I asked when he turned back. "You're expecting to be *renewed*, and becoming reacquainted with someone you once loved is *distracting*? Don't you have any shame—or, for that matter, taste? How could you say those things with a straight face?"

"I had the strength to keep my face straight because my heart is pure," he answered primly, then lost it to a grin. "Not to mention the fact that I've had to stretch the truth once or twice in the past. I told that sweet lady nothing that would hurt her, so why get into a bother? Or do you have personal objections to what I said?"

"Aside from the fact that I'm not your wife?" I said, trying to think fast. "What other objections would I have?"

"Don't ask me." He shrugged in answer, heading for the table and the chai. "We *are* supposed to be getting acquainted—in a way, reacquainted—and I expect this rest stop to renew me. The passion part you've been trying to supply, so I wasn't even lying about that. What else is left?"

His attention was on pouring chai into the cups, so I didn't bother shrugging or shaking my head. I *did* have the strangest feeling, though, almost as if he had begun backing me into a corner. Which was ridiculous, since he'd even refused to consider sleeping with me . . .

"I don't think they'll charge more if you sit down to drink your chai," he said, gesturing to the cup he'd moved in my general direction. "Taking advantage of this lull will work better if we do it off our feet."

There wasn't much to say to that either, so I moved to a chair and sat. When I picked up my cup, I couldn't help noticing that he had moved his own chair about a foot closer to me before doing the same. We sipped chai in silence for a moment, and then I turned my head to find that green gaze directly on me.

"Why are you staring at me?" I couldn't help asking, trying not to show how uncomfortable it made me. "Do I have a smudge I haven't yet found out about?"

"I'm not staring, I'm looking," he answered, just as though what he said made sense. "I enjoy looking at you, and seeing all that vitality and aura of competence. When a woman like you decides a man is good enough for her, it makes that man feel three times better than he is. And three times worse if she won't even look at him."

"I've looked at you," I said with a dirty grin I had to fight for. "Back at the oasis, when we were bathing. A woman would have to be crazy *not* to look at you, built as well as you are. Any time you need a reference, you just come to me."

"What a man is can be found only on the inside," he responded, still as serious as he had been. "People's outsides are for an initial attraction, something to bring them together the first time. After that only what he *is* counts, since that's what keeps the woman beside him. Or the man beside her. Diamonds can be packaged in paper, and garbage packaged in gold."

"I've heard that saying," I muttered, trying frantically to think of something else—on another subject. It was true Tiran d'Iste was beautifully made as a man, but that only inspired the sort of lust I'd encountered before. What I'd *never* run into was the way he never boasted even when he told you how good he was; the way he took things as they came and dealt with them calmly and competently; the way he shared an experience even when most of the doing had been his. He was a man who made you want to get to know him better, and therein lay his greatest danger.

"It's a true saying, and that's what makes it good," he went on. "I've met a lot of beautiful women in my professional life, but none of them had that—something special on the inside. And none of them was interested in what *I* was really like. As long as they could share my glory, nothing else mattered. It took a long while for me to realize I needed a woman with glory of her own. Then we could trade."

He covered his faint grin with his chai cup as he sipped, hopefully not noticing that I looked away rather quickly. I'd never experienced such pure torture as sitting there and talking to the man, discovering with horror that I liked everything I heard. The part of me that wanted him— no, *every* part of me wanted him; one part just wanted more—was ecstatic with anticipation, and I simply *had* to do something to break the mood.

"I think I can understand why so many women saw nothing but the outside you," I commented, bringing my gaze back to him. "You *are* somewhat overwhelming, but it's not only that. Your eye color, for instance, is such an oddity, it's hard not to stare. When I first saw you, I couldn't believe you'd entered a full-range competition with the expectation of winning. In our kingdom, even those who can't do more than chameleon-change are more—normal."

I watched his jaw tighten more with everything I said, but I couldn't let myself think about how insulted and hurt he must feel. I needed him to be insulted enough to stop talking to me, to give me the chance to get a better grip on myself. As self-defense went the effort was low, but it was also all I had.

"You might be right," he said in a voice that was almost a growl, the eyes I'd spoken about cold and hard. "A lot of people take one look at my eyes and decide I'm useless. I had that the entire time I was growing up, in a kingdom not much different from yours. The other kids would laugh at me no matter what I accomplished, trying to make me believe I'd never be their match. When I got to the point of being better than they were, they stopped laughing, and that left only the nastiness. Most people won't thank you for showing them they're second-rate."

"And then they blame *you* for being better," I added, finding it impossible to stop myself. "They laugh and call you empty-headed when you first start to try, sneer

about time-wasting while you're learning, then call it luck
when you begin to know what you're doing. After a while
it becomes obvious luck has nothing to do with it, and that's
when they start calling you a freak. But not to your face.
They don't want to lose teeth so they keep the comments
to themselves, but they make sure you know that's what
they're thinking."

"And when you finally can't take it anymore and leave,
you know they're glad to see you go," he said very quietly,
one hand coming to cover mine. "That's what hurts the
most, I think, to know they're happy rather than regretting
what they did. They put you through hell for being different, but they never lose sleep over blaming you for their
lacks. I can see now you've gone through the same thing,
but not because of your eye color. It must have been worse
being female. Men can sometimes grudgingly acknowledge another man's superiority, but never a woman's."

I freed my hand from his as I closed my eyes, wishing
that crying could accomplish something useful. I'd now
found out that he shared the biggest hurt in my life, and
almost for the same reason. I wanted to cry my heart out
for both of us, then find comfort with his strong arms
wrapped around me. Obviously I was too tired to think
or feel what I should, but I didn't know how to make
it stop.

"Let's find something more pleasant to talk about," he
said, briskly patting the hand I'd pulled away from him.
"Have you ever heard of a place called Fain? It's so far
out that the Sighted consider it perfect for games, it being
almost completely a place of magic. You can't even get a
fire to burn, not unless it's a magic fire. I visited there once
with a friend, and—"

A knock at the door interrupted him, and then our young
friend Rinni was back, as front-runner for an older, larger
boy. The second one carried a tray loaded with plates, and
the expression on his face was one of exasperation. I didn't
know why until the woman from downstairs bustled in
behind the tray bearer.

"Oh, I'm so sorry," she said to us, wringing her hands. "That boy——! Rinni, you were supposed to wait to be invited in after knocking, not just knock and walk in! This gentleman and his wife are entitled to their privacy!"

"Why?" the boy asked dismissingly. "All they're doing is sitting and drinking chai. And you *said* they were hungry."

"It's all right, ma'am," d'Iste said with a chuckle as he stood, soothing the woman's embarrassment. "In this instance the boy is right, so there's no harm done. We knew the food was coming, so the worst you would have interrupted is a kiss. I'm sure you know it's not all that terrible to see a man kiss the woman he loves."

Without warning he bent down to put his hand under my chin, and then his lips were on mine, gently demanding. It was a leisurely taste of my soul that he took, unhurried despite its brevity. Every bone in my body melted from the poleaxed shock, and then he was straightening again.

"You see?" he asked with another chuckle. "No harm done to any of us."

The woman laughed gently and answered him, but her words were lost in the roar filling my head. "No harm done to any of us," he'd said, but he'd lied. I no longer felt the chair under me or the floor beneath my boots, the cup in my hand or the sword hanging at my hip. Every ounce of my awareness was tied up in how much I wanted that man, how much I *needed* him. He and I had shared danger and pain; all of me now demanded that we share an equal amount of joy.

When I finally realized my eyes were closed and I opened them, we were once again alone in the room. The tray the boy had been carrying was on the table, and a number of mouth-watering smells rose up at me from it. Tiran d'Iste was just coming back from the door, apparently having closed it again behind our former company. I tried to let the lure of the food entice me away from different needs, but it wasn't any good. I was going to be a damned fool, and nothing in the universe would be allowed to stop me.

"Now that was nice of her," the object of my intentions said as he stopped at the table. "Our privacy *was* interrupted, so this first bottle of wine is on the house. If we want one *we* pay for, we'll have to order another."

He turned the bottle around to look at the label, a lock of his long black hair falling across his forehead. His shoulders were so broad they strained the material of his tunic, but they were also perfectly in proportion to the rest of him. I left my chair and walked around the table to him, and he looked at me with questioning in those incredible green eyes. It must have been my silence that puzzled him, but I didn't leave him in the dark for long. I had to use both arms to pull that stubborn head down, but once I did I kissed him with everything I was feeling.

And he wasn't able to refuse me that, at least. His arms came up to crush me to him, one hand in my hair, one on my back, his response to the kiss faster than instantaneous. He practically devoured me as I tried to do the same to him, and all sense of time was lost to the wild mindlessness of it. We tasted each other to the core, nearly to the point of destruction, and then he used his hold on my hair to free himself.

"That was . . . more than I ever imagined it could be," he said huskily, looking down into my eyes. "I thank you for the experience, but I think we'd better do something else now. Flesh and blood can stand only so much, and I passed that point ten minutes ago."

"Absolutely not," I said, more than aware that our bodies still touched. "This time I won't take no for an answer. If you try it I'll turn around and walk out of here, and the next time I see you I'll come at you with everything I've got. And I don't mean kisses and hugs."

"You're threatening me?" he asked with both brows high, surprised rather than angry or annoyed. "Isn't forcing yourself on someone usually considered rape?"

"Call it whatever you like," I answered with a shrug. "I tried being nice and then I tried being sexy, but you weren't interested in anything but your twisted sense of pride. How I feel now is *your* fault, and I refuse to let your misconceptions continue to torture me. The only decision you have to make is whether we separate or make love, but whichever it is, we'll be doing it *now*."

He stared down at me in silence, but I could see his mind working behind those eyes. He couldn't believe I was bluffing, because it's easy to see when I mean what I say. And I did mean it, every word. He was the one who had started it all, but I was the one who would finish it.

"No, right now is out for both options," he finally decided, not the least trace of uncertainty in him. "The first thing we're going to do is eat that food, and while we do, you'll rethink your position. If by the time we're finished, you still want what you say you do, we'll see about getting it for you. That should be fair enough."

"I thought I made it clear that fairness didn't enter into this," I said. "I don't need to 'rethink' anything, and I'm not interested in 'seeing about' getting what I want. I said—"

"And *I* said not now," he interrupted, his tone fractionally harder. "I realize that as a princess, you can't help being a spoiled brat, but I don't happen to like brats. And I also never take them to bed. That's one of the things you have to understand, that if it happens, *I'll* be the one taking *you* to bed. If the idea disagrees with you, after we're through eating you can use the door. Or not, just as you please. But right now it will be the way *I* please."

He finally let go of me to take my arm, and I was walked back to my chair and *urged* into it. That's another problem with men like Tiran d'Iste—stubborn as a rusty shutter, and set on doing things their way. If I hadn't been so really tired . . .

But I *was* too tired for gestures, and I did need to get that problem straightened out. I watched balefully as a plate of food was set down in front of me, another was put in his place, and extras like the fresh-baked bread and the cheese spread were placed within reach of both of us. There wasn't anything to argue with until he sat and reached for the bottle of wine, and then I shook my head.

"No wine for me, thanks," I said, reaching myself for the bread. "If I decide to walk out of here, I'll want a clear head."

"You consider that a strong possibility?" he asked. "I thought you were more interested in a different kind of activity."

"But you gave me something to think about," I pointed out, spreading cheese on the bread. "A couple of some-things, in fact, so right now there's no way of knowing. But I do like to be prepared for all eventualities, so I'll make do with the chai."

He hesitated for a moment after hearing that, then put the bottle down unopened. I hadn't mentioned that I also wanted a clear head if I didn't leave, at least as long as it was possible to have one. I had decided to do something my better judgment would have hated if it was still working, and blaming it on too much wine would have been too convenient an excuse. If it happened there would *be* no excuses, and I needed to understand that.

The cheese was mixed with raw egg and sugar to make it spread more easily, and that also made it incredibly good. The main dish was a thick stew with plenty of meat and vegetables and heavy brown gravy, and was close to the best I'd ever tasted. It hadn't really been that long since the last time we'd eaten, but all the running and walking and Shifting we'd done made it seem like a week. Once I started I found I wanted to shovel the food in, but also wanting to avoid indigestion made me take it slow.

And then there were those items I was supposed to think about. If I really meant what I said and talked *him* into it, then he would be the one who took *me* to bed. From my point of view that sounded ominous, but not because of anything *he* might do. I'd discovered a fragile hope in me that once I'd tried him in bed, the attraction I felt would be greatly lessened. Or would disappear entirely, an even better outcome.

But being taken to bed wasn't the way encounters had worked for me in the past. It had always been my decision that had made it happen, and I'd been the one in control. It was true the initial decision would be mine this time, too, but it wasn't possible to control a man like Tiran d'Iste, and he'd made sure I knew it. What if I found I liked it that way even better? As crazy as my reactions had been lately, I wouldn't put it past them, so what would I do? I couldn't simply change my mind and keep my distance, not and also expect to keep my sanity. His draw was too strong, too demanding . . .

"Well, that was very satisfying," the object of my rampaging thoughts commented as he sat back in his chair. "It looks like you also enjoyed the food."

That made me realize I'd eaten the second half of my meal without noticing, the only thing left being the chai in my cup. I smiled vaguely and picked up the cup, and he was back to looking at me very closely.

"So, has your thinking brought you to any decision yet?" he said next, his tone very neutral. "If you need more time, we could get some sleep before talking about it."

"I don't need more time," I told him, putting the cup down. "Tell me what you think we need to talk about."

"Well, for starters, I'd like to know why you're being so abrupt about this," he obliged. "The fact that I don't want a fling with the woman I intend to marry should please you, but it doesn't. I'd like to know why that is."

"Maybe it's because there's no guarantee your intentions will work out," I said, scraping at the tablecloth with one fingernail. "Or maybe it's because I think they *will* work. If I have to decide whether or not to marry you, I'd like to have something to base the decision on. And don't tell me again I won't have a choice. There's always a choice if you know where to look."

"Okay, that's a subject we can argue about at another time," he allowed. "But it still sounds to me like all you want to do is use me. Am I supposed to enjoy the idea of being used?"

"Most people consider this sort of situation mutual use," I answered, raising my eyes to his face. He was so strongly handsome that looking directly at him was close to being painful. But it was also more than physical attraction, a lot more . . . "I get the feeling you're still not interested—or not willing, to use your own word. If that's the case—"

"Now hold on," he interrupted, raising one hand. "Hurrying through life makes you miss half the fun of it. I didn't say I wasn't willing. All I'm trying to do is understand your reason for wanting this. If you have a good one, I'd like to hear it. If it's no more than a matter of curiosity, I'll have to say thanks but no thanks. I'm past the point in life where you tell yourself it's a compliment. I've already had too many compliments like that."

Looking at him, I could believe it. The wives and daughters of his employers, the employers themselves if they happened to be female, any woman who was in a position to take advantage of his being there. It hadn't occurred to me that some men were cornered as often as beautiful women, or that the man involved could get just as tired of it. Men weren't supposed to be that fussy . . . as if they were less intelligent, and therefore less human . . .

"I apologize if I made you think it was just curiosity on my part," I said, beginning to feel terrible. "I know what that's like, and also believed I was too noble to ever do it to someone else. But maybe I'm finding out I'm not too noble, and maybe there was more curiosity involved than I wanted to admit. Let's just forget about the whole thing—"

"I said don't be in such a hurry," he interrupted again, this time not letting me get out of the chair. His hand on my arm shifted to a grip on my hand, and then he leaned back again, still holding it.

"Curiosity in itself doesn't happen to be a crime," he went on, his thumb moving over the back of the hand he held. "It's natural to wonder about someone who attracts you, but that shouldn't be the only thing you feel. Is your sole interest in how well I'll do in comparison to the other men you've tried?"

I hesitated a moment then shook my head, telling the absolute truth. I also had the feeling I'd stepped into quicksand up to my knees, but there was nothing whatsoever I could do about it.

"So your interest runs deeper than the desire for another passing good time," he said, his voice now softer. "My poor bruised ego thanks you for that, but I'd still like to know more. Is this purely a physical thing, or is that sharp mind of yours beginning to become involved? Do you want me, or do you want *me*?"

There was no urgent demand in the question, but his eyes were watching me so carefully that a thrill of fear ran through me. I did want *him*, not just the man who happened to be with me, but I couldn't say the words. How he felt had become important to me, but I simply couldn't say that.

"So that's what you're afraid of," he murmured, raising my hand to his lips. "You're afraid of finding that 'something special' between us, but it's gotten to the point where you can't refuse to look and see if it's there. Since that answers my question, why don't we take that look together."

He stood up then, and used the hand he held to draw me up after him. I could taste terror in the dryness of my mouth, but he was right about my need to look. Somewhere deep inside I already knew what I would find, but I had to take that look to be sure . . .

My hand firmly held in his, I was led over to the bed in a way that made me feel like a complete novice. Once we got there I expected to be turned loose, but instead he drew me close and wrapped me in his arms.

"When you're with me, I don't want you to be afraid of anything," he murmured, only just touching his lips to mine. "I won't ever let anything hurt you, and that includes me. We'll chase that fear away together, and make sure it doesn't come back."

He gave me a fractionally longer kiss, and then let me go in order to reach to my swordbelt. When the weapons were off he carried them to a nearby table, put them down along with his own, then came back.

"I don't know how it's been in *your* experience," he said, "but mine has never included a sexy way of taking off a woman's fighting boots. What say we each take care of our own?"

"Another disappointment," I said with a sigh, working to hide my amusement. "I've scoured the male population of my kingdom, looking for just one man who can be sexy in taking off my fighting boots, but all to no avail. When the competition is over, I may have to make it a quest."

"That's how a lot of quests get started," he agreed, sitting next to me on the bed to work on his own boots. "But if you do that, you'll have to examine hundreds, maybe even thousands, of men across the worlds. Sounds like a lot of dull, endless repetition to me."

"I know, but when you begin a quest, you have to expect to suffer," I answered, this time finding it impossible to hide my grin. "All those men, one after the other—it's a dirty job, but somebody's got to do it."

I tossed away my second boot, carefully watching it rather than the man next to me, but the gesture didn't help. He stood up, pulled his tunic off over his head, reached down, and lifted me into his arms.

"There are certain rules a woman in my bed has to follow," he lectured while I gasped and clutched at his neck. I wasn't used to being picked up like that, but rather than drop me he acted as if I weighed nothing. "The first and most important rule is that *I'm* the only man she's supposed to be thinking about. That's unreasonable of me, I know, but it's still not subject to debate."

He put one knee on the bed, lowered me to the center of it, then lay down beside me.

"The second rule is that lovemaking is serious business," he murmured, his lips coming to my neck and ear. "No laughing out loud, no joking, and above all, no giggling."

That was when his tongue tickled my ear, forcing a forbidden laugh out of me. The thought itself made me laugh even more, and I saw his grin as he watched me. That ridiculous list . . .

And then I realized my hands were on his arms, his body gently holding mine down. He was made out of warm, flesh-covered stone, and I no longer considered the conversation a welcome delay in facing my fears. Desire was rushing higher than fear could go, so hot it even burned terror away. I reached up and ran my hand through thick, unruly black hair, and his grin went the way of my laughter. Green eyes looked at me with such intensity that I felt like shivering, and then we were sharing a kiss that was neither light nor brief.

Dizziness swirled over me immediately, racing through my blood, turning to insanity, then jumping to him. His mouth and tongue tasted me while his hands caressed and explored, and all I could do was hang on and let myself be swept along. His least touch turned me mindless as well as weak, and right then there was nothing "least" about it. He touched me deliberately and provocatively, possessively and excitingly, arousing me even as he drained me of will and strength.

After a timeless time we were both free of our clothing, but don't ask me how it happened. All I knew was how much I wanted him, and I was near frenzy by the time he came to me. Oh, endless life, the feel of him inside me! Like nothing ever before experienced, like pure desire in the shape of a man. We moved together with the insanity that held us both, exploded together, then began all over. I think I whimpered when he started to bring me after him again, but only because I didn't think I could stand it. If he'd asked I probably would have wanted to sleep first, but we were well beyond asking and allowing.

He carried me back up to the heights with him, kept me just short of screaming with delight for forever, then finally let it end. "Limp rag" is too firm a description for what was left of me, but I think he held me in his arms for a while. All I know for certain is that I blinked once and then was gone into exhausted sleep.

*   *   *

Tiran awoke to the sound of a clock striking somewhere, the dark of deep night unbroken around him. Unbroken around *them*. A shadow Alex lay to his left, facedown and sound asleep, and he turned to his side to touch a hand to her hair. He would have felt stupid saying aloud that there had been magic between them, but that was exactly what it had been. Magic he'd never had before, but intended having many times again.

"I knew you were meant to be mine, knew it the minute I first saw you," he whispered almost soundlessly, letting his fingers touch her silken hair. "You gave me more of a fight than some armies I've faced, but I now have the most important win of my life. You won't be able to deny you felt what I did, won't be able to forget it any more than I can. From now on we belong to each other."

Alex made a small sound and stirred where she lay, but other than that there was no response. Tiran hadn't expected a response, at least not until she woke again. He intended to repeat what he'd just said, wanting to hear her admit he was right, finding it all he could do not to wake her. The struggle had seriously drained his stores of self-assurance, but as soon as she admitted the truth everything would be fine.

And then I can concentrate on wrapping up this competition, he thought with a sigh, turning onto his back again. Since we've already started our honeymoon, we really should get the marriage ceremony taken care of. Before you, my girl, get cold feet again. As though anything about you can be cold. Soft, yes, smooth and delicious, definitely—I wonder how it will be when we're not both exhausted . . . before breakfast ought to be a good time to find out . . .

Tiran was feeling too aroused to slide back down into sleep, but he also realized he was too warm. Not a breath of air was stirring, even with the windows left open. The windows. He couldn't make them out in the dark, not even their outlines. As a matter of fact he couldn't see anything, just as though the bed were wrapped in flannel . . .

He brushed his arm out to the right, but touching cloth quickly calmed him. The bed-curtains were drawn—that was why it was so warm and he couldn't see anything. He also couldn't remember having drawn them, but he must have done it just before falling asleep. To save Alex embarrassment if that boy Rinni just walked in a second time. Of course. It made sense, but wasn't needed any longer. The boy must have been put to bed hours ago . . . and hadn't he locked the door after the food was brought . . . ?

Tiran sat up and brushed at the curtains to find their center, but that turned out to be harder than expected. It was almost as if they'd been sewn together, which was more than annoying. He'd have to stand up and fight with the curtains, maybe even wake Alex with the messing around. And she needed the sleep, just as he did . . .

That was when he heard the sound above him, above, as a matter of fact, the entire bed. As if something large and heavy were beginning to move, something with sharpness that cut through the material of the canopy with a snicking noise. Large, heavy, sharp, above them . . . curtains locked closed all around . . . By the EverNameless, he'd actually forgotten that this place might be a trap. "Might be" had definitely become "was," and they were caught but good . . .

CHAPTER ELEVEN

"Alex, wake up!" Tiran hissed urgently, a hard hand on her shoulder. "We have trouble, so don't waste time asking questions. Can you Shift to fly form?"

Rather than answer him in words, Alex blurred and effectively disappeared. Taking his own advice Tiran also Shifted, and it was barely in time. What he'd heard easing through the material of the canopy suddenly threw away hesitation and came crashing down, meeting the bed at enough points so that nothing should have escaped.

Standing in the deep valley his concentrated weight caused in the quilt, Tiran looked with faceted eyes at the forest of giant shadows all around him. Luck had kept one of those shadows from plunging into the place where he was, but it hadn't yet saved them. He had to make sure Alex was all right, and then they had to get out of there.

Cautiously he Shifted to mouse shape, and there was still enough room for his body. Now he could see something of the metal spikes that had driven into many points on the bed, and also felt less pressure than he had. Going very small was dangerous, and the longer you stayed small, the more dangerous it became. Mouse form wasn't easy, but there was less chance of exploding like a volcano than in fly form.

222

Getting across the quilt and around the spikes wasn't easy, not at his weight in such a small form, but he fought free of a last valley to see a small dark form watching him. A heartbeat later there was another mouse blinking back at him, which made his whiskers twitch. The newcomer was a girl mouse, but they didn't have time for that now.

When they finally reached the curtains on Alex's side of the bed, Tiran used sharp, tiny claws to hold a section of it still, and then he took a bite. Two additional bites made a hole big enough for him to fit through, and as soon as he launched his mouse body toward the floor, he Shifted back to natural. The fall wasn't as far for his own form, and as soon as he hit the wood he rolled. If anyone was in the room a moving target would be harder to reach, and Alex would need room for her own drop.

Moonlight lit the darkened room enough for him to see by, and even as Alex came through, he was already gathering up their clothes. They dressed quickly beside the table holding their weapons, armed themselves, then moved to the wall behind the door. They were all ready to go, but not until they made some attempt to find out what might be waiting.

"What in hell is going on?" Alex asked very softly from beside him. "I know I was the one who first said this place was probably a trap, but I have to admit I changed my mind. None of this fits in with what we saw."

"I know," Tiran answered just as softly. "It makes less than no sense, but look at the room. Is it the lack of light that makes me think it's changed?"

Alex took a moment to look around, and then she sighed.

"The lack of light makes it worse, but this isn't the room we first saw," she agreed. "The window curtains look like they're dripping blood instead of being patterned, the windows themselves look like the teeth of something living, and the bed looks like one of those plants that wraps itself around you before beginning to feed. And if I'm not misremembering, this polished wooden floor tried to suck at my bare body."

"It felt that way to me, too," Tiran said, constantly glancing at the shadows around them. "Whatever this place has become, it's time we left it behind us. We'll work our way down and outside, and if anyone tries to stop us, we'll remember this isn't the same inn we arrived at."

Her nod looked casual and businesslike, a reaction that shouldn't have surprised Tiran but did. He wasn't used to thinking of women as anything but people who needed to be protected, and that despite what he and Alex had already been through. Intellectually he knew she could take care of herself; emotionally he knew no such thing. He was going to have to work on a compromise between those two views, otherwise getting along with Alex would not be very easy.

He loosened his sword then reached for the door, but it began to open before he touched it. He and Alex quickly stepped back as lamplight began filling the room, and then three forms entered. Under other circumstances he would have said three people, but somehow the term no longer applied. Even from the back, the woman and the two boys looked different, and their first words confirmed the feeling.

"First meal is mine, I think," the boy Rinni said, sounding completely mature and distantly amused. "Which one should I choose, I wonder?"

"You know very well which one you'll choose," the woman said, faintly annoyed. "You'll gorge on more than half of the man, making it necessary for *me* to finish with the woman or end up still hungry. If I'd known you had peculiar tastes, I never would have accepted you in the nest."

"You should have asked before it was too late," the boy-thing answered with a chuckle. "I wouldn't have been able to lie, and that's what really bothers you. You never thought to ask."

"If you two don't stop going through this same argument every time, *I'm* going to find a different nest," the older boy said, his voice cold with annoyance. "You should have done this, I should have done that, as if it really matters. Do you hear *me* complain when the guests are all male?"

"We can't all have the same—equal-interest appetite that you do, Dranka," the woman told him dryly. "You do have a slight preference for females, but males will suit you almost as well. I, on the other hand, can't abide female flesh, but it *is* better than starving. And speaking of starving, how long are we going to wait before opening the curtains and rewinding the mechanism?"

"We're going to wait until most of their blood has drained out," the Rinni-thing said with exaggerated patience, as though he'd said the same words many times before. "It won't take more than another few minutes, which means we'll be through just before dawn brings the change. I've always thought it unfair that dawn forces us back to our other selves, but sunset doesn't release us. Having to wait until midnight wastes hours that could be better spent."

"I'll bet *they* made use of the time," the Dranka-thing said with a laugh. "They should have thanked us for using a drug in the wine that didn't take effect until they fell asleep. If it had cut them down sooner, they would have missed their final pleasure. But we won't miss ours, will we, Chiri? Since Rinn eats first, we frolic first."

"And then you'll frolic with *him*," the woman—apparently named Chiri—said, shaking off the fingers that had come to her face. "You're the only one of us who gets enough of everything, Dranka, and I'm becoming tired of it. Why can't *I* . . ."

By that time Tiran had drawn Alex out into the hall with him, the door the three had left open an invitation he hadn't cared to refuse. He'd gotten a glimpse or two of a large number of unusually sharp teeth in the mouths of their visitors, and the woman had held the lamp with a hand ending in claws rather than fingernails. He and Alex would certainly be able to defend themselves in some way against the three, but there was no sense in taking unnecessary chances.

Moving down the stairs close to the wall eliminated the vast majority of squeaks the steps might produce, and no one showed up to block their way. It finally came to Tiran that the sons the inn-mistress had mentioned were just as real as the repairs they'd supposedly been in the middle of. No hammering, no sawing, no smell of fresh paint, but he hadn't doubted her story for a minute. Show a man a woman past her prime in the company of a young boy, and every bit of caution he has flies right out the window.

Feeling more than disgusted with himself, Tiran led the way to the front door and through it. He would have been surprised if it had been locked, after their hosts had been so nice about giving them that free bottle of wine.

"You know, it's a good thing you got shirty with me before our meal," he whispered to Alex as they trotted toward the road. "If we'd shared that wine the way we shared the jug in the rain, neither one of us would have won the competition."

She made a noncommittal sound that could have been agreement, but didn't add any words. Luck had really been with them for this one, even more than it had up until then. If he hadn't awakened when the clock began striking, they could have been—

"Alex, something isn't making sense here," he said as they reached the road and started across it. "I thought that entrants caught in traps are supposed to be left there until the competition is over, and then they'll be released. What sort of release would we have gotten from *this* trap?"

"The permanent sort?" she asked in turn, looking at him with a frown. "I hadn't remembered about that, mainly because this isn't the first time we've come close. Even that rock tunnel could have killed us, if we'd been forced to stay there long enough without food and water. It looks like someone has made the competition more than ordinarily interesting for us."

"Not 'us,' " he responded with a headshake, suddenly and utterly convinced. "Me. I'll bet any amount you name that this trail is supposed to be mine, and you were meant to be elsewhere. As your friend Baron Sellin told me when he and I first met, I'm considered the one to beat among the entrants. If someone wanted to beat me badly enough and he didn't care to take any chances . . ."

"Then he would have had this trail gimmicked," Alex finished. "It couldn't have been meant for *me*, because he would want the prize in good enough condition to be claimed. But wait a minute. What if the object was to *stop* the competition rather than win it? Then the recipient of all this *was* supposed to be me."

"But who would want the competition stopped?" Tiran asked, considering the point. "The only possibility I can think of is that Vilimi, Lord Arthon. He's really lost it over you, but not so far that he'd want *you* hurt. He probably believes that with me out of the way, you'll be able to eliminate any other finalists. That means this trail is still meant for me, and is one I'm not supposed to find the end of."

"Only if your guesswork is true," she countered, stopping near the entry they'd already used and turning to look up at him. "Personally, I think you're seeing rivals behind every tree and rock, but not because they're there or responsible. Sellin is a blowhard who talks a better game than he plays, and Arthon is having fun with a meaningless attempt at seduction. I can't see either of them arranging something like this."

"Maybe you can't see it because you refuse to look," Tiran couldn't keep from pointing out, stung by her comment about rivals. Damn it, after what they'd shared there shouldn't have been even the *thought* of rivals! "Sellin isn't a man you can dismiss with a shrug, and Arthon is deeper than you make him out. Underestimating people and situations is a good way to get killed, but you enjoy twisting things to conform to your opinions. Changing the opinions instead is too far beneath you."

"I see everything I need to," she shot back, her tone cold and distant. "*You're* the important one and I'm just along for the ride, so why don't I take two steps back from your exalted presence and just stay there? The practice will undoubtedly do me good."

"What are you talking about?" Tiran asked, confusion now swirling around him. "And how did this turn into an argument? I thought that after what happened between us—"

"I don't care to discuss that," she said immediately, still cold and distant. "Not now, and maybe not ever. How about calling a break on the time-wasting, and giving me a hand in finding the trail?"

She turned away from him again with that, and began Shifting through test forms. Tiran was totally bewildered, not to mention speechless with shock. She didn't want to *discuss* what they'd shared, not now and maybe not ever? Was it possible she hadn't felt it the same, hadn't been taken the way he'd been? Could he possibly have hurt her? If he had he'd never forgive himself, but . . .

But if he'd hurt her, he would have known. The flare of guilt and horror died again as common sense asserted itself, reminding him that he wasn't exactly inexperienced with women. He'd learned how they would react to the various things he did, and also whether or not they were enjoying it. Granted, he'd been more emotionally involved than ever before, but he hadn't been dead. He knew without a doubt that Alex had enjoyed herself.

So what was her problem? He sat down in the damp grass to watch her Shift, letting his mind touch one idea after another, finally running into a possibility that felt solid. That fear he'd noticed in her, the one he'd been certain he understood. She'd been afraid of finding something real with him, and now that they'd tested the possibility, she was trying to start a fight. That had to mean she was beginning to fall in love with him in spite of herself, and that was her problem. But why? And what could he do about it?

"We have a problem," Alex announced abruptly, almost reading his mind. "I can't find the trail."

"You got nothing in *any* of the forms?" Tiran asked, frowning as he shifted mental gears. "But you went through every possibility. Where does that leave us?"

"In a world where midnight brings out the ghouls," she said, crouching in front of him. "If the pattern is started over here, the trail should be visible. But the pattern's already repeated twice, and now could be something else to confuse us. The big question is, what would the something else be?"

"I see two possibilities," Tiran answered, scratching his chin with a thumb. "Either the trail can be found only through a sense we haven't used before, or we're supposed to combine two or more of the ones we *have* used. It's also possible we're supposed to use pure deduction, but we'll leave that as a last resort. It would fit better at the end of the trail."

"I've already gone through a lot of the combinations," Alex said, reaching down for a blade of grass. "Sight and hearing, hearing and smell, smell and sight. Not all of them, of course, but a lot. Doing all of them one by one will take forever, so let's start with the unused senses. Should we include anything beyond taste and touch?"

"Not until we eliminate those," Tiran said, stirring in preparation for standing up. "Number six is usually a matter of opinion, and we don't know how the trailmaker saw—Hey! I don't believe it can be this easy."

He'd put his hand to the ground before getting up, and had immediately felt the vibration. That he hadn't felt it through his boots or his body said he'd found the trail, but it definitely seemed too easy. Just touch the ground and go?

"It may be easy, but it isn't obvious," Alex said, moving her own hand from place to place on the ground. "I can't feel this with anything but my palm and fingers; it wasn't there to bare feet in Shifted form. And the vibration seems to be strongest in *that* direction."

She nodded along a line deeper into the woods, one that led directly away from the inn. If they'd found the trail as soon as they came through the entry, they wouldn't have ended up risking their lives. But they also wouldn't have had a chance to eat and rest—and learn something important—so they'd taken the right direction after all.

"If that's the way, then let's get to it," Tiran said, standing up to brush leaves and grass off himself. "The sooner we get to the end of the trail, the sooner we can take a real rest."

"Why don't *you* give it a rest?" Alex said sourly, already having straightened. "Every other sentence out of your mouth is an order, and I'm getting tired of it. If you're looking for someone to push around, go back and choose one of those ghouls. You'll find it easier doing that than succeeding with me."

"Someone to push around," Tiran echoed thoughtfully, looking down at her. "Aside from insisting we stick together—which I think I've earned the right to do— when have I pushed you around? When have I even hinted I wanted to?"

"When we have the time to make lists, I'll answer your question in detail," she returned, but despite the dark Tiran was sure he saw her flush. "Right now, let's get on with it. Once I'm out of here, I'm going to soak in a tub for a week."

The last was said in a mutter as she moved off, calling for nothing in the way of a response. Tiran followed, trying to scratch the itch of curiosity, but it was too far out of reach. Had she accused him simply to start another argument, or was there a reason behind the complaint that he'd missed? Right then he couldn't tell, but maybe after some time had passed . . .

They moved through the woods at a decent pace, the strong moonlight helping quite a lot. Every once in a while Alex would bend to check the direction, and then they would continue on. She made no attempt to talk to him, and her silence was more brooding than thoughtful.

Tiran found himself growing impatient, but forced the emotion down. Eventually Alex would *have* to talk to him, even if she didn't want to. Pushing her right now would be foolish, not to mention useless. Let her get used to the idea of what had happened, and then he could help her to accept it.

A good chunk of time went by, and then they noticed they were coming out of the woods. Tiran had been faintly surprised when they weren't attacked by anything, but it was a good thing he hadn't decided that meant they were home free. As they left the trees behind, they discovered something else that would soon be left behind. The ground under their feet.

"They've got to be kidding," Alex said, standing at the edge of what was a large canyon and staring across. "If this was the right trail that has to be the right entry, but how the hell are we supposed to reach it? Climb down a mile, trot across another mile, then climb back up? It isn't possible."

"It has to be possible," Tiran said, stepping aside to avoid Alex's wildly blowing hair. Across the wide span of dark, empty air and about twenty feet down, a faint glow insisted an entry was present. It was more than tantalizingly out of reach; even in the dark he could see that climbing would be out, in natural form or any other. There had to be a way to reach it, but just then he couldn't think of one.

"You're right, it does have to be possible," Alex said suddenly, her eyes narrowed. "When we first got here it was daylight, and I think that was a clue. Have you ever gone soaring?"

"Only off cliffs over deep water," Tiran answered, abruptly unhappy with the conversation's turn. "Even in condor shape it doesn't always work, and if the water isn't there, you go splat. How much soaring have *you* done?"

"Enough to be willing to try it here," she responded, her tone telling him she'd made up her mind. "But not until the sun is up. I want every bit of an edge I can get. We can take turns storing up some more sleep, and then we can get on to the next part of the trail."

"Assuming we survive this part," Tiran countered, but the words made no impression on her. If there had been any other option he would have shown her what being pushed around was like, but without another choice, putting his foot down would have been useless. He was trapped, and in more ways than one.

"Do you want to sleep first or second?" Alex asked, moving back from the edge to look around for a good spot. "I'm wide enough awake that I don't mind taking first watch."

"Then it's all yours," Tiran agreed, not about to give her grounds for yet another argument. If she needed to be in charge for a while, then let her do it. If he couldn't trust *her* to keep a proper watch, he couldn't trust anyone. "Wake me in a couple of hours, sooner if you have to, especially if I start to roll over the edge of the canyon."

"Too bad you added that last," she murmured as she followed him to the foot of the nearest tree. "If you hadn't . . ."

She let her words trail off with a smile in her voice, and Tiran didn't have to ask what she meant. Ignoring it all, he took off his swordbelt, lay down in the grass, then pillowed his head on his arm. With his weapons close to his free hand he had no other provision to make, and was quickly asleep. Soldiers learned how to do that, a knack most of the worlds envied.

He was awake as soon as the hand touched his shoulder, but it was only Alex calling him for his turn at watch. He sat up to rub his eyes, and by the time he took his hands down, she was already curled up on the ground. So much for any possibility of conversation, but maybe it was just as well. She did need to get some sleep, and he had thinking he wanted to do.

By the time the sun was completely up, Tiran had given up trying to think of another way to reach the entry. Soaring on bird wings was probably the only way for those who weren't magic users, but he still didn't like it. It wouldn't have been easy trying it if he'd been alone, but he actually hated the thought of Alex risking her life. If only it were possible to stay there or turn back . . . but even if it were, she'd never agree . . . the end of the trail demanded that they find it, *she* demanded . . .

Tiran sighed and turned away from the canyon rim, the sight of a small ribbon of water at the bottom having done nothing to reassure him. If either of them fell from that height, even a good, deep river would not help. But what choice did they have? They had to go on, and *he* had to win.

He stood over Alex's sleeping form for a moment, wishing things could be different between them. No, make that *normal*. Things were already so different—if he had to face her in the finals, there was no telling what could happen—specifically, to him. He knew *he* couldn't hurt *her*, not ever, not for any reason . . .

Dropping down on one knee, he gave in to the sudden urge to taste those lips again. Bending over let him reach down to kiss her, not the least regret in him for taking advantage like that. What he really wanted to do was make love to her again, so the kiss should be an acceptable compromise. She stirred and murmured with pleasure, her lips quickly responding to his, and then she came more fully awake—

"What the hell do you think you're doing?" she demanded as soon as she'd pushed free, those silver eyes blazing up at him. "I was sleeping!"

"And I was waking you," he answered with a grin he couldn't swallow. "You weren't complaining to start with, so what's bothering you now?"

"You're what's bothering me," she growled, sitting up in a way that sent Tiran quickly to his feet and backing away a couple of steps. His emotions said she couldn't hurt him, but his mind knew better. "I don't like being taken advantage of, and if you ever try something like this again, I'll say it in a way you'll never forget."

"*You* are what I'll never forget," Tiran said, that sense of impatience forcing the words from him. "We sing together like a waterfall and a summer breeze, but you've decided to ignore that. I don't know why, and frankly, I'm getting to the point of not caring. Since the woman I love also loves me, I won't let anything or anyone come between us. Not even her."

"You're making assumptions with the usual result," she answered steadily enough, but was no longer meeting his eyes. "No one has even said anything about liking, not to mention love. As a working team we're fair to middling, but that's as far as it goes. I don't feel what you do."

"You're lying, and we both know it," Tiran countered at once as she stood, relief and elation filling him like rain in a barrel. "It has to be something serious that's making you lie so we'll need to talk about it, but first things first. There's a trail we have to follow, and then we can take a togetherness break. Just like the one last night."

She turned and hurried wordlessly off to some nearby bushes, her swordbelt held in her hand, and that brought Tiran's grin back. He'd gotten a glimpse of her expression when he said he was going to make love to her again, and if ever a woman was willing and eager—For her own reasons she was refusing to admit it, but that was perfectly all right. He'd find out what was bothering her, and they would fix it together.

Tiran was prepared for something of a wait, but Alex was back and ready in just a few minutes. They walked silently to the canyon rim, looked out over the edge, then Alex Shifted into condor form. Tiran did the same, but made no effort to launch himself. This was one of the times he wanted Alex to go first, and he would bring up the rear.

Alex spread her wings and leaped into the glistening morning air, and Tiran held his breath until it was clear she'd caught a thermal. She planed away in a lazy spiral, heading for the entry in a roundabout but necessary meander, and that made it his turn. He'd hated flying since his best—and only—friend had fallen and died when they were boys; fear was a cold and heavy knot around his insides, but over the years he'd taught himself to do what was necessary.

And right then, flying was necessary. Or soaring, which, for him, was worse. No control, nothing to use the bulk

of his skill on, chancy and dangerous and subject to the
vagaries of thin air. He wished he could close his eyes—
had to remember to spread his wings wide—just step off—
there's nothing to it—if you die she'll have to go on
alone—

And that thought launched him over the edge, reaching
to catch the air with his wings, legs tucked up, sound
whistling past his ears. It was warm in the sunshine, and
the warmth wrapped gentle hands around him, smoothing
his feathers, sending him circling. His wings touched the
air as his fingers had touched the ground, letting him know
that this *was* the trail. Follow it and succeed, lose it and—

Tiran didn't need to be told that birds don't sweat, but
for an unending string of minutes there was one that did.
He sweated trying to follow the path Alex blazed, sweated
keeping his eyes off the ground so far below. Alex seemed
to be enjoying the time, maybe even taking longer than necessary . . . Tiran sweated and clenched nonexistent teeth,
soothing himself with the promise to beat her if she
was . . .

And then she was heading directly for the faint gleam of
the entry, almost invisible in the bright light of day. She
swung down at it from slightly above, gauging time and
distance, ready to fold her wings and slide through. Down,
down—and then she was gone, safely into the entry and the
next world.

And now he had to do the same, only he wasn't certain he
could. His body trembled with strain, desperate to keep the
air from spilling out of his wings . . . plunging him down
to that ribbon of water on the canyon floor . . . just the way
others had fallen . . . He couldn't . . . couldn't . . .

"Your Majesty, Limis has good news," Merwin said,
drawing Reynar back from brooding. "He's found the key
to the changes made in Tiran d'Iste's trail, and feels certain
he'll be able to change it back."

"*Will* be able to change it back," Reynar said, picking up
on the point immediately. "Why isn't he already doing it?"

"He said he'll need Sisal to speak the spell with him, one of them to suppress the original spell, the other to make the change and protect it. No sense in canceling what was, only to have it re-form as soon as you look away. His words, Sire. He's gone to help Sisal comb through the bystanders, which will speed up the process. As soon as they find the miscreant, they'll get to work on their spell."

"While I deal with the one responsible," Reynar said, this time causing poor Merwin to flinch. The king had little idea what his expression was like, but he could guess. His smile would be the worst of it, definitely the worst . . .

CHAPTER TWELVE

I shifted as I sailed through the entry, hit the ground rolling, and from there to my feet. I almost lost my sword and dagger with that maneuver, too much water having warped and stretched the sheaths. I pronounced a few nasty but very satisfying words under my breath, glanced around at the dusty but unpopulated landscape, then gave my attention back to the entry. I'd made it through, but Tiran was still on the other side.

Tiran. Thinking of him by name like that made me furious, but I no longer had a choice. The night before had changed everything, and not simply for the worse. For the horrible, for the unthinkably awful, for the one thing I'd dreaded more than anything. I hated him for being more than I'd ever imagined a man could be, hated him fiercely . . .

But that wasn't all I felt, and he still hadn't come through the entry. I'd enjoyed the soaring more than ever before, though somehow I'd gotten the feeling he *wasn't* enjoying it. And maybe even having trouble. It was hard picturing him not being able to do something, but what if he panicked and fell? What if he—

My mouth turned dry and I began a step to return to the entry, but that was when he came flying through. His Shift was enough too late that it threw him off-balance, and

237

instead of doing as I had, he landed hard on his right side. I waited for him to get up, but all he did was roll onto his back and lie still.

"Tiran, are you all right?" I asked, seeing that his eyes were closed. "You didn't—break anything, did you?"

No answer. He lay there dragging in lungfuls of air, and didn't say a word. For a very long moment I couldn't understand, and then suddenly it all came clear. I walked over slowly to crouch beside him, then took his hand in both of mine.

"It's all right," I said softly with assurance in my voice. "It was a terrible thing to have to go through, but it's over now. You're finally safe, and you won't have to do it again. You made it, and now it's behind you."

"So *you* say," he muttered, but his breathing slowed a little and his eyes opened. He also realized he was crushing my hand with the grip he had on it, and loosened up a bit. "Thank you. That was just what I needed to hear right now, and I appreciate your making the effort. I don't just hate flying, it also scares the hell out of me."

"So I noticed," I said, starting to get mad again. Most people are ashamed of the things that frighten them, usually going out of their way to hide all trace of them. So what does Tiran d'Iste do? Lies there obviously having been terrified, and *admits* it! It was enough to make you want to hit him with something hard; the situation would be unchanged, but it would make you feel so much better about it.

"Give me another minute, and then we can get going," he said, tightening his hold on my hand to keep me from getting up. "You know, it's a good thing you went first. If I hadn't had my woman to follow, I'd still be standing at the rim of the canyon shaking."

"Like hell," I growled, pulling my hand free before straightening. "I'm not your woman, and even if you'd been alone you would have made it through this entry. Tell your stories to someone who'll believe them."

"Now there you go again," he said, sitting up to run a hand through his long black hair. "Every time you open your mouth lately, you're blaming me for something else. Would you like to tell me what you really think I'm guilty of?"

I caught a glimpse of annoyance in those green eyes before turning away, closing the subject in the only way I could. Was I supposed to tell him he was guilty of overwhelming me in bed, of casually taking the control I usually had and making me want more? He was the man women usually dream about, an absolute dominant who was so sure of himself that he found it unnecessary to try to control others. Except in bed, where he proved his right to do anything he pleased. One taste and I was already hooked, ready to believe he was the man born to be my other half.

But that wasn't what I was looking for, what I couldn't afford to let myself be tempted by. If I gave in we would never live happily ever after, but he refused to see that. Maybe if I told him how *I* saw it . . . No, a man couldn't be expected to understand, not even one like him.

"Turning your back on a problem only puts it in a position where it can unexpectedly sneak up on you," he said after a moment, the sound of his rising coming with the words. "Facing it lets you dispose of it more easily, especially if you have the help of someone else. Someone who cares. Tell me what's bothering you, and let me help with getting rid of it."

"Now there's an offer I can't refuse," I said, turning back to look up at him. "What's bothering me is you, and now that you've been told, I expect your help in getting rid of it. Start helping."

"What I've started doing is fantasizing about how much fun it might be to beat you," he replied, his tone very dry. "I doubt if anyone would deny you could use a beating, but I've been telling myself it isn't something to build a relationship on. Love is what you build on, and I'd much rather give you that. Let's take a break, and then we can get back to your problem."

He started to put his arms around me, but pure panic has the blessed benefit of helping you to move faster than normal. I was out of reach almost before he could blink, and fully intended to stay there.

"Don't you dare touch me," I hissed, silently admitting that if he did I was a goner. "We're not here to take breaks, we're here to find a trail. If you're not interested, then I'll continue on alone."

"No need to get wild," he murmured, those green eyes studying me so carefully that I felt as if he were seeing into my head. "If you'd rather take that break later, I can wait. But after a while anticipation becomes frustration, so let's get with it. This time, I think, we have to follow a taste."

"Right," I muttered, really needing to look away from him. I'd had one taste of what he could do, and another might make it impossible to remember what I had to. But I wanted that taste and had a feeling he knew I did, and that was why he refused to let the subject drop. Anticipation and frustration. Damn him, right down to his boots.

"Now isn't that interesting," he said from behind me, and I knew our previous topic had been temporarily shelved. "Are you getting what I am, or is my imagination playing tricks?"

Since I didn't know what he was getting, I stuffed everything of a personal nature into a mental box and began to look around. The world we'd come into was a dusty one, a gentle wind blowing the dust around. In this particular spot trees were more the exception than the rule, but there was a good deal of scrub brush. Soft, low hills dipped in and out in all directions, the very blue sky had a couple of lazy white clouds, and the morning sun was warm and comfortable. There was no immediate sign of a road or people, but a small flock of birds wheeled happily through the air to our right.

And then, as I began turning slowly, I spotted the first bush. It was small with thick yellow leaves, and a faint odor of nicely cooked meat was coming from it. That in itself was unusual enough, but there were three other bushes just like it, all with different scents. One was fresh-baked bread soaked in butter, another was eggs and bacon, and the last was cheese and fruit. Four bushes making a ten-foot square, not to mention making my mouth water.

"But this is smell rather than taste," I pointed out, bothered by the difference. "And it's also very obvious. If those bushes belong here, I belong in a sewing circle."

"You're right about it being obvious, and also about the bushes not belonging," Tiran said, his voice as thoughtful as mine. "The part about it being smell, though—Are you saying you can't taste the food those things are projecting? I can, and that's only one of the two possibilities."

"What's the second?" I asked, forced to admit I could also taste the food. And there was something else about the idea, something I was right then missing.

"The second possibility is that we're supposed to actually taste the bush, or at least a leaf or two," he said. "In some way the taste would be different, and that difference would tell us which direction to choose."

"That's a little *too* creative," I decided, frowning at the bush that smelled like meat. "If the leaf isn't made out of meat it won't taste like meat, and it might even be poisoned. In fact, the more I think about it, the more convinced I become that it's a trap. If we use it right, we get pointed to the trail; if we don't, we get poisoned or misdirected. With things the way they are, one mistake can be as fatal as the other."

"Okay, I'm convinced," he decided in turn. "Tasting the leaves is as obvious as the presence of the bushes, which means it's definitely too obvious. We have to taste without actually tasting, and figure out our direction from that. Along with deduction."

"The kind of deduction we only half used last time," I pointed out, realizing my inner mind had been thinking about that. "We found the trail by accident when you touched the ground, but we could have found the same by being logical. After all, we did get to the point of deciding the previously unused senses were now being used. But here—here we might have trouble."

"Because we're being offered *too* much," he said, nodding as he looked from one bush to the next. "But we should also be able to confirm our final choice—if it's the right choice. If we can't decide any other way, we'll have to work backward."

"That assumes not all the choices can be confirmed," I said, shaking my head. "We can't depend on that, not this late in the game. We'll have to choose one of those bushes by logic, confirm the choice, then go with it. Doubting our deductions can keep us here better than the tightest of traps."

"I'm not sure I agree, but we can argue about it later," he said with a sigh. "Now we need to make a logical choice that can be confirmed. Shall we start with the question of which of these dishes we would sit down to right now if we could?"

"Right now it seems to be getting on toward lunchtime," I answered, glancing up at the sky. "Many people have cheese and fruit for lunch, but we missed breakfast. On top of that, we didn't come through at the *proper* time. We spent part of the day and all night in the previous world, not to mention the bath break we took at the oasis. In order to choose that way, we'd need to know what sort of schedule we're *supposed* to be on."

"Then that's our answer." He nodded to show he'd already come to the same conclusion. "Since it's impossible to decide when we *should* have come through, we have to say it could have been at any time. Three of those bushes represent meals, and meals are usually eaten at specific times. It doesn't matter which of those dishes you have at the meal, you're still having the meal."

"But one of them represents something you would take at any time, even for a snack in passing," I added in support, both of us looking at the bush that smelled like fresh-baked bread. "If that line of logic holds, we ought to be able to confirm the choice. So how are we supposed to do it?"

"Good question," he muttered with a frown. "That logic we've been using so freely says it should have something to do with taste, but *whose* taste? Ours, or a Shift form's?"

"Ours," I responded at once. "The meat is cooked, so are the eggs and bacon, and so forth. If we Shifted, the choice might well turn out to be the cheese and fruit. Do we want to drag in that sort of confusion?"

"Thanks anyway," he said with a shake of his head. "I have enough of my own kind of confusion. So the taste has to be ours, without any enhancement. If that's so, let's start tasting."

He walked toward the bread-bush, but not, as I thought at first, to pull off a leaf to eat. He stopped in front of the bush, inhaled deeply, then made noises with his mouth and tongue.

"I love fresh bread with butter melted into it," he said. "The taste always reminds me of home when I was very young. My mother would bake me a small loaf all my own, and I would eat it while I followed her around the kitchen. Come and get a taste of this, and you'll know what I mean."

I started toward him, attracted more by what he'd said than by a love of bread, but then I stopped. His idea was a good one, but I'd thought of a way to confirm some of my previous guesswork.

"I think I ought to try 'tasting' one of the other bushes first," I said, drawing a look of surprise from him. "I have a feeling the first bush you try had better be the right choice, because you're going to be stuck with it. It won't help much to know that, but it *will* confirm their sneakiness."

"And knowing just how sneaky your opponent is, is always an extra point for your side," he agreed. "I'll try the rest of them, and then you'll take your shot."

He went to the three other bushes in turn, "tasted" each of them, then stepped back with a nod toward me. I began with the bacon and eggs, using it as the breakfast I hadn't had. Inhaling above the bush made me feel as though I had a mouthful of crisp bacon and eggs scrambled just right, and I couldn't help trying to chew them. There was nothing there, of course, but the taste was marvelous.

After that I tried the other bushes, which turned out to be a major disappointment. The meat was dry and overdone, the cheese and fruit had definitely been sitting around too long, and the bread—if the butter wasn't rancid, then the bread itself was way beyond moldy. A quick second sniff of the bacon and eggs told me they were just as good as the first time, and that pretty much settled it.

"Apparently they anticipated someone trying to work backward," I told Tiran as I reluctantly left my breakfast. "That bread you enjoyed so much really turned my stomach."

"And I couldn't handle bacon that was half raw and half burned, or eggs that were drippy as well as spoiled," he told me with a grin. "The first one you try is the only one that appeals to you. If we hadn't used logic to make our choice, we'd be in the middle of an argument now."

"Or on our way in the wrong direction," I said. "Since we happen to know the right direction, let's start using it. I wasn't all that hungry before, but now I'm ravenous."

"That makes two of us," he said, the grin changed to a smile. "If we don't find some place reasonably close where we can buy a meal, we'll have to Shift and hunt one. At the very least, there are birds."

I nodded to show I'd seen them, then started out in a line directly past the bread-bush. According to the sun the direction was southeast—if direction ran the same in this world. Hopefully we would be out of it before the question became relevant.

We trudged along over the low hills in silence for a while, my attention on looking for signs of something other than birds that could be hunted. There didn't seem to be much, but that wasn't the disappointment it might have been. We'd have to Shift in order to hunt, and a couple of minutes' worth of thought told me I'd be better off starving. I'd seen Tiran in animal form while I was a

member of the same species; the next time I would either
go completely feral, or hand myself over to him without
the slightest argument. Since I had a very strong hunch
which of those things would actually happen, I'd damned
well stay in human form as long as—humanly—possible.

"Do you have a wedding gown already made for you?"
my companion asked suddenly. "It just occurred to me that
you might have to have one made, and that would delay
the wedding. I hate the idea of needing to wait, but that's
not something that should be rushed. My mother told us
she wore *her* mother's gown, but even then the alterations
took time."

The rush of excited anticipation sweeping through me
was appalling, even more so in that I hadn't expected the
feeling. The majority *I* didn't want to marry anyone, but
that one traitorous part inside had gone completely over to
Tiran's stand. It believed he would win the competition no
matter what, and gloried in the thought of the wedding to
follow. I felt a strong disgust over that sort of mindlessness, the sort that considered only today, never tomorrow.
Stretch out in the sun and enjoy the warmth, forgetting
all about the storm that's due and getting closer by the
minute.

"Well?" he said, obviously not caring for my silence.
"Aren't you going to answer me?"

"There's no gown, because there won't be a marriage," I replied, deciding against beating around the
bush. "I don't want to marry anyone, and as you pointed
out, I'm used to getting what I want. We spoiled brats
always are."

"As long as you're sure you know what you want," he
said, ignoring the fact that I looked at the landscape rather
than at him. "Don't you think it's time we discussed the
subject, just so we know more fully where we stand? Yesterday was very special for me, and I happen to believe it
was the same for you. Refusing to discuss it doesn't change
that, it only makes it worse. Tell me what you have against
marriage."

"Tell me what *you* had against it," I countered, kicking at a small stone in my path. "If you were already married you wouldn't be here right now, so what kept *you* from indulging? And don't try to claim you couldn't find someone willing. You still don't have that, but it isn't stopping you."

"No, there were any number of women who were willing," he answered slowly, considering the question. "I'm not poor and I'm not a nonentity, and a man in my position can always find willingness. Obviously I was the one who was unwilling, because none of those women was the right one. I suppose you can say I was waiting to meet *you*, and now that I have I'm downright eager. Can you honestly say you never thought about meeting the right man?"

"Yes, I think I can," I responded, examining the words to be sure they were true. "Men were never unknown mysteries to me, not even before I started trying them in bed. Some were all right to talk to, most were too ready to boast about skills they didn't have or talents they *wished* they had. I could never understand why girls were so eager to tie themselves to them, to give up everything they might be for a secondhand existence. Personally, I'd rather be dead than spend a lifetime in boredom."

"I can see it never occurred to you that the right man would not let you be bored," he said, a hint of excitement in his tone. "You would be in love with him and he with you, and that would make all the difference. Together you would be able to accomplish anything."

"Like what?" I challenged, hating the way the same road had to be traveled over and over. "Would I be free to go and do anything I liked, or would he want me to stay with him while he did as *he* liked? And even if he did go with *me*, how long would he find it amusing to tag after me? And he *would* be tagging after me while I took a good long look around. There are things I've decided to do, and if I let something keep me from doing them, I'll end up hating myself forever."

"Forever's a long time," he said with a sigh, the trace of excitement gone. "And how can a man who really cares about you want to make you hate yourself? I can see where you're coming from, but I can also see you're on the wrong road. The greatest benefit of being in love is that it turns two individuals into a single entity that never has to be alone again. They both want the same thing, and what pleases one pleases the other. *I* know it works like that, but you still have to learn it. And you will."

Without warning I was suddenly in his arms, swept close and being kissed before I had any idea it would happen. My response was so immediate it was horrible; I felt as if I'd been waiting an eon for that kiss, and now that it was here I had to join in with complete abandon. My hands were pressed flat to the broad strength of his back, our bodies touched at as many points as possible, our mouths trying to merge us even more. He held me with the complete assurance of unchallenged possession, draining all my strength of will and taking it for his own. I couldn't have stopped him to save my life, but after too short a time he raised his head.

"You feel exactly the way I do," he stated, arms still supporting me, hands still caressing. "Alex, you and I are two halves of the same coin, a thousand times blessed because we've found each other. Most people live their whole lives without finding their true mates; throwing away what we have would be a crime against the universe. We'll work it out between us to your complete satisfaction—that you have my word on. And in case you were wondering, I never break my word."

The murmur of his voice was like a caress in itself, the green eyes looking down at me reflecting the sunlight of promised bliss. I didn't want to push myself out of his arms but I did it anyway, took a deep breath, then started walking again. It took a moment for me to regain my proper balance, and by then he was walking beside me again.

"This time I don't hear you insisting nothing happened," he remarked after another moment. "Are you ready to admit you want me as badly as I want you, or do I have to prove the point again?"

"You did this to me on purpose," I muttered, so deep into self-disgust that I was nearly drowning. "I didn't want to be in love with anyone, but you didn't care. You went right ahead and took advantage of me, and now it's too late to change anything. I hope you're really proud."

"Hey, don't do that," he protested, having turned my face to him and seen the wetness I could feel in my eyes. I wasn't actually crying—not yet, anyway—but he seemed to think I was. He pulled me to him for the second time, but only to hold me in the circle of his arms. He was trying to comfort me, apparently having no idea how far from comforting it really was.

"Alex, you can't blame either one of us for this," he said, stroking my hair and patting my back. "Once we met it was inevitable, because we were meant to be together. If we weren't, nothing I did could have made it happen, and you must believe that. My taking you to bed would have been just another fling, not the final bonding it was. I was hoping it would happen; you were hoping it wouldn't. Happily for both of us, I turned out to be right."

"You were hoping," I said, raising my head from his chest to look up at him. "I practically had to rape you, and all the while you were hoping. Because you knew there would be this—this—bonding, or maybe 'chaining' would be a better word. You made me force you into bed, the place you intended to end up all along, and I was supposed to think you were doing me a favor. If that's your idea of a favor, remind me to tell you where to put it."

This time I pushed at him with the heels of my hands, forcing him back with a grunt for the jab in his ribs. He was also flinching from the words I'd thrown at him, understanding a little too late that he'd said a little too much.

"All right, I'll admit I maneuvered you into the place I wanted you to be," he said as I stalked off, following immediately behind. "If it had turned out I was wrong I would owe you an apology, but I wasn't wrong. You and

I belong together, and when you calm down you'll see it's the truth. I won't apologize for refusing to lose the woman who's my other half."

Heavy stubbornness was coloring his tone by then, the unmistakable sign of a man who was used to getting what he wanted. Tiran d'Iste was a survivor and a winner, and this time what he'd won was me. I was so furious with myself for falling into his trap that there are no words to describe it, but I wasn't the only one the fury was aimed at. He was the one who'd set the trap, and I'd never forgive him for doing it.

"You don't look like you're calming down very much," he said after a few minutes of brisk walking. "I'm glad you're not crying, but this is almost as bad. Are we going to have another fight?"

"No," I answered shortly, still keeping to the same pace. The only thing I wanted just then was an end to the competition, or at least to *that* part of it.

"Well, if we aren't going to fight, let's make up from the last fight," he said, his grin so strong I could hear it. "I've been looking forward to that break I promised you."

This time I didn't answer, mostly because I couldn't trust my voice to hold steady. Damn the man, I *did* want him, and that was also his fault. Why couldn't he have turned out to be no better than the others I'd tried? Because he was meant to mean more to me than all the others combined . . . ? Because he really was my other half . . . ?

"Now you're looking depressed and miserable," he observed with a sigh. "Is that what the thought of my lovemaking does to you? If it is, we'll have to talk. I don't ever want to be the cause of making you feel like that."

"Your concern comes a little late," I couldn't help pointing out, words I regretted almost immediately but refused to take back. How I felt *was* his fault; circumstance might have turned it into something he'd never intended, but if he hadn't shown up to begin with . . .

I forced myself away from unprofitable lines of thought, concentrating on where we were going and enjoying the silence my companion was now engaged in. We still hadn't come across anything like a road, but we topped one rise to see some kind of structure in the near distance ahead.

Another few minutes of walking brought us close enough to recognize the structure as a series of pavilions, with a fancy fence and gate between them and us. The fence was wide decorative swirls that couldn't have kept out an infant, and the gate stood open, with a single man seated at a table in front of it. The man wasn't busy doing anything at all, but he didn't look up until we stopped in front of the table.

"Welcome-to-the-pleasure-halls-of-Lord-Misten-bless-ed-be-his-name," the man said all at once, a memorized speech rather than an actual greeting. "Entrance fees must be paid in gold."

"Gold?" Tiran echoed, brows going high. "You can't have many people entering at those prices, unless the ones around here are all wealthy."

"Those are not local prices, they're stranger prices," the man answered primly, cold dark eyes in a narrow face. He wore a green robe patterned in gold, but didn't seem comfortable in it. "Can you deny you two are strangers? Go ahead, try to deny it."

"Of course we're strangers," Tiran said with a faint smile that bothered the seated man. "But where we come from, 'stranger' isn't another word for 'fool.' Thanks anyway, but we'll forgo the pleasures of your pleasure halls."

The man actually let us turn and begin to walk away, possibly thinking we were bluffing. When he saw that we weren't, he dropped his own bluff.

"All right, all right, you can come back now," he said testily, unhappy about being pressed. "I'm supposed to get gold from strangers if I *can*, but silver's better than nothing. Three silver for each of you."

"Three silver for both of us, and no more bargaining," Tiran told him flatly without walking back. "That's more than I want to pay and more than you need to get, but I'm too tired to waste any more time. Say yes or no, but understand first that you won't get a chance to change your mind."

"Yes," the man grudged through gritted teeth, his eyes no longer quite meeting ours. "I thank you for your generosity, lord, and beg your pardon for needing to ask for the silver now."

Tiran dug into his swordbelt as he ambled back, then dropped three silver coins on the table in front of the man. I didn't know why he was acting so high-handed, and wasn't certain it was a good idea. Making enemies so casually in a strange place can be hazardous to your health.

"A thousand thanks, my lord, and please be good enough to enter," the man whispered, gathering up the silver that Tiran had tossed on the table. "This miserable creature hopes your visit will be a pleasant one."

Tiran made no attempt to answer what had become pure groveling, putting a hand to my back instead and urging me through the gate. He continued to say nothing until we were almost halfway to the series of pavilions, and then he sighed.

"No, I'm *not* sure that was the smart thing to do, but I had no choice," he said, somehow reading my mind. "I've been in that kind of situation before, and trying to treat the man like an equal proved to be a mistake. Did you notice that he's a slave?"

"No," I answered, surprised and a little shocked. "What makes you think he's a slave?"

"That collar around his neck, under the robe," Tiran said, looking around rather than at me. "It's there for anyone who knows enough to look, but otherwise isn't obvious. When I spoke to him as though he were free, he all but sneered in my face. Treating him like dirt got him bowing and scraping and also soothed him. He'd been put back in the place he knew he belonged, and by doing that I also established my own place."

"That has to be one of the sickest things I've ever heard," I couldn't help saying. "Settling so completely into slavery that you resent anyone who tries to get you out of it. Actually believing that that's where you belong."

"For him, that *is* where he belongs," Tiran responded with a shrug. "It's his opinion that counts in a situation like this, and fighting it is a waste of time we don't have. I'm hoping that going along with the expected will at least get us a meal before the trap starts to close. And it *will* close, so let's keep our eyes open. No indulging in anything that isn't absolutely necessary."

I started to ask if that was the extent of his orders, then changed my mind. Not only didn't he know he'd annoyed me, he wouldn't have understood there was anything to be annoyed *about*. Men who were that used to being in command never did.

We crossed lush grass on the way to the pavilions, and even before we got there we were able to hear soft, sweet music. The pavilions were large rooms walled with sheer silk in pastel colors, some roofed, some not. Figures moved around inside, and one of them came to hold the silk aside before we found it necessary to do it ourselves.

This time there was no doubt about the man being a slave; nothing in the way of clothing obscured the shiny collar around his neck—or any other part of him, for that matter. Long blond hair and gray eyes, chest and shoulders bulging with muscle down to a lean, trim waist, below that the landscape growing even more interesting. I don't know what my expression was like, but the slave lowered his head and eyes and smiled.

"Behave yourself," Tiran growled low, smacking me once, hard, on the backside. "That's a pleasure you would not be indulging in even if we had the time. I'm a generous man, but there are some things I refuse to share."

"You try that again, and you'll be sharing your blood with the carpeting," I snarled, having trouble keeping my voice down. I'd tried kicking him after the smack, but he'd had no problem avoiding it. "I don't belong to you no matter *what* your opinion is, and I'll be damned if I let you act as if I do. You—"

"All right, enough," he interrupted, but not because I'd convinced him. "This isn't the time or the place, so let's save it for later. And don't think we won't be getting back to it."

The look in those green eyes refused to acknowledge the anger in mine, which simply confirmed my earlier conclusions. Tiran d'Iste was a problem I didn't need and one I refused to have. One way or another, I *had* to win that competition.

There were individual couches casually arranged in small groupings around the pavilion, but there were also cushions thrown down in piles on the thick, furry carpeting. The male slave had the company of three female equivalents, dressed in wisps that teased rather than covered, and suddenly they were all over Tiran. Or maybe I should say all around him. They seemed much too timid and shy to be all over anyone, and their coaxing in offering him a couch had a lot of begging to it. The big man himself smiled indulgently at the display, then went along with the coaxing.

Which for some reason got me even angrier. I didn't really *care* that he was making a fool of himself by encouraging them; it was just so embarrassing to watch. I'll never understand why grown men eat up that poor-little-helpless-me garbage when they certainly ought to know—I cut off the thought and turned away, then stalked across the floor to an armless couch near a wide glass table. The table held a fancy tray with sandwiches, so I helped myself to one and sat on the end of the couch to eat it.

The male slave came over to ask if I wanted something more elegant than sandwiches to eat, but I wasn't in the mood for elegant. Or wine, which he really tried to talk me into. I sent him after a pitcher of water just to get rid of him, then went back to swallowing down sandwiches. There was a lovely little breeze blowing through the pavilion that encouraged you to sit back and relax, but I wanted to finish eating and get out of there.

But that desire didn't seem to be shared by my companion. One of his three handmaidens had been sent to get some of the sandwiches I was eating, while a second sat behind him on his couch. The one behind massaged his shoulders while the one in front held a sandwich for him to take bites out of, and the third would probably have been kissing his feet if he hadn't sent her somewhere. The cozy little scene was enough to have turned the food inedible— if I'd had any idea what I was eating.

After a little while the male slave came back with the water and poured me a cup, then crouched next to me to hold it until I wanted it. He was really beautiful and his smile said he was ready to do anything I asked, but I no longer wanted to ask. It was as though my initial interest in him had been a reflex reaction of sorts, one that no longer applied as it once had. It felt as if my standards and aims had suddenly shifted, narrowing down my range of desire to a single—

"Forgive me for staring, mistress, but this slave finds you very beautiful," the man beside me said abruptly, his deep voice held low. "This pavilion is only for greeting and entertaining new arrivals until they decide what they'd like to do. There are a great number of pleasures waiting to be experienced in these halls, and I would be deeply honored if you would allow me to show them to you."

"I'm not much in the mood for pleasure right now," I told him, taking the cup he held and sniffing before tasting. The water was fresh and cold, without the least hint of anything that might have been added. That didn't mean nothing *had* been added, but I felt reckless enough to drink it anyway. If it was poisoned and I died, then I'd no longer have to worry about the competition.

"Possibly a warm bath would help to change mistress's mind," the slave murmured, leaning a little closer. "I'm fully trained for the bath, mistress, and the ladies of my master's house consider me extremely adept. It would please my master to have you confirm or deny that."

"And you wouldn't mind much either," I observed, finding it impossible not to notice. He really did want to bathe me, and the thought of being completely clean again was a heavy temptation. But the additionals, what would happen besides the bathing—my body was responding to the nearness of the slave, but he wasn't the one it really wanted . . .

Abruptly I got to my feet, then strode over to a small fountain on the far side of the room. Just a few feet beyond the fountain was pale pink silk separating the room from the lawn-green of outdoors, the opposite side of the way we'd entered. To the left and about five feet away was yellow silk, a non-wall distorting the view into the next pavilion. Someone large stood on the other side, someone who wore too much to be another slave. I could still hear gentle music coming from somewhere, soothing music that wasn't doing a damned thing to relax me.

Which wasn't the music's fault. I took another sip of my water, trying to be honest about the way I felt. Harried, depressed, irritated, impatient—that's how I felt, along with a whole stew of other emotions too mixed together to classify. I was also back into self-disgust, and this time there was a really good reason for it.

I'd been outraged when Tiran had shown jealousy over the way I'd looked at the male slave, yet five minutes later I'd wanted to hit him with something hard. And only because of the way he was acting with those girls. Right now I was staring at a fountain, but not because of how pretty it was. There was something else I couldn't bear to stare at, something that made me feel bewildered and hurt . . .

"This can't be what he felt when I looked at the slave," I whispered to the fountain. Only a small plume of water danced into the air, but it was made up of two smaller plumes that merged into one. Two into one, two individuals becoming a single entity. But what if one of the two had a really good reason for not wanting to merge? What if that reason was a promise of misery to come, no matter how happy the merging started out being? I was more certain than ever that Tiran would never understand, but that didn't make the coming misery any less inevitable. It would be so much easier to give up and let it happen, but would that be fair? To anyone at all?

"I said that wasn't adequate." A raspy male voice broke into my thoughts, for a minute making me think the man was talking to me. I immediately turned my head to the left, only then discovering I was wrong.

The figure I'd seen through the yellow silk was obviously a guard of some sort, proclaimed by the sword he wore and a size that was an easy match to Tiran's. He also had on an outfit that was mostly leather, one that was meant more to impress than to protect. He and his heavy boots and dark scowl were easily visible now, the silk having been moved aside by the missing third of Tiran's female admirers. The girl carried a large basin filled full with water, a thick towel draped over her shoulder, and a look on her face that was agonized terror.

"Please forgive me for not kneeling to you properly, master," the girl begged in a low, trembling voice. "I was ordered not to spill the footbath, and if I tried to kneel properly—"

"And you think that lame excuse will let you get away with slighting me?" the man interrupted with a snort. "Is it supposed to matter to me that you'll be beaten if you spill any of that? I want a proper acknowledgment of my mastery over you, and I want it this instant."

"Don't waste your time, honey," I said as the pale, trembling girl began looking around for a way to get to her knees without losing some of the water in the basin. "He couldn't be considered something special even if everyone in the world went to their knees. Mastery? Him? Don't make me laugh."

The man's skin darkened with anger, his full attention now on me. That was what I'd been after, of course, and the smile I wore was a real one. I dislike taking out my frustrations on those who don't deserve it; it's much more fun using those who beg for the spot, especially if they should also happen to attack.

"Why are you speaking to me like that, lady?" the guard asked, clearly struggling to hold his temper. "If you were one of those fools who worry about slaves, the gate slave would have alerted us. Since you aren't, I don't understand what you're trying to do."

"What I'm trying to do is start a fight," I told him pleasantly, looking him over from light brown hair to dark brown boots. "I thought you'd be bright enough to understand that. But first I want you to tell me something. What happens if the gate slave lets you know that the new arrivals worry about slaves? Do you make them serve themselves, and from leftovers at that?"

"No," he answered, scowling even more. "We send a squad to welcome them, then give them a chance to learn firsthand about the life of a slave. If you don't care enough about your freedom to be jealous of it, you don't deserve to have it. And I think you've had a little too much to drink. Your wearing a sword doesn't mean you can use it, especially against someone with skill like mine."

"That's very true," I agreed, now grinning at him. "I usually *can't* use my sword against someone like you, but only because I hate taking advantage of the helpless. But your infantile ideas on freedom make you a special case, so I'm considering you an exception. Pay attention now, and see if you can follow this: pushing around someone who isn't free to respond is the act of a coward. If you want to show how brave you are, try doing the same to me."

I'd spoken the words slowly and clearly, wanting there to be nothing in the way of confusion, but he didn't immediately jump forward in attack. I'd forgotten the truism that if you're sincerely ready to fight you usually don't have to, and had also made the mistake of meeting the man's eyes. His skin had darkened again with anger, but the fact that I really wanted him to come at me held him back. Those who enjoy pushing around the helpless usually do turn out to be cowards.

And then I could literally see him figuring out what to do. He put two fingers in his mouth and whistled piercingly, then looked at me and grinned. All doubt and hesitation were gone, shrugged off as he straightened his shoulders, raised his head. A high-pitched battle cry came from his throat, and then he was racing toward me with arms outstretched.

CHAPTER THIRTEEN

Tiran, watching Alex through half-closed eyes, saw her leave her couch and slave and walk to the small fountain on the other side of the pavilion. The slump of the slave's shoulders said he hadn't been invited to follow, and that made Tiran feel like laughing aloud. He might have reacted a little too strongly when Alex had shown interest in the slave, but the past few minutes had changed her anger to thoughtfulness.

And he knew exactly what she was thinking about. The three girl slaves were precisely the kind of women he'd given his interest to in the past, the kind he'd used to distract himself until he'd found Alex. But rather than brush them aside he'd encouraged them, and Alex hadn't liked that idea at all. For a moment he'd wondered if his silver princess would leave him undamaged, but then she'd stalked away to a couch of her own . . .

Where she'd spent her time thinking. It had hopefully come to her how painful it was to see the person you want for your own showing interest in someone else. If they'd had freely given promises between them it would have been different, but uncertainty breeds more of the same, and insecurity as well. She'd kept saying she didn't want him; now, it seemed, she was learning differently.

The third of the girls meant to serve him had excused herself and hurried away somewhere. Tiran hadn't known where and hadn't really cared, but now he could see her coming back through the silk separating them from the next pavilion. He watched idly as he finished the last of his latest sandwich, food that was hopefully safe since it had been there even before they'd arrived.

And then Alex was talking to the guard who'd stopped the girl, what he could see of her smile making Tiran suddenly very nervous. He would have recognized it as a challenge from a mile away, and the guard clearly saw it the same. The man frowned but pulled back without moving, and that made Tiran feel better. The guard was a good deal bigger than Alex, but apparently he was bright enough to know that size wasn't always the winning edge.

But just as Tiran was relaxing again, the guard let go with what *had* to be a signal whistle, and then he was charging at Alex with a yell. Tiran was off the couch so fast he scattered the girl slaves, but happily it didn't matter that he was half a room away. Rather than being startled by the man's yell or frozen in fear, Alex ignored it. She tossed away the cup she held to free her hands, set herself, then caught one of the guard's outstretched arms. The twist and heave were so well done they looked effortless, and then the guard was flying past her shoulder to crash to the floor beyond her feet.

The furlike carpeting might have been easy to walk on, but it didn't do much to protect a thrown body from the flooring beneath. The guard lay stretched out and moaning, still conscious and therefore aware of the pain. His scabbard wasn't hung from lockets, so his hilt had done its own damage when he went down. Tiran stood a few feet away, more amused than angry. The guard should have known better than to tangle with a woman like Alex, and she'd thoroughly taught him the error of his ways.

And then the amusement disappeared as other guards came running into the pavilion from all directions. There were five of them, each one at least Tiran's own size, none of them pleased to see one of their own on the floor. Their eyes came to him as their hands reached for sword hilts, and Tiran suddenly knew that they thought *he'd* dumped the guard. Faint amusement touched him again, coming with the knowledge that he wasn't about to disabuse them. If they were looking for someone to take their mad out on . . .

And they were, but they got more than they bargained for. They hadn't even quite cleared their scabbards before Alex was beside him, her own sword in her fist and a faint smile on her face. Tiran's hand tightened around his hilt as worry about her safety flashed through him, but then the worry was pushed aside by confidence and satisfaction. He had no doubt that Alex was better than any of the guardsmen edging closer to face them, and having her willing and able to stand with him gave him a high like none he'd ever experienced. She was a woman he could share everything with, and the exhilaration that that knowledge brought was incredible.

By the time the five newcomers were close enough to circle them completely, the sixth man was back on his feet and had joined his friends. He wasn't all that steady, but now that he had some support he was letting his anger control him. Tiran and Alex stood roughly back-to-back, each watching half the circle and as much more as they could. Six to two should have been safe enough odds, but if the guardsmen had sent for even more reinforcements . . .

But they hadn't. They spent a moment or two apparently reassuring themselves that they had nothing to worry about, and then they attacked. One glance told Tiran that they knew nothing about tandem fighting, and then *he* was attacking the nearest three rather than defending. The ability to Shift-fight had served him well in the past, once even helping him to best five men like himself. That win had become part of his reputation . . .

One man lunged at him while the other two backed; blocking the strike and then going in over his guard ended the man fast, and that made one down. The remaining two had learned how little decorative leather did to protect, and now they were afraid. Under other circumstances Tiran would probably have let them go, but doing that when they'd certainly return with a dozen friends would be suicide. And murder, considering that Alex was with him.

The two men tried attacking together. Tiran blocked a cut from the one on his right, caught the one on his left with the backswing, then finished the other almost without effort. These men really weren't very good at all, and something about that bothered him as he turned to check on Alex. Even as he watched she finished the last of her three, then turned to face him with a grimace.

"I don't think I've ever felt more like a butcher," she said, vocalizing his own thoughts. "What were these cattle doing wearing swords, not to mention trying to use them? I knew that first one was a coward and a bully, but I expected *something* in the way of skill. He did worse with a sword than he did bare-handed."

"Was that why you challenged him?" Tiran asked, noticing that the man who sprawled again on the carpeting no longer had to worry about pain. "What made you decide that?"

"I heard him trying to give that girl slave of yours a hard time," she answered, silver eyes somewhat less than friendly. "If you're going to collect them, you really ought to keep a closer eye on them. Anyway, when I interfered the man didn't understand what was happening. Since we'd been cleared by the gate slave, he knew we weren't the kind of fools who are soft on slaves."

"And what would have happened if we hadn't been cleared by the gate slave?" Tiran asked, heavy suspicion beginning to writhe under the surface of recent events. Alex began walking toward the table holding the sandwiches, snagging a blue silk scarf from a statue as she went. Tiran followed to get his answer, but kept his eyes moving in all directions as he did so.

"If the gate slave hadn't cleared us, they would have tried to enslave *us*," Alex finally said as she stopped beside

the sandwich table. Putting her sword down, she began to
throw sandwiches into the blue silk scarf, obviously taking
enough for two. Then she tied the silk closed and hung it
from her belt, a sack that was secured and would not get
too much in the way. "With that in mind," she added, "not
to mention what we just did, it might be a good idea to be
on our way now."

"A very good idea," Tiran agreed, waiting until she
had picked up her sword again before beginning to move
toward the far side of the room. "The girl slaves are hiding,
but that male of yours has disappeared. I'd rather not be
here when he gets back with help. Even cattle can take you
down, if there's enough of them."

Alex made some sort of sound, but it was too neutral
to be considered agreement. Or disagreement. Tiran had
wanted her to say something about the slave not being hers,
but Alex was being her usual self where cooperation was
concerned. Finding the trail or defending against attack—
no problem and no argument. Reassuring him or giving
him the least encouragement—don't hold your breath,
d'Iste. When it isn't cooperate or die, it becomes cooperate *and* die.

Tiran cleared his mind of inner dialogue as he stepped
outside, alert for the appearance of other guardsmen. Right
then there weren't any, so he led off southeast, the direction they'd been going in when they'd come across the
pavilions. His sword was just as ready as Alex's as they
crossed the thick green lawn, both of them hurrying but
not running. The object was to get out of there, not bring
people after them for no reason other than curiosity.

When they reached the fence on that side, they
slipped through without bothering to look for a gate.
The sun hadn't done much moving in the sky, and
maybe that was because they hadn't been in the
pavilion very long. Whatever, it was a bit of help
they wouldn't be ignoring. After another look around,
Alex wiped her sword on her pants and resheathed it,
and a few minutes later Tiran did the same.

They walked for a while looking over their shoulders, but time passed with nothing in the way of pursuit showing up. Tiran was just beginning to wonder if it could be that easy when they got a surprise.

"Could that really be the entry?" Alex asked, apparently having the same idea as Tiran. "I'm feeling too suspicious to believe it."

"Then let's take a few minutes out and discuss it," Tiran said, scanning the low, scrub-covered hills they'd come across. "But let's also stop a little closer to the entry. We want it handy in case we need it in a hurry."

Alex nodded and moved to a point about twenty feet from the entry, untied the sandwich sack she'd made, then sat in the grass. Tiran took a spot opposite her, the entry to his left, the way they'd come to his right. When the sack was open he helped himself to a sandwich, then sank down into his thoughts. His eyes were still on sentry duty, but his mind had gone off to poke at a mystery.

"What are you thinking about?" Alex said after a number of minutes, the words sounding like something she hadn't been able to keep from asking. "If it's none of my business you don't have to tell me, but—"

"Don't be an idiot," Tiran broke in, almost impatiently. "I'm not going to say one minute that I want you to share my life, and the next tell you that what I'm thinking is none of your business. Sharing doesn't work that way— and besides, it certainly *is* your business. I was thinking about this latest trap, and how it had more than one level. As a matter of fact the levels overlapped, and each one was aimed at me."

"How did you come to that conclusion?" Alex asked with a frown. "I remember you saying you'd had experience with the sort the gate slave was, but what has that got to do with the rest of it?"

"It works as follows," Tiran said, organizing his thoughts as he reached for another sandwich. "The last time I dealt with a slave like the one at the gate, I insisted on treating him as if he were free.

What would have happened if I'd done the same again?"

"They would have sent a bunch of guards to enslave us," Alex answered promptly. "Or at least they would have tried. Whatever, it wouldn't have been a time of carefree fun."

"Right," Tiran said with a nod. "But I'd learned a lesson the first time, and didn't repeat my mistake. So we made it to the first pavilion and inside, and what did I find waiting there? Not one girl slave but three, and all of them exactly the sort of woman I've shown a preference for over the years."

"Now that you mention it, it does seem odd that there were three females and only one male," Alex said, her brows high. "You would think all transient guests would be given the same number, especially since those people expected the slaves to be abused. If I'd damaged my one slave and didn't immediately have another to take his place, they couldn't have argued the legitimacy of my complaint."

"But *I* had three slaves, a large enough number to allow one of them to go off after something," Tiran said. "When she came back, there just happened to be a guardsman there to give her a hard time. What do you think he would have done to her if you hadn't interfered?"

"At the very least, he would have made her spill that water," Alex replied. "From what she said, spilling even a little of it would have gotten her big trouble, maybe right on the spot. But he also could have decided that whatever she tried didn't suit him. At that point, he probably would have hurt her himself."

"And that would have brought *me* into it, especially if you weren't there," Tiran said. "I might have been able to treat the gate slave as a slave, but I'd never be able to stand around and watch a woman being hurt. That guardsman was fairly big, but when you challenged him the first thing he did was call for help. He would have whistled a lot sooner if *I* was the one he had to face, and that brings us to the number of guardsmen who responded. Along with him, there were six."

"Obviously that means something to you," Alex observed, watching him take another bite of the sandwich. "Does it tell you anything specific about whoever made these traps so deadly?"

"It tells me that the individual knows my reputation," Tiran responded after he'd swallowed. "Some years ago, when I was still in the process of building that reputation, I happened to find myself in the position of needing to face five men at the same time. Their aim was to stomp me into the ground, mine to keep it from happening. By using Shift-fighting techniques I was able to best them, and then people began to say I could take any five men my own size.

"Letting a boast like that circulate is dangerous—it tends to bring would-be challengers out of the woodwork—but it's also too useful careerwise to ignore. I had to think of a compromise, so I did. Anytime someone mentioned that I was supposedly able to take any five men my own size, I would smile and agree, then add, 'But not six.' After a while, people began adding the response themselves."

"And those six were all your size," Alex said, brows raised high. "But that makes it even more of a mystery. They might have been big, but they certainly weren't good fighters. Who would be stupid enough to think a specific number alone is enough to replace skill?"

"Someone who isn't a fighter himself," Tiran answered promptly. "If there had been fifteen or twenty guardsmen instead of six, chances are good that they could have taken both of us. Numbers do count for something, just as I mentioned earlier. The five I faced originally were good fighters, which was why I said that about six. One more and *I* would have been down, but because of the level of skill, not because of the number. A non-fighter might not understand the difference."

"I'd be more inclined to think our culprit isn't bright enough to understand," Alex remarked with a shake of her head. "And now that I think about it, I'll bet he also doesn't understand what Shifting really is. All those traps that were so deadly—any one of them would have had us if we couldn't Shift, but since we can they weren't all that bad. So our culprit is someone who can use magic, who wants to use your reputation against you, who isn't a fighter or very bright, and who doesn't know what's involved in Shifting. Who does that describe?"

Tiran was about to say he didn't know, but he suddenly had the feeling he *did* know, although it didn't make any sense. Lord Arthon or Baron Sellin should have been involved . . . maybe they'd hired someone . . .

"Now, how about that," Alex said. "I think I just found the original trap in this world, or at least the second half of it."

"What are you talking about?" Tiran asked, pulled away from his thoughts to see that she was squinting upward. "What more of a trap do you need than the pavilions?"

"I'm willing to bet the pavilions were supposed to be nothing but a good time," she said, bringing her gaze back to him. "We were supposed to spend more than a short time there, eating, relaxing, and maybe even doing some fooling around. When we came out we'd have to orient ourselves by the sun to find our direction of march again—and that sun isn't moving the way a sun normally does. I think it's slowly spiraling across the sky, which means using it for direction can throw you off completely."

"Unless you're very lucky or didn't stay long enough, and it's in the same quadrant," Tiran agreed, doing his own upward squinting. "I could be wrong, but I think taking anything but the proper direction will get you lost, not lead you to a phony entry. At this point it's a toss-up, but we have no way to double-check the conclusion. I say we take the chance and use the entry."

He looked down in time to see her rising to her feet, the sandwich sack already tied and ready to be attached to her swordbelt.

"Since there's no choice, why not?" she said with a shrug, sounding more tired than ever before. "Sitting here wondering or wandering around searching are two corners of the same dead end. I want this over and done with."

By then Tiran had also risen, but not to start for the entry. He reached out and took her arm, then gently pulled her to him.

"Alex, everything will work out just fine," he said, trying to put complete assurance into the words as he stroked her comfortingly. "I know you don't think so now, but you're tired and confused about everything that's happened. Once we're out of here and the competition is over, you'll see I'm right."

"Will I?" She raised her head from his chest to look at him with those beautiful silver eyes. "First you save my life, then you make it something that belongs to you. I didn't want any part of you, but I'm being drawn in despite that. It's not only you I have to fight now, but myself as well. How is all *that* supposed to work out right?"

"It can be done if you just give me a little help," Tiran answered, wishing desperately that he could banish the pain in those eyes. "Tell me why you feel you have to fight, love. Why can't you just enjoy what we've found together, working with me to make it stronger? What are you fighting against?"

"I'm fighting for my life and my sanity," she responded, pushing reluctantly out of his arms. "*For*, not against, Tiran. And I think it's time we went through that entry."

And ended that conversation, Tiran finished silently. He didn't really understand the point she was trying to make, but there was something tantalizingly familiar about the distinction she'd pointed out. Once they were out of there he'd have to think about it . . . assuming that was the proper entry, and they weren't walking into another trap . . .

He glanced up at the sky again, checked the area of hills in the direction they'd come from, then walked with Alex to the waiting entry . . .

* * *

"Your Majesty, there's a problem," Merwin reported, now sounding as tired as Reynar felt. The king had been pacing around, pausing now and then to stare at the entry that had swallowed Alexia and Tiran d'Iste. He probably should have sent some of his guard to follow and help them. Why hadn't he thought of that sooner?

"What is it now, Merwin?" Reynar asked. "Please don't tell me the miscreant can't be found. After all this time—"

"No, Sire, it isn't that," Merwin hastened to reassure him, more concerned than frightened. "Or, not precisely that. Limis and Sisal have narrowed it down to five people, three men and two women. The miserable wretch behind all this is clever, but we'll catch him."

"How can there possibly be that kind of confusion?" Reynar demanded, turning to stare down at the smaller man. "All Limis and Sisal have to do is tell which of the five is a magic user. They can't all be magic users, since we don't have that many living independently in this kingdom."

"Your Majesty, from what I gather, the miscreant managed to spread his aura and share it with four others," Merwin replied, just short of biting his lip in vexation. "All five read the same, but only one of them is guilty. Our people won't have trouble separating them out, but the process will take time. Limis prefers canceling the spell on d'Iste's trail first, and then he and Sisal will begin eliminating."

"All right, I'll agree that that takes precedence," Reynar fretted, running a hand through his hair. "Let them give what help they can to Alexia and d'Iste, and then they can separate out the one responsible. How soon will they be starting?"

"They've already started, Your Majesty," Merwin answered, then turned to point. "See, over there. First they merged their power, and then they spoke the spell. It should already be taking effect..."

CHAPTER FOURTEEN

Simply stepping through the entry didn't seem to be a good idea, but I'd had enough of diving and rolling. I settled for going through fast and ending in a crouch, and a moment later Tiran had done the same. We were both poised and ready to Shift or dodge, and it looked like both might soon be necessary.

The world around us was jungle, a heavy, threatening jungle that seemed to be waiting for us to make the first wrong move. Mostly green all around, with creepers on the ground and lots of noise from unseen fauna. It was also hot, and that despite the way the treetops hid the sun.

"And now we get to decide in which direction to go," Tiran said softly, green eyes moving all around. "Does any of this give us a hint about what sixth sense is being used? If they decided to make it luck, I'll be lodging more than a strong protest."

"If anything, it's more a matter of 'Good luck trying to get through,'" I responded with the faint amusement I felt. "This place reminds me of a battle zone waiting to happen, traps on top of traps with more traps in between."

"The feeling that says you're about to walk into an ambush," Tiran clarified with a nod. "I know exactly what you mean, because I've experienced the feeling before—hey! Maybe that's it!"

"Maybe what's it?" I asked, now faintly annoyed with his look of revelation. I realized I wasn't allowing myself to feel any emotion more than faintly, but that was good. Plenty of time to wax outraged or hysterical once the last entry was behind me.

"Maybe the sixth sense is the survival instinct," Tiran answered, moving just a little where he crouched to my left. "We all have the instinct for survival, but some of us have it really strong, and some of *those* have even taken the training. Instinct works better when you have survival training to bolster it."

"And showing how well you can survive whatever comes at you is supposed to be the purpose of this competition," I said, suddenly agreeing with him completely. "Now all we have to do is—"

I was about to mention finding the trail, but just then the entire world around us—*shifted.* There was no sound, no flashes of light, just the impression of a brief hum in the ears and a flickering in the eyes. Nothing moved including us, but suddenly we were crouching in a changed world.

"Well, well," Tiran commented as he looked around. "About time, I'd say, but better late than never. Whatever was done to make this trail more dangerous, I'd say it's now been stopped. This is a normal jungle— if jungle can ever be considered normal—and we've even got a visible path."

"They found the distorting spell or whatever was used and canceled it!" I exclaimed, absolutely delighted. "Limis and Sisal, I love you! You've made it possible for me to get a bath before the end of the century."

I doubted that the two sorcerers could hear me, but I was too pleased with the prospect of getting out to care. Without the distortion, it shouldn't take long to finish the competition, and then . . .

"Have I ever mentioned how many bath connections *I* have?" Tiran asked mildly, arms draped across thighs. "I don't want to sound like I'm boasting, but if you stick with me even two baths a day aren't out of the question. There aren't many men around who can promise that to a woman and really mean it."

"There aren't many men around crazy enough to *think* of promising that," I countered, trying not to laugh. When he said things like that, it made me want to put my arms around him and—Suddenly the amusement was gone out of the discussion, at least for me. "I think it's past time we got moving," I said, glancing up before rising out of my crouch. "Do we follow the trail we can see, or do we look for a less obvious one?"

"I'd say we follow what's there," he answered with a sigh, also straightening up. "If we're supposed to survive whatever's thrown at us, avoiding it won't accomplish the same thing. Let's both of us keep our eyes open, and spring any traps with something other than ourselves."

"Good idea," I muttered, finding it impossible to look at him. I no longer had to see the pain he felt; just hearing his voice made me feel what he did, and it was rapidly becoming unbearable. I wrapped my arms around myself as he turned away, refusing to think about how much better it would feel if it were *his* arms instead. I already knew what I had to do, and if I got the chance, I would. Even if the urge not to was getting stronger . . .

Whirling confusion doesn't do much to help you survive, but it took a short while before I was able to push it away and concentrate on my surroundings. By then we had left the entry well behind, and had even spotted some traps. They were established to the left and right of the trail, and would have been less easily seen by someone paralleling the trail rather than walking it. Shortly after that the trail widened out, and all parallel traps seemed to disappear.

Leaving nothing but the traps on the trail. Dead falls and spring traps, camouflaged pits and trip wires, you name it and somewhere it was there. We all but crept along one step at a time, testing the ground before we trusted our weight to it, making sure nothing was coming down from above. Once we had to drop flat to keep from getting scooped up in a swinging net, but both of us saw it coming in more than enough time.

But despite all that, it came to me how easy the going was compared with what we'd already been through. Shifting was unnecessary and so was fighting; we had to stay alert and rely heavily on recognizing the suspicious, but it wasn't impossibly hard. And it wasn't dangerous. At worst we could have gotten slightly hurt; most often the trap was a simple one, designed to hold what it caught without harm until someone came by to release them.

It had to be those realizations that crystallized the idea. I wiped sweat off my forehead as I continued to look around, my mind working as my eyes scanned our surroundings. If I had to face Tiran in the finals, it would be all over for me. The question of skill aside, I'd never be able to force myself to do anything that might hurt him, and I'd probably end up blaming *him*. I didn't want to do that, not when someday we might . . . when it might become possible for us to . . .

I couldn't finish the thought. The need to step carefully over the edge of an exposed root was a good excuse to bring me back from distraction. What I was about to do would probably ruin any possibility of something strong and lasting developing between Tiran d'Iste and me, but I had no choice. Going along with him would also produce disaster—that, I couldn't be more certain of. Better to end things before they went too far . . . less pain that way, for both of us . . . even though they might have gone too far already . . .

How I managed to spot the perfect opportunity in my mental state, I'll never know. The sound of small bodies racing through the treetops and scrambling through the brush was distracting, as was the look of some overhanging vines just ahead. Tiran was paying a lot of attention to that, probably suspecting a two-pronged attack just as I was. The unseen beasts would be a diversion, causing us to ignore the vines, which would then close the trap on us.

And then I happened to notice something to the left of the trail, beyond Tiran. There was a lot of scattered grass and twigs just as there had been all along, but in one spot I could see something that looked heavier than a twig. It was peeking out from under the grass in one place only, and the polished yellow and brown looked remarkably like bamboo. Could somebody have dropped a staff there, leaving it to be covered over . . . ?

And then I woke up to the truth. The animals in the trees were only the first diversion, and we were supposed to notice the vines. They must be arranged in such a way that the best manner of avoiding them would be to step off the trail. There hadn't been traps parallel to the trail in quite a while, and none that we'd seen right next to it. Stepping off would be easy and natural . . .

"Tiran," I said, plunging in before I lost my nerve. "Tiran, let's stop for a moment. We're almost up to those vines which have to be a trap, and I want to tell you something before we tackle them."

"I dislike being critical, but your idea of a good place to take a rest break needs rethinking," he said, flashing me a quick grin. But he did stop, and even glanced at me again. "Is something wrong? All that silence you were producing goes beyond simply concentrating on the trail."

"It . . . isn't exactly that something is wrong," I faltered, having no need to wonder why I was losing the language. How do you say good-bye to someone when it might be for the last time? When you don't really *want* it to be the last time?

"Tiran, I want you to know how sorry I am that we had to—get to know each other—just at this time." I was hashing it up badly, but once started I couldn't afford to stop. "If it had been somewhere else—even a couple of years from now—What I'm trying to say is that I'll never forget what we went through together, and it meant more to me than you'll ever know."

By then he was frowning with confusion, not to mention probably getting suspicious. I'd said too much and too little, and now had to get it done fast before he realized my intentions. But first there was something else I had to do, a selfish something, but absolutely necessary. I stepped close to him, circled his neck with my arms, then began what would probably be our last kiss.

The speed he responded with almost drowned me, but the determination to finish what I'd started kept me afloat. I tasted him as deeply as I could, encouraging his own tasting of me, the experience immediately turning into something I didn't want to stop. But the time I had was limited, and that was no place to let things proceed to their natural conclusion even if I'd had the time. Much too soon I had to begin ending the kiss, and after some determined resistance he finally, reluctantly, allowed me to take one step back.

"If there's any swamp ahead, that's probably where you'll decide you want me to make love to you," he murmured with an uneven chuckle. "I don't know why you've suddenly changed your mind, but I thought I'd let you know that a swamp is fine with me. Any time, anywhere . . ."

He seemed to be about to kiss me again, and I simply couldn't let that happen. One more time, and I'd say to hell with my plans. Panic is wonderfully useful if you have the good sense—or the desperate need—to channel it, and right then I did. Before he could put his arms around me again, I turned sideways and bent, then put a shoulder into his middle with all my body weight behind it.

Under normal circumstances I couldn't have taken Tiran off his feet, not even with a running start. Size and balance would have made it impossible, but right then I had a couple of abnormal pluses on my side. The first was total surprise, which threw his balance off enough to let my attack send him staggering back a few steps. Solid footing would have let him regain his balance, but that was where the second part of my edge came in. Tiran staggered back, and with his third step there was a loud crunching, and then he disappeared through the hole in the ground caused by his fall.

Even though I was expecting it, seeing him disappear like that was upsetting. I hurried forward to peer through the hole he'd made, noticing that it *was* bamboo that made up the framework of the trap. Large, round sections braced a weaving of thin, small pieces, and the thin part was what Tiran had broken through. Enough light filtered down to let me see him at the bottom, still bouncing a little on a thick mattress of wide, rubbery leaves. Just as I'd hoped, he wasn't hurt at all, but he *was* a good long way down.

"Tiran, I'm sorry I had to do that," I called, seeing his shadowy face twist up toward me. "If there had been any other way . . . Don't worry, they'll let you out as soon as the competition is over. Until then, this should help."

I took the square of silk that still held a number of sandwiches, tossed it down to him, then moved back fast from the hole. He hadn't said anything, and I wanted to keep it like that.

Getting past the vine trap wasn't particularly hard. It was set to swing down and grab at anything passing under it, but it had to fold all the way back up before it could swing down the next time. Throwing four good-sized stones got me that information and the opening I needed, and then I was beyond the vines and continuing along the trail. Being alone helped a lot; the need for full alertness kept me from having the time to think about what I'd done.

I trudged through jungle for what seemed like hours longer, avoiding traps and snares and pitfalls, grateful for the survival training I'd hated but had still taken. Everything in my immediate vicinity was suspect, so it took a little while before I noticed that the number of traps was decreasing. Some of them still took thought rather than caution to get around, but they definitely grew fewer and fewer.

And then, suddenly and unexpectedly, there was an entry ahead. The twenty-five yards looked ridiculously short after what lay behind me, and I stopped to blot the sweat off my face with a sleeve as I looked at it. Was it smart to trust so obvious a presentation? Could this entry be a phony, with the real one hidden somewhere behind it? That was more than possible, so I had to take a few minutes to think about it.

I crouched down where I was to look around and think, and it didn't take long to come to certain conclusions. With the number of traps along the trail it was natural to decide that the entry was a phony, so that meant it probably wasn't. You need suspicion to carry you through the dangerous times, but you also have to know when to turn it off.

But not completely off. The fact that the number of traps had decreased probably meant there was another somewhere around the entry, waiting to grab the careless. The entry ahead of me was the one to be used, but had to be approached with a lot of caution. It hadn't been hard to decide that, but somehow I felt the conclusion would have been reached a lot sooner if I'd discussed it with someone—

I straightened up fast, ran a hand through my greasy, sweaty hair, then looked around for a way to test my theories. I still didn't have time to think about anything but the competition, and I had to keep that firmly in mind.

It took the use of stones and branches and about twenty minutes of inching forward, but I did find the trap. Fifteen feet in front of the entry, the ground was no longer solid; a solid-*looking* area stretched right up to where I wanted to go, but it was a strange kind of quicksand. It took the probing branch right out of my hands and sucked it down, the action so fast I had no chance to snatch it back.

"Damn," I muttered, staring from the quicksand to the entry. I was fair at broad-jumping, but fifteen feet was well beyond my limit. I looked up to see if there were any vines it might be possible to swing on, then immediately rejected the idea. I couldn't trust a vine not to break and dump me in the middle of that, not when—

And then I stopped to look at the quicksand again. The branch had been probing to the left when I'd lost it, and that meant I hadn't really checked out the boundaries of the trap. If there was a safe path through the middle of it . . . it would take intelligence to discover that and nerve to use it. At the very least it was worth a try . . .

I lost a large number of stones and another branch, but finally discovered that my hunch was right. Just left of center of the stretch there was a safe path, narrow and invisible to the eye, but still there. I tossed stones to mark it almost up to the entry, probed as far as I could with a branch, wiped at sweat again . . .

Then cursed myself for wasting time dithering. The idea of falling into that quicksand scared me silly, even though there was probably a nice safe place under it where anyone caught would be dumped and held. I knew that in my head, but my insides knew no such thing. If I fell I would be sucked down and down and down, no air, no light, not ever again—I shuddered and closed my eyes tight, spent a moment fighting to breathe normally, then went ahead and did it.

The path was *very* narrow, turning the fifteen feet into a mile or more. I watched where I was stepping rather than looking ahead, so when I reached the entry it came as a surprise. I wanted to move right straight through, but not knowing what sort of world lay on the other side meant I couldn't. Jump through fast ready for anything, that was the way to get it done. *Jump* through . . .

I landed in a semi-crouch a few feet from the entry, ready for anything but what was actually there. The noise—so startling and distracting—the movement and colors dizzy-making—and then most of them started to rush at me . . .

"Your Highness, you made it through!" came from all the throats of those coming at me, and then my father was pushing them all aside to pull me close and hug me. It took a real effort to understand that it was over, that I'd found the way back to the world I'd started from. Very briefly I considered that it might be a trick, but then my father stopped crushing me and held me at arm's length.

"Alexia, are you really all right?" he demanded, golden eyes trying to inspect every inch of me. "It took so long before they were able to cancel that interfering spell, I was afraid you would be—Are you really all right?"

"I'm tired and hungry and would kill for a bath," I told him, finally letting myself relax a little. "Aside from that I'm just fine, but not as good as I'll be once the finals are over. Anyone else make it through?"

"Baron Sellin and one other, so far," my father answered, then looked around with a frown. "But where's Tiran d'Iste? We know the two of you were together, so I don't understand—"

"Father, he's caught in a trap," I said, bringing those eyes back to me. "It happened after the interference was canceled, so it's a shame, but he'll be fine. How soon until the finals are held?"

My father stared at me without answering, but the look in his eyes said he knew it was *my* fault that Tiran was disqualified. I couldn't quite meet or respond to that silent accusation, and looking away didn't help at all. What I'd done hadn't been fair, but like it or not the necessity remained.

"Ah, Princess Alexia, how good to see you safely returned," I heard, and looked around to see Lord Arthon, Lord Moult, and Lady Wella. "Fregin sends his good wishes as well, and asks to be excused. There are still two contestants he needs to keep track of, and duty comes first."

"Yes, of course," I agreed, wondering why their smiles looked so strange. "Duty always does come first, so I'd appreciate your answering a question for me. Do I have time for a bath before the finals, assuming leaving the field is allowed? If it isn't, I'll just have to wait until—"

"Your Highness," Lady Wella said gently, stepping forward up away from two men who were no longer meeting my eye. "You have all the time you like for a bath or anything else. I'm afraid—my countrymen and fellow judges asked me to—My dear, the rules clearly state that a contestant must follow his *assigned* trail to its end, and your assigned trail was left untraveled. You fought your way through to the end, but along someone else's trail. We have no choice but to disqualify you."

"But . . . No, that's not—it can't—" I knew what I wanted to say, but the pity in her eyes told me the decision was final. Shock clanged in my head as I began to understand what had been said, to believe and begin to realize the consequences. I'd been *disqualified*—but two others had reached the finals—and Tiran was caught in a trap—

"Alexia, go back to your apartment and get cleaned up," my father said quietly, his hands to my arms from behind. "Get whatever rest you can, and when it's time for you to come back here I'll send for you. Until then, I want you to stay away."

So I won't interfere again, I thought as he urged me gently on my way toward the palace. I'd already interfered so badly that I'd wrecked everything, but the numbness inside me was making it difficult to think. Something to do—something to do—go back to my apartment? Sure, why not? What else was there to—

I looked up to see that I'd wandered a short distance away from where I'd been, toward the palace where there weren't any crowds. The numbness I'd felt was giving way to heavy illness, sickness so bad that I thought I'd throw up. I'd been so damned clever that I'd ruined everything, and what I'd passed through and survived was nothing compared with what was now ahead.

A marble bench stood in the grass about ten feet away, and it was all I could do to reach it and sink down on its end. My legs were so weak I knew they'd never hold me, my head throbbed with the worst pain imaginable, and the shudders passing through my body clacked my teeth together. I'd never been so frightened sick in all my life, and there was nothing I could do to make it better. My father would demand that I marry the winner of the competition, and I couldn't . . . couldn't . . .

I wrapped my arms around myself as I rocked forward and back, trying not to moan, trying to regain control. My only hope had been to win the competition, and now that hope was dead. I'd lost the chance to do what I'd dreamed about for so long, and to hope that someday Tiran and I could—Gone, it was all gone, and the only thing left was to curse myself for surviving the deadlier traps. If my life had to be over, it would have been better having it over completely.

I sat there with my head in my hands for another moment or two, and then it came to me that I did still have a choice. I'd told Tiran there was always a choice for those who knew where to look, and I realized my mind had come up with a last-ditch escape. If I had the nerve to use it. Or the desperation. I considered desperation for a couple of minutes, checked on nerve, then got to my feet and sighed. My final escape route scared me almost as badly as what the future held, but the key word was "almost." My choice was clear, and there was no sense in wasting time.

Leaving the palace grounds unseen wasn't hard, and getting to the city was even easier. The horse I borrowed was easy-gaited and fresh, a lot fresher than its rider. What I really wanted to do was lie down somewhere and sleep, but that would have to come later. Yes, later I'd have lots of time to sleep.

The High Magistrate was hearing a case when I reached his courtroom, and there were even a few people in the audience watching the proceedings. I interrupted someone's discourse when I rode my horse through the doors, and the High Magistrate immediately began purpling with outrage.

"How dare you!" he thundered, red eyes blazing even more as he recognized me. He was a man of middle years, but so stern and implacable that most thought of him as old. His sense of fair play was as sharp as a blade's edge, and the idea of anyone getting away with breaking the law was enough to make him throw fits.

"Why shouldn't I dare?" I tossed back at him mildly, letting him see how amused I was. "You can't do anything to me, and we both know it. It doesn't even matter that this is the second horse I stole. My father will get me off just the way he did the first time."

"His Majesty didn't 'get you off,' " the man growled, fighting to control himself. "He gave me his word that the matter would be seen to in another way. The competition—"

"Ah, I see you remember that it's being held right now," I said with a grin when he broke off. "It happens I completed the course myself, but they didn't like that. They knew I would win in the finals if they let me compete, so they pulled some stupid rule out of the air and disqualified me. Well, they can disqualify and name winners all they like. I'm not *about* to go along with their final decision."

"Then you're here to accept your term at hard labor," he said, his eyes still directly on me. "The first thing you'll do is get off that horse, and then—"

"Forget it," I said with a snort. "If you don't know what you can do with your hard labor, I can tell you in words of one syllable. I came by to see your face when I wished you—and the rest of this crummy place—a fond farewell. I'm leaving the kingdom, but I may come back someday. When I do, I'll be sure to stop by and say hello. I'll probably even bring my newest horse."

I laughed at him then, showing my contempt for his belief that he had any authority over me, and this time he paled. The High Magistrate was supposed to have absolute authority in his courtroom, over everyone and anyone accused of breaking the law. He'd ceded part of that authority by making a deal with my father, and somewhere deep inside that must have rankled. He stood slowly behind his bench, raised an arm that was actually trembling, and pointed at me.

"You, Princess Alexia, have admitted before this court that you're guilty of stealing not one horse but two," he pronounced, the words as slow and steady as a metronome. "You've refused the punishment offered by your father out of his love for you, and you've refused to repay society for your trespass with the sweat of your brow. You leave me no alternative but to sentence you to the ultimate punishment, to protect the innocent from any future depredations. By order of this court, you will hang from the neck until dead."

"And you think my father will let that happen," I scoffed, making sure my expression didn't change. "He's involved with the competition right now, but as soon as it's over and dinnertime rolls around, he'll start looking for me. If he finds out you've sentenced me to hang in the morning, he'll trot on over and get me out. Are you silly enough to believe you'll refuse a royal command?"

"Out of courtesy and respect, this court would never consider refusing the Sovereign its cooperation," the High Magistrate said in a grinding but oily purr. "However, it also happens to be the duty of this court to protect the Sovereign in every way possible. Presented with a fait accompli, the king will grieve, but his grief will soon begin to pass. Your sentence will be carried out tonight at sundown, not tomorrow at dawn. Take her away, and be sure to remember her capabilities."

Hands reached for me from all sides, the hands of bailiffs and guardsmen. I pretended to struggle as they pulled me from the horse, removed my weapons, then dragged me out. We went down, of course, but this time I wasn't put in a cell with anyone else. I was thrust into a glass-lined cell designed to hold a full-range Shifter, the door was closed and locked, and I was finally alone. A lamp burning low on the wall showed a cot, a stool and a bucket, and nothing else. I went over to the cot, sat down, then stretched out.

"And that takes care of that," I whispered, closing my eyes. The cot wasn't in the least comfortable, but it was good enough for the few hours I'd be using it. Tomorrow the High Magistrate might realize that *he'd* sentenced me to hang, but I was the one who had named the time as tomorrow morning. And then had forced him to make the change to this very night. He was very angry, surely enough to carry him through the time until sundown.

Sundown. I found it impossible to believe that this would be the last sundown I ever saw, but one small part of me believed and that part was crying. I was so damned tired that I wished it were already over, the ache and fear and regret already behind me. Afraid? Yes, I was afraid, but that had been the only honorable thing left for me to do. I couldn't marry whoever won the competition, and I couldn't turn around and walk away. I had a debt to pay, and if my life had to be forfeit . . .

I noticed then that the tears had spread from the original small part, and now were rolling down my cheeks from under my lids. I finally had the time to think about Tiran, but it hurt so much that I didn't know if I could. Saying good-bye to life was easier than needing to say it to him; the thought of accepting any other man had become inconceivable, and nothing would ever change that. The last kiss we'd shared—it really would be the last—I'd never see or touch him again—if I'd had to live, I might not have been able to stand it—but I wasn't going to live—

The sobbing started then, toneless music fit for a funeral dirge, a useless effort to match all the rest of the uselessness I'd accomplished. I'd never even gotten to really know him, and that loss was the worst of the bunch. Next to that my life meant nothing . . . less than nothing as it was almost over . . . only a few empty hours to go . . .

*   *   *

Tiran heard the sack of sandwiches land somewhere in the pit with him, but he didn't bother to look for it. He still fought to accept the idea that Alex had actually done that to him, knocked him into a trap and gone on alone. It had to be a joke, her way of teasing him for being less alert than she'd been. She'd be back in a minute with a vine or something, and then she'd—

But what she'd said, both before she kissed him and after he was in the pit . . . He'd been trying to figure out what she could be apologizing for . . . it had definitely been an apology . . . the second time no doubt about it . . .

"Alex?" he called, standing up to listen for sounds of her coming back. Standing on those rubbery leaves was hard, but they'd certainly done a good job of breaking his fall. He couldn't possibly have gotten hurt . . .

"Alex!" he roared, finding it impossible to kid himself any longer. "Alex, you get back here this minute, or I'll—"

Choking down the rest of the words was hard, but threatening someone from the bottom of a pit was ludicrous. He already felt enough of a fool, and if he didn't find some way out of there . . .

"But how the hell am I supposed to get out?" he muttered to himself, using the small amount of light leaking down to examine his prison. The pit was a good fifteen feet deep, more than that wide, and its sides sloped down and *back* from the top. In order to climb one of those sides you'd have to get under it and move outward as you went up, clinging to it like a spider on the bottom of a web.

But a web had the advantage of being sticky, and a spider weighs almost nothing. The sides of the trap were compacted dirt that would crumble if climbed, and Tiran would still weigh more than two hundred pounds even if he Shifted form. Nothing he could change to would let him go up those sides, and that was the reason for the shape of the trap. It was meant to hold a full-range Shifter, and that was exactly what it was doing.

The next few minutes weren't pleasant for Tiran. He went from one side of the trap to the other, cursing every time the rubbery matting almost made him fall, examining walls that refused to give him a clue about how to get out. And he *had* to escape, there were no two ways about that. He had a redheaded female to catch up to, and when he did . . .

Rage doesn't do much to help you think, but determination is sometimes strong enough to overcome that. There was no way out, but he still had to find one; as he stood in the middle of the pit looking upward, thinking that thought, he knew well enough what it would take. If he could just Shift into a bird that really flew, he'd have it made. But his kind of bird could only soar, just as he'd done to reach that entry, and soaring in a pit was stupid . . .

And that was when the idea came, a stupid, desperate idea, but one that might work. One that he'd have to *make* work, otherwise it was all over. Alex certainly ought to win in the finals, but what if she didn't? What if someone like that Baron Sellin won, and she had to marry him? After that cute little trick she'd played Tiran would have enjoyed beating her for an hour, but that didn't mean he wanted to lose her. There was something driving the girl, something she refused to talk about, and next time he'd *make* her discuss it . . . !

But first he had to get out of there. He looked around to be certain he stood in the middle of the pit, silently thanking those responsible for making sure that any entrant falling in would not get hurt. Their method of ensuring safety might help get him out again . . .

He immediately began to jump up and down. He started slow and easy, needing to get the feel of the bounce produced by the rubbery leaves, needing to find his balance. As soon as he did he began helping his rate of rise, kicking off harder and stretching upward. That part also had to be taken slow, and he had to watch for the time he reached his limit. The leaves let him bounce high in the air, but not high enough to reach the bamboo framework covering the pit.

When Tiran reached the same approximate height three tries in a row, he knew it was time for the next part of his plan. The stupid, uncertain part that might not work . . . Shut up, you fool, and just do it. Ignore the sweat dripping down your face and the heaviness of the air, and give it the best try you can. Bury all of those old, painful memories and let them finally die . . .

The next time Tiran went up, he was ready. He waited until he was *almost* to the top of his rise, and then Shifted with every ounce of speed he could muster. The giant condor he became had only a little room beyond its wing spread, but it was enough. Just as he reached the top of his rise he beat those giant wings powerfully, twice, and then he was Shifting back to grab for the bamboo framework. He still couldn't really fly, but his wings had gotten him up the necessary few feet.

And his hands now had a grip on one of the heavier bamboo poles. Tiran hung there for a moment to catch his breath, at the same time watching the pole he held and the ones it was bound to. There had been the chance that his weight would bring the whole framework crashing down, but apparently the poles rested solidly enough on firm ground to prevent that. The framework trembled, but it didn't come apart.

Which wasn't to say that it wouldn't, and that meant Tiran had to get moving. The bamboo was far too smooth to make his damp-palmed hold a secure one, not to mention the fact that his strength would be gone sooner rather than later. And there were crossings he would have to pass, places where the bamboo was tied to other poles both large and small. Better get moving right now . . .

Height was something that had bothered Tiran ever since the time his boyhood friend had fallen to his death. He fully expected that it always would, which was why his hand-overhand progress along the pole surprised him. Once he'd started his nervousness left him, confidence building and taking its place with every surge of his arm muscles. It was almost as though having fallen such a distance safely now let him dismiss a second fall, and through dismissing it, he also lost the fear of it.

He reached the hole he had fallen through faster than he had expected to. Possibly it was overconfidence that made him swing his body and legs up immediately to reach the free air and ground beyond, maybe only a remnant of memory that still urged him to get quickly to safety. Whatever, Tiran immediately regretted the move. As he swung past the broken ends of the thinner bamboo, they raked his left side like a line of knives. Hissing with the pain he finished twisting and shoving himself up and forward, and once he sat on the ground beside the pit he was able to inspect the damage.

"Nice going, fool," he muttered as he saw the blood welling out of three deep gouges and two shallow ones. "You could have kicked that garbage out of your way first, but it wasn't important enough to bother about. Now you've got something that *is* important enough to bother about."

But what he didn't have was something to put over the wounds, not to mention to stop the bleeding. After a moment he lowered his torn tunic back into place, then stood up. He'd find his way to the next entry and through it, and if the weather in the next world permitted it, he'd tear up the tunic itself for a bandage.

Tiran had to ignore the pain as he made his way along the trail through that jungle, but that wasn't the hard part. Feeling his strength dribble out with his blood was worse, but at least he wasn't yet to the staggering point. He got safely past all the traps in his way, noticed when the number of traps grew fewer, then reached the point of being able to see the entry.

And also saw the remnants of Alex's efforts to reach the entry. Branches and stones still lay scattered just in front of a stretch of suspicious-looking ground, and Tiran had to spend only a minute or two experimenting before he understood. The stones leading to the entry showed the only safe path through the quicksand, so he began to follow it. Narrow, it was really narrow . . . had to be careful not to fall . . . dizzy, but couldn't notice that . . . keep going and get through the entry fast . . .

Tiran stumbled through into warm late afternoon, and stood for a moment blinking at the scene in front of him. Lots of people, lots of noise, no one noticing him and then more and more who did. Rushing over, slapping him on the back, yelling congratulations, catching him as he began to fall . . .

CHAPTER FIFTEEN

Tiran opened his eyes again to see that there were fewer people around him. He knew he hadn't been out for long, but someone was putting a bandage to the gouges in his side. Even as confused and light-headed as he felt, that didn't make any sense.

"You're wondering why you're being bandaged rather than healed," a voice said, its owner obviously reading his thoughts. "No, don't try to sit up yet. Give it another minute."

"Your Majesty, I'd like to know what's going on," Tiran said, having recognized the king's voice, but he did stay where he was. Trying to sit up had made him dizzy, and when his vision cleared he saw the king crouched to his right.

"What's going on is that the first part of the competition is over," Reynar told him, his voice low and serious. "Everyone who started is now accounted for, either in a trap or here and ready for the finals. Counting you, the finalists number four."

"And Alex is one of them," Tiran said, the heavy weight of worry leaving his mind. "She came through before me, so she's safe. But that doesn't explain—"

"Tiran, listen to me," Reynar interrupted, golden eyes fiercely intent. "Yes, my daughter came through and is safe, but no, she isn't a finalist. The rules say you have to follow your own trail back here, and she followed yours. She was disqualified, and I sent her to the palace to wait for the results of the finals."

Tiran took that in along with the attitude of the king, then rolled to one side and forced himself into a sitting position. The man who had been bandaging him was finished and gone, which meant the conversation was more or less private.

"And the reason I'm being bandaged rather than healed has to do with the finals," Tiran said, knowing it for a fact. "Tell me."

"All entrants successfully completing the first half of the competition must enter the finals just as they were when they left the last entry," the king answered, sounding as if he were reciting something memorized. "The only exceptions to that are the matters of drinking water and the bandaging of wounds. Finalists may be given water to drink and bleeding wounds can be bandaged, but nothing else. Healing you would be the same as disqualifying you—unless you decide you're too badly hurt to continue. If you are, I'll get someone over here right away."

"Thank you, no," Tiran said, running his hand through his hair. "Your first instincts were right, Your Majesty, and I won't be giving up until I can't move any longer. I hope you'll forgive me for saying that if Alex was here now, I'd probably strangle her."

"Then my guess was right," Reynar said, half relieved and half outraged. "She *was* responsible for your being in the trap she mentioned. If I'd been certain—Here, have some water while I figure out how we can both strangle her. And if you really were in a trap, how did you get out?"

Tiran accepted the jug of water and drank from it, then shook his head.

"It's a long story, but getting out was what caused these wounds," he said, gingerly touching his bandaged side. His tunic lay on the ground to the left, partially draped over his weapons belt. "How long until the finals start? The longer I have to wait, the worse it will be."

"It's only a matter of minutes now," Reynar answered, glancing around. "My sorcerers have been spending the time since your appearance working some spells, but they're still having trouble. The one responsible for trying to ruin the competition came here and was trapped, but they can't tease him out of the group of five they've narrowed the choice down to. Why don't you stay here and rest while I check on what progress they've made."

"I have a better idea," Tiran said as the king straightened. "I've been thinking about the way the trail was made more dangerous, and I may be able to help you find the one you're looking for. Give me a minute."

Picking up his tunic and swordbelt before standing was hard, the coordination required for the two acts almost more than Tiran could manage. The king's hand on his arm steadied him once he was up, but the sweat on his forehead showed the effort he was making.

"Tiran, are you sure you can go through with this?" Reynar asked quietly, his concern having grown. "It won't do anyone any good if you die trying to win."

"If I don't win, I might be better off dead," Tiran answered, meeting the king's eyes. "If I lose and live, I'll probably end up disgracing myself by doing something dishonorable. Alex means too much to me for me to give her up without a fight, and right now I'm facing the easier battle. Winning here means I still have the one with her ahead of me."

"There's nothing I can say," Reynar replied with a sigh. "If only this competition hadn't been necessary . . . Well, that's water under the bridge. Let's see if walking a short distance brings some of your strength back."

Tiran nodded and let the king head him in the proper direction, and then paid attention to regrouping his energy. Sitting in one place would be easier on his body than moving around, but it would also make him stiffen up. If he overrode the pain and moved slowly and carefully, it should do more good than harm. He told himself that as he walked along, but at first he had trouble believing it.

The distance to where they were going really was short, and Tiran knew they'd arrived when he saw the crowd. A large number of uniformed guardsmen surrounded two smaller groups, and one of the smaller groups also surrounded the other. Everyone bowed when Reynar came up, and one of the men from the small group doing the surrounding stepped out to meet them.

"Nothing yet, Sire," the man said, looking vexed. "We'll break through his spell eventually by sheer strength, but right now we're still fighting to get a grip on it. It's not so much powerful as devious."

"I'm not surprised," Tiran said, interrupting the king without realizing it as he examined the five people in the centermost group. "And they all look so helpless and pathetic, you can't spot your quarry by appearance. It's too bad for him, but I can. There's your man, the one trying to hide behind the larger woman."

The man Tiran pointed to screamed and tried to run, but the guardsmen weren't about to let that happen. Warded as they were by powerful sorcerers, they grabbed the guilty party without fear and dragged him in front of the king. He was short, thin, and delicate-looking, and couldn't seem to decide between fear and rage.

"How did you know this was the one?" Reynar asked Tiran while he stared at the miscreant. Such an innocuous, useless look to the wretch, and yet people were dead because of him.

"His name is Encar, and I knew because he and I came to this kingdom together," Tiran answered, moving his tunic and swordbelt back to his right hand. "Since he isn't supposed to be good enough to do more than open gates for us, it took me a while to get around to suspecting him. Would you like to explain the mysteries, Encar?"

"You muscle-bound oafs *need* an explanation, don't you?" the small man sneered, now more angry than frightened. "I'm not surprised that *you* don't understand, Tiran; you always were so easy to fool. Of course I was able to do more than open gates and take you through, but what business was that of yours? If you'd known, you probably would have asked me to *do* more."

"And you preferred to collect gold without the need to earn it," Tiran said with a nod, his own anger rising. "The times I lost good men when a competent magic user could have saved them—that wasn't any of *your* business, because you were paid no matter how many men died."

"Which was exactly as it should be," Encar responded, narrow chin rising. "You were the only one I had to concern myself with, and you always survived without my help. You're the only one I ever found who could, but I should have known better than to trust you. The instant my back was turned you betrayed me, and I'll never forgive you for it."

"Betrayed you?" Tiran, totally confused, frowned into the venomous glare being sent at him. "All I did was pursue a personal dream. How can you possibly see that as betrayal?"

"Don't you play the innocent with me!" Encar shrilled, trembling in the grip of the two guardsmen holding him. "You know there was a commission waiting for you to arrive and accept it, and at least one more beyond that! All that gold was sitting there waiting for me to come and get it, but *you refused to go!* If that isn't betrayal I'd like to know what is, but I fixed you! You didn't care that if you died I'd be left all alone, so I fixed it so you *would* die.

But you didn't! Why didn't you die? Why?"

Encar's voice had risen to a screech, and he was literally beginning to foam at the mouth. Disgust and illness rose in Tiran as he glanced at the king, but Reynar was looking toward the man who had earlier approached them.

"I think that's clear enough," the king said in a voice that went beyond calm. "I was looking forward to taking care of this, but it's obviously beyond even my jurisdiction—and I can't decide whether I'm pleased or sorry. Sisal, it's in the hands of you and your brothers and sisters now. Please see to it."

"At your command, Your Majesty," Sisal acknowledged with a bow, then turned away to beckon to the others of his group and the guardsmen. Encar was screaming again as they dragged him away, and Tiran felt a need to sit down that had nothing to do with his wounds.

"The only reason he failed was because his laziness kept him from learning that I was capable of Shifting," Tiran muttered, still shocked and confused. "I knew he was self-centered, but to see the worlds only in their relationship to *you*—!"

"No, Tiran, he wasn't just self-centered," Reynar disagreed, putting a sympathetic hand to his shoulder. "The man is totally insane, and eventually we might have to end him. They'll strip him of every memory he has and try to start over and build a healthy personality, but there's only a small chance of success. Our conclave of the Sighted doesn't care to waste someone with the Sight, but if they can't change him they *will* put him down."

"He was the ultimate spoiled brat, and next to him even Alex is sweet and reasonable," Tiran said with a headshake. "It makes me wonder what kind of disease he was born with or caught, that he would turn out like that."

"Most of the time it's the combination of no conscience and the depredations of indulgent parents,"

Reynar answered, his tone sour. "If you have no conscience and your parents are too hard on you, you grow up prone to committing violence on everyone you meet. If your parents spoil you, though, you learn how to manipulate people to get what you want. In both cases they're only taking what they consider is due them, but the outlook isn't sane. If you're not taught to cooperate with and support society no matter what your personal bias is, you're unsane and not likely to survive."

"I'll take your word for it," Tiran said, also taking a deep breath. "What happens now?"

"Now you'll sit down for five minutes," the king responded, and this time the words were an order. "If you're going to compete in the finals, you have to be able to stand without help."

Tiran realized it was Reynar's hand that was making it possible for him to remain erect, so once again he nodded. He would go someplace and sit down, and when it came time to fight he would . . . he *would* . . .

Tiran got to sit down for longer than five minutes. The four finalists were seated together in chairs arranged on the far side of the speakers' platform and below it. Ten feet in front of the chairs was a large, roped-off area, and beyond that stood the crowds. They'd waited all day to see the end of the competition, and now it was ready to start.

Lord Arthon spoke for the four judges, announced the finals as officially begun, then called out the names of the first two entrants to return. The first man was someone Tiran had seen but never spoken to, and the second was Baron Sellin. The baron looked annoyed that he hadn't been the first to get back, and he glared at his opponent when the man was asked to state his choice of battle. First back earned first choice, and the man immediately chose bare hands.

"Good thinking," Tiran muttered at the decision, the third man beside him nodding briefly. As a baron, Sellin would be expected to have more experience with weapons than most men. Facing him bare-handed negated that experience, at the least making the confrontation more equal, at best giving an edge to the first man. Sound strategy, and it should have worked.

But it didn't. As soon as the two men faced each other in the roped-off area, Tiran knew the first man was done. His stance was confident and aggressive, but Sellin had the balance and moves of a highly trained fighter. He let the first man tire himself out with attacks that never reached their objective, and then caught him with a blow to the heart region, followed by a spinning kick to the head. The first man went down, and didn't get up again.

"Looks like it's my turn," the man next to Tiran said, a faint gleam in his eyes as he stood. Tiran had the impression the man was better at hand-to-hand than Sellin and knew it, but the baron must have also known it. As the winner, he was entitled to make the next battle choice, and he chose swords.

"Yes, your turn to go down," Tiran murmured in belated answer as he saw the way the third man held the sword given to him. He was familiar enough with the weapon to make *some* kind of showing, but it definitely wasn't his strong suit.

And Sellin took advantage of that fact. Once again he conserved what strength he had left by letting his opponent do all the attacking, spending his own effort only on defense. It wasn't long before the other man started stumbling, and then it was Sellin's turn. He beat aside the other's guard and lunged, but didn't kill the man as he so obviously intended to do. The man stumbled again at just the right—or wrong—time, and instead of being skewered got a slice along the ribs.

But that still put him out of the contest. Sellin stood aside and rested while a Sighted healed the injured man before helping him from the fighting area, and then the baron's gaze came to Tiran. Two down and one to go, his faint smile said clearly. You're a fool to think you can face me as you are, and I'm ready to prove it to the world.

"The final meeting will be between Baron Sellin and Tiran d'Iste," Lord Arthon announced, almost as if he were confirming Sellin's silent challenge. "The winner of this meeting will be the winner of the competition, so will Tiran d'Iste please step forward into the arena."

Easy for you to say, Tiran thought, aware of the stiffness and pain waiting for the first of his movements. Sellin wasn't being overconfident by viewing himself as the ultimate winner; anyone looking at Tiran could see the shape he was in. But Tiran was a professional, and when your life is constantly on the line, you don't leave your survival to luck. You plan carefully for all contingencies, and make your own luck.

Years earlier, Tiran had come close to dying by having to fight while badly wounded. He'd won only because he had been that much better than his opponent, something that couldn't be counted on for any future time. With that in mind he'd thought long and hard, and finally came up with a very unorthodox idea. He'd never heard of anyone trying it, but when he'd tried it himself, it had worked. For some reason it had drained his energies fast and so could be used for only a relatively short time, but it could still be used.

And the time to do it had arrived. Without moving Tiran *Shifted*, but not to another form. His Shift was into his own form, but one that he visualized as unwounded! In a way it was like Alex's game of Monster, where she Shifted into a horrible, repellent version of her own self. Tiran was still Tiran, but with a very important difference.

"No!" Baron Sellin shouted when Tiran stood and headed for the fighting area. "Didn't you judges see that? He did some kind of Shifting, and now he isn't wounded! That's cheating, and I want him disqualified!"

"This competition is for full-range shape-shifters," Tiran countered, pausing to look back and speak directly to the judges. "Since Shifting is required it can't be disallowed, especially since I'm exactly as I was when I got to the end of the trail. My wounds might not be visible, but they're still there. Unless there's a specific rule against doing this, I claim it's fair."

The four judges moved together, and each of them spoke briefly. Arthon nodded and asked a question, the other three answered, and then the conference was over.

"It's our unanimous decision that, since no rule specifically excludes this sort of action, it's legal and acceptable," Arthon announced, causing the crowd of onlookers to cheer. They all seemed to approve of Tiran's unorthodox idea—all, that is, except Sellin. When Tiran turned back to him the baron held his sword in a white-knuckled fist, and his eyes were filled with the intention to kill.

An attendant brought Tiran's sword to the fighting area, and a moment later he and the baron were facing one another. Sellin had stripped off his tunic before the first match, and that left the two of them bare-chested.

"How will you feel when I replace those wounds you think are gone?" Sellin asked in a murmur as he circled with Tiran. "Remember how much they hurt, how hard it was for you to move? It's going to happen again, and I'm the one who'll do it."

Sellin's grin was a good part feral, but Tiran ignored it the way he ignored the man's words. Some men liked to *talk* their opponents into losing, and Tiran had experience facing that sort. They were usually good enough to best most comers, but needed an extra edge to bolster their confidence. There was a chance Sellin *might* win the fight, but Tiran wasn't about to help him do it.

This time it was the baron who attacked first, probably because of Tiran's lack of response. He'd tried to make Tiran fear him even before blades were crossed, and when that didn't work he decided to use steel. It was a move of desperation rather than sound strategy, and he found that out when Tiran parried his attack and nicked his swordarm before he could withdraw.

"Damn you!" Sellin hissed as he touched the small wound with his left hand, his fingers coming away blood-covered. His face had paled more than a wound that size could account for; obviously he knew as well as Tiran that his swordarm would now be weakening rather quickly. If he was going to win the fight, he would have to do it fast.

And then he looked at Tiran's face, and a good part of his anger dissolved into pleased anticipation. Tiran knew Sellin was seeing the sweat on his forehead and the strain in his eyes, two dead giveaways he had no control over. He didn't have much time before he collapsed, and now Sellin knew it. The only thing the baron had to do was drag out the encounter, and time would win the fight for him.

Which meant that Tiran couldn't wait. Sellin's first two opponents had wasted their strength in attack, and now it was Tiran's turn. But he couldn't afford to waste what he didn't have, and he was a better fighter than those other two. He adjusted his grip on the hilt of his weapon, put his mind fully on the fight, and then began to take the battle to Sellin.

At first the baron tried to play the same game of defense only, but you can't do that with someone who's better than you. Sellin found himself defending frantically and then was forced to respond, needing the aggressiveness of attack to keep his guard from being breached. It didn't add a whole lot to the safety of his position, but it did save him from immediate defeat.

Tiran smiled as he continued to press the baron, but only because that was part of his way of fighting. A calm and easy smile was often more effective than a fancy passage at arms, but this time there was nothing behind the smile. Pain and exhaustion were trying to slow his swordarm, and dizziness was trying to tangle his feet. But he would continue on one step and movement at a time for the next year if necessary, and would not stop until he had been declared the winner.

And that, too, Sellin was able to see in his eyes. The baron's complexion went gray as the wound in his swordarm continued to bleed, strength draining away with every movement in defense or attack. For the first time his inner fear was visible, the fear he'd undoubtedly felt all along at the prospect of having to face Tiran. He surely considered himself a better fighter than anyone else there, his reputation unblemished . . . and now a professional was about to ruin it all and make him look like a fool . . .

Sellin, Baron West, was clearly a man of pride with no sense of perspective to balance it. Rage and humiliation threw him at Tiran in attack, everything he must have been taught about remaining calm in combat forgotten. He was going to show the upstart . . . teach him a lesson for not staying out of the way of his betters . . . especially now, when the man was all but dead on his feet . . . force an aching arm to move, slash aside that infuriating guard and aim for the middle of that chest . . .

Tiran let his guard be knocked aside, rode with the attack to parry in his turn, then extended in a lunge most sword fights don't allow for. It was a move usually made only with foils, but the opening had been there and his reflexes had sent him to take quick advantage of it.

Sellin grunted as pointed steel entered his chest, the surprise on his face still mostly anger. He tried to bring his own weapon into play again, and discovered it was impossible; the surprise grew as his fingers opened and his knees buckled, sending him weaponless toward the ground. Tiran let go of his own sword, unable to withdraw it and barely able to stand. That last effort took everything out of him at once ... blackness was starting to cover the world ...

"Somebody catch him!" Reynar roared, and half a dozen men jumped toward a Tiran who was about to follow the late Baron Sellin to the ground. Where the man had gotten the strength to fight and win Reynar didn't know, but he wasn't about to let the effort be wasted. The four judges had come down from the platform to stand beside him, and he quickly turned to them.

"If he's the official winner, say so and order him healed," he instructed a worried Lord Arthon. "If you waste any time at all, he could die."

"I couldn't possibly allow him to die," Arthon answered with flat-voiced determination, then ran forward to make the announcement and get help to Tiran. Reynar didn't realize that only Moult and Fregin had followed Arthon until Lady Wella put her hand on his arm.

"Don't worry, Your Majesty," she said in a soft voice. "We're too grateful to Tiran d'Iste to let him die, especially when Fregin can prevent it. He'll be just fine, and I'd like to take this opportunity to offer you our apologies."

"Apologies for what?" Reynar asked, turning to look down at her. "You and the others couldn't possibly have been better guests, not to mention fairer judges. I mean to let your own monarch know how well the four of you have done in the matter of establishing friendly relations between our kingdoms."

"If you should do so, we'll be most grateful," Wella answered with a smile. "That, however, doesn't change the fact that we owe you two distinct apologies. One is for our suspicions about this competition. We were certain that you would attempt to influence our decisions at some time, but you never did. It upset you to see Princess Alexia disqualified, but you made no attempt to interfere."

"It wouldn't have been proper for me to interfere," Reynar said with a faint smile of his own. "I asked the four of you to be judges in the hopes that you would render fair decisions no matter who was involved. Since you did exactly that, I couldn't very well decide to change my mind."

"Many in your place would have done so anyway," she maintained, her words insisting on the point. "The second apology owed you is a more personal one, even though it was part of my job to learn just how strong a man you are. My kingdom has had some unpleasant experiences, you see, dealing with monarchs who were supposed to be strong, decisive leaders. By the time we learned they were wishy-washy and easily swayed by others, it was too late to amend the trade treaties we'd signed with them."

"Which is why you did—what?" Reynar asked, seeing the flush in her cheeks but not understanding it. "Was something done I'm unaware of? As far as I know, there's been nothing that should cause embarrass—oh."

"Yes, you remember now," she said, her expression rueful. "You see, Your Majesty, I have a—talent—that I'm able to exercise at will, and when we spoke alone that time—It takes a very strong man to resist me— we had to know if your word really could be relied on. You have no idea how much I regret having had to do that—"

"All right, dear lady, be calm," Reynar said with a chuckle, patting her twisting hands. "My kingdom has had the same sort of bad experience, and it would certainly have helped to have someone with your— talent—working on *our* behalf. As long as I passed the test, that is."

"Oh, you certainly did!" the woman exclaimed in relief, making Reynar chuckle again. "You were wonderful, Your Majesty, and my report will say exactly that."

Reynar would have added something else, but the crowd noise had been getting out of hand the last minute or two. He turned to see what all the cheering was about, and found that Tiran d'Iste was back on his feet and being congratulated by everyone in reach. The way he stood said he could still use a good night's sleep, but he was no longer wounded and much of his strength had returned. He accepted the acclamation of those around him, then excused himself to come over to the king.

"Your Majesty," he said with a formal bow. "Thanks to Lord Fregin I now feel I might even survive the next and, hopefully, last battle, so I present myself before you as the undisputed winner of this competition. May I ask where my bride is?"

"I sent for her when you stepped out to face Sellin," Reynar answered with a grin, Lady Wella laughing softly at his side. "I see now why you made fighting your career. Another man in your place would have waited a short while before plunging into the fray again."

"It's been my experience, Your Majesty, that those who stop to catch their breath also begin questioning their sanity for being in the place they are." Tiran's grin was as wide as the king's, a substitute for mentioning the eagerness inside him. The most important fight was still ahead of him, but if he managed to win *that* one . . .

"Then by all means, let's not stop for anything," the king agreed with a laugh. "As soon as she gets here, I'll make the announcement—"

King Reynar had started to look around in the direction of the palace, but suddenly all amusement disappeared as he fell silent. He looked at the man hurrying toward them, Tiran realized, a man who seemed to be very upset. Tiran's first urge was to demand to know what was going on, but that was stupid. Obviously even the king didn't yet know, but in another moment they'd both be finding out.

"Your Majesty, Princess Alexia has apparently disappeared," the man gasped out with a bow when he reached them. "The palace guardsmen are certain she didn't enter, but we checked her apartment anyway, as well as other locations. There isn't a sign of her."

"Blast that girl!" the king growled as Tiran's insides turned cold. "When I get my hands on her—! Isn't there *anyone* who saw her and the direction she took? There have to be hundreds of people on these grounds, especially today. You can't tell me not a single one noticed a red-haired girl wearing weapons!"

"Lord Merwin is using a contingent of the palace guard to question as many people as possible, Sire," the man responded nervously. "He's certain he'll find more than one witness, so it shouldn't be much longer before—"

The man broke off when the king suddenly looked beyond him, and Tiran followed Reynar's gaze to see someone who might be Lord Merwin hurrying toward them. Another man accompanied the lord, but in the small amount of daylight left, Tiran wasn't sure whether or not he recognized him.

"Your Majesty!" Merwin puffed as he all but ran to them and bowed. "This is terrible! How can I tell you—!"

"Damn it, man, just get it said," Reynar ordered, obviously trying to keep from biting off the small man's head. "Did you find out where she is? If she's gotten involved in another escapade, I'll—"

"Your Majesty, no!" Lord Merwin said quickly, shockingly interrupting the king deliberately. "Please don't say anything you'll—Princess Alexia took a horse from the stables and went to the city. This man here has been trying to find someone to tell about what happened, but some of your guard officers have been . . . unsure about bringing him to you. They—"

"They tried to make me pay to see you, King," the man interrupted in turn, not about to be diplomatic. His clothing wasn't new, but it also wasn't shabby enough to make someone believe he was penniless. "They refused to listen to anythin' I had to say, not unless I came up with silver for 'em. I don't have no silver with me, an' it would have taken too long to go an' get some. I been waitin' a couple of hours, an' now it could be too late."

"Too late for what?" Reynar asked much too softly, his rage obviously not aimed at the man he spoke to. "And don't worry about those guard officers of mine. In a very short while they won't have any need of silver whatsoever."

"It's the princess, Your Majesty," the man answered with a gulp, eyes wide over new understanding of what royal anger actually could mean. "She come into the High Magistrate's court while I was there, waitin' to see what kind of sentence my cousin would get. Wouldn't care myself, Garmin's never been worth anythin', but his ma—"

"Please," Tiran interjected, speaking before Reynar could explode. "Just tell us what happened."

"The princess rode her horse in, an' then laughed at the High Magistrate," the man went on quickly, not too dim to take the hint. "She kept sayin' the High Magistrate couldn't do nothin' to her, an' she was goin' to leave town with another stolen horse. She kept pushin' at him and pushin' at him, until he wouldn't take any more. He had her arrested, an' then sentenced her to hang."

"And I'll bet she made no effort to fight being arrested," Tiran said, furious with the girl he loved despite the fact that he understood her motives. "I told her once that her sense of honor would never let her simply walk away from this problem, that she would have to pay what she owed. She countered that there was more than one way to pay up, and this has to be what she meant. She's decided to pay with her life."

"Right now I'm tempted to be the one who takes that life," King Reynar growled, heavy vexation covering him. "I try to make a point of not interfering in the High Magistrate's jurisdiction, but now I'll have to talk to him for the second time. When I get that girl back she'll pay for this—that I swear by everything I hold dear. And I think I'll let her spend the night in a cell; it might teach her a lesson."

"Your Majesty, please," Lord Merwin said, actually looking ill. "You still don't have the entire story. Princess Alexia must have expected you to intervene, so she took steps to prevent it. She—taunted the High Magistrate so strongly, he announced that it was his duty to protect you from her. Rather than sentence her to hang in the morning, he—he—"

"It's set to be done at sundown," the city man finished when Lord Merwin found it impossible to speak the words, his tone filled with compassion. "Don't know if there's any time left now . . . this kingdom's been good to me an' mine, so I tried comin' here as soon as it happened . . . wouldn't want one of *my* girls dyin' without me knowin' about it . . ."

Tiran saw the king go pale, obviously sharing the same terrible chill that wrapped its hands around his own heart. Sundown. His Alex had been sentenced to die at sundown . . . it was just about that time right now . . . they couldn't possibly get there until it was too late . . . even magic couldn't keep the sun from setting . . .

"Horses," the king whispered, his voice clearly trembling in spite of that. "If only Sisal and Limis hadn't left . . . Get the fastest horses in the stables . . ."

"I've already ordered them to be brought, Sire," Lord Merwin answered, turning to look behind himself. "See? Here they come now, along with your personal guard."

The king made no answer in words, instead immediately pushing forward toward the approaching men and mounts. Tiran was right beside him, trying to believe they would get there in time, trying to fight the illness that was turning his personal world as dark as the outer one. Could he really lose her even before they had the chance to like each other? It had been coming, he knew it had, if only they were given the chance—

If only she didn't die. It was too stupid to think about, too frustratingly idiotic to even consider. Tiran pulled himself into the saddle of the horse brought for him, sending it quickly after the one the king was moving into a gallop. His body still ached and his head was beginning to hurt, but he wouldn't have stayed behind even if he were still wounded. Which in a way he was. Magic healed the outer wound, but the toll taken on the body in strength and the effort to rebuild . . .

Why did she have to see death as the only way out? She was a stubborn, unreasonable brat who had refused to tell him why she felt as she did, and the thought made Tiran angry. She would have called him every name imaginable if *he'd* tried to handle a problem alone, but she thought she was entitled to do anything she pleased.

The darkening landscape whipping past him brought a peripheral dizziness, but Tiran banished it from his awareness. They *had* to get there in time. He hadn't told her how much he really loved her . . . not so that she understood and believed ... What would he do if she wasn't there to share his life with him? How could he make her happy if she died?

"Please, beloved, we'll find an answer to your problem," he vowed in a whisper. "Together we can do anything ... please don't go ahead without me ... at least wait for me to come with you ..."

Tiran knew he would go anywhere, just as long as she was there to go with him. If it couldn't be in life, then it would have to be in death ... which might not be all that far away from him either ...

I lay on the cot trying not to think, but time passes so visibly when you're waiting for something. There was no clock in the cell to tick, but my imagination made up for that. I could see and hear the minutes going by, each one like a grain of sand in an hourglass, each one decreasing the pile of those that were left. They dropped away into the infinity of forever, one at a time forever gone.

I had to keep my muscles locked to stop the trembling, so filled with terror that I could understand why people that frightened often wet themselves. In a little while I was going to die, and even though it was what I wanted, I couldn't control the fear. It shook me like a rag doll, worse than anything I'd ever experienced. I didn't want to change my mind, but even if I did, it was far too late.

And then I heard a sound I thought I was braced for, the sound of someone opening the cell door. My heartbeat went from a shivering thud to a gallop, and for a moment I thought I would pass out. I lay trembling even while terror froze me in place, my eyes glued to the door that was being opened. A guard pulled it back out of the way, and then the High Magistrate stood in the opening.

"Your Highness," he pronounced, like a death bell tolling. "The afternoon runs away before us, and evening is almost here. Are you ready?"

I'll never know how I forced myself slowly to sitting without throwing up, but I finally managed it. My feet were on the floor and my arms were wrapped around myself, leaving nothing to do but nod stiffly to his question. I would have spoken if it had been possible . . .

"So you're ready," he said, studying me closely. Then he turned his head and said, "Do as I ordered earlier," stepped into the cell, and let the door be closed again behind him. We two were now alone, but I didn't understand why.

"Allow me to congratulate you, Your Highness," he said after a moment. He stood motionless with his arms folded, his hands invisible inside the sleeves of his robe. "I pride myself on being a man not easily manipulated, yet you recruited me to your cause with very little effort. And caused me to misjudge you, which should have been even more difficult to accomplish. You're a very . . . unusual young woman."

"I—don't understand," I managed to get out, hating the fact that the waiting wasn't over. "You said it was almost sundown—can't we get started *now*? I want to start now."

"Your Highness, it's over," he said with more gentleness than he was supposed to be capable of. "I was angry and outraged for quite some time, but then I calmed down and was able to think again. After considering the matter at length, the only question I had was whether you truly meant to go through with it. It was possible you were playing your game for appearance's sake, but I've now satisfied myself that you weren't. Your intention was to satisfy the demands of honor by giving up your life."

I stared at him very briefly before closing my eyes and putting my hands over them. The way he'd used the past tense in describing my intentions—he'd not only figured out what I'd done, he'd decided not to let it happen. Knowing I wasn't going to die produced a relief that weakened my knees and set my head spinning, but the disappointment washed those feelings away. My last chance to get out from under was gone, and needing to live would prove how much worse it could be than having to die.

"I find myself deeply touched by your plight," I heard, controlled compassion behind his words. "I won't pretend that I understand it completely, but your desperation must have been extreme to force you to this pass. Perhaps if we discussed the matter, a less final solution could be found."

"The only choices left to me are impossible ones," I said, not quite sure why I was answering him. "Either I ruin my life by marrying, or I ruin it by spending years working as a prisoner. Either way I'll end up crazy and bitter, and I'll certainly reach a point where honor begins to mean less than escape. From then on it will all be downhill, and there's no telling how many people will get hurt. Why do innocent people have to suffer, when it can all be avoided if I die right now?"

By then I was looking at him again, willing to beg if that was what it took. I loathed the idea of hurting innocent people, but it had become just about inevitable that I would.

"I can see you really believe what you've said," he declared, those eyes probing deep inside my head. "That, however, doesn't make it true. No matter how strongly you doubt the possibility, there's always the chance that a satisfactory compromise can be found. I think we'll try *that* first, and save resorting to extremes until—"

He was interrupted by the sound of the cell door opening, an action that apparently surprised him. The guardsman who had opened the door didn't come in, but it was obvious he had news of some sort. The High Magistrate walked over to him, listened for a moment and nodded, then looked back at me.

"I sent one of my court officers to inform His Majesty of your whereabouts," he said. "I expected that he would have to go all the way to the palace, but it seems he encountered the king just a short distance away. He's now being shown to my guest chambers, and it would be best if we joined him."

So that was the end of that. Even if the High Magistrate hadn't caught on, there was a good chance my father would have arrived in time to stop the hanging. Everything seemed to be piling up against me, and I was beginning to wonder why I'd bothered. I stood up to follow the High Magistrate out, but it took a couple of steps before my body remembered how to accomplish walking straight.

"Your Highness, are you all right?" the High Magistrate asked, his hand to my arm. "You look so drawn and tired—were you given anything to eat or drink during the past hours?"

"I didn't want anything," I answered, telling the absolute truth. I couldn't imagine ever being hungry again, and the thirst wasn't so bad that I couldn't ignore it. What I really wanted was a dark, silent place deep underground where I would be left completely alone, but I wasn't likely to get that.

The High Magistrate let the guardsmen lead the way while he walked beside me, and it wasn't long before we reached his guest chambers. Four members of my father's personal guard stood outside the door, but they made no attempt to stop the High Magistrate and me. One of them opened the door for us—onto a scene of agitated confusion.

"What's going on here?" the High Magistrate demanded automatically, for the moment forgetting that one of his guests outranked him. The crowd of guardsmen and attendants parted to show my father on one knee beside an unmoving body, someone who looked just like—

"Tiran!" I couldn't help gasping, and then I was forcing my way through that crowd of idiots to go to my knees beside him. Under his tan he was horribly pale, and he was very deeply unconscious. "What's wrong with him?" I demanded, one hand to his face as I looked at my father. "What have you done to him?"

"What have *I* done to him?" he countered in outrage, golden eyes flaring. "He was hurt trying to get out of the trap *you* maneuvered him into, and even though he's been healed, he's been pushing too hard. We came here from the palace at top speed, and that was obviously the last straw. As soon as we confirmed the fact that you were all right, he let himself collapse."

I looked down at Tiran again, well beyond feeling anything as simple as guilt. I didn't even have the right to be worried about him, not after the way I'd wrecked things. None of my plans had worked, not even keeping this man safe; my shooting score was perfect, with not even a single arrow hitting its mark.

Just then one of my father's attendants came in with the High Magistrate's sorceress-healer, and she chased everyone away from her patient. I walked to one corner of the large room, deliberately paying no attention to what was being done to Tiran. Nothing about him was my concern any longer, and the sooner I accepted that, the better.

My father spent a couple of minutes talking to the High Magistrate, and then he came over to me. He studied me silently for a little while, possibly waiting for me to speak first, but when I didn't he refused to follow my example.

"Aren't you going to ask who won the competition?" he said, a disturbance behind the evenness of his words. "Now that you're going to live, you should be concerned again."

"I don't give a damn who won," I answered, leaning against the wall with one shoulder and not looking at him. I would have enjoyed lying down somewhere, but it wasn't important enough to mention.

"You don't care who your husband is going to be?" he pressed, almost in a coaxing way. "If people find out you said that, you'll be drummed out of the women's guild. At the very least, a woman is supposed to be curious."

His gentle teasing was too familiar to be anything but painful just then. I stared at the chair I stood near, and fought with all my strength not to cry.

"This is ridiculous," he said, faint exasperation now coloring his words. "You're not dead, and you're not going to be. You're going to live and continue with your life, and I want to see some sign that you understand that. Ask me who won the competition."

I lowered my head just a little more, and didn't say a word. I didn't care who had won, but distantly I sympathized with the man. He expected to get a wife for his efforts, but he'd have to make do with her land and wealth. Poor thing, the disappointment would probably crush him.

"I can see your stubbornness hasn't changed," my father said after taking a deep breath. "That's some-thing we'll be talking about along with a number of other topics, but this isn't the time or place. First we'll get you and d'Iste back to the palace, and then—"

I glanced up to see what had made him break off in mid-sentence, finding it was the healer coming toward us. I had the urge to hold my breath until I heard what she would say, but I really didn't have the strength.

"Your Majesty," the woman said with a curtsy, then gave one to me. "Your Highness. I'm pleased to report that the man will be fine, once he's allowed to sleep away his exhaustion. I've made sure that he won't wake until it's all right for him to do so, which means you needn't worry about moving him. Just be reasonably gentle, and you won't disturb his sleep."

"We thank you for your efforts, madam," my father told her with a smile. "We've already arranged for the use of the High Magistrate's coach, therefore shall we depart immediately. Be assured that a more substantial indication of our satisfaction will be sent you."

"Unnecessary, Your Majesty, and for that reason welcome," the woman said with a smile and a bow of her head. "Allow me to add that Her Highness is scarcely in better condition than the man. She, too, should rest as soon as possible."

"We mean to see to it personally, madam," my father said, and then his hand was wrapped around my arm. "We bid you a pleasant evening."

The last thing I wanted was to go back to the palace, but my father didn't care. I was given Tiran's horse, with half the escort left behind to accompany the coach he'd be in. The silent ride was much too short despite being hard as hell, and once we got there I was taken directly to my apartment.

"You're all but falling off your feet," my father said after he'd escorted me inside. "I want you in bed right now, and I'll have food sent up. Tomorrow we'll get this straightened out once and for all."

Sure we will, I thought as I watched him leave. Who's supposed to bring the magic wand to make that happen? And I don't feel like going to bed, so I won't.

I went over to my favorite chair and sat instead, getting nothing in the way of satisfaction from the defiance. I was so tired I'd probably find it impossible to sleep . . . even though it was night outside . . . the perfect time to sleep . . . so tired . . .

CHAPTER SIXTEEN

Waking up in bed seemed perfectly natural, until I remembered I'd fallen asleep in a chair. I was also somewhat cleaner than I had been, but I still hadn't had the bath I'd wanted. Whoever had undressed me and put me to bed had done a job that was only just adequate, but that was fine with me. The urge to be clean and comfortable had disappeared with my appetite, and even a long night's sleep hadn't returned them.

I sat with my head in my hands for a little while, trying to see past the fog of depression, then gave it up and went to get dressed. A new gown of golden silk hung in my dressing area, probably because of some official function or other that was scheduled for later in the day. I ignored the gown and pulled on exercise clothes and boots, but not because I intended to exercise. All I wanted was to be left alone to brood.

I had barely gotten myself into a chair before my breakfast arrived, delivered by a chattering crowd of four house girls. Two of them fussed and kept asking how I felt, while the other two gushed over the delicious idea of my upcoming marriage. I stood it for about five minutes before ordering them out,

317

but they didn't leave feeling upset or insulted. They had nothing but sympathy for the "ordeal" I'd gone through, and made sure I knew they'd be back the instant I wanted them.

Normally that horrible a threat would have made me smile, but my face couldn't seem to remember the technique. I poured myself a cup of chai from the breakfast tray, carried it back to my chair, then returned to brooding. Brooding is never productive, but at times it can be satisfying in a comforting way.

A moderate amount of undisturbed time passed, the kind that you know won't be lasting very long. Bright sunshine poured in through the windows of my sitting room, telling me that all sorts of people would be sharing its enthusiasm. It wasn't hard to decide not to let them do it near me, but there are some people a decision like that doesn't apply to. One of them was the first to show up, and he glanced at my breakfast tray before coming to take a chair near mine.

"You're looking a lot better this morning, Alexia," my father said with a warm smile, briefly making me wonder why my mother hadn't already come by. Probably because my father wanted first crack at me . . . "I'm very glad to be able to say that to you, daughter. It may not have seemed like it lately, but I happen to love you very much."

"I know that, Father," I replied, looking down at my hands. I did know he loved me, but sometimes the most horrible atrocities are committed in the name of love. When you make a decision involving someone that's based on your preferences rather than on theirs, you'll probably end up ruining their lives no matter how much you love them.

"Child, we really do have to talk this out," he said with a sigh, and somehow I felt he would have been happier if I'd argued his loving me. "The High Magistrate told me you believe you have two options left open to you. You're not seriously thinking of insisting on being sent to prison, are you? You have to know I couldn't possibly allow that."

"That was supposed to be my only alternative if I refused to marry," I said, raising my eyes to his face. "What have you decided to put in its place?"

"Alexia, you *can't* refuse to marry," he said intensely, patience a thick blanket over him and his words. "All requirements of the competition aside, it's something your mother and I really want for you. Do you think we'd want something that would harm you?"

"What about what I want?" I asked, just for the hell of it. "Did you even bother to ask what that was? Or did you just grab a very handy excuse to force me into doing things your way? Tell me you don't know why I did what I did to start this whole mess."

"That's very much beside the point right now," he answered, but at least he had the grace to look uncomfortable. He did know I'd taken that horse to help our people against a swindler, but he'd chosen to ignore the motive. "The point that needs discussing is the fact that you're promised in marriage to the winner of the competition. I want to hear you tell me that you'll honor the obligation."

"Certainly, Father," I said after taking a deep breath, looking away from him again. "I'll certainly honor whatever obligations you think I have."

"You will?" he said, suspicion and disbelief flashing bright in his tone. "I'm delighted to hear that, but I don't feel reassured. *Why* don't I feel reassured?"

"I have no idea," I responded with a shrug, then leaned my head back in the chair and closed my eyes. "You should know that I won't break my word once I give it. You want me to marry the winner of the competition, so I give you my word that I will. All I ask is that the ceremony be held as quickly as possible."

"Damn it, girl, I want to know what you're *not* saying," he insisted, now even more upset. "The words

I hear are exactly the ones I asked for, but there's still something wrong. You haven't started agreeing with me, you've just stopped disagreeing."

"What else do you need?" I asked, too depressed to feel even slightly annoyed. "Since my refusal would be more than just embarrassing for you, I've given you my agreement. Did you think I would stand by and let people say your word was worthless? I don't want to do this, but you gave your word, so I will. Just don't make the time any harder on me by dragging it out."

"All right, I can't stand any more of this," he said, his voice uneven. "I haven't been so close to crying since—Alexia, I'm willing to bet that one of the things that's making you feel so hopeless is what's developed between you and Tiran d'Iste. You've fallen in love with him."

"Don't be silly, Father," I said, glad my eyes were already closed. "What would be the sense in falling in love with a man I'll never see again? I was worried about him last night because he saved my life during the competition. It's nothing more involved than that."

"Alexia, last night you knocked down three of my personal guard and two of my attendants," he said very gently. "You did it because they happened to be between you and Tiran, and didn't move out of the way fast enough. I was fairly certain you didn't realize you'd done it. You *are* well-mannered enough to apologize when you inadvertently walk over people's faces."

Under other circumstances the dry tone he'd used would have made me blush, but all that came to my cheeks was the gray of uselessness. What did it matter how I felt about Tiran? I had no memory of knocking people down, but it had been done in an effort to get to the side of a man I'd never see again.

"You're not interested in commenting on that?" my father asked after a moment. "Normally the lack would make me worry, but I think I understand. You've promised to marry the winner of the competition, and you don't want to dishonor your word by getting involved with another man. The winner is delighted you feel that way, and has come to thank you personally."

I realized then that the man must be waiting in the corridor outside my apartment, and that increased my depression. I didn't want to see him or talk to him, and I certainly didn't want him thanking me. I opened my mouth to say exactly that, but opening my eyes at the same time caused every word in my mind to disappear. Right there above me . . . bending over and staring down with hungry green eyes . . . no longer unconscious or unaware . . .

Tiran pulled me out of the chair and into his arms, but I was the one who started the kiss. I knew it wasn't right but I couldn't seem to stop myself, not when he was right there in front of me. I buried my hands in his hair and tried to swallow him, only vaguely realizing he was doing the same with me. I was pressed so tight against his broad, hard body that I could scarcely breathe, but feeling him against me was more important than breathing. I hadn't realized how much I would miss him, hadn't even let myself consider the thought.

But after a little while I was forced to consider a lot more than that. What I was doing wasn't fair to either one of us, and especially not after having pushed him into a trap. If my father hadn't been there I probably would have started tearing his clothes off, and the way he touched me said he was just about to forget we weren't alone. That in itself meant the kiss had gone on long enough—even though it was probably the last we'd ever share.

Prying myself loose wasn't just a matter of deciding to do it. Tiran didn't want the kiss to end, and he

was big enough to make his decisions stick. It was
a struggle to get both of my hands against his chest,
but when I pushed I also jerked my face away. That
got his attention, and to make it worse my father
found the situation very amusing.

"It was good of you, daughter, to show how little
you care about the man," he said with a chuckle. "I
know you've set *my* mind at rest, and I'm sure your
prospective husband feels the same way."

I hadn't needed the reminder, but hearing it anyway
made me pull back completely from Tiran and move
away. He liked that even less, and as his big hands
came to my arms from behind, he said, "Your Majesty,
don't." The half-growled words were almost an order,
but for some reason my father wasn't insulted.

"I suppose you're right, Tiran," he allowed, his
amusement lessened. "She deserves to be punished for
knocking you into that trap, but there *is* a difference
between punishment and torture. You can take care
of it yourself once the two of you are married."

"Father, what are you talking about?" I couldn't help
asking, his words making absolutely no sense. "Tiran
didn't win the competition—he couldn't have."

"That's what I was trying to tell you last night,"
my father said. "Tiran escaped from the trap you
tricked him into and completed the first half of
the competition, but he was hurt doing it. He was
wounded when he faced Baron Sellin, but that didn't
stop him from winning. We weren't able to heal him
until that happened, and then we found out what *you*
were up to. He pushed himself too far riding out with
me, and that's why he collapsed."

I turned around to stare up at Tiran, my jaw brushing the
floor. He was absolutely incredible, and for once I couldn't
think of a thing to say. He'd kept insisting that nothing
would stop him from winning, and nothing had.

"Let that be a lesson to you," he said in his deep
voice, trying to sound stern despite a faint grin. "Your

future husband isn't a man to mess with—as you'll learn in even more detail. You remember, I think, what I said would happen if you took off on your own again."

As a matter of fact he'd never *said* what would happen, but I wasn't in the least curious about what he had in mind. And he also had more than one score to settle with me, a fact emphasized by my father's renewed chuckling. So much for fatherly love and protection—as though any of that made a difference. Realizing that things had changed only for the worse brought me back to reality, and once again I found myself staring at my hands.

"Hey, we're not discussing torture and execution," Tiran said, faint worry in his tone as his hand came to my hair. "I don't know what you're picturing, but I'll be spending more time making love to you than beating you. There's no reason for you to look as though the world is coming to an end."

"I'm sure it's just lack of food doing that to her," my father said. "She was asleep before a tray could be brought to her last night, and this morning she seems to have had no more than that chai. I'll have a fresh tray brought, and you two can eat together."

"I don't think she's interested in doing that," Tiran observed as I moved away from his hand and went back to my chair. "As a matter of fact, she's looking worse than she did earlier. Alex, tell me what's wrong."

"Nothing's wrong," I answered, taking another sip of my chai. "I promised to marry the winner of the competition, and I will. Since that's what you want, there isn't anything wrong."

"Like hell," he growled, coming to crouch in front of my chair and stare up at me. "You've promised to marry me, but you still don't really want to. How can you love me but not want to marry me?"

Those green eyes demanded an answer, no doubt in them at all that I did love him. He wasn't wrong, but only about that. The rest—how could he possibly understand?

"What difference does it make whether or not I want to?" I asked. "I wasn't given a choice about this, I was told I *had* no choice. Is the fact that I love you supposed to make me forget that? I'm still being forced to marry, rather than being left alone to do what *I* choose."

"You've said that before, but never mentioned what you would choose instead," he replied, green eyes now serious. "I can't imagine what it would be that we can't do it together, so you'll have to tell me. What do you consider more important than marrying the man you love?"

"Justifying my existence in my own eyes," I answered, wondering why I was wasting my breath. He'd never understand . . . "I want to do something *worthwhile*, something that will make a difference to more people than just me. I'm able to do so much more than most—I have abilities many have never dreamed of. If I use those abilities to benefit only myself, it's cheating. And if I cheat others I also cheat me, because then I'll never know what I *could* have accomplished. Finding the man I'll always love is something only for me, nothing for anyone else. If I never make the effort to do more, how can I live with myself?"

He didn't answer my question, and the way his brows were knitted over troubled eyes said it would be a while before he did. But that doesn't mean I didn't get the argument I was expecting. My father has always claimed he doesn't know where I get my tendency to argue everything said to me, but no one else has ever had any doubt.

"Alexia, you can't be serious," he scoffed. "A woman doesn't have to prove herself the way a man does, especially when she's supposed to marry. And when she loves the man she marries, things turn out even better. You won't be living with yourself, you'll be living with *him*, and unless I'm completely mistaken, he won't find it hard to make you forget everything else."

"But for how long?" I asked without looking at him. "Six months of married bliss, a year or maybe two? After a while the fireworks of passion die down, but they're supposed to leave behind a stronger, truer love. What if they leave an awareness of loss instead, a memory of what was given up and left undone? That's when bitterness steps in, making you look around for someone to blame. Life becomes a lot less pleasant no matter who the someone turns out to be."

"And if I make you marry me because I love you, I'll be the one you blame," Tiran said. "That's why it doesn't matter that you love me now. Eventually the love will turn to hatred and loathing, and our life together will be ruined. That's worse than blaming someone you never really cared about, incredibly worse. No wonder you're looking at the end of the world."

"Nonsense, my boy, nonsense," my father blustered, seeing the tragedy in Tiran's eyes just as I did. "Women love to dramatize things and make monumental mountains out of tiny anthills. When the two of you are married she'll forget that nonsense, especially once my grandchildren start coming. If you weren't the perfect man for her, she never would have fallen in love with you."

"I think it's time someone told you how wrong you are, my dear," came a new voice, and then my mother was marching up to join us. "You claim to know how different Alexia is, but you still persist in treating her like our other daughters. At least Tiran knows better, and I don't think he'll be going through with the wedding."

"Nonsense," my father said again as he stood, this time adding a shaky laugh. "Tiran is much too sensible to let Alexia talk him out of his victory. She couldn't best him even by cheating, so now she's making up wild stories. He would have to be a gullible fool to believe what she says."

"Perhaps so, but what about believing in what she does?" my mother asked smoothly while Tiran's eyes narrowed just a little. "You men are supposed to be so quick to see things, but sliding something under your nose is no trouble at all. You heard what she said, but made no attempt to listen."

"What are you referring to, Your Majesty?" Tiran asked as he straightened and turned. "I thought I *was* listening."

"Then you must have heard her say she would marry the contest winner, but wanted the ceremony held as quickly as possible," my mother answered. "By itself that means very little, but my husband also told you that she hasn't been eating. Don't you two understand? She'll marry to keep her father from being dishonored, but she doesn't have to stay married if she starves to death."

Put like that my plan sounded ridiculously melodramatic, but neither Tiran nor my father laughed. What they did was look stunned and shocked, and then both of them were speaking at once. The babble was enough to give a tree a headache, and I couldn't help sending my mother a dirty look. I wasn't about to change my decision, but that wouldn't keep the two men from bothering me.

"All right, that's it," Tiran announced when my father paused for breath, running a hand through his hair. "I can understand preferring death to the prospect of coming to hate someone you love. Dying has got to be easier. If I'm a fool for believing she'll do it, then I'm also a fool who knows his woman. I'd rather give her up than see her dead, so the wedding is off. And I'll make sure everyone knows the decision was mine."

He turned to look at me with that, but this time I was the one too stunned to speak. He wasn't going to try to make me change my mind? After all he'd gone through to win?

"But what about my land and gold?" I blurted, thinking he must have forgotten. "You're entitled to that at least, so—"

"I—don't—want—it," he pronounced, still staring at me. "*You're* the only thing I wanted, and if I can't have you I don't care about the rest. Keep it yourself or give it away—I couldn't care less."

"Let's not be so hasty," my father said in a coaxing way, looking back and forth between us. "We're all making decisions based on emotion here, and that's always a mistake. If we sit down and talk it through, I'm sure you'll both come to see the wisdom in at least going through with the ceremony. Once you're actually married . . ."

His voice trailed off as he looked at us, undoubtedly seeing that we weren't buying his suggestion. It felt strange having Tiran's support *against* marriage, but having him on my side again also felt wonderful.

"I think you're going to have to tell them, my dear," my mother said in a smugly pleased way. "Technically you're not supposed to mention it until after the wedding, but if you don't tell them there won't *be* a wedding. The choice is yours, of course, but . . ."

She let the last word dangle like a fishing line in water, all but challenging my father to make a grab for it. He glared at her for a moment before closing his eyes and taking a very deep breath, and when he looked at us again, his decision was made.

"Obviously, this time *I'm* the one without a choice," he said, shifting his gaze to me. "I know you were seeing yourself cornered by well-wishing, Alexia, but there's a good deal more to it than that. I would have told you if I'd been allowed to, but I consider my word just as binding as you do yours."

"Father, is that supposed to mean something?" I asked, wondering if I'd somehow slipped through into the wrong world. "It sounds as if you're about to reveal some deep, dark family secret."

"I am, but it's not a *family* secret," he replied with a grin. "It all has to do with the competition, and what happens when you use it. Haven't you wondered why it's done so rarely, and how the tradition got started?"

Now that he mentioned it I realized there *were* things to wonder about, but there was no need to spend time on them. Not only was he ready to talk about them, he looked downright eager.

"Many hundreds of years ago, there were only a few kingdoms of people like ourselves," he said, urging my mother into a chair before sitting again himself. "Because of their small numbers and the fact that they were all distantly related, the rulers of these kingdoms met once a year. They discussed problems, passed on solutions to former problems, described what they were doing to give their people better lives—everything they could think of to help each other out while enjoying each other's company.

"Right from the beginning they realized the benefit in working with strong magic users and rewarding their help lavishly, so most of the rulers brought their favorites to the meetings with them. Sorcerers and wizards were considered interested parties, which means they were included in the discussions. More than once, one of them came up with a suggestion that was unanimously adopted.

"One day one of the kings had a problem that he didn't immediately share with the others. When questioned about it he said it was a family matter, and so shouldn't concern anyone else. The others urged him to talk about it anyway, and after a little more hesitation he told them about one of his daughters.

"The girl was still young, but even so the king could see trouble coming. She was very talented and highly skilled, and try as he might, the king couldn't find a man she could be matched with. Even most of her brothers weren't as capable, and the king wasn't about to make the girl settle for a man who wasn't at least her equal. He wanted her to be happy, but it didn't look like she would be.

"At that point, two of the other kings admitted they had the same problem. One's daughter was younger and one's was older than the first king's, but all three girls presented the same problem. There was no man available to make a proper match, and considering the natures of the girls, there was bound to be trouble because of the lack.

"No one seemed able to come up with a solution, and that worried all of the kings. Since they all pretty much shared the same bloodline, it wasn't unreasonable to expect that if *they* didn't have the problem, their descendants would. And a daughter who didn't fit in was a *big* problem, considering their positions. Even if one of them was too self-centered to worry about the girl's happiness, he *had* to be concerned about how her antics would make *him* look.

"The discussion went on for hours without any workable solutions being offered, and then one of the wizards stepped forward. He was a guest of one of the associated wizards and so had no real place there, but when he asked if he might speak, they allowed it. He had an enormous reputation as a wizard, being older and stronger than any other sorcerer or wizard there.

"He began by asking if all the rulers agreed they had a problem that needed a solution. When they gave him the obvious answer to his very obvious question, he smiled and asked if they were willing to strike a bargain. He was authorized to give them their solution, but it would have to be paid for. The universe demanded balance, and they would have to provide it.

"Half of the kings demanded to know how much gold it would cost them, while the other half asked who could have 'authorized' a wizard like him to do anything at all. Wizards did as they pleased according to the level of skill they'd attained; they weren't hired to 'represent' others like salesmen. That was the more important of the two questions, and those who had asked about gold immediately shifted sides. Any questions about money could wait.

"The wizard smiled at them again, then said he couldn't tell them who he'd been authorized by. It was something they didn't need to know, but he *could* tell them that their payments wouldn't be in gold. Gold and silver were human symbols of wealth and balance; not only did the universe have no need of them, it demanded more important things in their place.

"That gave the kings pause, but they still wanted to hear what the wizard proposed. After all, they could always refuse to agree to it. They told him to go ahead, and he told them about the idea of a competition. Only the best would enter it, and only the best of the best would win. There would then be suitable men for their daughters to marry.

"Most of the kings were impressed with the idea, but the king who had first brought the problem to light didn't agree. He pointed out that the best of those who entered the competition didn't necessarily have to be his daughter's equal. The man only had to be better than the other entrants, which wasn't saying much. And how was he supposed to get his daughter's consent to marry? If he tried ordering her to it, he'd probably lose half his guardsmen forcing her to obey.

"The other two with similar daughters admitted they would have the same problem. The girls were as strong-minded—read 'stubborn and opinionated'—

as they were talented, and would never agree to being quietly married off. And if the winner of the competition *wasn't* equal to or better than the girl involved, what he'd really win would be an abruptly shortened life span.

"The three kings spoke with such weary certainty that the others didn't doubt them. The wizard's solution wasn't any good, but he smiled again when they told him so. He acknowledged all their objections, but said they hadn't heard the whole proposal. He was prepared to guarantee that any time the competition was held, the proper man would appear and enter. No matter how far away the man normally was, he would be there to join the competition. That would be part of the deal."

Tiran had perched himself on the arm of my chair, and I couldn't help looking up to see his reaction. He'd just been told that entering the competition hadn't even been mostly his idea, that some force had brought him here and caused him to compete. If it had been me I would have been good and mad, but all Tiran did was raise his brows in surprise. I wanted to know why he wasn't angry, but my father was continuing.

"The kings thought about that, then granted it made a good deal of difference," he said after sipping from the cup of chai my mother had brought him. "They didn't know how the wizard could guarantee that, but they also didn't doubt his ability to come through. The next thing they were told was that *they* would have to find a way to commit their daughters to the marriage, preferably without the spilling of blood. As fathers they ought to know their daughters, and know as well the best way to handle them. If double-dealing became necessary, they had to remember it was in a good cause."

He glanced at me when he said that, but apparently didn't see the full agreement he seemed to be looking for. He must have realized he hadn't said anything yet to justify that belief, since he went on without a pause.

"Once all the kings had agreed the requirement was reasonable, the first king spoke up again. He hadn't forgotten that there would be a price to pay, and he felt it was time to find out what it was. He also had the strangest feeling, and so asked *who* would do the paying. He'd probably have no objections if it was himself, but . . .

"The wizard bowed and congratulated the king on his perceptivity, then explained in a gentle way that it wasn't possible for the kings to pay. Their daughters and the men were the ones who had to balance the gift. They'd have been given their ideal life mates, so they'd be required to give something back. It was only fair, after all."

"Even though they'd never asked for that—gift?" I couldn't help putting in. "Other people got to decide what was best, but they had to pay for it?"

"That was the exact objection one of the kings made," my father answered in a very—bland way. "If you're going to talk about fairness, it isn't very fair to rope people into schemes of your own and then make *them* pay for the privilege. Even if you think you're doing them a favor, they could very well disagree with you.

"The wizard granted the point, but said they still didn't know the entire story. It was all well and good to bring two highly capable people together, but the happiness they would find with each other was the least of what needed to be considered. The first question was, 'How many really capable people are there in the worlds?' The answer that everyone knew was true—'Not very many at all.'

"The second question, the wizard said, was, 'How many people in the worlds are in need of help to better their lives?' The answer to that one was, 'Quite a lot,' but with so few highly capable people to do the helping, what were their chances of *being* helped? Not very good at all, unless some kind of bargain was struck somewhere. And the bargain wasn't quite what the kings were thinking—"

"Your Majesty, can't you shorten this a little?" Tiran said, his tone telling me he'd held off commenting as long as humanly possible. "There's no real reason to think the kind of people you're talking about would just drop their own lives to give a hand to those who needed it. Human beings aren't built to be that selfless, and it's a damned good thing. People who spend all their time giving to others never accomplish anything."

"What about the happiness they accomplish?" my mother asked, her voice mildly curious. "Don't you think *that's* worth something?"

"I've found that happiness provided through the charity of others is very limited, Your Majesty," Tiran answered more gently. "If someone simply gives something to you, it rarely has any meaning or value. Helping you to help yourself is another story, but those who like to give tend to give that gift least of all. Possibly they don't care for the idea of losing those they can selflessly give to."

"That's rather a cynical way of looking at things, Tiran, but interesting nevertheless," my mother responded with a smile. "Especially the part about an outright gift being valueless. Reynar, my dear, Tiran is right. Can't you hurry the story a little?"

"Now I know where Alexia gets all that impatience from," my father stated with the expression of a martyr. "But if all of you insist . . . All right, I'm getting on with it! The bottom line is, once you two were married, you would have been offered the chance at something very special. There's a place among the worlds that has already been designated as yours, a place where you two will be recognized as the legitimate rulers. But . . ."

"But?" Tiran prompted when I didn't, having less experience with my father and his ways. "But we have to pay for it with our firstborn? But we have to promise *not* to give away our firstborn? But we have to stand on our heads and whistle the Song of the Stars backwards? I ask Your Majesty to pardon the shortness of my temper, but what if we don't *want* a place among the worlds to rule?"

"I didn't say it was yours to rule," my father replied with a wave of his hand for the annoyance in Tiran's voice. "I said you two would be recognized as the legitimate rulers, even though someone has long since established an illegitimate rule. The people in that place are miserable, having no choice but to be victims of the usurper, and aren't even allowed to leave the kingdom. If you wanted to claim what was yours, you would have to fight for it."

Tiran's willingness to argue went suddenly silent, which put an immediate gleam in my father's eyes. We'd just been told we could have our own kingdom—if we had what it took to win it for ourselves. I wanted to curse out loud when I felt a stirring of interest inside *me*, but my father didn't give me the chance.

"What's the matter, Alexia?" he asked at once. "Is something like that a little *too* worthwhile for you? You can't claim you won't be helping others, because you know very well that you will be. In a situation like that you can't help but make a difference—if your abilities are as exceptional as you claim. I won't say I like the idea of your getting involved in all that, but I also can't say you'll be happier if you don't. Tell me you'll be able to find something like that on your own if you turn this down."

I stood up fast to tell him exactly that, then stalked away to pace without speaking a word. The spark of interest I'd felt was now a growing fire, beginning to burn away all reluctance. Wandering around on my own, saving the gullible from cheaters and thieves—

how could that possibly compare with helping an entire kingdom of those who were desperate? Not just unhappy, uncomfortable, or slightly put out. Desperate to the point of agony and terror.

And Tiran. I'd almost knocked him off the chair arm when I'd stood, but I still hadn't missed his expression. Something like that would be more of a challenge than anything he'd ever faced, anything he ever would face for someone else's benefit. And even if he won, the challenge wouldn't be over. A country ravaged by an uncaring tyrant would need to be rebuilt once the tyrant was gone, and after rebuilding it would need defending . . .

"I would like to know what happens if the couple involved refuses the offer," Tiran said abruptly, interrupting my pacing. "What if they say thank you anyway, but we're going to be retiring to the country? What happens to that very involved agreement?"

"I don't know," my father admitted, making no effort to avoid the green stare locked to him. "In all the kingdoms and all the times the competition's been used, no couple has ever refused. Think about it, Tiran! We're not talking about men who spend their days gardening and women who just love to embroider their delicate gowns. The men and women who are made the offer need it as badly as their new worlds need *them*. They have skills to offer that most places don't want, especially not from the women. You were a professional fighter. How many women have recognized status in your field?"

"Two," Tiran answered after glancing at me. "One of them inherited her place after years of being second in command, but she had a hell of a fight before she was able to claim it. The other bought her place, and most people believe her outfit is run by her male lieutenants. It isn't, but that's what people believe."

"So there aren't many opportunities for a woman like Alexia," my father said. "She'll never fit into just any place; it will have to be a place she makes for herself. Would she be useful on a campaign like this, or can you get six male fighters who are as good or better?"

"Better?" Tiran said with a ridiculing laugh. "Better than Alex? I'd be lucky to find six who could hold their own with her. She wouldn't be useful, she'd be invaluable."

"How long have you known about this?" I demanded when my father's smug gaze moved to me. "I know now why you were so much on Tiran's side when he first appeared. But if you're waiting to be congratulated on how smoothly you set me up, don't hold your breath. Just answer my question."

"Once this matter is settled, I think you and I will have a discussion on manners," he murmured, hard golden eyes pinning me where I stood. "For now I'll just say I saw this coming years ago, and brought my problem to the meeting. I had to be convinced the solution was the right one, but once I was I went along with all of it."

"And now we need a decision from you two," my mother said quietly, her hand on my father's arm. "Will you go through with the wedding the way you're supposed to, and then accept the proposal? It took a while for me to understand that dangerous though it will be, it offers the only true chance for happiness that you two have. If you choose any other path, it's almost certain to lead to disappointment and heartache."

She then looked directly at *me*, Tiran and my father silently joining her. They were telling me that my decision was the one that counted, but I couldn't find much to feel flattered about. I don't like being manipulated, but if there was anything else at work there, I'd eat it without salt.

"If you're expecting words of wisdom, you're out of luck," I told them all, trying not to grumble.

"I don't like any of this setup and don't trust it, but here's what I'm willing to do: tomorrow or the next day Tiran and I can go to this place and do a reconnaissance, and then—"

"No," my father interrupted, his tone flat-voiced and final. "It has to be done the proper way, or it can't be done at all. First you two get married, then you agree to the proposal, then you gather what you need and go. All of it or none of it."

"You know, *I've* been considering what might happen if you refuse," my mother said before rising anger could make me snap out exactly that answer. "It stands to reason that two people like you and Tiran make a formidable combination, maybe too formidable to be allowed to stay together in a normal, peaceful realm. You know you were brought together by magical means none of us understand . . . what if you're separated in the same irresistible way . . . separated forever . . ."

I shouldn't have felt a chill that made me look immediately toward Tiran, but I did and it did. Since he'd been standing for the last couple of minutes, it took less than three strides for him to reach me. His arms pulled me close to his body to warm away the cold, but after only a moment or so he broke the silence.

"Alex, look at me," he ordered in a very soft voice, waiting until I did before going on. "We've talked and argued and argued and talked, but now it's time for a final decision. I know you don't want to feel that you *have* to marry me, and in all truth you don't. You can state your refusal, and then we'll never see each other again. I agree with your mother, so I'll repeat that. We'll *never* see each other again. If that's the answer you feel you have to give, go ahead and do it."

But understand exactly what you *are* doing, his green eyes added silently. You won't be able to change your mind later if you decide you made a mistake. You're a big girl now, and you claim to know what you want. If that's true, prove it by making a decision *now*.

"I hate the idea of marriage, but not as much as the thought of losing you," I said, loud enough for everyone to hear. "It's hell what a girl has to put up with, but what choice do I have? It could be months before another perfect man comes by, and I really don't have the patience to wait."

"You miserable brat," he said with a grin while my parents laughed in relief. "You'll regret adding that last part, just wait and see if you don't."

"Well, it looks like we have a wedding to arrange," my father said with heavy satisfaction, standing and taking my mother's arm. "What will you two be doing until the big day—or shouldn't I ask?"

"One of the things I'll be doing is sending for my company," Tiran answered with a chuckle as he hugged me tight. "I'll want them here and ready to go right after the honeymoon."

"What honeymoon?" I asked, pushing away a little to look up at him. "Why do we have to waste time on a honeymoon when we can do exactly the same thing after starting the campaign? And I didn't know you had a company. How large is it?"

"There are a lot of things you don't know about me," he answered, beginning to touch his lips to mine. "I do have a company and we will have a honeymoon, even if half the time is spent in planning. For the other half of the time, I don't want to worry about needing to keep my eyes open."

"That could be annoying," I agreed, my own eyes beginning to close from the touch of his lips and hands. "And you may have a very good point. I'll have to think about it."

"You do that," he said in a murmur, and then his hand moved under my tunic to glide slowly up my bare back. I gasped and tried to pull away, but he just chuckled. "Your parents are gone, so you don't have to worry. It's just you and me without an audience or attacker in sight."

"Well, that's a relief," I said, beginning to reach for him again, then I thought of something else. "Tiran, are you sure you're strong enough? I mean, you really had a hard time, and I don't want you to hurt yourself by overdoing it."

"You're absolutely right, I'm the next thing to an invalid," he murmured, his lips at the side of my neck as his other hand slid down into my trousers. "You'll have to be very gentle with me, otherwise I may faint."

I gasped again as he tickled my bottom, and found out for the second time that I couldn't push free. As an invalid Tiran was a complete washout, but he did have other uses.

"If you're feeling all that delicate, you should be in bed," I told him, trying to speak the words rather than moan them. "I happen to have one that doesn't eat people, but it's in the next room."

"A bed that doesn't eat people?" he echoed, raising his face to look down at me. "That doesn't sound like much fun, so we'll have to make up for it. If I can find the strength. Let's try."

The next instant he had lifted me in his arms, but this time I didn't gasp. I reached to his face to kiss him instead, and he almost walked into the wall rather than through the doorway. That made us chuckle, but he didn't tell me to stop. I had the feeling he'd never tell me to stop, not when I was showing him my love.

He carried me all the way to the bed, and he still wasn't straining when he put me down. We kissed and touched for a while, and then he raised his head and moved back just a little.

"In case you were wondering why men don't like seeing women in pants, this is the reason," he said, deliberately beginning to undress me. "If you were wearing skirts I'd already be under them, and that doesn't even count those blasted boots. And if you laugh, I'll probably beat you."

I did feel the urge to laugh, but only faintly. What I felt a lot more strongly was the need to get on with it, just what he had to be feeling. It was taking longer now that we belonged to each other than it was when we were still groping toward the truth.

"Here, let me do it," I said, beginning to sit up. "You take care of your own clothes, and I'll—"

"No, we'll be doing this the right way," he insisted, pushing me gently back down. "First we'll get rid of these boots, and then I'll show you what I mean."

He took off my boots and his own, and then he came back to me. I thought he would simply take my clothes off, but "simple" didn't apply to what he actually did. His fingers trailed up my body with his lips just behind as he slowly lifted off my tunic, then he did the same with my trousers. By the time I was able to kick them off to the floor I was moaning and clutching at him, but he wasn't ready yet to get on with it.

"Now you do the same to me," he whispered as he lay back. "My body belongs as much to you as yours does to me."

At first I didn't want to spend the time, but once my lips were touching him as I struggled to get rid of his tunic, I changed my mind. It was frustrating to have to take the extra time, but kissing him like that was marvelous. When I began to work on his trousers *he* was the one who moaned, and by the time they were off I had made up my mind. During our honeymoon I would definitely be wearing skirts.

And then he pulled me into his arms, no longer able to hold himself back. We kissed so fiercely our lips should have melted, but that wasn't the best part. Best was when he thrust into me, starting the incredible journey we would take together. There were no regrets, no hesitations, not even the shadow of a thought that this shouldn't be. It *should* be and it was, and then the dizziness took me into marvelous madness. Two separate halves had become a complete whole, one I had never imagined could be so good.

It took quite a long time to be over, but once it was I lay curled up in his arms, completely content. It was going to be something being married to this man, something I was already looking forward to.

Having Tiran in my bed at night and fighting next to me during the day, and afterward having a kingdom to rearrange to my own taste ... What more could a girl ask for?

Tiran let himself enjoy the taste of victory as he held Alex tight after having loved her, but only a swallow of it. He finally had her in his arms and promised to him, but they still had a ceremony to wait for and go through. Afterward ... afterward they would be a team, and would win against everything thrown at them. They would oust a tyrant, save an entire kingdom of victimized people, and then settle down.

He would have the woman he loved, a family and place of his own, a kingdom to rule where no one could argue his decisions ... What more could a man ask for?

SHARON GREEN grew up in Brooklyn and discovered science fiction at the age of twelve. A voracious reader, she qualified for the school library medal, but didn't get it because the librarian disapproved of sf. ("If you want to press the point," she writes, "you *could* say Lucky Starr, Space Ranger, got me in trouble in junior high school. It would be the literal truth.") Later, she earned her B.A. at New York University, where she got rid of an unwanted admirer by convincing him that she was from another planet.

Currently Ms. Green lives in Nashville, Tennessee with her cats and her Atari computer. A prolific writer, she is the author of over a dozen books, including *The Far Side of Forever*, the Terrilian Warrior series, *Lady Blade, Lord Fighter*, the Jalav series, *The Rebel Prince*, and *Dawn Song*, which is currently available from Avon Books. When she's not at her computer, she is engaging in one of her diverse hobbies: Tae Kwon Do (in which she has a purple belt), knitting, horseback riding, fencing, and archery.

RETURN TO AMBER...
THE ONE *REAL* WORLD, OF WHICH ALL OTHERS, INCLUDING EARTH, ARE BUT SHADOWS

ROGER ZELAZNY

The Triumphant conclusion of the Amber novels

PRINCE OF CHAOS   75502-5/$4.99 US/$5.99 Can

The Classic Amber Series

NINE PRINCES IN AMBER	01430-0/$4.50 US/$5.50 Can
THE GUNS OF AVALON	00083-0/$4.99 US/$5.99 Can
SIGN OF THE UNICORN	00031-9/$4.99 US/$5.99 Can
THE HAND OF OBERON	01664-8/$4.50 US/$5.50 Can
THE COURTS OF CHAOS	47175-2/$4.50 US/$5.50 Can
BLOOD OF AMBER	89636-2/$3.95 US/$4.95 Can
TRUMPS OF DOOM	89635-4/$3.95 US/$4.95 Can
SIGN OF CHAOS	89637-0/$3.95 US/$4.95 Can
KNIGHT OF SHADOWS	75501-7/$3.95 US/$4.95 Can

Three Wondrous Stories
of Adventure and Courage by

B R I A N

J A C Q U E S

MOSSFLOWER

70828-0/$4.50 US

The epic adventure of one brave mouse's quest to free an enslaved forest kingdom from the claws of tyranny.

REDWALL

70827-2/$4.50 US

A bumbling young apprentice monk named Matthias, mousekind's most unlikly hero, goes on a wondrous quest to recover a legendary lost weapon.

MATTIMEO

71530-9/$4.99 US

The cunning fox, Slagar the Cruel, and his evil henchmen have kidnapped the Woodland children, and Matthias and his band of brave followers must rescue their stolen little ones.

Coming Soon
MARIEL OF REDWALL 71922-3/$4.99 US